Winds of Change

Diana K Robinson

I have thoroughly enjoyed this book. Very well written, and the detail Diana has put into it is fantastic. I was immersed in the book and felt like I knew the characters! It's been a pleasure working on it.
  ~ Lauren. Editor, Publishing Push

This is a work of fiction. Names, characters, places, and incidents either are the product of the author's imagination or are used fictitiously. Any resemblance to actual persons, living or dead, events, or locales is entirely coincidental.

Copyright © 2022 by Diana K Robinson
All rights reserved. No part of this book may be reproduced or used in any manner without written permission of the copyright owner except for the use of quotations in a book review.

Contact dianarobinsonauthor@yahoo.com
Diana K Publications – https://dianakrobinson.com
First paperback edition
Book design by Publishing Push

ISBNs
Hardback: 978-1-80227-820-0
Paperback: 978-1-80541-050-8
eBook: 978-1-80541-051-5

To my husband for his patience and encouragement. To my family, who read the second draft and still encouraged me! To my chief editor, Tim Macilwaine — I could not do this without you, and to my other editors, a huge thank you.

This trilogy is dedicated to all Rhodesians who so bravely fought a war alone. Thanks to the author of this poem, who says it so well.

DIDN'T FIGHT FOR FUN
BY SYDNEY E. LASSMAN
IN WORLD WAR ONE WHEN THINGS WERE BED,
AND ENGLAND NEEDED MEN,
WE RALLIED TO OUR COUNTRY'S FLAG,
RHODESIANS ANSWERED THEN.
AND MANY ASKED US AS WE WENT, "WHOSE BATTLE DO YOU FIGHT?"
"OUR COUNTRY NEEDS US," WE REPLIED, AND FOUGHT WITH ALL OUR MIGHT.
AND SOME CAME BACK, BUT HUNDRED NOT,
BUT YOU MUST UNDERSTAND
WE DIDN'T FIGHT FOR FUN, MY LAD, WE FOUGHT TO SAVE OUT LAND

TWO DECADES PASSED AND ONCE AGAIN, THE CALL TO ARMS WENT OUT.
RHODESIANS ANSWERED AS BEFORE – WAS EVER THERE A DOUBT?

WHERE DID WE GO? WHY EVERYWHERE! ON LAND
AND AIR AND SEA,
WE FOUGHT IN EVERY BATTLE, AND WE HELPED TO SET
MEN FREE
AND SOME CAME BACK, BUT THOUSANDS NOT, BUT
YOU MUST UNDERSTAND, MY LAD, WE FOUGHT
TO SAVE OUR LAND.

THE YEARS ROLLED BY, AND ONCE AGAIN,
THE BATTLE CRY WAS MADE,
THIS TIME RHODESIANS FIGHT ALONE – FEW COME
TO OUR AID.
BOTH YOUNG AND OLD, BOTH BLACK AND WHITE,
WE'LL KEEP OUR COUNTRY FREE
AND MAKE IT SAFE FOR EVERYONE – NOT JUST
FOR YOU AND ME
YES, SOME WILL LIVE, AND SOME WILL NOT, BUT YOU
MUST UNDERSTAND
IT ISNT ANY FUN, MY LAD, TO FIGHT TO SAVE OUR LAND

Chapter One

1977

IVAN FELT their misery deep in his gut, it was his misery too. Five o'clock marked the end of the workday. He stood at the door to the sawmill office watching the cutters return from the forest. He shivered. Not from the cool breeze evening brought in, but something icier and more menacing.

Here at Blue Winds forestry estate, in the eastern highlands of Rhodesia, happy banter, singing, and whistling from log cutters once marked the end of a long day. Today, the cutters were silent. Their shoulders drooped, not only from tiredness but the insurgence of terror within the forests where they worked. The mood brought on another realisation. Every morning, he'd hear the school children set off barefooted, travelling lightly over frosted earth at this time of year. This morning Ivan strained to hear them. Like their parents, cheerful banter, singing and giggling had quietened.

He hated the thought the disgruntled rumblings of political activists had grown into a fierce bush war, sweeping the nation, causing bloodshed and chaos effecting everyone, even the happy little singing children.

Guerilla's armed with machete's threatened his workers now.

Vowing to cut off their ears and lips if they didn't comply with an ideology most of Ivan's men didn't understand, let alone support.

The men were frightened. Vulnerable and defenceless. Access into the forests was easy for the terrorists.

The estate foreman approached. "Good evening, Sir."

"Good evening, Misheke. How much timber was cut today?"

"Less than yesterday, Sir. The men are not happy, as you can see." Misheke didn't venture a more explicit explanation. He assumed Ivan knew.

"I'm aware. Let's try to keep things as normal as possible for now. I'll see you tomorrow at six. Stay well."

Ivan locked the office, zipped his Parker jacket, and hurried back to the house to get out of the cold. Autumn was approaching, and the eastern highlands were cooling down rapidly. At the kitchen door he scraped caked sawdust from his boots and entered the warm, cosy kitchen.

Fillimon, the family cook of many years, smiled, offering his usual happy greeting, exposing a mouth almost devoid of teeth.

"Evening Fillimon. What's cooking?" Ivan asked. The delicious smell of dinner wafted in the air, held there by the warmth within the room.

"Ilish stew." Fillimon couldn't pronounce the 'r' in any English words, mostly because of his lack of teeth.

Ivan's voice must've woken the family Labradors. They bounded into the kitchen to say hello. Bessie's golden, otter-like tail thumped against Ivan's legs. Benjie, the more needy, stuck his nose straight into Ivan's crotch, demanding attention. The two dogs always welcomed Ivan home in this way.

"Baas!" Fillimon spoke louder than he'd meant to. "The terrorists have come to feed in our compound." He warned, speaking in Shona, his native tongue.

Then Margaret burst into the kitchen. "Have I interrupted something?"

"No, not at all, just calming the dogs as usual, and Fillimon was telling me he's feeling his age, especially as it is getting colder." Ivan smiled at his wife of nineteen years and led her to the sitting room. It would have been considered rude of Ivan to have betrayed Fillimon's warning in front of Margaret. War was man's talk.

Every evening at around this time, Ivan and Margaret would sit together, sipping tea, discussing the day and preparations for the following one. One of the few routines he hoped wouldn't change, even with the bush war and terrorists. When he and Margaret married, she was adamant she wanted to be an active part of the farming operation, and she was. She farmed with Dorper sheep and had done so for the last fifteen years. Ivan had always admired her animal husbandry practices and she shared her thoughts on the flock as part of their evening conversation.

Fillimon had lit the fire in the sitting room, taking the chill off, and the last rays of sunlight drifted through the expanse of bay windows. Margaret never drew the curtains until the sun had set. She loved watching the sky changing colours. On the tea tray in front of them was a plate of Fillimon's delectable shortbread, which Ivan never tired of eating.

He tossed his tattered hat down on the arm of his inviting giant-sized armchair and fell into its folds, stretched his long legs toward the fire, raked his fingers through his matted hair, and listened for the sound of the backdoor closing. Fillimon leaving for his home, a walk of over a kilometre away.

Ivan picked up a slice of castor sugar sprinkled shortbread and took a bite, spreading a fine scattering of white grains over the coffee table, then shared Fillimon's warning with Margaret. "Fillimon mentioned there have been terrorists inside our compound. The mood at the mill, and watching the men this evening, confirmed guerillas are in the forests too." Though he didn't want to worry Margaret, but it was vital she know.

He chomped on the cookie, chewed, and swallowed, scarcely tasting the treat. "I've been watching for the tell-tale signs that this bloody war is on our doorstep." He hated having to share his fears and absent-mindedly brushed the biscuit crumbs from his shirt. "So, I think it's necessary, just as a matter of precaution, that Fillimon go home at varying times now, and before four-thirty. It's not fair to ask him to stay longer, don't you agree?"

Margaret nodded, having just bitten into her own slice of shortbread, swallowed and sipped her tea. "I'll let him know in the morning. And I called the security fencing people. They'll be here next week." She sighed. "I have mixed emotions about being surrounded by an ugly, 2-metre-high diamond mesh fence."

"I understand. Horrid thought, isn't it?" Ivan stood, grabbed another shortbread, and wandered to the bay windows.

The indigo mountains in the distance had a wintery, dusty pink haze from the setting sun. "Sad to think the people who want us dead, live in those beautiful mountains. It's contradictory, somehow. Who would've have thought...... a war." Ivan remained at the window, staring at the view. A view he never tired of gazing at.

"Running operations in our forests is going to be a challenge, isn't it?" Margaret pushed her thick auburn hair away from her eyes. "Fear. That simple little word can manipulate even the most powerful. It worked for Hitler." She took the last sip of tea and put her cup and saucer on the tray. "What are we going to tell Melonie? She'll be home from school in a few days, and she can't ride through the forests alone anymore."

Ivan wandered back to his chair. "We've raised a sensible, seventeen-year-old daughter with an abundance of good old-fashioned common sense, she'll understand. But not just in the forests, she shouldn't ride anywhere alone."

Collecting Mel from her boarding school in Umtali, the border city closest to them, usually coincided with a bulk shop to restock the farm store. "What about the store." Margaret asked.

"You have concerns about the store?" Ivan asked.

"Yes. Should we keep it open, or close it? The store is a perfect draw-card for terrorists to mingle with the locals." She stood. It was her turn to pace in front of the windows. "Dressed like farm workers they could filter into gatherings without raising suspicion. They could pretend to be from neighbouring farms or masquerade as job seekers. It's an ideal setting for them to gather intel."

Ivan knew Margaret's concerns were real. He hated the thought of disrupting life on the estate for so many people if they closed the store. "Let's do the re-stock. I'll pop into the army base and speak to Captain

Hall. And talk to Phil from PATU (Police Anti-Terrorist Unit) too, before we decide. And getting the stocks will avoid arousing suspicion."

Margaret stopped pacing. "You're right. And too many people would suffer if we closed it, especially Eric, and Agnus."

Ivan loved Margaret for many reasons, but her concern for others, like the storekeeper and his shelf-packing assistant, Agnus, was one of the many.

A FEW DAYS LATER, Ivan pulled to the curb in front of his daughter, Mel. A pile of suitcases stacked beside her. She waved to her friends and wasted no time hurling her cases into the open back of the truck, then she jumped in and smacked a kiss on Ivan's cheek. "Hi, Dad."

"Hello, my girl. Happy to be going home?" He shifted the truck into gear.

"Always. You know that. I'm going to bounce on Firelight, gallop off, and feel the wind on my face." She pulled the elastic band from her hair and shook the mop of long auburn locks loose. The colour matched Margaret's.

She glanced at her father. "What's wrong?"

Ivan didn't expect to explain the issues at the compound so soon, but Mel was a perceptive girl. "A few nights ago, Fillimon told me the terrorists have been in our compound."

Mel's gaze fixed on his face.

Ivan drove out of the school grounds, travelled down the main road from the school, then turned onto Milner Avenue, and drove out to Grand Reef Fire force base. Tree-clad mountains surrounded the city and many of the avenues were lined with glorious Flamboyant trees. When they flowered the entire canopy became a dome of brilliant scarlet. "Before we collect Mum, I'm popping into the army base to find out more and report the gook presence in our forests and compound."

So far, he felt he'd relayed the worst of news in the best way he could. It was the next words he knew would be the hardest for Mel to hear. "This means no galloping off on Firelight or Spindle on your own."

As he expected, Mel's face crumbled. Tears spilled from her emerald eyes. She looked down at her hands, pressed them between her knees and rounded her shoulders. She nodded, even as a tear stained her skirt.

She sniffled but straightened her shoulders. "I guess I'm not surprised. An army Major visited school last week. He addressed the assembly and warned the war is on our doorstep."

She wiped her eyes. "While I stood listening to the frightening things he said, I couldn't digest the thought it would directly affect us. He said the eastern part of the country has been declared an operational zone. Operation Thrasher, he said."

Ivan's tight chest loosened. At least Mel had been partially prepared. "Quite right," he said. Hoping he sounded strong and sure. "What else did the Major talk about?"

"He warned that the school is going to implement emergency drills when we get back from holiday. And being on the border with Mozambique, Umtali could come under mortar attack, so the students need to be prepared."

Her hands fisted in her lap, then clenched and unclenched. A sign he knew meant she was more worried than her tone conveyed. She went on. "He said, us farm kids are exposed to the possibility of being caught in ambushes and farmhouse attacks. He also warned landmines are being laid in farm roads and showed us images of what to look out for."

Her brow furrowed, her lips formed a tight line, but no more tears, thank God.

She continued. "It's scary, Dad. Everyone was silent as he spoke. After he'd finished, we were divided into groups and taught the army alphabet in case we need to use a radio. That was fun." Her brow unfurled and he detected a hint of a smile. She shifted in her seat and her hands relaxed. She looked at him. "I now know the whole phonetic alphabet off by heart." A light-hearted proudness filled her tone.

He didn't want to break her bit of happiness, but he knew he had to tell her all the facts. "Sounds like you learned a lot from the army Major, so you'll understand when I say life at home has already changed, Mel. A security fence is being erected around the house and garden soon. Mum has also applied for an Agric Alert radio system."

He reached over and squeezed her hand. "When the radio's

installed, you can chat to neighbouring friends using the phonetic alphabet."

He smiled, but he knew he had to reinforce his earlier warning. "And Sweetie, I meant what I said just now, you'll have to ride with Patric. You cannot go out alone."

Silence hung heavy. Finally, Mel spoke, soft and wistful. "Why is the war so hot in our area now? Why can't people live in peace, like we have been?"

Ivan decided not to soften the truth, facts might help. "Well, the Portuguese have been chucked out of Mozambique. Frelimo, the new Mozambique ruling party are now harbouring and actively supporting terrorist incursions into Rhodesia."

Ivan gripped the steering wheel, politics and the current situation irked him, badly. "This makes it dead easy for terrorists to hop across the border and create turmoil and hop back again. Our farm becomes front-line. There's no one between us and the border. This fight is all about them wanting majority rule and ending colonialism, sweetheart."

Mel didn't say a word.

He wasn't sure if that was good or bad. He parked outside the military base. "I won't be long. You'll be okay waiting?"

"Yes Dad, I'll be fine." She pulled out Romeo and Juliet from her pack. Her English literature set-work book. "I'll immerse myself in a different sort of drama."

Chapter Two

The next morning, Mel rushed to give her horses a hug, but her mum intercepted her passing through the hall where the dog baskets lay. In her haste she nearly tripped over them.

"As soon as you've said hello to your horses, please pop down to the store and help Eric, Agnus and me, unpack and re-stock the shelves." Mel allowed a pout to surface. Re-stocking the store had never been her favourite past-time, but she did it, mainly because she could fill her pockets with sweets.

She ran down to the stables, arriving outside Firelight's stable, breathless. It was always the first thing she'd do on the first morning home.

The line of four thatched stables stood in front of a backdrop of pine trees. A kiss and a cuddle for Firelight, a dark bay Thoroughbred cross Connemara gelding. Her favourite horse. Then she moved to Spindle, cooing affectionately to the little chestnut mare. Then she approached Sid who put his ears back. "You grumpy old sod, no wonder Dad called you Sid." (Short for acid.)

She skipped him and went on to Smiler, who reached out to her. He loved kisses from her for he knew what followed, handfuls of chopped carrots and apples.

Sid and Smiler were Patric's two stockhorses.

Knowing her mother was expecting her, she dashed to the tack room, scooped a handful of horse cubes, and shoved them in her pocket. She'd emptied her pockets of the fresh treats and ran down the line of stable doors once more. She put four cubes in her hand and fed each horse the extra treat, then raced to the store to help, as her Mum had asked.

The store, a good kilometre and a half from the stables had been built next to the farm entrance. Easy access for locals without interfering with the daily operations of the sawmill and farm.

Being a good hockey player, she covered the distance quickly. Catching her breath outside the store, she looked up at the signs and smiled.

She fondly remembered the day it opened. She was eight years old. Still hanging on the front wall above the tin-covered entrance were old, dented billboards advertising Eno's Liver Salts, Coco-Cola and Surf washing powder. The signs hadn't weathered well, but they had a special worn look her mum liked. It gave the store a character, she always said.

"Ah, there you are." Margaret smiled at her daughter, standing at the entrance to the store trying to recover regular breathing.

"Hi Eric, Hi Agnus." She greeted and moved down the long wooden counter to the hatch opening, lifted it, picked her way over the boxes strewn on the floor, and closed the hatch.

"Mum, why does everyone always leave the boxes ready for unpacking right here where we can trip over them?" Margaret shrugged her shoulders. Behind the counter shelves ran from the floor to a foot below the tin roof.

"Grab the stepladder and stack the cigarettes by brand," her mum said.

"And after that, Mum?"

"Matches, tea and fresh bread."

"Okay, that's quick." She glanced at her watch. "I'm meeting Patric at the stables at ten."

Almost out the door, Mel stowed a handful of chocolate éclair toffees in each pocket. One for Patric and one for her. She was too late for breakfast, so she trotted down to the stables and got there in time.

Mel was looking forward to her ride. Sheep in the northern part of the estate were being checked for foot rot. Her task for the day.

She hadn't been to that part of the estate for ages.

Patric was waiting at the stables with Firelight and Sid saddled. Not to delay further, she swung into her saddle, and they walked off down the road past the sawmill. Firelight flattened his ears as they past. He hated the sound when a pine log was pushed into the waiting teeth of the sawblade.

Nudging Firelight, she drew alongside Sid and scooped the toffees from her pocket.

"These are for you, Patric."

"Thank you, Mel." Patric leaned out the saddle and pocketed his share.

"Where are we turning off?"

Patric pointed to a path ahead. Mel knew the route. It led through the first and oldest pine plantation. Though she normally rode the track alone, this time she let Patric lead the way.

Sunlight offered speckled light on the path beneath the canopy of mature trees. As they entered Mel felt the drop in temperature. Even though mid-morning had passed the sun held less heat in the early autumn. Goose bumps rose on her bare arms.

The damp and years of intwined pine needles covered the path. Though it was soft underfoot, it made it treacherous for the horses. It was safe enough going uphill, as they were now, but she thought of the journey back. Unshod hooves slipped easily on the matted pine needles.

Patric stood in his saddle and turned to face Mel.

"Shall we canter?" He asked.

"Yes. That'll be nice. I'll follow you."

He broke into a slow canter. Trailing Patric made her feel unusually comforted. She'd known Patric all her life and she hoped if anything happened, he would protect her. What *anything* constituted she wasn't sure, and she didn't want to find out while they were riding. Trapped in the forest wouldn't be a good place to encounter terrorists, she thought.

The sheep and horses had been under Patric's care for as long as Mel could remember. She'd never really thought about Patric as a tutor and caregiver, but he'd been that for her. He'd taught her how to feed and groom her horses when she was six years old. He'd also taught her how to avoid getting her horse or herself tangled up in a barbed-wire gate when opening it. Keep the wires taut. And he always offered to saddle up for her, although this was something she preferred to do herself for the most part.

Suddenly, Patric stopped.

A near collision avoided, she shouted to Patric. "Hey. Warn me when you're going to stop." She shrieked as she hung onto Firelight's neck.

Patric spun Sid around and went to help. "I'm sorry, Mel. I'd forgotten you were following." He uttered bashfully while Mel pushed herself back into the saddle, thankful she hadn't fallen off.

Then she laughed. "Did you miss the turn-off to the dam?"

He nodded and looked embarrassed. Mel wondered if his thoughts were on the increased terrorism and what he'd do if they happened upon a group of them in the forest. He seemed eager to get out of the forest as fast as he could, but the pathway down to the dam was steep and narrow. It wound its way between heavily set tree trunks and large granite boulders.

Riding behind Patric on Sid, Mel enjoyed watching Sid's hip sway on the downhill. A sure-footed pony who seldom slipped. He'd past this way more times than Mel could count.

"Oops," Mel chuckled as Firelight's hind feet lost their grip, almost sitting on his haunches, he scrambled to find his footing. "I'm jumping off, Patric." She shouted and led Firelight down the most slippery part, then clambered onto a boulder and re-mounted.

"Are you okay, Mel?"

"Yes, thank you, Patric. Firelight isn't used to this like Sid, but we're nearly there, hey?"

"Yes. Not much further before we are onto level, harder ground."

Mel noticed Sid's ear prick forward. At first, she thought he'd seen unwelcome movement in the forest and her tummy lurched, but thankfully he was looking straight ahead. He'd seen the dam beyond the open grassland. Sid loved swimming.

"Hey, Patric, Sid's seen the dam. You better not let him roll."

Patric laughed. "It's difficult to stop him. He's a naughty boy in water."

"I know. I'll stand away from you, cos I know he'll splash me."

The forest opened onto a narrow stretch of alpine grassland. Mel took in a deep breath. She loved the smell of the wild herbs that grew in these parts and welcomed the sun on her bare arms. The horses picked up the pace and when they reached the edge of the water, Firelight pulled the reins through her hands, waded in, and dropped his head to drink. Patric steered Sid away from Firelight, but his splashes still caught Mel's legs. She squealed.

"Patric, stop him. This water's freezing."

Patric was trying, but Sid was determined and struck at the water with his right front leg. Patric pulled his head up and moved him out of the water. He let him drink from the edge.

"Good idea, thanks Patric." Mel said and moved Firelight from the deeper water.

The route to the top, northern paddock crossed the dam wall. The track was almost as steep as the one coming down, only this time they were out in the open fighting their way through thick bracken that tangled around the horse's legs. This and the contrasting temperature brought out a sweat on the horses.

Mel relished the warmth. "Nice and warm out here. I got cold in the forest and now I'm wet."

"You'll dry quickly." Patric said.

"It's lovely up here. I didn't get too wet, don't worry, Patric."

The climb to the summit took fifteen minutes of hard riding. The horses were breathing heavily when they reached the top.

Patric bounced off Sid and opened the wire concertina gate which led into the paddock where the sheep were.

"Thanks, Patric, it's so nice having you do the things I hate."

He laughed. "I taught you how to do this." His expression enquiring.

"I'll open it on the way back so you can see I haven't forgotten."

Patric smiled.

While he was tackling the gate, Mel sat on Firelight gazing at the view. In the middle distance to the south stood Inyangani, the highest mountain in Rhodesia. It stood dark against a backdrop of cloud. She'd always wanted to climb it with the mountaineering club at school, but the war had stopped all excursions to the mountain. She watched now, as the roll of cloud moved and rested along its crest.

To the east, in the far distance, hazy from the rising heat, were the mountains in Mozambique. The same ones they could see from the sitting room window.

To her right she looked across the top of the vast expanse of her father's forests and mourned for the peaceful past. Now, hiding somewhere within those six thousand hectares of pine plantation, terrorists moved and hid, having come in from their hiding in the mountains she'd been looking at. She shuddered. They were the people who wanted to destroy all their lives.

She and Patric rode across to the first flock of sheep grazing not far from the gate. Patric wove Sid through the flock, scattering them. He needed to check if any of them were lame from foot rot. This caused by grazing in areas that are too wet - a vile smelling disease sheep are prone to. This was one paddock where the sheep didn't suffer badly from the disease. It was drier at these heights, though soon, they too would be blanketed in a fine mist that only lifted around mid-day.

None in this flock were lame. Melonie counted them and noticed Patric was counting too.

"How many?" She asked.

"Twenty-six." He answered.

"Yes, I got that number too."

He pulled a sharpened twig from his pocket and scratched the number on his toned, strong forearm. It showed white against his black skin.

Melonie laughed. "Hey, isn't that sore?"

He shook his head without answering.

"Well, you won't lose that list, will you?" She chuckled.

They rode on to find the next flock. In this paddock lay scattered remnants of ancient stone ruins, thought to have been built by the Nyika and Karanga tribes. Mel watched where they trod.

"Hey, Patric, do you know the history of these stone ruins?"

"No, I don't, Mel. I respect my ancestors, but these," he pointed to a line of stone craft about half a metre high and fifteen metres long. Chevron patterns could be seen in places. "They don't interest me." He smiled apologetically, foot rot and sheep numbers were his concern.

On the other side of the wall, another seventeen sheep were grazing. According to her mother there should be a hundred and twenty sheep in this paddock.

"We've got a lot more sheep to find, Patric. Are your sweets finished?"

"No, I still have some. Would you like one?"

"No thanks, I still have two, but I'm going to be starving when we get home."

At the next flock they counted forty-six sheep quite well spread out. Only two were lame. Patric jumped off Sid and pulled the small can of spray from his pack.

"Hey, can I do it?" Mel asked and dismounted. The two horses stood side by side. They'd done this many times.

"Oh yuk, it stinks." She held her nose while Patric opened the cloven foot while Mel sprayed purple spray around the offending flesh.

It was after two o'clock when they finished. Melonie's concern was not the foot rot. Having scoured the countryside, they had accounted for a hundred and thirteen. There were seven missing. Searching for them had delayed them getting back by lunch.

In the past, if sheep were missing, they'd been taken by Leopard. Never seven, one or two.

Melonie shared her suspicions with Patric for the first time.

"Do you think terrorists have stolen them?"

Patric hesitated before answering. "Yes, I think so. We must take the short cut home, it's quicker."

"Okay. Are you worried, Patric."

"Yes, Mel. We are all worried." He looked at her with eyes that weren't seeing, they looked far beyond her. Then he shook his head.

"I've forgotten the route, so I'll follow you. I guess it'll be a fast ride back to the stables then."

"Not too fast." Patric smiled. "Only one gate, and don't worry. I'll open it. I'm quicker than you." He teased.

They got to the stables just before three o'clock. Mel untacked and rubbed Firelight's back, lifting the haor so it cooled quicker.

"Will you do the rest, Patric? I'll let Mum know the numbers."

Patric gave her a sign with his thumb as she ran off.

Back at the house, Mel walked into the kitchen sweaty and hungry. Her mother was there. "Hi Mum, there are seven sheep missing in the top paddock. Patric and I searched. Only three with foot rot, which was good."

"Seven?" Mum repeated and pulled a plate of lunch from the oven. The food, still nice and warm, Mel tucked in. A handful of toffee's hadn't sustained her.

"Yes. And Patric and I both reckon they've been stolen by terrorists living in the area." Between bites, she said, "I think Patric's on our side, Mum. I chatted to him about training the horses to be calm when being fired off. He said he'd help me. Is it still okay for me to use your 9mm pistol?"

Margaret sat at the table, amused by watching Mel devour her food. "Yes, of course you can use it." But her brow creased, and she tapped her forefinger on the table.

"What are you thinking, Mum?"

"Before any training starts, you and Patric will have to bring all those sheep to the home paddock tomorrow. Seven missing is a lot of money. We can't afford to lose more."

"Okay. Patric and I will herd them down here in the morning. Yippee, another long ride."

Margaret shook her head. "You're a remarkable young lady. Where do you find the energy?"

"It's all the toffees I've been chewing." Mel said playfully and put her knife and fork together. "Thanks Mum, that was yummy."

THE NEXT MORNING Mel and Patric headed out early, taking the same route. Rain had fallen over night, but the day had dawned clear. Everything in the forest seemed more charming, more vibrant, more alive. How fresh the forest looked. The sweet scent of wild jasmine smelled stronger. The contrasting colours of orange and luminous green lichen clinging to the surface of granite boulders, seemed brighter. She'd always appreciated the wonders of the forest, but today it seemed more special. Under normal circumstances, the forests filled her with a sense of calm. She remembered playing fairies with an imaginary friend here. Everything within the forest was mystical, but the war had changed all that now. She squeezed her eyes closed and a tear ran down her cheek. She wished, that when she opened them, the harmony and magic would be restored. Instead, her mother's 9mm pistol holster tap-tapping against her side reminded her that hidden in the forests lay a sinister threat. She looked up, swallowing the rising lump in her throat and took a deep breath. Perhaps because she may never ride this way again?

When they reached the summit, the view seemed clearer. The mountain wasn't veiled in cloud, it had a soft purple haze, but the clouds that brought rain last night were gradually filling becoming ragged, menacing clouds. To ease the discomfort of her thoughts, she chose to focus on little clumps of delicate, papery pink and yellow 'everlasting' flowers growing on the edge of the road, stretching toward her, begging to be picked as she used to do. But not today. They had sheep to move.

It took an hour to gather them and push them down the steep track toward the dam. From the dam they herded the flock along the road beside the forest. The track through the forest too narrow to drive over a hundred sheep through.

"Mel," Patric shouted. Her reverie suddenly interrupted, and her body tensed. Her hand automatically went to the butt of the pistol.

"Quickly, chase those sheep."

She relaxed when she realised Patric's shouts were to alert her to four escapees darting from the flock right beside her. She quickly cantered forward, driving them back to their mates.

The gate to the home paddock was not far down the road. Once all the sheep were safely through the gate, Mel and Patric wandered back to the stables devising a training program for the horses and agreed to begin the following day.

Mel felt a little nervous wondering how the horses would react to gunshots near them. She hated the thought of frightening them at such close quarters.

She stood with her back to the stables and let off the first shot. As expected, the horses jumped forward, eager to break out of their stables. Spindle stood at her stable door shaking, pawing at the door. The other three weren't quite as nervous. Mel could see Spindle was no war horse.

It took another four days of intermittent shooting around them before Mel dared shoot off the back of Firelight and when she did, she was pleasantly surprised. His ears flicked back and forth but he absorbed the sound through tense muscles and didn't jump forward as she'd expected. Sid and Smiler behaved in much the same way. It was only Spindle she couldn't fire off, so she never did.

Chapter Three

A KNOCK on the front door interrupted breakfast. Ivan jumped up.

"Ah, it's the security fencing people." He said, looking out the window.

"Oh good. Although I've always hated the thought of being imprisoned by a security fence, now they're here, I find the thought oddly comforting." Margaret's shoulders visibly relaxed.

Ivan opened the front door and greeted the foreman in charge.

"Good morning, Mr. Johns." The foreman reached to shake Ivan's hand.

"Morning. Thanks for getting here so early. I'm off to the sawmill. My wife is here. She'll pop out every so often. She's rather sensitive about her garden being hacked back. Please ensure your workers keep in mind if they need to cut anything. You'll see we have cleared the perimeter but there may be areas where the clearing isn't enough."

"No problem, Mr. Johns. I'll make sure they're careful."

"How long do you think it'll take to surround the house, before your team moves to the sawmill?"

The foreman looked about, assessing the perimeter of the house and garden. "I'm not sure. I've not seen the area cleared yet, but I guess about two to three days. It'll be at least a week or more to complete both."

Ivan nodded. "I'll let you get on, but before I go, let me show you where we want the gates."

The foreman followed Ivan down the driveway. "Off-set to the left of the front door. I guess this is about seventy metres." Ivan stopped and put a cross in the sand with his foot.

"We'll do the double gates first, then the pedestrian gate. The supports need to be concreted in and dry before we can put any tension on them. If I follow you to the sawmill, show me where you want the main gates and the two pedestrian gates, and we can get the holes dug for them all today."

From there Ivan walked down to the mill with the foreman and marked where he wanted the gates.

"My wife and daughter will pop out every so often to see how your chaps are doing."

"Very well. Thank you, Mr. Johns." He turned and walked back to the house.

When the eight o'clock news came on during breakfast announcing that a farmer had been killed during a stonking on a farmhouse in Mtoko, Mel ran out the house and down to the stables. She didn't want to hear more. Knowing she had a setwork book to finish before going back to school, she wandered back to the house after brushing Firelight and letting him go in the paddock near the stables.

But the lunchtime news broadcast brought more bad news.

"At least no-one's been hit around here. Hopefully the fence will keep the buggers out."

"Do you think it will, Dad?"

"It'll certainly help, Mel. They can cut through it, but it'll take time. There's been recent talk of effective fence monitors which I'm going to investigate. I meant to ask earlier, have you heard from the Agric-Alert yet? About the radio?" Ivan asked Margaret.

"No, I'll give them call this afternoon, but they said there's quite a waiting list."

Seated in the sitting room after lunch, Margaret poured two cups of coffee. Mel had gone back to her room.

Half an hour later, Fillimon scuttled into the room to clear the table. Ivan noticed his twitchy behaviour. On the way out, the coffee pot toppled off the tray, shattering on the parquet flooring.

Ivan jumped up to help. "What's troubling you, old man?" He placed a hand on the cook's shoulder.

His head was bowed. Fillimon hated breaking anything. "I'm sorry, Sir. Sorry. Sorry" He apologised in his accented English and rushed to the kitchen.

Ivan picked up some of the chunkier bits of the coffee pot and followed him into the kitchen.

Fillimon placed the tray on the table. "Baas, there's talk in the compound again."

The muscles in Ivan's stomach knotted and he clenched his jaw.

"They say the bad men are coming back. You 'member Solomon? The man who deserted."

"Yes, I do. A cocky youngster who always argued."

"Yes, he's a freedom fighter now. All of ten days training." Fillimon jested in broken English. His hands shaking.

"When are these men supposed to be coming?"

"I don't know, Sir." In his nervous state he broke into Shona, his mother tongue. "The talk is they come to recruit young men, spread fear and propaganda. When they visit, they are cruel, Sir. Very cruel. We have no protection in our huts. They smash the doors open, demand food, rape our wives and daughters and take our sons." Spittle flew from his mouth, he wiped his lips with his sleeve, then hurried back to the sitting room with a broom and pan.

Ivan stood for a moment digesting what Fillimon had said. Ivan spoke Shona fluently. There was nothing to be misunderstood.

Most of the staff were housed in brick-and-mortar homes. Despite this, some still opted to live traditionally in thatched wooden rondavels, leaving them even more vulnerable. Beside most of the houses stood chicken coops suspended on wonky poles, held in place with faith, hope and bits of scrounged wire mesh. Rabbit and guinea pig cages were scattered here and there too. An extra source of protein, and most of the workers had a vegetable patch.

As usual, Fillimon laid the wood in the fireplace, but before leaving he informed Ivan, he had learned terrorists were expected to infiltrate the compound at full moon. Solomon would be with them.

A full moon would appear in three days.

AT SIX A.M. THE following day, Misheke rung the gong. A rusty old plough disc, that hung from a tree near the compound. As foreman, it had been his job for years. With a piece of metal rod, he struck the gong six times. The metallic rippling sound filled the air, momentarily drowning the din of the overpopulated cockerel colony that competed in waking the sleeping workers.

Ivan had woken moments before the gong sounded. His favourite time of the day. He crept to the bathroom to change, not wanting to disturb Margaret. When Ivan went to bed, he'd left Mel and Margaret in the sitting room. They were working through Romeo and Juliet and had obviously been late to bed. He knew this because Mel was normally in the kitchen first and Margaret always stirred at six.

Standing on the veranda with his tea he would soon hear the farm children on their way to school, but he remembered, they were all on holiday. He'd have to wait to listen to their cheer when school reopened, and cheer he prayed he'd hear.

He wandered down to the sawmill office, shoulders rounded, feeling the burden of the terrorist threat. The foreman had advised Ivan the security fence around the house would be finished tomorrow.

Unlocking his office, he sat at his desk and picked up the phone. "Morning Phil, I hope I haven't called too early?"

"No, not at all. What's up?" Phil, a dear friend, and head of the local PATU (Police Anti-Terrorist Unit) needed to know what Ivan had been told.

"I've been informed our compound is to be raided by gooks at full moon."

"Oh shit. Not good, but forewarned is forearmed, they say."

"Certainly is, and our security fence will be finished today, thank the Lord. But it's full moon in three days. Not that it means in three days the compound will be attacked. It could happen tomorrow night, or when the moon is waning."

"We've already put in place more roving patrols in the district, and I'll soon be calling on you to join the night patrols twice a week. We need all the men we can get with the two extra vehicles."

"Ready to help, but after full moon. Can you arrange regular patrols around the estate over the next few nights? Might put the bastards off."

"Yes, of course." Cheers, mate."

Ivan put the phone back on its cradle and wandered around the mill. The gate uprights were in and sturdy. Misheke was there to greet him. They discussed the sections to be cut that day.

***

BANG. BANG. Ivan woke. Only one thing made those sound - gunshots.

"Jesus wept." He threw back the bedclothes and jumped out of bed. He picked up the Uzi machine gun on the floor, placed beside the bed for this eventuality. Despite the pre-planning, he hadn't expected the attack tonight.

Margaret slithered from the bed onto the floor and sat with her back resting against the side of the bed. She picked up the FN rifle beside her and placed the weapon across her knees and waited for Ivans instructions.

Since Fillimon's warning, Ivan, Margaret, and Mel had gone to bed each night prepared. The Uzi for Ivan, despite being lighter than the FN, it's a fully automatic weapon, unlike the FN. Mel had gone to bed with Margaret's 9mm pistol.

Ivan inched close to Margaret and urged her trembling fingers into action. "Put a bullet in the chamber."

BAM.

A rifle grenade blasted into the side wall of the bedroom, rocking the house. Windows could be heard breaking. Glass littered the floor and the room quickly filled with swirling dust and debris.

Ivan's ears were ringing. Checking on Mel or defending the hole in the wall? Ivan's instant dilemma. He chose to run through the swirling dust to the hole in the wall, only just big enough for a man to get through, but access would be difficult. Preventing terrorists from entering their room was, for him, the immediate priority. Margaret was safe sitting where she was for the moment. He guessed Mel would be hiding in her room.

Holding the Uzi at hip height he emptied the entire magazine, shifting the barrel in a one-eighty-degree arc through the hole. The rat-a-tatting from his gun vibrating in his hands sent pins and needles through his fingers and a message to the gooks outside.

Silence.

He unclipped the empty magazine and threw it across the bed to Margaret. Then he pulled the full one from his pocket and clipped it in place. He was a farmer, not a fighter, but he'd do anything to protect his family. The silence was telling. He hoped the quick retaliation had caught the terrorist in that return blast of gunshot, and unnerved the others that were sure to be somewhere outside.

Ivan crossed to where Margaret sat. With shaking fingers, she'd reloaded the empty Uzi magazine.

"Are you okay?"

"Yes. Here, shove this in your pocket. Let's get to Mel." She handed him another full magazine, grabbed the FN and they ran down the passage to Mel's room.

"Mel." Ivan called out at the door.

"Under the bed, Dad."

"Clever girl." He bent down. She was clutching the 9mm pistol and the two dogs were pressed against her. They shook uncontrollably and she whimpered, "This is so scary. What should I do?"

Before Ivan could answer, the living room was being battered by gun shots.

"The terrorists have re-grouped. Stay where you are for the moment. Hang in there, sweetheart. I must go."

He turned to Margaret. He didn't want his family split, but to save their lives, it was necessary in the moment. "The gaping hole in our bedroom wall is a dangerous point of entry. If I start firing from the sitting room, they'll know where I am. It's a decoy. Can you cover the hole?"

"Yes, okay. I'm taking Mel with me. Between us we can protect our room and fill empty magazines. All our spare ammo is in our room."

"I wish we had that radio right now." Mel's voice echoed against the sounds of war coming from outside. She crawled out from under the bed and commanded the dogs to stay.

Rushing through the open sitting room door, Ivan quickly sidled toward the bay window. He poked the tip of the Uzi through the curtain and pushed it to one side. The smell of cordite filled the room as he emptied the full magazine through the broken window. Adrenaline pumped furiously. He quickly replaced the magazine and waited. Shooting from outside ceased for a few seconds then began again, coming from the side of their bedroom as Ivan suspected it would. He raced back to support his wife and daughter. He saw they were facing the onslaught bravely, but he couldn't leave them there alone.

Then the shooting from outside slowed to a few single shots.

Ivan quickly grabbed the FN from Margaret. "You two are doing well. Keep loading, I'm going to need a steady supply." He jumped over a mound of brick rubble and stood at the gaping hole once more. Thick dust had settled, though the finer dust still lingered even though fresh, cold air breezed into the room. His nostrils filled with the smell of fragmented earthen bricks and cordite and caught in his throat. He coughed, then fired the FN on rapid fire. Empty bronze cartridges spewed across the room. With each double tap, return fire came hurtling back. The gooks were determined to gain access to the house through the hole they'd blasted in the wall. Then shots rang out from the other side of the house, forcing a hasty decision. Did he dash to defend that side, and hope that Margaret and Mel could manage to keep the gooks out of their bedroom, or did he stay with them?

He stayed. Margaret grabbed the empty magazine and passed up a full one. He leapt across the room to the hole and fired four more shots. Deafened, he quickly rubbed his right ear with his index finger. He hadn't realised the shooting from outside had stopped. It was his own shots he was hearing.

Squatting beside his wife and daughter the night went eerily quiet. They froze. Immobilised by fear and uncertainty, they prepared for more. Ivan felt for Margaret's hand and squeezed it. She responded by returning the pressure and felt for Mel's hand.

"Don't move." The sound of him clipping in a new magazine was the only sound they heard. He moved back to the edge of the gaping hole. Holding his breath in anticipation of the next bullet to be fired.

Nothing happened. The night had returned to her quietness.

"What's happening?" Mel whispered to her mother.

"No idea. At least when they're shooting, we know where they are. This silence is unnerving."

Ivan heard the two of them speak, but he waited in position. His finger twitching on the trigger. The silence continued. "What the fuck," he said under his breath so they couldn't hear him swear.

The silence continued.

Resting his frame against the side of the wall, he thought he heard voices coming from outside.

"Good God," he spoke aloud. "Did you two hear my name being called?"

"Yes, Dad, I did." Mel answered, and the call got louder.

"Ivan. Ivan. Are you okay, mate?" The voice boomed from the direction of the main security gates some eighty metres away from where he stood.

Ivan didn't recognise the voice at first, his ears still buzzed. The call sounded again. It was Phils voice.

Ivan heard Margaret's loud sighs of relief over his.

"Give me your hand, sweetheart. My legs are so weak from fear, I can't stand up." Margaret said. Ivan offered his hand and pulled her up. Mel was already tucked into the other side of her father. He embraced them both, praising their bravery.

"Let me go down and open the gate for them." Ivan said.

Margaret held his forearm, not wanting him to leave them. "Be careful." She warned.

Ivan stood at the front door and answered. "All present and alive," he called out then hurried to unlock the gate.

The moon was indeed full, just as Fillimon had warned. Ivan unlocked the gates without needing torchlight. "Thanks for coming, chaps, it was getting hairy, and we were running low on ammo."

Ivan pushed the gates open and the PATU Bedford truck drove in and parked. Seven armed men scrambled out. Phil detailed four to check the fence perimeter, and three to examine the outside of the house. Moments later a voice could be heard calling from the pedestrian gate.

"Ivan, man down at your pedestrian gate."

Had Ivan managed, by some stroke of luck, to hit one of the terrorists? It was well known that during a contact, wounded terrorists often pretended they were dead, but weren't and lay in wait clutching a hand grenade. When the enemy soldier neared to inspect, the terrorist would pull the pin, killing them both. This was great reward in the minds of terrorist commanders, but it hadn't happened here.

Ivan rushed across the garden to the gate. "Howzit," he greeted the men. "How did you chaps get here so quickly?" He asked, addressing them all.

One of the men answered. "We were on routine patrol not far from here and heard the shooting. The gooks must've heard the vehicle and fucked off fast."

"Thank God for that. At the time it felt like the battle lasted hours. It was probably no more than fifteen minutes." Ivan was staring, unseeing, at the body lying face down on the ground.

"Hard to believe that in such a short time they managed to fuck up my house. Windowpanes shattered, glass everywhere and they blew a fucking great hole in our bedroom wall." Ivan knelt beside the corpse and shone his torch on the body.

"Now who do we have here?" Two dark holes in the bodies back still oozed blood. Ivan rolled the body over, then recognised who it was.

His guts twisted. He fell back on his haunches. Not a gook, his friend and cook, Fillimon. "Jesus wept."

Nausea and sadness thrust into his solar plexus. A deep mournful sob escaped from within his throat, sucked from his heart. The woeful sound ricocheted through the surrounding trees.

"Fuuuck. This is Fillimon, our cook." He threw his arms to the heavens. A dear, loyal man lay dead. A man he'd known and loved all his life. Then a thought struck him. Two bullet wounds in Fillimon's back. The two initial shots that woke the household. Fillimon must've been on his way to warn them, and he'd never know the level of Ivan's gratitude.

WINDS OF CHANGE

Phil put his hand on Ivan's shoulder. "I'm sorry, Ivan. We'll move his body to the compound a little later."

"Thanks Phil." Ivan stood and wiped at his eyes.

"Are Margaret and Mel, okay?" Phil asked.

"Yeah, they managed darn well. But this," he pointed to Fillimon's body, "this will knock them hard, just as it has me."

Ivan turned away and began a slow walk back to the kitchen. Revealing the news of Fillimon's death was not going to be easy. Not to Margaret and Mel and, the mere thought of having to tell Doris, Fillimon's wife, made him feel queasy.

Phil called to Ivan. "I'll catch up with you shortly. I want to join my men checking the house perimeter." Ivan didn't stop walking, instead he raised his hand, the index finger pointed upwards.

When Ivan entered the kitchen, Margaret stood beside the kettle, waiting for it to boil and Mel sat at the table, lost in thought, a glazed look in her eyes. "Phil and the others are checking the outside of the house. They'll be in shortly."

Margaret turned to the sound of his voice.

"What's the matter?"

He'd just get it done. Tell them the wretched news. He sat next to Mel and took each of their hands in his. "The first shots we heard killed our beloved Fillimon at the pedestrian gate."

Margaret's lips quivered.

"Noo. Not Fillimon. Nooooo." Mel dropped her head to the table and cried.

Ivan hugged Mel. Her sorrow cracked open his own heart again and he stood and held Margaret. She finally spoke but Phil, who'd just entered the kitchen. "Thank you for rescuing us." Her shoulders shook and she left the kitchen. Mel pushed her chair back and ran after her.

Phil walked over to Ivan. "Do you want me to come with when you tell Fillimon's wife?"

Then another voice boomed. It was one of Phil's men assigned to check the outside of the house. "Ivan, you got two of the bastards."

Ivan looked to where the voice had come from. Then the man entered the kitchen. "Did I? Where?" Ivan responded.

"Right outside the hole they blew in your bedroom," the man said.

Ivan's expression changed. It was exactly what he'd thought they'd do. Try and gain access to the house through that hole. He heaved a sigh. He'd made the right decision at the time.

"Two down, thousands to go." Bitterness raged in Ivan's tone.

Now to tell Doris that her husband was dead. Ivan raised his shoulders and stretched his back. "Let's get this terrible job done, Phil."

Back at the pedestrian gate once more, Ivan knelt beside Fillimon's body and uttered his final farewell. "Sorry old man, you saved our lives, I wish I could've saved yours."

Ivan stood. Now dread churned in his gut and he swallowed hard. He walked the road to the compound with Phil beside him.

Halfway down the road, a man ran toward them. Terrorist? He and Phil leapt from the road and crouched in the long grass.

"I think I recognise that gait." Despite the light offered by the full moon, it was still too dark for Ivan to make out who it was.

The man drew closer. It was Patric. Moving back onto the road, Patric fell at Ivan's feet.

"Sir," he blurted. "Misheke and……" he broke off. It was obvious something terrible had happened. Ivan prompted the hysterical Patric. "What about Misheke?"

"They…. they're…… all…dead," he stammered.

Ivan closed his eyes for a moment, then he turned to Phil. "Let's go to Misheke's house first, then on to Doris." Sadness giving way to fury. "Come on, Patric, stand up and come with us."

They continued down the road to the compound, following the foot path to Misheke's house. The door to the house was ajar. Taking two steps onto the small veranda, Ivan peered through the open door, then spun around, and puked over the edge of the veranda. Wiping his mouth on his sleeve he faced Phil and Patric. No words left his lips, and he flared his nostrils, like an angry bull. Strewn across the floor lay eight disfigured bodies, hacked to death with pangas and bayonets. Misheke, his wife, their four children, his father, Kenneth, and Misheke's mother lay dead in pools of blood. These were people Ivan loved. People he'd known all his life. People who did not deserve to die and certainly not this way. A burning rage filled his chest and the bile in his throat lingered hot and painful.

"Why?" The word whooshed from his mouth like an angered dragon. Stepping off the veranda, he came to stand beside Patric. His jaw clenched so tight it pained him. He put a hand on Patric's shoulder. "Fillimon was killed too. Mown down at the pedestrian gate."

Patric's knees gave way. He collapsed onto the top step and sobbed like a child.

"I'm so sorry, Patric. I must go to Doris," Ivan finally said as he moved off the veranda. The metallic smell of blood stained his nostrils.

Patric could only answer with a nod.

Phil and Ivan left Patric to deal with his grief. As they neared Doris's house, only thirty strides from Misheke's, Ivan uttered, "I cannot believe what I've just seen. Fucking savage. No-one deserves to die like that." Anger rose again, like a bush fire burning in his throat. The intensity of his emotion gave him the strength to deliver the worst news anyone can carry to another.

Ivan knocked on the door. Fillimon and Doris had been together forty-two years, living at Blue Winds. She pulled the wooden door open. Ivan spoke in her native tongue and shared the horrific news.

She stood in stunned silence, then she began to wail. Low and pitiful to begin with, then the sounds gradually rose in volume till her lament reached a bone-chilling crescendo. A song of anguish that echoed across the community.

Ivan and Phil left her with the promise to look after Fillimon's body. On his way back to the house, nauseated from exhaustion and what he'd witnessed, Ivan threw up again. This time it was bile and he spat the toxins of the past hours into the grass.

The visions of Misheke and his family now carved into his brain. A vile memory that could never be erased.

Ivan wiped his mouth. "Unforgiveable barbarism."

Chapter Four

IN THE HEART of the village, Chief Rex Sithole peered through the small window into the depths of the tree line, his eyes scanning for any signs of movement. A thin crescent moon and a sky full of stars, cast an eerie glow.

Joe's formidable gang of four emerged from the bush. Like silent ghosts, armed and dangerous, they dashed across the open space toward Rex's hut.

Joe's movements were as concise and commanding as his orders, and as weighty as his imposing frame.

Rex moved to his chair in the centre of the hut. A rattle on the hut's loose hasp alerted him

that Joe stood on the other side of the door. Rex fought a spasm of dread that gripped his gut. Familiar beads of perspiration rose on his forehead, and resentment, bitter and rancid filled his throat. A measure of fear produced a splurge of adrenaline, giving power to his voice.

"Yehbo Yakavhurika," It's open, he called in his native tongue of Shona.

The door creaked. Rex held his breath. There was no escape from the tangled web of fear, hatred, and confusion, but his life depended upon keeping the status quo.

Joe's head peeked through the crack to determine only Rex occupied the small hut and pushed the rickety door. The scrape of the door across the floor and Rex's crackling fire were the only sounds to alert unwanted ears to Joe's presence.

Joe's men, eyes as wary as Joe's, and sunken with hunger, filed into the hut. The hut walls were a mixture of plaster and cow dung offering welcoming warmth against the biting temperatures outside. Joe's men nestled their cold buttocks on the floor. Rex remained seated by the fire. Joe pinned him with a stare, searching Rex's watery, smoke-stained eyes looking for any trace of betrayal. Rex didn't worry. None existed, none ever would after Joe threatened to cut off his ears back in the early seventies when the terror insurgence moved from rumbling unrest to more serious warfare. Despite the passing of years, Rex remained confused by their modus operandi of pure adulterated hate. It saddened him. Rex had no hatred in his heart being too wise to feel such pointless emotion. Rex knew it led to bloodshed and heartache, as was happening now. He knew Joe's life would end in misery.

During an earlier visit, Rex had watched these five men speak of the coming of the Kingdom of Zimbabwe. A utopia created in each man's imagination that made them giddy with blood lust. Not in Rex's mind.

"The white dogs were here?" Joe's words rang as more of a statement than a question, and Rex cringed.

"Yes. On routine patrol two days ago. There were more of them this time," he said truthfully.

Joe silently analysed Rex's expression searching for a blink of an eye or a twitch at the corner of his mouth, as if he could read his mind and know the truth of Rex's words. Joe, an intelligent, brave man, took no chances, not even with Rex.

The aroma of Rex's home-cooked meal caught Joe's attention. Rex could see the hearty smell of the tomato relish was on Joe's mind. He kept looking at the fire. A low flame traced the bases of the two three-legged cast iron pots that straddled the fire.

Rex knew Joe and his men would be famished. Not one of them carried an ounce of superfluous flesh. Joe reached for a chipped, pale yellow enamel plate. Beside it lay a misshapen serving spoon. He scooped stiff maize porridge known as *sadza* from the first pot, moved to the second and removed the lid. After scooping a large portion of relish over the *sadza*, he nodded to his men.

They rose, one by one, and served themselves before settling back on the floor. Since Joe commanded the single eating spoon Rex owned, the men used their dirty fingers to shovel steaming hot *sadza* into their mouths. Within minutes, gravy and maize meal crumbs littered the hut's floor.

Beside the large cast-iron pots stood a hissing, boiling teapot. Rex had set out five enamel cups for the visit.

Joe rose. He wrapped a soiled cloth around his fingers, then gripped the heated handle and poured a cup of sweet tea. He sipped. "Mushi," Good, he said in his native tongue. After another mouthful. "Mushi sterek." Very good. "Your efforts will be rewarded." His eyes turned hard, "but you failed in your recruiting," his friendly tone morphed into menacing.

Rex willed his trembling body to still. *Show no fear.*

"This task is more difficult now, Comrade Joe. We have recruited most of the boys from the mission schools in the district. If we recruit more, security forces will grow suspicious." His heart pounded.

Joe stretched his legs towards the fire and waved away Rex's excuse.

"No problem. We have new targets." A nasty grin wrinkled the corners of Joe's mouth.

"New Targets?" Dread slid up Rex's spine. "What are they?" He asked with a confidence he didn't feel.

"Girls," Joe said. "Girls can train to fight for our freedom as well as boys."

Rex bowed his head. Recruiting the fairer gender would pose greater problems. A lot of the girls were either pregnant or had a baby.

Rex coughed. "The difficulty with recruiting girls between fifteen and eighteen years of age is tradition. You and I know they must prove their fertility at that age." Rex waited for Joe to explode with anger and ugly threats, but he didn't. He couldn't deny that the chief was right.

"Strong girls of fourteen will also do."

"Very well. I'll seek girls this week. I cannot guarantee how many I'll get."

There was no point in further lamenting the difficult task Joe demanded. Instead, he listened to the men talking of their perceived freedom in the Kingdom, where no king existed.

The chatter soon quieted. Each man sat with their silent thoughts. Outside, the wind howled, and the temperatures inside the hut seemed to drop by the minute.

Joe stood. "Time to leave."

His men lumbered to their feet. Now warm and satiated, they didn't appear too enthusiastic about leaving the warm hut.

Rex pushed out his chair. "Thank you for visiting."

Joe offered a curt nod. "You have your orders."

Rex burned with indignation at the reminder. He forced calm into his voice. "I'll have more recruits within the week."

"One week." He repeated Rex's promise.

The men filed out of his hut, then he pulled the rickety door shut and locked it. Only when he was certain they were gone, did he exhale the toxins of fear stored in his chest. He lowered himself onto his reed mat. His limbs weak from exhaustion, closed his eyes and forced sleep as the last of the fire's embers burned away.

**

Solomon stirred, and his bamboo mat on the floor creaked. He sat up, rubbed his eyes then opened them, he could see nothing. It was dark and cold inside the hut. Fumbling for the box of matches he'd left beside him, he struck one and lit the candle standing upright on the floor. Before blowing out the flickering light, he held the tiny light over his watch, a gift from Joe Mbutu - 12:14 a.m. A little past midnight. Excitement had brewed for a long time, and now, finally, it was time.

The gift of the watch marked the beginning of his new life. Soon he'd be fighting for the cause, the promise of freedom. When the battle was won, he'd come back and claim the estate. Blue Winds would be his, in recognition for his contribution to the war effort. Joe had promised. He would not need to work for a boss again, he'd be the boss. Victory was not far off for the freedom fighters. Joe had promised this too.

Already dressed in loosely fitting, torn jean, a T shirt, and a blue hoodie tracksuit top, he pulled on his soccer boots, the pair he'd stolen from the store. *The estate store will be mine too.*

He stood up, grabbed the cash he'd saved hidden in the thatch of the hut roof and counted the money again. One hundred and forty-seven dollars. He whistled, proud of himself. Soon he'd earn double that as a freedom fighter. The thrill of anticipation sent a quiver through his muscles.

He slid the money down the side of his boot, then spread a thin blanket on the floor and bundled spare clothes onto it, folded the corners inward, and tied the bundle with rope he'd stolen from the mill. He felt no remorse for his thieving ways. If anything, he was proud of himself for not being caught. The storekeeper had eyes everywhere.

Pinching out the flame, he left the hut and closed the door. He would reach the given rendezvous point not long after sunrise. Joe would be there waiting for him.

Solomon ran through the Blue Winds compound and joined the road on the edge of the forest. It was a longer route, but not as dark as the path through the forest.

The blanketed bundle bounced on his back, prompting a recollection of when he first met Joe, a fierce militant. Everything Joe had said to Solomon in the forests that day came back to him as he hurried along the road.

'We'll see all the white colonial pigs either killed, maimed, or running across borders. We'll watch them scuttle away like the vermin they are.' Those words made Solomon smile. To him Joe seemed superior, even to God.

Now, running in an easy jog, Solomon was looking forward to meeting Joe's commander, Antonio Budu. Joe was one of Antonio's top men. Solomon would fall under their joint command.

Solomon ran for hours. The sun began to rise, it's rays striking pink lines across the skies. He stopped frequently to check the map from Joe. Maybe an hour to go now. Solomon found an ancient mango tree with the girth of a hippo. He rested his back against the bulky, dark sienna coloured trunk, closed his eyes and let his breathing regulate, then sipped the last of his water.

"Tonight," he said aloud, "I'll draw inspiration from the words of

Chairman Mao." Saying his thoughts aloud boosted his confidence. He patted the bundle, inside was the Little Red Book. He allowed himself ten minutes rest and almost fell asleep. Alarmed he'd dozed off he checked his watch - 5:40 a.m. Not late. Following the well-worn path to freedom made him stand and rejoice. He jumped, snapped his heels together with joy and shouted and off he went again.

A quick glance at the route map and instructions, he could see a building that fitted Joe's description. Solomon slowed to a walk. He approached the building with caution, and entered what appeared to be an old, dingy bar. The stench of stale liquor and fermenting Chibuku beer mingled with stale cigarette smoke that still hung in the air, indicating the bar had customers last night.

Tired, rusty old sheets of corrugated iron, full of holes, posed as the roof. Shafts of light filtered in, cutting through the smoky haze. The walls were built using large cement blocks and strips of frayed hessian nailed to wooden window frames acted as curtains.

Solomon stood with his back to the door. He could just imagine the conversations that would've taken place in this room, then Joe's voice boomed behind him.

"Comrade Solomon. You made it."

Solomon spun around. "Yes, Sir."

The two men clasped hands.

"Follow me," Joe ordered.

Solomon trailed Joe in a comfortable jog, moving down a dusty road that led through the village. The first large village they'd encountered so far just inside Mozambique. An occasional dog came to see them, barked, then retreated. They passed through banana plantations, skirted fields of cassava, and covered distance inside indigenous forest.

They arrived at the camp built within these dense, ancient forests just after 9:00 a.m. Joe had told him, for security reasons, most of the rooms lay underground, making it hard to determine the size of the camp.

"The Commanders office." Joe said, pointing to a building on the far side of a red earthen parade square swept clean by new recruits. They crossed the parade square and took the steps to commander's office door.

Joe knocked.

"Yes." Came a bellow from inside.

Joe opened the door.

"Aah, you're back. Enter, enter." The commander beckoned.

They entered and stood beside each other facing the commander.

Antonio was a large man, pasted, greasy black cropped hair and a dark olive skin. He was clean shaven. A military requirement. His wide girth spread, filling the chair with no room to spare. Born in Beira to a Portuguese mother and a local father, a businessman with a reputation for dubious dealings.

"Sit," Antonio demanded.

The two men obeyed and pulled out the chairs. The seats, once covered in maroon vinyl was old, hardened and torn, the sharp bits standing up that dug into their legs when they sat. On the walls were ancient, yellowed topographical maps of Mozambique. One of the corners had peeled away from the wall and hung loosely, flapping in the occasional breeze.

"Am I to believe this man is Solomon Tlale?" Antonio asked Joe, looking over Solomon with eyes that penetrated without expression.

"Yes Sir, this is him." Joe answered.

Antonio continued speaking to Joe as if Solomon didn't exist. The commander praised Joe for the work his freedom fighters had accomplished along the border with Rhodesia. He also praised Joe for the damage he caused at Blue Winds estate recently, even though the freedom fighters lost two men, mown down by the colonialist, Ivan Johns.

"That's war. It happens." No remorse reflected on Antonio's face. "You've done good in the Honde Valley. The tea farmers are scared, but they are too stupid to leave." Antonio laughed. His enormous gut bounced like jelly. "Our ZANLA (Zimbabwe African National Liberation Army) forces are committed and brave. Recruiting more young men and women is going well, but we still need more. We received twenty-two women from Chief Rex. A very good job, Joe."

Antonio breathed deep. "Now listen carefully." He eyed Joe. "Orders from the top are to increase ambushes on farm roads. Hamstring cattle. Destroy irrigation pipes and pumps belonging to whities." His jowls vibrated. "Destroy morale in the TTLs (Tribal Trust Lands) and farm compounds. Decimate rural cattle dips built by the colonials. Gut mission stations. Kill the priests, rape the nuns, they're easy targets." He spewed raucous laughter sending a chill down Solomon's back. "Plant landmines in farm roads and Anti-personnel mines on well used paths." It seemed not to matter to Antonio that most of his victims on the roads and paths would be innocent black women and children. It shocked Solomon, but then he realised that's the cost of war.

"Attack the Johns homestead again. I want my prize. Do not fail again." This last instruction raised a smile on Solomon's face. He would be on that mission.

The two men left Antonio's office. Joe guided Solomon to his quarters underground.

Solomon hadn't been on the first attack of Blue Winds estate. He'd been in Tanzania undergoing intensive guerilla warfare training. He returned at the end of April as a ruthless soldier. Antonio wanted Solomon as his man for the plan to retrieve his prize.

Solomon knew the layout of Blue Winds farm, and the inside of the house. The next attack would be timed carefully, Antonio wanted no mistakes. And his warning left Joe and Solomon with no confusion about what Antonio would do to them should they fail.

Over the next week, they were to bury large amounts of arms and ammunition in the forests belonging to Ivan Johns.

A week after Solomons return Joe advised that the next morning, five comrades and himself were going on a risky mission. Soaked with anticipation and sweat, Joe's order to move out brought fear to the pit of Solomon's stomach. Joe likely saw Solomon's terror despite Solomon's recent training.

"Move it," Joe warned as the five men slowed to a walk. "No stopping, run." They jogged down the narrow path toward the forest after crossing into Rhodesia once more. The load each man carried in hessian sacks was heavy.

Two of the main sell-outs had been killed in the first attack on Blue

Winds, but there were more that lived in the compound and worked in the forests. Solomon couldn't afford to be seen by any of the men he used to work with. They would notify Johns, blow their cover, and the caches would be discovered, so they had to lay them when the workers had gone home, or at night.

In the months since leaving Blue Winds, Solomon had drawn much inspiration from the words of Chairman Moa's writings. Last night he'd held the Little Red Book between clammy hands and read another passage. There were many words he didn't understand, but those he did he stored to memory. Twenty years old, with only basic education, the concepts of socialism, Marxism, communism, or any other *ism* was beyond his grasp, except colonialism. That he understood.

Hiding below the forest canopy, the men rested until dusk. They'd watched the labourers leave. Their mission tonight involved burying the sacks of arms and ammunition in marked caches which they'd use in their planned future attacks, not just on Blue Winds, but other farms too. They had an hour of daylight left to dig unseen in the forest.

Chapter Five

Down at the sawmill Ivan yelled. "Flick the red switch." He watched in horror as Joseph's arm flew in bits through the air like bloody missiles. The saw stopped.

Ivan ran to Joseph. Arterial blood pumped out of the stump and smudged the sawdust he lay on. Powered by adrenaline, Ivan ripped off his jacket and cotton shirt. Using the shirt as a tourniquet, he tightened it around the stump to stem the flow from the severed artery. Then he wrapped his parker jacket around Joseph to keep him warm. Shock and the rapid loss of blood could kill him. This was a dire emergency.

"Call the madam," Ivan bellowed. One of the mill workers ran to the house. Stammering, he briefly explained what had happened. Margaret ran to the bathroom, grabbed the first aid kit, a bundle of towels and bandages, and raced down to the mill.

"Oh, my goodness. Here, take all this, let me get you some new clothes." She turned to rush back to the house. Shivering Ivan said, "while you're at the house, call the hospital, tell them I'm on my way in five minutes."

"Emergency admissions"

"Hello, it's Mrs Johns here, from Blue Winds Estate. My husband is bringing in a worker whose arm caught in a band saw. Sucked into the saw before it could be stopped. The stump is close to the shoulder. We've bandaged it as tight as possible to stem the bleeding."

"No! How terrible. We'll be waiting, Mrs Johns."

Margaret hurried through to the bedroom, pulled a clean shirt and pullover from the closet and another jacket for Ivan, jumped into the car and drove to the mill. She covered the back seat with a blanket and towels. Workers carried Joseph to the car and laid him on the back seat. Margaret covered him with blankets while Ivan quickly put on the clean clothes and jacket. He'd got really cold, and his teeth chattered as he jumped in behind the wheel and sped off.

To keep Jospeh from slipping into an unconscious state, Ivan spoke to him as he drove.

"Hold on Joseph. Don't go to sleep."

"Yes Sa," Joseph uttered from the back seat. "Too......too.... much pain, Sa."

"I'm sure. I can't go faster, Joseph. Don't fall off the back seat. Hospital staff are waiting."

"No Sa, I ...... won't fall."

Ivan asked Joseph questions in his mother tongue to keep him awake. It was normally a forty-five-minute drive to the Inyanga village hospital. Thirty-five minutes later they arrived. The emergency team raced to the car, lifted Joseph from the back seat, onto a gurney and wheeled him to theatre within minutes.

The village government hospital was a small rural hospital. On his way to admissions, Ivan prayed they'd save Joseph's life. After he completed the necessary paperwork, Ivan drove home slowly, deep in thought. When got back to the farm he drove to the mill first. Margaret was still there.

"What are you doing here?"

"I stayed. Someone had to direct the dazed, horrified workers. These poor men didn't know what to do next. Two men cleaned the saw with disinfectant we found in your office, and I got two to dig a hole to bury the bits of offending flesh and blood-soaked sawdust. I sent the rest of them home. How's Joseph?"

"He was whipped off so fast, I have no idea. Let's call the hospital later. We have no other mill worker of Joseph's calibre to stand in till he gets back. If he survives." Ivan rubbed his forehead. He wasn't convinced poor Joseph would live.

"He's been the head sawyer for five years and what a wonderful, humble, softly spoken man. He rarely makes mistakes. I don't know what happened to his concentration today, but I can only surmise he's not sleeping well for fear of another attack on the compound." Margaret listened on the verge of tears. Ivan knew Joseph better than her and this news made it all worse.

One of the men who'd dug the hole came across and greeted Ivan.

"How's Joseph, Baas?" He asked.

"I'll let you all know in the morning. Thank you for helping dig the hole and clean up here. I'm going to close the mill. You chaps head home."

"Thank you, Baas."

Ivan locked the mill security gates, and he and Margaret wondered home. Nausea tugged at the pit of Margaret's stomach as they walked. Margaret rubbed her arms from the chill as they stepped into the kitchen. Simon was standing by the stove, dumbfounded.

"Madam, Baas, will Joseph die?"

"I certainly hope not. We don't need to lose another excellent staff member. Is that water boiling?" Margaret asked, pointing to the large black kettle that lived on the Aga stove.

"Yes, it is, madam. I'll make tea for you and Baas." Simon quickly jumped to action.

"Thank you, Simon. You're a wonderful replacement for your dear uncle, Fillimon. How we miss him."

"I miss him too." He bowed his head and wrapped his hand around the hot kettle handle. "I'll bring the tea for you."

Margaret and Ivan wandered slowly through to the sitting room. Both with their own thoughts on the tragic event at the mill.

Margaret had just finished her tea when the phone rang. She ran to answer it. It was the hospital. Joseph had died in theatre. She staggered back to the sitting room and collapsed into her armchair and sobbed. Ivan knew then that Joseph had passed.

Simon heard their distress and knocked quietly, hesitant to disturb them.

"Yes, Simon." Ivan said.

Simon entered and picked up the tea tray. "Is Joseph alright?"

"No. He's just died." Margaret murmured through her tears.

"That's terrible. I'm sorry. Very sorry." He lingered. "I'm not supposed to tell, but the terrorists were at Joseph's hut two nights ago. They threatened to cut off his lips if he didn't feed them."

"What?" Margaret's head spun, tears still wet on her cheeks. "Good God." She moaned, angered by the war and all the bloodshed and heartbreak it brought. Ivan sat silently by, suffering from the shock of witnessing the accident and the anger that penetrated deep within his soul.

"No madam, no good God." Simon's perspective.

Ivan looked at Simon now. "What else is going on in the compound?" Now Simon had bravely revealed those truths after losing his uncle as a sell-out, Ivan felt it fine to ask.

"There's talk that many weapons have been hidden in the forests recently." Ivan went cold. He felt the chill run through each part of his body.

"Has anything been mentioned about another attack on us?"

"No, Sir. I shall tell you what I hear."

"That's very brave, Simon, but we don't want anything to happen to you. Please be very careful." Margaret warned him.

His focus reverted to Margaret. "I don't care, madam. Telling you all I hear is defending the memory of my beloved uncle, Fillimon. These people are evil. They need to be stopped."

Ivan answered. "They certainly do. Thank you, Simon. Your loyalty is commendable. We wish we could do more to protect you all in the compound."

He didn't reply. Hurting and angry, he bowed his head, backed away from where he stood holding the tray, and left the room.

Ivan and Margaret glanced at each other as he left. Stunned, staring into space for a moment, Margaret whispered, "arms caches in our forests."

Ivan's shoulders were hunched. He was pale and exhausted. "I'm grateful to Simon, but right now I can't get the sound of Joseph's screaming from my head. I left all the blankets and towels at the hospital. They'll incinerate them."

Margaret took a deep breath. "Good. I couldn't bear having them back anyway." They sat silently, mulling over their own thoughts on Simon's revelation.

Ivan spoke first. "Did Simon mention which sections of the forest the caches have been hidden? I wasn't really concentrating then."

"No, he didn't. You'll have to ask him."

A restless night followed and, in the morning, Ivan strode down to the mill before the gong sounded. He unlocked the security gates and opened his office. He sat in deep thought in the quiet of the early morning. Not even the pleasure of listening to the bird calls lightened the burden he carried. He dreaded telling the workers of Joseph's demise.

Chapter Six

A WEEK after Joseph's accident Ivan and Margaret felt they had to get off the farm, have a round of golf and socialise with local farmers to help them settle taut nerves.

Feeling refreshed, they entered the pub. A glowing fire welcomed them into the warmth and friendly banter. Friends and associates offered an insight into numerous new tricks on protecting themselves and their home in the event of another attack.

The equipment that interest Ivan most were the fence monitors. Sensors attach to the security fence in various spots around the perimeter. The monitoring station is installed in the house. Those who'd already purchased the device said the best place to fit the monitor was above the bed in the master bedroom. The monitor beeps loudly when the fence is tampered with and wakes the occupants.

Ivan and Margaret agreed to getting the equipment urgently. Ivan also thought a few Adams grenades would be a valuable investment, though it meant building protective walls in front of windows that neither of them wanted, but knew it would be sensible, particularly in front of the bedrooms.

After Simon's warning Ivan arranged to meet the local District Commissioner. The DC's office was a typical rural government building. The inside, painted in a dreary cream colour, with enamel paint so shiny you could almost recognise yourself in its reflection. Green or brick red enamel painted on doors and window frames. You could not mistake a government building.

On entering the building, they noticed, stuck scattered on the walls, gazetted laminated posters. 'Keep Big Ears Out.'- 'Rhodesia is Super.'

Manning the reception stood a tall, arrogant looking man dressed in khaki uniform. The gold buttons on the tunic shone. He stared at Ivan for a moment longer than could have been deemed polite.

"Good morning, we have an appointment with the DC. Johns, is the name." Ivan said, but the obvious insolence from the young man had not gone unnoticed. He left his desk and sauntered down the passage.

Ivan looked at Margaret. She could see his annoyance by his clenching jaw. The man returned and with his index finger, beckoned they should follow. Walking down the passage behind the uniformed receptionist he ushered them into the DC's office.

"Good morning, Ivan. How can I help?" DC Birch asked, seated in his chair, his ample stomach stuck out so far, the edge of the desk dented it where his invisible waist might once have been. Too fat to observe common manners which prickled Ivan's already touchy mood. To make matters worse, Ivan noticed DC Birch staring longingly at Margaret.

"It's me you need to focus on." Ivan snarled. Birch's eyes shot back to meet Ivan's. His nose and cheeks turned a deeper shade of purple.

"Yes, yes, yes, go on." His cheeks wobbled in time with his lips. Ivan and Margaret pulled out the chairs and sat.

A Scope magazine lay open on his desk, the centre spread, a voluptuous semi-nude blonde. Ivan struggled with the urge to grab the man by the scruff of his neck and tell him what he thought of him. He calmed him anger and told the DC about his concern.

"There's an increasing number of terrorists in my compound and forests." For reasons unknow, Ivan stopped speaking, stood, walked to the door, and closed it. The reception clerk, eager to hear what the Johns had to say, had been standing beside the open door. He had a meeting with Joe and Solomon at Naidoo's trading store in the village that evening.

"Another terrorist meeting, eh?" A supercilious grin appeared on the DC's face as he watched Ivan walk back to his chair. "Are you sure the information is accurate? Not some idle *kaffir* wanting to stir the shit because he sees you're a bit twitchy."

His patronising tone turned Ivan's face a deep angry red. "Firstly, there's no need for derogatory language. My staff are loyal. So loyal some have died for us., and because of that and the last attack on our homestead, we have every right to be twitchy." Ivan seethed, his fists balled, and his jaw clenched painfully from suppressed anger.

Ivan's comment didn't deter the man. "Christ, Ivan," Birch stretched back in his chair, expanding further at the waistline. "How many farmers in Kenya were betrayed by their so-called *loyal* staff and were slaughtered in cold blood by the Mau-Mau? You're living with blinkers on, my friend."

"One thing I need to make abundantly clear. I'm not your friend." Ivan could take no more of this unhelpful idiot. He knew all about the Mau Mau. Margaret had experienced the indignation imposed on the white farmers in Kenya. She was a young girl of six when they were thrown out of the country and she and her parents had moved to South Africa.

Ivan stood. "If you're not going to give me your full co-operation, I'll take this matter higher, or take the law into my own hands." Ivan seethed. His hands twitched by his sides.

Birch smoothed the front of his khaki tunic, expecting Ivan to launch over the desk. He braced himself for the event. "Take the law into your own hands Johns, and you're a dead man."

Ivans lips curled. Thrusting a well-defined jaw forward, he snarled. "You'll be a dead man if you don't act on this report and send it through to JOC (Joint Operational Command) HQ in the next fifteen minutes."

Birch coughed. "Where did you say your loyal *kaffir-boy* said the gooks are hiding arms?" His tone even more patronising.

"My eastern plantations. Our most mature forests. The area covers approximately five thousand hectares of forest close to the border. I want security forces deployed in our area to carry out a thorough recce and support PATU. They cannot cover such expanses effectively, and I need to harvest timber. It is my income. Do you hear me?"

"For Christ's sake, Johns. They'll need to deploy a fucking battalion to find those gooks and their cache's." A contemptuous grin spread, pushing bulbous cheeks up the side of his face.

"Well deploy a fucking battalion, then. The army is there to assist us front line troops - commonly known as farmers." Ivan couldn't take any more of the DC's contempt. He turned to Margaret. "Come on, let's get out of here."

DC Birch rose from his chair. The effort was so extreme, he finally got himself upright and farted from the exertion. Breathing heavily, he spoke. "I'll.... do what...... I can." There was no apology for the rude release of unwanted gasses.

Once the Johns had left the office the DC rested his weight on his right arm and slid the left desk drawer open and pulled a half jack of brandy from within. He unscrewed the lid and took a large swig of the amber liquid.

Ivan and Margaret had not gone more than a few strides down the passage when Ivan stopped and looked at Margaret. "I'm going back. I want to watch him write out the memo, then I'll know it's been done."

"I'll wander back to the car. I cannot bear to look at him again. Give me the car keys." Margaret said.

Ivan fiddled in his jacket pocket and handed her the keys, then marched back to Birch's office just as he took a swig of neat liquor. Caught in the act, he swallowed and stared at Ivan.

"Drinking on duty gets people in your position instantly dismissed." Ivan warned, enjoying the fact he could now manipulate the disgusting thug.

Sweat beads covered the DCs brow and burst, dripping onto the blank memo pad.

Ivan unclipped the parker pen from his pocket and handed it to Birch. "Write. The memo's priority is *'Immediate.'*"

Ivan watched him write, then Birch dialled a single number on the telephone dial. A young lady rushed into the office. "Yes, Sir." She stood near Ivan. Birch tore the memo off the pad and handed it to her. "Have this message sent to Brigade HQ immediately. It's Top Secret."

"Yes Sir." She took the memo and left. So did Ivan.

When he got back to the car and sat in the driver's seat, he turned to Margaret, "What a truly awful creature."

"Did he do as you asked?" Margaret enquired.

"You bet, he did. I caught him swigging on a bottle of brandy. He knows better than to do nothing and I'm going to follow up with Phil when we get home."

THE FOLLOWING week the garrison town of Umtali, where Mel's school is located, became a new target. Reported on the national news the town had been pounded by mortars and rockets. Phil called shortly after the announcement was made.

"You'll be pleased to know the school escaped the mortars." He put Ivan's concerns to rest.

"Thanks for letting us know. Margaret was about to call the school. Something's been niggling at me after we spoke last week after the meeting with the DC. I'm suspicious of the front desk clerk. I reckon he's feeding information to the terrs. If you need leverage with that ghastly arsehole, I caught him drinking neat brandy. He keeps it in the left desk drawer."

"Is that a fact? Everyone wants him out. I'm damned sure he's in cahoots with the terrs and this information ties in with your suspicions. I'll make sure I get to the bottom it and get him booted out."

"Thanks Phil. Much appreciated." Ivan placed the receiver and seconds later it rang again. It was the security fence monitoring system company. They wanted to do the installation.

"Yes. Absolutely. The sooner the better. We're home all day." Ivan felt relief fill him. He told Margaret they were expected a little later that morning.

Margaret's nerves, still on edge from the news of the mortar attack on Umtali, welcomed the men inside when they arrived.

A few Adams grenades were still left to install.

When Ivan got home that evening, he appeared slightly more relaxed. "With the security fence up, fence monitors everywhere, flood lights in the garden, walls across our windows and Agric Alert buzzing in the passage, our home has become another Fort Knox, but at least we can protect ourselves against another attack."

Margaret glanced at Ivan. "It's going to take weeks to get used to the incessant buzzing from the monitor above their heads."

"I know, but when the perpetual sounds of the night become entrenched in our sub-conscious, the slightest deviation will wake us in an instant. Forewarned, remember. That's life on the front lines."

APART FROM THE exception of a military Bedford truck being blown up by a landmine, killing the driver and three military personnel only eighty kilometres from Blue Winds, the district had been quiet.

"This period of quiet is a relief in some way, but in other ways, not. It's a bit eery. What's next?" Margaret mentioned to Ivan as they wandered hand in hand from the mill to the house for lunch. "Mel will be home soon for the mid-term break. It's hard to believe our little girl is in her last year at school."

"Where have the years gone?" Ivan shook his head in wonder. "Not just because she's our daughter, but my goodness, she's grown into a beautiful young lady, hasn't she?" He said proudly.

"She certainly has, even though she behaves like a tomboy most of the time." Margaret chuckled.

After lunch, in the sitting room, Ivan picked up the newspaper. He browsed through it. After a few minutes of reading, he shouted, "Good God, Margaret. Reporters really know how to skew the truth. They've no idea what happens on the ground in this ghastly bloody war. This horrid reporter," he looked closer at the name, "Brian Jefferies. The creep has sly, belittling comments on Ian Smith's declaration that before the war, the black population in Rhodesia were some of the happiest in Africa.

Margaret pulled the needle and thread through her tapestry and rested her hand on it. "Well, if our staff are anything to go by, he's quite right. They were, until this bloody war took hold of the rural native folk, frightening the life out of them."

"Radicals, like this idiot, are my pet hate, I'm afraid." The newspaper shook in his hands. Margaret smiled, wondering how he could read.

His voice boomed again. He moved the paper away and glanced across at her. "Before this rotten war a wonderful comradery existed between most blacks and whites. This man gets me going. Bloody Brit know-it-all who's never lived a week in the country." Ivan took a deep breath. "Blacks and whites farm side by side, they mine side by side and now we fight to save our country from falling into communist hands, together. RAR (Rhodesian African Rifles) are some of the finest soldiers in the world. They're bloody brilliant. They fought in Burma too."

"Look at this! Just look at this." He turned the newspaper around for Margaret to see a picture of a white American senator sitting with, 'representatives from principal Zimbabwean liberation movements.'

"Who the hell is this person? I thought America was against communism and terrorist insurgence." Ivan looked closer at the caption. "Senator Joseph R. Biden. Who the hell is he? And what does he think he's doing cosying up with these bastards?"

"Sweetheart, perhaps you should stop reading," Margaret suggested, though she knew his political tirade got rid of tension. It was best to let him finish reading.

"Black leaders throughout Africa have mastered the art of oppressing their people. They are brilliant at it. That kind of thing's simply not in our DNA. Scooping the GDP into private Swiss bank accounts, not giving a thought to the starving populace. Generally, their own kind. It's despicable." He put the paper on his lap. "There's only one thing Ian Smith strives for - maintaining our standards, no matter colour or creed. If the natives think they're frightened and hard done by, wait till they experience deeper fear that comes with mass unemployment and guaranteed starvation. If ZANLA take over there'll come a time when only twenty per cent of the population will be earning, inflation will be rampant, there'll be no farmers left to feed the populace, and export top quality produce, as we do now. The GDP will plummet." Ivan realised he was holding his breath and he stopped talking and took in a deep inhalation of air.

"Put it away, my love. Bundle it up for when we have fires again soon. Simon can light up Senator Biden's opinion and let it go up in smoke." She said affectionately. "It's not doing you any good reading the newspapers. You said yourself, *what bullshit.*"

Ivan gazed at her. "You're quite right. I worry about Mel and what her future holds. I worry about our workers in the forests, and while they sleep at night, unprotected. I worry about our income, which has already been radically affected. The gooks won't win the war, but they might win an election if it comes to that, but you can guarantee it'll be rigged in favour of ZANLA, and in ten years the country will have been brought to its knees."

Chapter Seven

Mel was home from school. She and Patric rode the fence lines and discovered more sheep had been stolen. Fifteen unaccounted for this time. A huge loss of revenue. They combed the paddocks and found where the fences had been prized open. The two bottom wire strands cut and pulled back, wide enough to drive sheep through, without the damage being too obvious. The tell-tale sign from a distance was the flattened grass.

Arriving back at the house after four, Ivan wagged his finger at his daughter. "You've been out all day."

"I know, Dad. Fifteen of mum's sheep have been stolen. We found where the fences were cut and fixed them." Mel brushed sweaty streaks of hair from her face. "I'm exhausted. I'm off to shower."

After an early supper Mel kissed her parents' goodnight and dragged the dog beds into her room. Benji and Bessie happily followed. They always slept in her room when she was home.

Not long after Mel left the room, Ivan and Margaret decided to get an early night too. They lay in bed listening to the gurgling, liquid sounds of frogs chatting to each other. Soon the screeching beetles joined the chorus. This nighttime lullaby captured by the fence monitors had eventually offered a soporific effect. When the sounds assured them nothing untoward seemed to be happening beyond the security fence, they fell asleep.

The deafening roar of an RPG (rocket propelled grenade) pierced the air, then a thunderous explosion woke them. Realisation immediately dawned as the impact shattered the brick wall of their bedroom again. Another attack.

Ivan scrambled out of bed and grabbed the Uzi. The sharp crackling of debris filled their room with more dust and debris than before. Dust billowed from the hole engulfing the bedroom, but Ivan noticed the hole was big enough for a man to climb through easily.

Camouflaged by swirling dust, Ivan flipped the safety off the Uzi. Three large strides, he stood to the side of the opening and fired into the darkness in a wide arc.

The dut, dut, dut sounds of automatic gunfire came hurtling back, echoing across the countryside. The quiet night had erupted. The sounds of war filled their home once more.

After emptying the first magazine Ivan darted back to the bed and grabbed the full magazine lying on the bedstand. He noticed Margaret was sitting on the floor with one arm over her head, coughing from the dust. He quickly clipped in the full magazine, leaving the empty one for her to fill.

The gunfire directed at the bedroom had stopped, just like before. Ivan wondered if one of the bullets had stopped the terrorist before accessing the house through the hole in the wall. This time it was big enough for a man to walk straight in.

"Are you okay?" Ivan asked Margaret. She was still sitting in the same place.

"Yes. The bas.... tards." She coughed. "Flying debris hit my head."

"Are you badly hurt?"

"No. Some skin off. Head wounds bleed like hell, but I'll be fine. It's not sore."

Ivan leapt back to the side of the wall and fired six rounds, then he went back to Margaret. The FN lay on the floor beside her. Blood was running down her face. He picked his way over the fallen bricks and plaster to the bathroom, grabbed a towel, and strode back to Margaret.

"Ominous, this silence. I don't like it." He handed her the towel. "Will you be able to guard the hole. I'll go check on Mel?"

"Yes, go." Margaret stood, holding the towel to her head. "I think my shoulder's been hit too, it's bloody sore suddenly."

Ivan hesitated. Torn between his wife's need and checking his daughter wasn't injured. "You sure you'll be all right? I'll be quick."

"Go, I'll be fine. I'll sit on the bed and God help anyone who steps through that hole."

"That's the spirit." He took the FN from her and handed her the lighter Uzi. Ivan found Mel at the radio. After the last attack, the three of them had decided, if another attack came, Mel would go to the radio. Still no more shooting from outside. This worried Ivan. Trapped in their home he had no idea where the next hail of bullets would come from.

"Bravo One, Bravo One, come in." Melonie broke the silence.

"Charlie two, go," came the comforting, crackling response.

"We're under attack, send in help." Mel sounded calm, but Ivan knew she couldn't be feeling calm.

"That's my girl. Get yourself armed."

"I am. I've got Mum's 9mm pistol. "Where's Mum? And what hit the house?"

"A mortar. The hole is bigger than me. Mum's sitting on the bed with the Uzi ready to shoot anyone who tries to climb through. Go to her, she'll need help reloading."

Leaving her station at the radio in the passage, Mel stood at the door to her parents' room, one of the outside lights lit the space. She picked her way over broken bricks and bits of plaster. Her mother fumbled with FN bullets, pressing them into the empty magazine.

Dut. Dut-dut-dut-dut-dut.

Gunfire from the kitchen side of the house.

They heard Ivan's return fire.

Mel sat beside her. "Mum, are you okay?" A large smudge of blood covered the top of Margaret's tracksuit top.

"It's my shoulder, I think a piece of sharp debris hit me. It hurts like hell. But don't worry about it. Take the Uzi, stand to one side of the hole and blast off a few shots. Keep the terrs from getting any closer. It'll take the pressure off dad." She handed Mel the Uzi.

Mel hefted the Uzi to her hip.

"Give me the 9mm, I'll guard this side of the house and refill magazines."

Standing beside the hole, Mel fired, then jumped back across the fallen debris. She helped her mum manoeuvre herself along the side of the bed to the bedstand and pushed herself up. "Press the outdoor flood light switch." She said to Mel.

Two floodlights lit the garden. Enemy gunfire ceased. Then Margaret triggered the first Adams grenade, and they could hear shrapnel scatter over the lawns and hit the barrier walls.

The sounds of the explosion settled, followed by silence. Mel grabbed a handful of tissues from the bedstand, lifted her mum's tracksuit and packed the wad of tissues over the wound to help quell the bleeding.

"Are you going to be alright here on your own, Mum?"

"Yes, you go and help Dad. I'll be fine."

She left her mum sitting on the bed reloading and met her dad in the kitchen. The shooting began again. This time bullets were hitting the sitting room walls. Mel followed her dad into the sitting room. They made their way toward the curtained windows when the house was rocked by another explosion. Debris showered down on the tin roof covering the veranda. Then the shooting ceased.

"That's the second Adams grenade Mum has triggered. Creep back to the radio and call again. We need help."

Mel did as her dad instructed. With shaking hands, she called.

"Bravo One, come in please."

Seconds later her call was answered. "Bravo One, go."

"We need help urgently. Are the army on their way?" Mel heard the fear she felt in her own voice.

"Back-up is on the way, over." The response came back, and she felt comforted, but her body still shook.

Mel clenched her jaw and balled her fists. She didn't want to leave her station by the radio but decided to check on her mum.

Passing her father on the way, he shouted, "going to the kitchen."

"Right. I'm going to mum. Have you seen her shoulder?"

"Yes, I have. Get her some pain tablets from bathroom cabinet." Ivan cried out.

Mel crouched at the door to her parent's bedroom and clambered over the rubble making her way to the bathroom. She stood, pulled a box of painkillers from the cabinet, and grabbed a toilet roll then went back to her mum.

"Shit Mum, you're badly hurt." Mel noticed how much blood had oozed from the shoulder wound.

"I'm okay, sweetheart." Margaret tried to sound convincing.

"There's so much blood from the wound on your head, Mum."

"It's because I rubbed hair out of my eyes and the graze started bleeding again. It's my shoulder that hurts." She moaned loudly.

"Here are some painkillers." Mel shouted above the noise of gunfire and handed the box to her mother. Margaret opened the packet and pressed two tablets out of the foil. She reached for the glass of water that still stood on the bedstand. Though there was a covering of fine dust, Margaret swallowed the tablets and the dust while Mel rolled off a wad of toilet paper and pressed it down hard on bleeding head wound.

"I think the gooks must know we've got the hole in the wall covered. Hopefully we're safe in here."

Margaret held the bundled sheets of toilet paper in place. It stuck. She placed the pistol on the bedstand and went on reloading magazines. Mel stood nearby, her ears ringing. A conundrum, did she stay or help her father? Then she heard him coughing loudly.

"I'm going to help Dad." She leant down and shouted to her mother, worried about leaving her, but she knew her dad needed extra fire power. She found him in the kitchen and handed him two full magazines.

"Where do you want me, Dad?"

"Go to the sitting room. Sneak the barrel of your Uzi through the curtains and the broken window, and fire off a whole magazine in an arc.

That'll keep the buggers' heads down. Then race back to the radio. We need help. I reckon we're almost out of ammo by now."

"Okay, Dad. The last radio message said help was on the way."

Mel held the gun to the window and pulled the trigger. Suddenly she felt immortal, but the sensation soon passed. She raced back to the radio, pushed her back against the wall, slid to the floor and placed the machine gun next to her. Picking up the radio mouthpiece, she called. Only minutes had passed since her last call, but it felt longer.

"Bravo One, come in."

"Bravo One, go."

"When did the army leave? We're almost out of ammo. Over"

"Help should be with you in five minutes. Out"

Mel felt like crying, they could be dead in five minutes. She felt frustrated by her lack of military readiness, both with weaponry and radio procedures, although she knew correct radio procedures weren't expected from the operators manning the receiving stations. They had to deal with panicked wives and children often.

In the heat of battle time stretched. Every second felt like an eternity and each minute she knew was critical. Would they hold out? Scared, Mel's body began to shiver as she listened to bullets pepper the walls of the sitting room again, ricocheting off the veranda's tin roof. She prayed none of the bullets fired by the terrs were tracers. Dad had told her about tracers, so had the army major who'd addressed the school. They would set the roof alight. She didn't want to die in a blazing inferno as the house burnt down.

Should wondered if she should go back and help her dad. She put the radio mouthpiece back on the stand and stood at the radio station, her head tilted to the floor, then she looked up. Shaking in terror, a figure loomed in front of her. She lifted the Uzi, ready to fire. "Dad!" She shouted with fright, having nearly pulled the trigger. The fear reached her toes and they tingled; she'd nearly shot her dad.

"Have you got spare magazines?" he asked.

"No, Mum's got them." She slipped to the floor, weakened from the relief of not pulling the trigger. Ivan shuffled quickly through the rubble in their room and took two full magazines from Margaret. Passing Mel, seated at the radio, he headed to the kitchen, then the shooting began again. She could hear windows shattering and her dad's return fire, sporadic this time, conserving ammunition.

***

Solomon, Joe, Jacob, Herbert, and Enoch crept stealthily toward the John's house, silhouetted against the night sky, dark and silent within, the occupants sound asleep. The silence of the night made Solomon's body tingle with excitement and anticipation.

Solomon pulled the folded fence cutters from his pocket and carefully snipped the fence, making as little noise as possible. Joe and the rest of the men filed through the opening after Solomon. Standing in the garden about thirty metres from the master bedroom, Joe fired the RPG. (Rifle Propelled Grenade) The grenade ripped a hole in the master bedroom wall. From where he stood, it looked big enough to climb through. He turned to Solomon, who was grinning. Joe raised his thumb.

Joe rushed forward while Solomon led the other to their positions around the house, but just as they scuttled off a barrage of lead ripped into Joe's flesh, flinging him backwards landing close to where Solomon stood. The others quickly moved round the side of the house as Solomon crawled to Joe. He was already dead, too many bullet holes to count.

Solomon hurried to the others. "We've failed, again, Joe's dead," He shouted to Herbert then fired at the house. Return fire came zooming back.

"Hit the kitchen, I'm going to see where Jacob is." Solomon ran around the side of the house to the sitting room. Firing was coming from inside the room. He reached Jacob. He stood still, the AK he held remained silent.

"Enoch is dead." Jacob uttered.

"Joe's dead too. Keep firing, I'm going in." Solomon bolted to the front door and bravely opened it, darted through the hall, and cautiously approached the passage. He knew his way in this house. He'd been inside once before. There she was, sitting on the floor next to the radio, talking into it. Solomon lifted the barrel of his AK and fired into the ceiling above her, and then at the walls over her head. Large chunks of ceiling fell, crashing down around her.

Powered by anger at the loss of his comrades, especially Joe, he lifted the AK up and down from his hips, firing randomly at the walls and ceiling. Then he ran forward, rammed a dirty cloth into Melonie's mouth and brutally dragged her from the radio, through the hall and out the front door.

Herbert kept firing at the kitchen, likely keeping Ivan pinned there, giving Solomon time to get clear of the house and through the opening he'd cut in the fence with Mel in tow. Mel's struggles slowed him down. He yelled to Herbert and Jacob. "Prop your Aks on your shoulder. Point the barrel backwards, keep your finger on the trigger and *mhanya*. (Run) Meet me on the other side of the mill."

Solomon dropped his AK. Herbert would get it. He threw Melonie over his shoulder, held onto her arms and one leg. This had been their plan, now his life depended on keeping Mel over his shoulder and making a hasty escape.

All he saw in his mind's eye was Antonio. He couldn't face the commander without the girl.

Solomon moved as fast as he was able to with the writhing Mel hindering his pace. By the time he reached the mill, some of the fight had left her, but she'd manage to free one hand and yanked the cloth from her mouth. Her screams and cries were absorbed by the surrounding trees.

"Let me go, you filthy pig," she beat on his back with her fist.

Solomon had had enough. He threw her to the ground. Though he knew her name, he wasn't going to let her know that.

She struggled for breath. He didn't wait and punched her hard. The blow to her head, knocked her out. He leaned down, picked her up like a rag doll and threw her limp body over his shoulder. Shortly after this, Herbert and Jacob caught up. Herbert was carrying Solomon's AK, and the three men sprinted for their lives.

***

Ivan found Margaret her trying to step over all the rubble on her way to the bathroom when the shooting stopped. Each step was obviously difficult. Ivan helped her over the debris. Margaret washed her face and hands of dried blood, then they made their way to the passage to look for Mel.

Dust still churned in swirls. Bits of ceiling dangled precariously from the roof. And the radio mouthpiece dangled, covered in a thick layer of dust. The Agric Alert was unmanned, and the table was littered with bits of broken ceiling, and chucks of painted plaster from the wall.

Where was Melonie?

Gripped by an uneasy panic, they rushed to Mel's room. The dogs had vacated their baskets and were hiding under the bed, shivering. Bessie and Benji crawled out from under the bed and wagged their tails nervously, then followed. On reaching the radio, Ivan noticed the Uzi lying on the other side of the table, covered in dust.

He broke out in a cold sweat. Suddenly the radio burst to life. He answered. "Bravo One, go." Margaret stood close to him.

"Hi Ivan, army eta less than three minutes. Out"

Ivan replied. "Shootings stopped but we can't find Mel. Out".

They needed to find Mel. The army may be just too late. He turned to Margaret. "I'm going to search the rest of the house. Go to the sitting room, it's not full of dust, just be careful of the glass shards." Ivan said.

"Do you think the gooks have gone?" Margaret asked, her lips quivering and dry.

"I think so, but it's hard to tell and could be quiet on purpose."

"My ears are still ringing. My shoulder throbs and my throat is parched. All the dust. I'm going to wander slowly through to the kitchen and get something to drink, then I'll go to the sitting room. You and Mel can meet me there."

Ivan disappeared down to the end of the passage and peered into the first guest room. No Melonie. Onto the next room. Empty. He checked under the beds as he called her name. She may have hidden there after the last blast of gunfire and been deafened. Mel wasn't in any of the spare bedrooms. He hurried to the office. Panic had begun to rise. Where could she be? He didn't bother with the pantry and made his way back to the sitting room. Margaret sat alone.

She looked up at Ivan, tears were running down her cheeks, carving pathways through her dusty face.

"Where could she be?" The dogs sat obediently at her feet. They also looked up at Ivan with expectant expressions.

"I've no idea. Did you check the pantry when you were in the kitchen?"

"No darling, the door was open. She would've heard me pouring water."

Ivan frowned. His worst fears nudged at him again.

"Surely she wouldn't be on the veranda." Margaret said. Ivan needed to check and took several large strides from where he stood and peered through the unbroken sliding glass doors which lead onto the veranda. He couldn't see her anywhere, but he saw the lights of the army vehicles approaching. Fear bit ferociously at the pit of his stomach. She was either lying dead somewhere or the terrs had taken her.

He turned back to Margaret. "Darling, I'm sure the terrs have abducted her." Ivan was on the verge of tears, "but the army have arrived."

"Nooo," Margaret cried out. "They couldn't have. Not our Mel, she'd have fought them like a caged leopard."

"She may not have had the opportunity to fight them, sweetheart. The army will be at the security gates. They'll need to act fast, chase after the gooks and bring her back." His tongue travelled over his parched lips. "I'm going down to open the gates."

The dogs followed Ivan out the house.

Ivan turned to leave and ran to the front door. It was open. The terrorists must have taken Mel out the front door while he defended the kitchen and Margaret guarded the hole in their bedroom wall.

"Fucking bastards," He murmured as he strode down to open the gates, shielding his eyes from the vehicle headlights.

"Ivan." Captain Clive McIntyre called and jumped out the Crocodile, (a modified armoured military vehicle) followed by a 4.5 Mercedes truck filled with army personnel.

"They've abducted our daughter, Melonie," Ivan shouted, shaking uncontrollably. The men jumped from the vehicles, ready for action.

"You, you and you," Clive shouted, pointing to three of the soldiers.

"Take the two trackers and pick up the spoor. Go." The soldiers had heard Ivan say the terrs had his daughter.

"They would've gone down past the mill," Ivan indicated the direction the men should take.

"On our way." One man shouted, and five men took off.

"Jesus Christ. I'm sorry, Ivan. I wish we could've got here sooner. I'm going to call for more trackers." Clive said and jumped back into the vehicle, grabbed the handset of the radio mounted on the dashboard. Ivan heard him report what had taken place at Blue Winds estate and waited for him to finish.

"Come on up to the house," Ivan said.

"Thank you. First let me get these men deployed." Clive instructed the four remaining soldiers to check the perimeter of the security fence, then the gardens around close to the house.

Clive followed Ivan through the front door into the hall. He noticed the ceiling hanging down. "What the fuck happened there?" Clive asked finding it odd the way the walls had been peppered with gunshot and the ceiling had fallen in.

"I wish we knew. My thoughts are one of the terrorists got into the house, because the front door was open and fired into the ceiling above where Mel sat at the radio then grabbed her. I was in the kitchen and Margaret was in our bedroom. I heard the gunshots, but it's all so disorientating. Shooting was coming at the house from every direction."

They walked into the sitting room. Margaret was slumped in her chair. Ivan introduced her to Clive, then asked, "how's the shoulder?"

"Not good. Now the adrenaline has worn off it's extremely painful."

"What happened?" Clive asked with concern sounding in his voice.

"A shard of debris hit when the bedroom wall exploded. Nicked some skin off my head too." Margaret explained.

"I haven't had a good look at it yet, but from the little I've seen, it looks nasty, and I think I need to get Margaret to hospital." Ivan said to Clive.

Clive put a hand on Ivans shoulder. "We'll get your daughter back, you get you wife to hospital."

Margaret sniffed. "Ivan, give me a hand to get up. I'll pack a little overnight bag." Desperation and pain reflected in her dusty face. Just as she was taking the first uncertain step toward their room, one of Clive's men shouted.

"Ivan, you got one of the sonofabitches right at the hole in your bedroom wall."

Ivan and Clive followed Margaret. Clive whistled when he stood at the door. "Jesus, what a mess. That's some hole. Just as well you got him. One more stride and the fucker would've jumped through."

Ivan remembered the moment. It had been identical to the last attack, only the size of the hole was different.

Clive and Ivan climbed out the hole, while Margaret pulled her nightie, gown and slippers out of her wardrobe and a change of day clothes. Picking her way carefully over the debris she made her way to the bathroom to get her toiletries.

Ivan and Clive approached the body lying on the grass. There were five bullet holes oozing blood. Then another call sounded. "Man down over here." The call came from the sitting room side of the house. Ivan and Craig walked around to the veranda.

"Two down. I wonder how many there were." Ivan said, viewing the body of the dead terrorist.

"You got yourself two AKs'." One soldier remarked.

"No bloody use to me without bullets." Ivan said and turned back to Clive. "I need to get Margaret to hospital. Can I leave you and your men. Lock the gate when you go."

Ivan walked quickly back to their bedroom. "I'll pack the case for you, sweetheart." He pulled one from the top shelf of the built-in cupboards. "Clive and his men will stay here for a while and will lock the gate when they go."

It didn't take Ivan long to pack the things Margaret had put out, then he helped her to the car.

Clive called out. "Drive safely. Keep your eyes peeled." He warned while Ivan settled Margaret into the car.

THE JOURNEY to the hospital in Umtali seemed to take longer than normal. Margaret had fallen asleep leaving Ivan with his sad and angry thoughts. He felt helpless. Anxiety filled him. He didn't want to think about what the gooks might do to his daughter. Then he wondered why they'd been attacked twice. Eventually he pulled up outside the emergency entrance at the general hospital and woke Margaret.

"We're here, my love." He put a hand on her forearm and shook it gently. She opened her eyes slowly and moaned.

Ivan opened her door and helped her out. Inside the trauma unit the doctor ushered her into a curtained bay, and she sat on the bed, blotching the clean white covers with dust and blood. Under instruction from the doctor the nurse quickly inserted a canula and administered an injection for pain, then she handed Margaret a gown.

"Take off your clothes, then pop on this gown."

She left Ivan to help Margaret take her clothes off, then the doctor pushed back the curtain.

"What happened to you, Mrs Johns?"

"Our farmhouse was attacked by terrorists. I think a chunk of plaster, or a brick hit me," she explained. He checked her head injury then moved to the shoulder wound and had a good look. He turned to Ivan, "I'm Doctor Hitchens. I'll take care of your wife."

"Thank you, Doctor."

"This is a nasty wound. We need to get you to theatre. It'll need more than just stitching. Half an hour, perhaps a bit longer, in theatre. I'm very sorry to hear what happened to you." Then he addressed Ivan again. "Are you alright?"

"Yes, I'm fine, but we lost our daughter in the attack."

"Shot?"

"No, abducted. The fuckers got into our home and took her. We last saw her sitting at the radio calling for help."

"That's horrifying news. My deepest condolences. I'll give you a sedative, Mr. Johns. Do the army know? You two must be in terrible shock. I'll watch carefully when you are under anaesthetic."

"No sedatives for me, thanks Doc. Just look after my wife." Pale and shattered, Ivan made his way to the visitors lounge and fell asleep. He woke an hour later and asked a nurse if Mrs. Johns was out of theatre, and which ward she was in.

"She's just come out of theatre. They are wheeling her down to Ward 3c."

"Thank you." Ivan caught up with the nurse pushing Margaret. She was fast asleep. He left the hospital and headed home to begin a lonely and agonising clean-up operation.

No Margaret. No Melonie.

Chapter Eight

EARLY DAWN OFFERED SOME LIGHT, and respite from the dark moonless night, as Solomon, Herbert and Jacob reached the Gairezi river crossing. A heavy mist hung over the rushing water and hid the stepping stones. Solomon balanced on each slippery rock, treading with care. Finally, on the far bank, he plopped Melonie on the grassy verge, her body limp and still, her head flopped to the side.

The water's edge allowed access to fresh mountain water. All three men knelt, scooping the icy water into their hands and drank.

Solomon wiped his mouth and looked at Melonie's still form. His gut spasmed. Had he hit her too hard? No matter. She'd wake eventually.

"Herbert. Your turn to carry the girl," he said as the sun began its eastern ascent. Herbert bent, lifted Melonie, and slung her over his shoulder.

Solomon hoisted Herbert's gear over one arm. "Run faster," Solomon urged, "as fast as we trained." If they stepped up the speed of their pace, sharing the load of carrying Mel, they could get to Mozambique in an hour. Solomon, Jacob, behind him, and Herbert in the rear travelled over rough terrain as they climbed into the hills away from the river and made-up time.

Tired now, Solomon trudged over the last rise, ready for the downward slope but he worried about Mel. She should've been conscious by now. He really didn't care if she lived or died. She'd fought him like a viper and nearly escaped, but the commander wanted her alive.

A non-delivery, and he'd die. That simple.

The ragged column of exhausted men reached the crest. It wasn't the summit. Jacob's turn to carry the burden of Melonie. One more gentle incline to the top, then Solomon moved faster along a cattle path. He zigzagged through metre high, golden tambuki grass that clutched at his pants. The dry grass razor sharp, cutting into the skin of his arms. Dried out seed heads of the tambuki grass towered over them, hiding them. Fifty meters ahead, low branches of short, dark green Mnondo trees spread wide. Hidden beneath this tree canopy, Solomon signalled the men to stop, rest their aching legs and burning lungs.

"When's this girl going to stir?" Herbert asked. "I think you hit her too hard, comrade." He hoisted her onto the other shoulder.

Solomon didn't answer. The urgency now - getting to the first village in Mozambique. Once they arrived at his friend's village and located her hut, their spoor (footprints) would mingle with the others villagers' footprints. If they were being tracked, which Solomon knew they must be, the trackers would surely lose their trail.

Solomon's turn to carry Melonie. He made the exchange and Melonie groaned. Relieved, Solomon jogged on, setting the pace, thinking with sadness about the loss of Joe. Joe had been the buffer between Solomon and Antonio. Now Joe was dead. Solomon didn't like Antonio, nor did he trust him, but bringing Antonio the prize he'd requested - Melonie, Solomon hoped would elevate his status with the commander.

Twenty minutes later they emerged from the Mnondo forest and Solomon felt the first stirrings of excitement. It gave him an energy boost. He moved faster. The village drew closer.

Solomon's friend would be waiting. She'd promised to keep Melonie in her spare hut, feed, and water her for twenty-four hours while Solomon and his men rested.

***

Melonie hung on, too terrified to think of escape. Her tummy pained her more than the throbbing in her head. She found it difficult not to cry out, knowing the dangers that screaming would invoke. Solomon may hit her on the head again and do permanent damage, or he'd kill her.

The longer Mel was conscious the clearer her dire situation became. She tried to calculate the distance they would've already covered. She compared the speed of their running to the speed of her horses in a good walk.

Using the dawn to help her math, she figured they must've travelled at least thirty-five kilometres from Blue Winds boundary. If she was anywhere close to accurate, they were in Mozambique. The thought pained her, and she suppressed the urge to cry. The AK47 rifle banging against the man's opposite side proved a constant reminder of the danger she faced. Would they kill her in Mozambique, she wondered. Awake and more alert, aside from the emotional pain, the shoulder of the running man who carried her dug into her intestines. Unable to take the pain any longer, she cried out. "Stop."

Solomon set her on her feet onto the grassy verge beside the path. He gripped her arm with vice-like fingers, expecting her to attempt an escape. She shot him a fierce feline glare. The bright early morning light hurt her eyes. She squinted and thought she recognised this man. Impossible.

Trembling, Mel took a shaky step. Solomon released some of the pressure on her arm. She lowered herself to the ground. Shock attacked her muscles, and her body shook violently. She lay back, breathed deep and rubbed her aching stomach.

Less than a few minutes passed, and the man shouted, "You run."

"Run? I can hardly stand," she said.

"Move," he warned.

Mel got to her feet and took a few uncertain steps. Her world spun; the grass rolled as if in waves. Her vision blurred, and tears ran down her face.

"Run," the man's voice rang with anger. His face filled with rage.

"I can't." She clutched her head with one hand, her stomach with the other. Irritated, he hauled her up. She thumped her fist into the man's back and wiggled her legs, as she worked to slow their progress, but she soon sensed his frustration in his tightening grip on her legs. He shouted, "Hey, hey."

They ran on till eventually he dumped her on the verge where she lay in prickly, dry grass, and sucked in quick breaths. Mel eyed the man opposite her. Even in her woozy state, she knew she'd seen this man somewhere. Then suddenly she realised. He'd worked at the mill.

"Bastard." She flung the word at him as if it was spit.

"White whore," he said with venom in his tone.

Seething, Mel closed her eyes and considered her options. Her brain still numbed, and her throat parched, she glanced across at the other two men. Flies buzzed around their noses and lips desperate for moisture. The rising sun would soon scorch the land.

Preserving what strength she had, she lay still. Mel had heard the name Solomon. It was he who seized her by both arms.

She pleaded. "Please, put me on your back. Your shoulder digs into my stomach. I might puke all over you."

Surprisingly, he obliged and carried her piggy-back style, holding her ankles. She wrapped her arms around his neck, and he trotted onto the path.

Sordid thoughts of dehydration and dying flashed in her mind. She kept telling herself not to panic. Inhale, exhale.

Calculating the minutes that passed was impossible, but it hadn't seemed too long before they arrived at a hut in a village. A young woman and a swarm of naked kids met them. A small village, Mel thought, seeing only a cluster of about twenty huts, rooves thatched with dry banana fronds. This confirmed they were in Mozambique. The dusty air caught in her throat making it hard to swallow. The kids danced about her, fascinated by seeing a white woman in their village. Melonie, only barely able to stand, let the woman take her hand. She led Mel into a dark, empty hut. The only light filtered through a small windowpane that didn't open. The woman never spoke. She left and locked the door.

Melonie slumped to the floor and wept for the first time. The floor, cool on her cheek, offered welcome cooling from the heat and humidity.

She realised the more she wept, the thirstier she got. She sat up and wiped her tears away. Weeping like she had also sapped energy.

The door rattled, unlocked and the young woman entered. She had a kind face and a youthful body wrapped in a colourful sarong of many vibrant colours, and secured at the back of her neck. She knelt in front of Mel. Mel understood this gesture, a cultural gesture of respect. She handed Mel a white enamel cup filled with water.

Mel sniffed, the water smelled strange, but she drank, praying it wasn't poisoned or leave her with dysentery. One of the naked kids entered, carrying a mug and a banana and handed it to the woman, then ran out the hut chuckling. The mug, filled with a hot, sloppy maize meal porridge had been sweetened, Mel tasted. The woman stood and backed out of the hut without uttering a word and locked the door. Having her thirst and hunger partially quenched, Mel fell asleep.

She woke to the same woman hauling her to her feet and dragged her outside.

"Run," she said, taking Mel's hand. "You must run. We must meet Solomon." The woman pulled Mel along.

Mel managed three steps, but her legs had no strength, her knees sagged.

"Run. We must meet Solomon," the woman urged.

Instead, Mel walked, taking in deep breaths.

The woman seemed to understand Mel had little strength. She took Mel's hand again and walked with her. They wove their way through scattered huts to the perimeter of the village. The woman found a footpath through fields planted with sesame and cassava while Mel thought about escape plans. She asked the woman for the name of the village, how far they were from the border, and her name. She squeezed Mel's hand, offering no information and met the man on the edge of the field. This must be Solomon.

Obviously irritated by being kept waiting, Solomon grabbed a fistful of Mel's hair and pulled her to his side.

"Lift her, Jacob." He ordered the younger of the two men to carry her, thankfully, piggyback. Solomon uttered something to the young woman and hurried on their way.

Soon they entered a cool indigenous forest. Trees more than forty to fifty metres high towered above them. If the circumstances had been different, Melonie would've enjoyed the experience, but with escape plans in mind, she focused on the landmarks. She would need to remember them for her journey out of Mozambique.

Shortly after midday, they arrived at what appeared to be a terrorist camp. Solomon now carried her. He strode across a large open square of hot red earth that shimmered in the rising heat, to a door. He knocked.

The door opened. "Seu prêmio, your prize, commander," Solomon announced, and dumped Melonie on the floor as if she was a sack of potatoes. She winced.

Prize! She said to herself. I'm no fucking prize, she swore under her breath. The word *prize* conjured up some ghastly visions.

She lay in a crumpled heap at the commander's feet. Her lips tight, holding in her anger and excruciating thirst. She thought of her parents then. She knew they would be frantic.

She glanced at the man. A victorious smile stretched across the commander's deeply tanned face. Melonie instantly hated him. A frightening look glazed his eyes and wrinkled the corners of his lips. His mouth open, he stared at her, then turned to Solomon. "Where's Joe?"

"Dead." Solomon replied matter-of-factly.

Mel listened to Solomon and the commander's conversation. So, Joe was the terrorist who'd led the attack on Blue Winds. Did Dad kill Joe? The thought pleased her. If Joe had got into the house, he would've likely murdered her parents.

The commander wore a weird expression she couldn't work out, but it lit his face, then disappeared, as quick as lightening in a storm. After a strange moment of silence, he said, "Good job, Solomon. Joe taught you well. You'll be rewarded. Now go."

Solomon left and the office door banged closed.

"Aaah," the commander sighed. "Delivered alive. You are very beautiful." He towered over her. And muscles trembled. She gritted her teeth, but shuddering had taken control of every fibre of her being. She focussed on the toe caps of his boots.

He crouched beside her and grunted words in a language she assumed must be Portuguese. The language she knew they spoke in

Mozambique. Unexpectedly, he poked a missile hard finger into her upper arm. She dared not to flinch. He poked again, harder.

Mel rubbed her arm. "Ouch. Leave me alone. Get away from me." He smelled foul. She wanted to wretch. Her eyes bored into him. He'd puffed up his chest like a courting pigeon, then cooed mockingly.

"Come now, talk nicely, my little beauty," he urged.

Melonie pushed backwards with her hands and shifted her stiff, sore body away from him. She fixed her gaze on his dark emotionless eyes. She wouldn't show fear. He stood, grunting, too fat to crouch for long.

"I need water." She gasped through her drought-filled mouth, swollen tongue, and cracked lips.

He bent and looked into her eyes. "You want water, huh?"

Ugh. Body odour again. He smelt worse than a rotting rat. His black hair was cropped in a military style. Smeared with grease from never being washed. Mel couldn't imagine going days without washing her hair. The odious smell of dirty hair, obnoxious body stench and halitosis had her holding her breath and leaning away from him. He stood and saliva rushed to her mouth. Almost about to vomit, she swallowed quickly.

The extreme humidity made his disgusting body smells hang in his office. The stench stuck in her nose. A pitch-black stroke of a moustache underlined his nose and met the creases of his blubbery, veined cheeks. The most repulsive man she'd ever seen.

He strutted to the door, yanked it open, bellowed something in Portuguese, and slammed it shut. Melonie prayed he'd called for water.

He returned to where she sat on the floor and his eyes burned into her. Feeling exposed, she reversed farther on her bottom and leaned her back against the wall. She drew her legs up in a vain attempt to protect herself.

A knock reverted his attention. It *was* the delivery of life saving water. He stood beside his desk, held the water jug high above an enamel mug and trickled the water slowly into the vessel. Teasing her.

Cruel, she thought, hoping he'd not drunk from the mug. He continued torturing her and poured the water back into the jug, then repeated the punishing ritual. She put her head on her knees, pretending his stupid act didn't affect her, but in truth she couldn't watch any longer. Then he walked over and nudged her with his boot. "You want?" He held the mug in front of her face.

"Yes." She grabbed the mug, spilling some, then sipped the cool water, remembering to go slow, not to down it in her state of weakness and dehydration. Savouring every sip, she finished and asked for a refill.

He obliged.

She finished the second mug of water.

"Get up, bitch." His tone suddenly angry and fearsome.

"I can't, my legs are too weak."

Retaliation was quick. He sunk the dusty toe cap of his military boot into her side.

She wailed, gasped for breath, and held her ribcage.

He leaned over her, his stinking breath wafted up her nose again. She held her breath.

A chilling, icy threat lay within his evil dark brown eyes. She snapped her head to one side, his breath too overpowering.

"A fighter." He sniggered, yanked her arms away from her chest and hauled her to her feet. She stood, rigid as a statue. Then he rubbed a hand over her left breast. Mel hissed like an adder, humiliated and angry but too weak to strike.

"You're mine, white bitch." He hurled the words at her like machine gun fire.

"Never." Melonie spat on his shoe, trying in vain to wrench free of his grip.

He laughed, grabbed the front of her torn tracksuit top and slid his large hand inside, cupping her breast. He held his hand there and she squirmed trying unsuccessfully to get away. Then he pinched her nipple. She wanted to die. Her lips quivered, but she would not cry.

He pushed her to his desk then hoisted her up. She screamed, terrified of what he might do next. He ripped her tracksuit pants down. Mercifully her pyjama pants still covered her. Frantic, she fought. So weak her strength was soon sapped.

Each second, tumbled into the next. A hollow sense of detachment came over her when she saw his enlarged penis. She braced herself for the inevitable. Her tense legs hung over the edge of his desk.

He moved closer, panting loudly, he violently penetrated her virginity. She cried out as he tore into her, jerking backwards and forwards as he drove deeper inside her. After more agonising thrusts, he orgasmed, stood still, breathing heavily, then he pulled out of her, and collapsed in his chair.

The pain and insufferable agony that followed she would never forget, nor forgive. She sobbed, deep guttural, crushing sobs. He'd violated her soul. Her womanhood taken in a most horrifying rape. Saliva frothed and caked on the edges of her mouth. A rabid hatred boiled. Her cries took on a different sound now. Cries of anguish, like the last wail of a hunted, dying antelope.

He pushed her off the desk onto the floor. Used, limp, exhausted and ashamed she simply whispered, "Water."

She found her tracksuit and pyjama pants and put them on. The stench from his fluids mingled with her blood. Her stomach was cramping, the contents roiling, she wanted to puke.

Covered, she leaned back against the wall and squeezed her eyes shut. There were no more tears, he'd taken them too. Shivering from shock and horror, a wave of nausea brought another rush of saliva to her mouth. She suddenly felt dizzy, and the room began to sway. Conquered. Lifeless. Worthless.

She needed to rid her body of the filth he'd savagely injected into her. "I need the toilet."

He nodded and walked to the door.

In her struggle to stand, a trickle of urine and semen ran down the inside of her pyjama pants. Sweat wet her armpits and moistened the small of her back. Salty rivulets dribbled from her brow into her open, parched mouth.

He stood at the door and shouted more Portuguese words.

Two men ran into the office.

"Take her to my room." The commander instructed.

The two men, dressed in military drill, escorted her, helping her along. One on either side of her, they held her arms. A walk of about fifty yards stretched into eternity. She stumbled, and her legs gave way. The pain between her legs excruciating. The two soldiers helped her back to her feet.

The building, long and wooden, housed his room. One of the men opened the door. The room reeked of the commander's filth. Inside, she noticed a screened-off area where she spied a large iron washtub. The soldiers left, closed the door, and locked it.

She hobbled to the tub and saw the toilet. She'd not peed much in the last two days, but having drunk two mugs of water, her kidneys wanted to work again. She sat, grateful for a western design toilet, and relieved herself.

Feeling bleak and defeated, urgently needing to clean herself in the tub, she'd noticed no running water fed the tub, only the toilet. The room was sparsely furnished and untidy, what she expected from an evil man with no morals, and no idea about personal hygiene.

A wooden bed, with a lumpy mattress stood against one wall. A dirty grey sheet covered the mattress and a floral bedspread folded at the foot of the bed had two dirty grey pillows heaped on top.

Beside the bed was a bedstand, which looked homemade from old wooden crates, on it an enamel candle holder. Glued to the base with melted wax was a candle and next to it a box of matches. She sat on the bed and picked up the box of matches. She slid the box open and to her relief, a few unlit matches remained. Her weapon of mass destruction, she smiled.

A spark of courage surged through her, giving her a little strength and inspiration. A dual paned, weathered wooden window frame let the light into the room. Faded, tatty curtains, once vibrant now hung torn and thin. It was all she needed, apart from a bath and a few days rest with plenty of food and water while she planned her escape. Deciding not to stay on the bed, in case the horrid man came back, she sat on a rickety wooden chair. She thought her tears had dried up, but she couldn't help herself, and cried some more. Sobs of indignation, fatigue, and pain, but simmering inside her now, a tiny ray of hope. She glanced again at the box of matches.

Suddenly the door burst open. His gross bulk filled the space of the open door. She cowered. He held a plate with a mound of *sadza*, covered in what appeared to be a meaty sauce. Even in such dire circumstances, the aroma brought a rush of saliva.

"Eat," he shoved the food at her. Melonie took it from him and shovelled the meal into her mouth with the wonky handled spoon provided. He watched her famished feeding frenzy, but she didn't care. When she'd finished, he ordered her to bathe.

"I can't, there's no water in here."

"It will be brought, my little pi...je...on." He pronounced with a French brogue.

She winced. Not again, please, please, please, not again, she prayed. A knock on the side of the open door announced the arrival of the bath water.

"Yes, pour it in," he ordered. The first jug of steamy hot water was poured into the steel bathtub. Three more followed, then two jugs of cold water. The men all left, closing the door, and locking it.

Melonie sighed with relief. She could regain a sense of calm and safety, if only for a short time. She'd had visions of the commander watching her bathe, then assaulting her again. Her body involuntarily quaked.

Before removing her clothing, she checked to make sure she was alone, no one watching, peeping through the window. On the side of the tub a bar of *Lifeboy* soap balanced. She hated its carbolic smell. But the smell reminded her of home. They sold it in the farm store and the thought of home wrenched at her.

Peeling the dirty, torn clothes from her body, she left them on the floor and climbed into the tub of warm water. Her torn ankles and feet burned, the sensation a weird sort of pleasure. She lowered the rest of her body into the sanitizing water and scrubbed at herself with soapy fingertips, trying to rid her body of all the filth of her nightmare. Ingrained dirt from the last few days fell off her as a by-product. The blisters on her feet burned and the loose flaps of skin swished.

She looked about. No towels. She stood and let the water run off her before stepping out of the tub and patted herself dry with her pyjamas, then tossed them into the bathtub and scrubbed them clean of the commander's filth. She longed to put on clean clothes. Pulling on her dirty tracksuit she hung up her washed pyjamas, draping them over a makeshift washing line made of string. They'd soon be dry in the heat of the room.

Cleaner than she'd been in days, her belly full, and enough water to sustain her, she sat on the chair, rested her head against the wall and fell asleep.

From somewhere far off Melonie heard his voice. Startled, she woke, pushed herself upright and grasped either side of the seat. Eyes wide in fearful anticipation, she watched the commander enter the room. Through the open door, the early evening skies softened. The light of the sun being her timekeeper.

Don't panic. Inhale, exhale.

"My little whore slept well, I see." The commander sneered. Angered, Melonie wanted to yell she wasn't his whore. Instead, she kept quiet and stared at the floor. He carried another plate of food. He didn't know it but feeding her played into her escape plans perfectly. She took the plate. Another mound of *sadza* covered with wild spinach, tomato, and onion relish. The first taste, a little too salty, but she devoured the food and the nutrients she needed.

Standing at the door, the commander surprised her by saying, "Your room." He closed the door and locked it.

She let out a long and grateful sigh, then collapsed on the bed and slipped into a deep sleep.

In her sleep she heard her screams, they grew louder in her head, and she felt herself spasm and writhe in the nightmare. Plagued by the last forty-eight hours, Melonie woke, choking on another anguished cry. Her eyes flew open. She sat up. The room held no-one else, though she could've sworn, *he* was there. Sweating from the nightmare, she took a long drink of water. Assured no-one was there she lay half asleep and planned her escape. The humidity and heat had lessened. Could it be early dawn?

The key turned in the lock. He entered the room and smiled, then walked across to the rickety chair and sat.

"Oh, my pi... ge... on, you delighted me late last night."

"Your screams, they woke me next door. I quietly unlocked your door and sat in this chair." So he had been in her room. "I watched you writhe in your nightmare. Oh, so erotic, you aroused me. I slipped down my night shorts and spasmed with eroticism. I hoped you'd wake to watch how you satisfy me, but you continued crying in your sleep. I snuck out of your room, empty."

Mel wanted to cover her ears, but she didn't dare in case he hit her or jumped on top of her. She lay still, her heart pounding, revolted by his words, but grateful he'd not raped her again. She wouldn't allow him to assault her again. She'd kill him if he tried.

He stood. "I'll bring your breakfast." And he left, locking the door once more. She got up, folded the bedspread, and returned the pillows to their usual place. Though Mel had slept, the thought of what may happen after breakfast made her body flush and sweat. Bubbles of perspiration rose on her forehead and nose.

The door opened and a welcome cool breeze blew in. The disgusting monster had returned holding a bowl of porridge. He handed it to her, said nothing, then he left. The porridge was sweet like pudding and gave her an energy boost.

He never returned for the rest of the day.

That evening he arrived carrying her supper, only this time he sat watching her eat. When she'd finished, he stood, wrenched her plate from her hand, and dropped it on the floor.

"Hmmm." He glowered, unbuttoned the fly of his military pants.

Mel froze. She felt a surge of adrenaline flood as her senses heightened with a feeling of impending doom, triggered by a fright-fight response. Just let him touch me.

He slid his trousers down with his underpants. Erect, he shuffled to her, playing with his penis.

NO. NO. NO. NO. She sat up and swung her legs over the side of the bed.

He grabbed her hair, pushed her head down and forced his penis into her mouth. She bit down hard, then vomited her supper all over his legs.

The commander cried out. 'Cadela.' He yelled. Beads of sweat formed on his brow. His face crimson with anger.

Her strength restored, she leapt up and launched a foot deep into his crotch.

He instantly collapsed to the floor, coughed, and spluttered Portuguese words, likely swearing from the torture she'd dished out.

Grabbing the wooden chair with both hands, she smashed it over his head, splintering the chair into pieces. Clutching one of the chair legs, she jumped on top of him. His eyes streamed and rolled from the beating to his head. She pinned his arms with her knees and rammed the end of the chair leg into his throat. She held down, mustering all her strength while he kicked and floundered, fighting to free his arms to get her off but his massive stomach hindered him. Pressing into his windpipe, the chair leg broke the skin and blood gushed out. Choking, she'd weakened him.

The sudden exertion combined with ample adrenaline allowed Melonie to push the wooden leg deeper in. Sweat dribbled off her face and landed in droplets against his skin. A glazed, lifeless look appeared in his eyes as he looked at her. Blood still trickled down the sides of his neck. The fight oozed out of him. His body went limp, and his eyes closed.

For a moment, horror filled her soul. What had she done? Then her father's words flashed. 'Kill or be killed.'

Wasting no time, she pulled her tracksuit over her pyjamas, yanked the sheet off the bed, thinking she may need it, quickly filled a military water bottle she'd found, then grabbed the box of matches and tucked them into her pocket.

She pried open the window and squeezed through. Once outside she struck the match, cupping it with one hand she held the flame to the tatty edge of the threadbare curtain. The flame lit the fabric. Satisfied her plan to torch the building and the commander would work. She'd noticed the camp was not fenced when they'd brought her in. She sidled along the building and peered around the end. Just bush lay beyond. She made a dash for cover and disappeared into the night.

Chapter Nine

Margaret stirred in the cold, quiet hours of early dawn. Confused and disorientated she rolled her head from side to side. Nothing felt, or smelt familiar, then she tried to sit up and a sharp, stabbing pain in shoulder brought the memories of the attack rushing back.

"Mel." She cried out, weeping quietly. The horrors brought on a sweat. Her daughter, brutally taken from their home. Where was she? She couldn't bear the thought of how terrified, hurting, exhausted and hungry she would be at the hands of vicious captors. Tears streamed down her face, welled from her soul.

She pressed the red 'help' button. A nurse came rushing to her aid.

"What is it, Mrs. Johns?" The nurse asked.

"Can you help me sit more upright?"

"Certainly." The nurse braced her arms under Margaret's and manoeuvred her into a more vertical position, stacking the pillows comfortably behind her. "Is that better?"

"Yes. Thank you. Please bring me painkillers, my shoulder is really hurting."

The nurse nodded, scuttled off and returned holding four tablets and a glass of water. Margaret took them, willing them to work quickly.

"Was the wound deep?"

"Yes, apparently. Whatever it was that hit you, went in quite deep, damaging muscle and chipped a bit of your shoulder blade. I'm not surprised it hurts. It may take a few months to heal fully."

"Oh really? Do you know if my husband is coming to fetch me this morning?"

"He called in earlier. I told him Doctor Davis is seeing you at eleven. He'll call back then." The nurse smiled warmly. "You have been through terrible trauma, Mrs. Johns. Try to rest. I am sure you'll have news of your daughter very soon."

It wasn't long before the pain killers and sedatives took effect. The nurse never woke her for breakfast but woke her just before the doctor arrived. While he briefed Margaret on her wound and how to care for it, Ivan walked in. He shook the doctor's hand, then leant down and kissed Margaret's forehead. "Hello, my angel. How's the shoulder?"

"Sore, but the painkillers have helped a lot. Doctor has been telling me how to care for it. What to do and not do."

Doctor Davis spoke again. "I'll send you home with painkillers and antibiotics. Finish the course, and whatever you do, take it easy."

The nurse had already packed Margarets few possessions. Sliding herself off the bed, Ivan held her good arm and walked her to the car. Still groggy from sedatives, she asked, "have you heard anything yet?"

"Nothing yet. Phil said the trackers have crossed into Mozambique. They'll find her, my darling. The report suggested Mel was carried most of the way to throw trackers off their trail. It has apparently slowed them down. The army have two skilled Bushmen with them. They know what to look for."

Assured by the news, her eyes droopy, she laid her head back and slept.

"Sweetheart, we're home." Ivan gently shook her. Her eyes opened sleepily.

"I'm dreading walking into our home." Margaret whispered, looking at Ivan. He couldn't answer, instead he jumped out, opened the car door, and helped her out. She steadied herself while Ivan held her.

"I know you're dreading this. I had the same feeling of despair after I left the hospital. Simon's been amazing. Took one look at the state of the house, dashed back to the compound, and rallied up a team of ladies to help clean. The builders are repairing our bedroom wall, so we'll sleep in the big spare room for now. The smell of wet cement is awful, and the broken windowpanes won't be in for a few days. I picked up the cut glass and putty before collecting you. Phil arranged a roving night patrol around our perimeter fence to keep us safe."

Margaret took an unsteady step. Holding her, Ivan walked with her to the sitting room, lowered her into her chair and called Simon.

Simon knocked on the side of the open sitting room door.

"Ah, Simon, please organise a tray of lunch and a cup of tea."

"Yes, Sir. How is the Madam?"

"I'm glad to be back. Simon, what's for lunch?" Margaret answered.

Simon smiled broadly. "I've made the madam's favourite, Chicken a la King."

Touched by his thoughtfulness, she smiled at him. "How sweet of you, Simon. Thank you." She laid her head back, thinking how fortunate they were to have such wonderful staff. She closed her eyes and prayed for Mel's safe return. A little later she heard Ivan call out.

"Simon, bring lunch when it's ready, please."

"Yes Sir." Simon answered from the kitchen. Minutes later he brought in a tray with Margaret's lunch, then darted back to the kitchen to get Ivan's tray.

Margaret took a mouthful and savoured the flavours. "Simon makes this dish just like Fillimon used to. It's delicious."

Telephone calls were relentless. Friends and neighbours offered help and support. Surprising Margaret, some arrived bringing baked goodies, flowers and words of love and kindness. Phil from PATU, popped in too. He kept them informed on military intelligence feedback relating to Mel.

That first night home, after taking her antibiotics and sedatives, Margaret slept soundly. Ivan lay next to her wishing he could sleep. In the eery hours after midnight, senses heightened, he heard every creek in the house, and the rustle of wind outside amplified the feeling of acute vulnerability. He began to question his belief in God, life, humanity, and himself. His thoughts regularly interrupted by ghastly visions of the danger Mel was in. Of all the crippling emotions, anger and helplessness were the biggest takers.

Margaret woke around nine. Simon heard her cries. Standing respectfully at the bedroom door, he asked, "Shall I call Master?"

"Yes please. Thank you, Simon."

Simon rushed down the passage, crossed the veranda and found Ivan in the office.

He knocked. "Sir, the madam is calling for you." Ivan thanked Simon and went to Margaret's aid. Restricted by her injury, she needed his help for almost every task.

"Morning, sweetheart. Did you sleep well?"

"I certainly did. Those tablets knocked me out. I can't believe how late it is. Have you heard anything new?"

"Yes, I have. Phil called in. Trackers found Mel's footprints on a path about twelve kilometres inside Mozambique. Those little bushmen are closing in. I'm sure it won't be long, before we have our daughter safely home."

She held her mouth tight. Sitting on the edge of the bed she looked at her feet, nodded, then finally looked up at Ivan, refusing to let tears fall again. It was all she seemed to do.

"You're being so strong." He cupped her face in his hands and kissed her gently. "What do you want to do first?"

"Brush my teeth and have a pee." She attempted humour.

Ivan helped her dress and walked with her to the veranda. The smell of wet cement, window putty, turpentine, and paint too overwhelming to stay inside. Once she was comfortably seated, Ivan fetched her tea and toast and her book.

"Are you going to be alright here for an hour or two. I must get down to the mill."

"Yes, darling I'll be fine."

Margaret finished her tea and toast and reached for her book, reading one of her favourite authors, James Herriot. All Things Bright and Beautiful, the book she was reading and sequel to All Creatures Great and Small. Heartwarming and humorous. Exactly what she needed. Immersed in the tale, enjoying the warmth of sun on her legs and the author's descriptions of the four-legged and two-legged inhabitants of the Yorkshire Dales, she hadn't noticed the time pass.

Ivan stood watching her read. "Good book?"

She looked up. "Darling, you look exhausted. And now you've got the added burden of me being injured."

"You're not a burden, sweetheart. You're alive. It could have been worse. I'll take one of your sleeping tablets and knock myself out tonight."

"Good idea, that's what you need. Sleep."

IVAN WOKE JUST before the alarm sounded at six o'clock. Margaret stirred beside him.

"How did you sleep?"

"Well. Very well."

"I'm so pleased. You needed a full night's sleep." She kissed him.

Ivan stretched, jumped out of bed, and got himself dressed. "Do you want to get dressed now, or when I get back from the mill?"

"When you get back. I'm so enjoying my book. I'll lie here and read. Don't forget you have to change the dressings today."

Ivan nodded and left their room. After checking on the new sawyer, who seemed to be coping, he chatted to the foreman. They'd cut the required quota which pleased him. He was back to help Margaret by eight.

Sitting on the edge of the bed, Margaret was ready for the new dressing. Ivan carefully pulled back the plasters.

"What does it look like?"

"Clean. Nice, neat stitching job. One, two, three…" Ivan counted the stitches. There were eleven stiches holding the skin tightly. He was about to secure the new dressing when the phone rang.

"It always rings at the most awkward time." Ivan rushed to answer it. It was Ian, their closest neighbour. "Any news yet?"

"No, nothing new. It's a living nightmare, Ian. Can't speak, in the middle of doing Margaret's dressing."

"Okay. I'm off to town and wondered if you need anything?"

"That's very kind of you. We're going in on Friday, doctor wants to see Margaret."

"Debbie is home all day if you think of anything, giver her a tinkle." Ian hung up. He'd known Melonie since she was three days old. He felt helpless and angry and couldn't imagine what it must be like for Ivan and Margaret.

THE RELENTLESS STRAIN WAS BRUTAL. Trackers had lost the spoor and pulled off the search. Finding Melonie Johns became a 'special ops' infiltration, to be done by Selous Scouts, Phil reported, standing in Ivan's office at the mill. Ivan felt drained. Rhodesia *wasn't* so super anymore, but he felt encouraged that Selous Scouts were going in. They'd find her.

The following day Clive McIntyre called in at the house.

"Good news. Selous Scouts have found spoor not far from a marked terrorist camp. They have a good idea it's where Mel is being held. It's just a matter of time now, Ivan."

"That *is* good news. Thanks Clive. I don't want to think about what our poor child must be going through." Ivan looked out the bay window to the distant mountains in Mozambique. "I'm a farmer, Clive, not a bloody killer, but I would feel no remorse killing the men who abducted her."

"I don't blame you, Ivan. Listen, I must go. I'll call back as soon as I have more news."

"Of course. Thank you so much for popping by."

Ivan wandered back to the house to let Margaret know. He allowed himself to feel more hopeful. That night their conversation silenced while they listened to the militia talking, their voices being picked up on the fence sensors. They spoke in Shona. Ivan was fluent. Margaret had a reasonable grasp of the language.

The militia spoke of horrific murders and shocking atrocities taking place in the Tribal Trust Lands. (TTL's) Melonie's story was just another to add to the long thread of misery the freedom fighters were bringing to the people of Rhodesia, of all races. A defining moment for them both. Theirs an insufferable loss, but there were thousands of other people suffering life-changing losses too. Consumed by their own grief, they couldn't think about so many others who were carrying burdens greater or equal to theirs.

"Did you hear that?" Ivan whispered.

"Most of it, yes. It's shocking what the black folk have been forced to endure at the hands of these so-called freedom fighters, who are their own kind. I sympathise, but it's hard to feel it when all I can feel is the emptiness inside without our precious Mel."

"I know. It's so much easier to feel sympathy for others when you're not needing it, isn't it? The gooks do what they like to the rural communities. It's too ghastly, and even worse being privy to conversations like this. Did you hear their opinion on being governed by a black government? That interested me."

Margaret shook her head. "I didn't understand most of it."

"Poor fellows have a skewed vision of their assumed utopia under majority rule. Sadly, at this point, they don't understand the bigger picture."

"I hate this bloody war, Ivan. It's so destructive. So pointless." The tone in Margaret's voice became a heart-breaking whisper. "We will get our Mel back, won't we?"

"Of course, we will." Ivan held her close to him, praying his words would prove to be true. They shared a sleeping tablet and drifted off to sleep holding hands.

Chapter Ten

Deep inside Mozambique, Lieutenant Stevens glanced at his night watch. His calculations were spot on. Eight-thirty p.m. Co-ordinates showed they were a kilometre from the terrorist camp where Melonie was reportedly being held.

A dark night and a cool breeze kept he and his men alert. The African bush is a mysteriously silent place when bugs, birds and reptiles are asleep. The stealth required for Stevens and his three men to move undetected and unheard required a clandestine skill for which they were trained.

Suddenly, a whiff of eucalyptus-tainted smoke filled the air. Lieutenant Stevens motioned for his men to halt. They crouched. Stevens stayed standing and gauged the wind direction, which being a mere breeze, wasn't easy. The smell grew stronger, and the dark night grew lighter. In the distance flames spiralled into the sky. Terrified screams echoed across the wilderness.

"Holy shit. Could it be the gook camp ablaze?" Lieutenant Stevens whispered to the soldier who'd moved next to him.

"Let's get the fuck out of here. Gooks will be fleeing in all directions." The soldier standing next to Stevens said.

Stevens and his men scarpered, running two hundred metres downwind, they laid low. Senses on high alert. Crouched in long grass, Stevens and his men waited and watched. The night skies lit by a growing orange glow.

Scanning the surrounding bush, Stevens saw something move. Human or animal?

"Hold your fire," he whispered to his men. He held his breath. His heart pounded. Had he seen a ghost? No, a sheet-clad figure came straight at them. Could it be Melonie?

"Jesus Christ, it's her. She must've set the camp alight," he said. Plucky chick.

In her haste to get away from the camp Melonie ran and ran and ran. Disorientated and frightened, she finally stopped.

"Psst. Melonie, over here," a voice beckoned.

She refused to move a muscle, and too terrified to answer. Who, in the middle of the Mozambiquan bush, in the middle of the night, would know her name?

"Melonie, it's Adrian Stevens, from Selous Scouts. You're safe now."

"Th... an.... k.... you," she spluttered. "I.... I.... can't believe ...... I never...... thought...... I'd be saved." The terror she held, dissolved. Overwhelmed, she collapsed into Adrian Steven's arms.

"We must get out of here, and fast. Did you set the camp alight?" Adrian Stevens set her on her feet.

She nodded.

"You foiled our hot extraction plans but thank you. Can you run?" He asked, looking at her, concerned.

"Yes, I think so." Relief powered the muscles in her legs. She took a step, her knees buckled. "I can't, my legs..."

"Jump on my back," Adrian said. "We have a collection point eight kilometres from here. We'll take turns carrying you." He chucked a pack to another man. "Wrap your legs around my waist. Piggyback."

She climbed on Adrian's back and held on tight.

He grabbed her ankles and ran. "In two kilometres...... we should be.... safe to stop. To rest." He sounded breathless, likely from carrying her extra weight.

The group sprinted on in silence. She chanced to look back every now and again. The sky brightened, dulled only by heavy smoke. Smoke that was all thanks to her.

After what must've been the two kilometres Adrian had mentioned, they stopped. She slid off his back and he faced her. It appeared he was trying to smile, but the black camouflage cream on his face had dried like clay, and his face barely moved.

Using the radio pack, he called someone. After listening he said, "We've got new co-ordinates for the rendezvous point." He lifted Mel onto another man's back, and the group traversed the terrain in a steady jog.

Adrian gave a signal and the group slowed to a walk. Adrian moved beside the man carrying Mel. "Are you okay?

"Y...es, I...'ll.... I'll be.... fine." Mel answered. "I'm....I'm sorry. I can't run. I'm sorry to......slow you......down." Her life and the life of these four brave men depended on swift movement. She knew this.

They walked on. Adrian checked his compass. "On course," he said.

She was transferred to another man, and they continued through the bush, skirting small villages. The strong smell of smoke could still be smelt.

Dodging open tracts of land, they hugged fields of cassava, and maize, ducked between papaya and banana plantations, and trotted through sparse indigenous forest, making sure they weren't seen. At a small rocky outcrop, they stopped and looked out over the landscape. Smoky orange smudged the sky.

Looking at the compass again, Adrian whispered, "Doing well chaps, we've covered nearly six kilometres. Just over two to the new RV. We'll take a short break here."

Resting against granite boulders, the men closed their eyes. Adrian pulled the A63 radio from its pack, relayed a message that sounded like code. Then he came and sat by Melonie.

"We've done well. Are you sure you're alright?"

"Yes, I'm okay, I think. I'm happy to be far away from that terrifying, disgusting camp, and its commander." There was venom in her voice.

"I'm sorry. You must've endured hell." Adrian's eyes showed he felt deep concern. "You did a splendid job, though. That camp won't ever operate again. Not only because you set it alight, but its position has now been exposed."

Melonie swallowed hard. She felt somewhat cheered by that information. But she would've like to hear the camp commander was dead. Then she would rejoice.

"Doing what you did must've taken a lot of courage. I admire you." Adrian said.

Yes, she'd been brave and courageous, but inside she felt hollow. "I've possibly killed a lot of people." Her dad's words came back to her again, *'Kill or be killed. This is war, my child.'* But even his words didn't soothe her conscience. It was only the commander she wanted dead.

"It's better than the other way round, my girl," Adrian said. "Try to sleep. We'll move out in about three hours. We're well hidden amongst these rocks."

Though Melonie closed her eyes, she couldn't sleep. The men slept. All but Adrian, who kept watch. To take her thoughts off what she'd endured, and what she'd done, she focussed on trying to hear the sleeping soldiers breathe. She must've dosed because she woke to the sounds of early dawn. Bird calls from every direction, sounding like they were having a party to celebrate the birth of a new day. That made her smile.

She sat watching the men, obviously battled trained they were alert and standing in seconds, not a groan or a stretch, almost like they'd never slept. She marvelled at their training and levels of fitness.

Adrian rested his hand on her arm. "I'm calling in fire force, they will sort out what's left of the camp. And we need to get you to hospital in Umtali."

"Hospital. I don't need the hospital. I need to go home."

Adrian smiled and the camouflage on his face cracked. "You're a brave one, but as you foiled our hot extraction plan, I have to go along with my orders. Army rules." He put his thumb up. "The hospital is the order. We expected to find you in a worse condition, even dead."

The word dead, echoed in Mel's hollowed out core.

"In fact," Adrian said. "We weren't even sure we could find you. Your gutsy escape saved our mission and likely saved at least one of our lives." He glanced at the other men.

Mel had been so caught up in what she'd been through and done, she hadn't had time to consider the risk these men had taken to rescue her.

"A chopper's due to collect us two klicks from here. Can you walk now?" Adrian asked.

Melonie nodded. She'd slept and soon would be with parents. A surge of adrenaline boosted her energy.

In single file, the group moved steadily, hiding amongst the trees. Four steely men and Mel. She'd heard of such men. Men trained to infiltrate enemy camps like ghosts. Unseen. Unheard. Soldiers who were revered, and who terrified the terrorists.

They stopped at the edge of a tree line where a grassy patch opened. At least fifty metres by fifty metres. Must be where the chopper will land, she thought.

"The chopper's on its ways." Adrian pointed to the grass patch. "It will land there. We must be quick, no delays. Melonie, if you don't feel strong enough to make the dash from here to the waiting chopper, tell me."

Melonie's thighs shook, her knees were weak, her feet sore from blisters. Her lips quivered; tears threatened.

Adrian nudged her gently. "Can you run to the chopper?"

"I don't know. I.... I think so. My legs, my feet."

He stared at her. His gaze reassuring and kind. "Listen. Can you hear the helicopter rotors?"

Wiping away tears, she smiled. She did hear them. Her rescue chopper. She would be whisked away from this horrid country. She would see her parents soon.

The helicopter hovered, kicking up dust and grass, then landed. Adrian pulled her to her feet and carried her. The wind from the blades tossed sand in her face. Her long hair swirled into a knotted mess. Quickly, they all boarded. The chopper lifted and buzzed away from her nightmare as the sun peaked over the horizon.

Chapter Eleven

THE SMELL of smoke woke Solomon. He jumped up and shook Jacob. He could see smoke drifting into the underground passageway.

"Hey, wake up, wake up. Smoke. Let's get out of here." He shouted.

Solomon pulled on his boots as fast as he could, fearful of being trapped underground in a cavern filled with smoke.

Grabbing his AK and a full magazine, Solomon bolted down the passage holding his breath. Jacob followed.

Outside they were met by a swirling inferno. Just about all the buildings on the other side of the parade square were ablaze. Jacob took charge. He waved to Solomon to follow him. They sprinted across the smoke-filled parade square, ducked around the side of the only building that hadn't caught alight yet, and raced over bare ground to a large collection of wild banana's a couple of hundred metres from the camp.

Pulling the wide fronds open, they climbed in, covering themselves with the succulent leaves. From there they watched the fire spread. It raced up tree trunks, crackled and spat as it climbed. A further move would be necessary at first light, Solomon considered.

Solomon watched cadres run, alight and screaming. Running fire-balls as the flames devoured them. "Nooo," he groaned, sick at the sight. A sight he'd never forget, then his eyes scanned for signs of Rhodesian security forces. They must have rescued the white girl, then set the camp alight. He wondered if Antonio had got away in time. It was his building that had already burned to the ground.

As full dawn broke the inferno had almost gone out. A few trees still burned, but there was little left of the camp. Solomon strained his eyes for movement.

Not wishing to reveal their position, but growing uneasy, Solomon spoke. "We'd better get out of here." Suddenly, the fire, caught by an early wind, flared up again.

Rising from the prone position, Solomon moved onto his hands and knees. At that precise moment, a high-pitched scream filled his head. Two Hawker Hunter jets swooped low overhead, then climbed almost vertically. He'd been warned by Joe what Hawker Hunter jets sound like. The noise of the climbing Hunters changed from the high-pitched screech of their approach to a head-splitting deep roar as they disappeared into the sky. The sound deafening, and the image terrifying.

He'd barely flattened himself beside their hide-out when the ground shook violently. A new sound. The sound of bombs exploding. Rocks and debris flew in all directions, tearing the banana leaves above them to shreds. The sound of the explosions filled Solomon with a fear he'd never experienced before. Miraculously he wasn't injured. He lay still, knowing if he survived this, the sounds and the terror of the moment would scar him for life. His ears were ringing but the silence that followed deafened. No sound came from the jets. All he could hear was the lone cry of a soldier in agony. It was this that made the silence so horrifying.

Instinctively, Solomon, having just learnt something about the speed of sound, realised if the Hunters were to return, they would, once again, be at their mercy. He had barely heard the screech of the approaching aircraft the first-time round. Where would the next attack come from?

It didn't take much for him to stay rooted beside the banana fronds.

Solomon strained his ears. He could hear another sound. The thud-thud of a helicopter in the distance.

"I can hear a helicopter," he said to Jacob.

"It's what the *Mukiwa,* those white soldiers, call, *fire-force.*" Jacob said.

"Yes, if an MAG gunner should see us, we're dead, comrade." Solomon advised, expecting the worst to suddenly erupt. It never happened, but the Hunters were not finished. They swooped in from the East with the sun behind them.

The screech, the roar and the momentous explosion of bombs forced Solomon to flatten himself again. Hardly time to cover their ears, much less to shoot. Bombs exploded, seconds apart. Solomon heard a sharp crack to his right and the soil leapt off the ground. The banana leaves writhed and danced as stones cut through the grove, tearing the trees to shreds. He prepared to die.

Then the silence. Solomon wondered if this was the silence of the afterlife. He submitted to it. Fear left him as if he were drifting. It felt like forever before he became aware of himself. He lifted his head and saw dust and smoke and realised he was still alive. He looked over at Jacob. His head had been flipped up, lying on its side, facing Solomon. His eyes were open, but there was a hole between them, where the eyebrows met. Blood oozed from the hole.

Mercifully, Jacob's death was free of pain, suffering and stress. That reality, apparently, was reserved for Solomon.

There were no more surprise runs by the Hunters and no sign of Fire-Force. Solomon lay where he was, grateful to live to fight another day. This day would be singed to memory forever. Disorientated, he retreated into the bush. It finally occurred to him, he was walking in circles. He'd noticed the fire had joined other fires caused by the bombs. He stopped and noted the wind direction. It blew in his favour, he retreated alone and scared.

Slowly but surely the terrorists regrouped to salvage, to bury the dead and to establish a new base. Solomon never saw Antonio again. None of the surviving comrades could account for the white girl. Solomon wondered. Had they both been blown to smithereens?

Chapter Twelve

The telephone rang. "Hello," Ivan's voice was tired from another night of staggered sleep. He glanced at his watch, not yet seven o'clock.

"Cheer up Ivan," Phil said. "I've got good news. Melonie is in a helicopter, on her way to hospital in Umtali."

"What? They've found her?" Ivan's relief flooded his voice, his nerves, and every muscle. "Hang on Phil, let me tell Margaret."

Ivan raced to the bedroom, his feet barely touching the floor. "They've rescued Mel."

"Oh my God" Margaret sat on the edge of the bed and her expression sailed from depression to elation. "Is she alright?"

"I believe so. Phil's on the phone." He took Margaret's hand and together they practically flew to the phone. "Phil. This is the best news ever." Ivan held the phone so both he and Margaret could hear. "Is Mel okay? Why are they taking her to hospital?"

"Lieutenant Stevens instructions were to have Melonie casevac'd to hospital. Apparently, she's in good spirits. Exhausted, dehydrated and struggling with shock, so hospital is the best place for her."

"We'll be on our way. Any idea what time she'll arrive?" Ivan squeezed Margaret's hand.

"No idea, but you two must be thrilled, and I'm happy to deliver this good news."

"I can't even begin to find the right words. Thanks Phil." Ivan hung up the phone.

He and Margaret hurriedly dressed and packed an overnight bag. Ivan gave Simon instructions to lock up the house.

Ivan drove at a speed he knew he shouldn't. Margaret reminding him they wanted to get to the hospital alive, so he slowed down.

They rushed to the reception counter at the Umtali Central hospital and asked where they could find Melonie.

The receptionist blabbed on and on about Melonie's exciting arrival. "You daughter was met by two nurses and a doctor."

"Which ward?" Ivan interrupted, desperate to see Mel.

"Oh, of course. She's in a private room. Go up the stairs, turn left down the passage, the last door on the right," the receptionist said.

Ivan and Margaret hurried up the stairs and found Mel sitting on the bed wearing a white hospital gown.

"Mum. Dad." Mel slid off the bed and fell into her parents' arms. Ivan held her tight, so tight he couldn't believe he was holding her again. Margaret's bandaged shoulder couldn't offer the same bear hug.

Mel pulled back and grabbed the back of her gown. "Why do these stupid gowns open down the back?" She laughed through tears and sat back on the bed.

Margaret hugged Mel again. "This moment...... it feels so surreal. I can't believe I'm holding you." Her voice carried tears and anguish and bottomless love.

Then Margaret's face filled with concern. "Oh my. We were in such a hurry leaving the farm, I forgot to pack clothes for you. We'll pop out and buy some nice new ones."

Mel touched Margaret's drooping arm. "Oh, Mum. Your shoulder. I can see you're still in a lot of pain. You should have the doctors check you out."

"I'm fine, sweetheart. It's well bound and I have pain killers. All that matters is you." She wrapped her arms around Mel again.

Ivan feared he'd need a crowbar to separate his wife and daughter.

A doctor entered the room. "Hello. You must be Melonie's parents.

I'm Doctor Smith. I've been the doctor assigned to treat your daughter while she's here. Melonie will be put on a drip shortly. We need to hydrate her, and I'll include a sedative and some antibiotics. She may be asleep for the rest of the day."

Ivan studied Mel. He could see the hollow, sunken look of her eyes. "Sounds the right thing to do."

Margaret let go and helped Mel wriggle beneath the sheets. She smoothed their daughter's hair and adjusted blankets.

"Doctor, may I have a word?" Ivan stepped to the door. The doctor followed and they stood outside the room in the passage.

"How is my daughter? I mean, I know you said she's dehydrated, but what else? Any injuries? Did the kidnappers hurt her?"

"All things considered, she's doing better than I expected. She did ask me not to tell you any detail. I'm sure she'll share with you and your wife in time. You have a very brave daughter. She's holding emotions close to her chest. Give her time to rest, recover, and heal from her ordeal."

Ivan understood and appreciated the doctor's advice. "Thank you, Doctor."

Back in Mel's hospital room, Margaret gazed at Melonie, as if she never wanted to let Mel out of her sight again.

A nurse pushed the drip stand close to the bed. From the hall came a commotion and Doctor Smith's voice. "Someone get the fucking press out of the hospital. Inform them there will be no access to Melonie Johns, she's endured quite enough."

Doctor Smith walked back into the room, his face red with anger. "Like vultures fighting for their place at the kill. Armed with camera's, tripods and note pads, eager to be the first to shove a microphone under Melonie's nose and pick at the carrion of her tattered emotions."

Melonie's eye widened. "Why would the press want to see me?"

Ivan hated to see Mel alarmed and used his most soothing voice. "Because you're a celebrity, my darling child. The whole country has been praying for your safe return."

"Really?" Melonie's face wrinkled in apparent disbelief. "Do I really have to stay here tonight? I'd rather just go home."

Doctor Smith smiled. "You've been through considerable trauma, young lady. Rehydration and sleep will help your body heal. Your parents can take you home after I've seen you in the morning." He shook Ivan's hand, nodded politely to Margaret, and left.

"Don't worry sweetheart. Just rest. Mum and I are here, staying close by."

Mel sank back on the pillow. The nurses connected the drip, added two syringes of medicine, and then left. Mel tilted her head to her parents. "I'm so glad to see you. I survived because of you... my...... wonderful parents. How......are.... the.... horses?" She closed her eyes and succumbed to sleep.

Mel woke late in the afternoon. A bowl of flowers, packets of biscuits, salt and vinegar crisps, chewy spearmints sweeties – her favourite, were stacked on the bedside locker. A warm gooey feeling filled her.

She heard a nurse saying, "I think Melonie is in denial. Probably the only way to cope with what she's been through."

Denial? Denial of what? Fear, pain, and humiliation tore into Mel's psyche. Anger and guilt ping ponged in her brain, but she intuitively knew she would deal with everything in time. She'd never forgive the evil commander, nor would she forgive Solomon. But she didn't feel any sort of denial.

The nurse walked in. "Supper will be served shortly. You had a wonderful sleep."

She gestured at the flowers and treats. "You've obviously seen your parents were here. They send love. They didn't want to interrupt any healing sleep you may need. They'll be back in the morning. Meanwhile, Doctor Lewis is here to see you."

"Who's Doctor Lewis?" Mel pushed herself further up in the bed.

"I'm Doctor Lewis, your appointed psychologist." He said and stood at the end of the bed. Mel looked up him, he was very tall, but he had a kind face and eyes that she thought reflected sincerity. She'd hear him out.

"I don't need a psychologist. I haven't gone mad." Melonie didn't hide the indignation in her voice.

"Miss. Johns, psychologists help deal with emotional difficulties, and my goodness, you've had more than a fair share. Stored trauma can ruin people's lives. I would hate that to happen to you. I'm not suggesting you went mad in that camp, though no-one would blame you if you had." His warm smile seemed genuine, and Mel found it reassuring.

"I'll never forget what has happened to me, Doctor. Fear came in many forms, starting at home with bullets flying, then terror when I was hauled from our house. The hell run from home to the terrorist camp was horrific, and then the pain and suffering I endured there." She shook her head back and forth, trying to stem the threatening tears. "My escape and then running into the Selous Scouts was a miracle. And I'm forever grateful for the Scouts."

The door opened and Mel's supper arrived.

"May I eat? I'm starving and it smells much better than *sadza*." Mel breathed in the aroma of deliciousness and then laughed.

"Yes, of course," Doctor Lewis said.

Mel lifted the lid covering her dinner. "Ooh, roast chicken." A rush of saliva filled her cheeks, and she grabbed the knife and fork and dived into her meal.

"I admire the pragmatic way you've dealt with the trauma you've endured. "Doctor Lewis said. "I'm confident, given time and support from your parents, you'll survive these horrors and get on with the rest of your life."

They spent the next hour discussing strategies for Mel's emotional healing.

Doctor Lewis stood from his chair beside the bed. "You're an amazing young lady, and I wish you everything of the best. And if you ever need to talk further, don't hesitate to contact me."

Mel smiled drowsily. "Thank you, I will."

Before the door closed behind Doctor Lewis, Mel's eyelids fluttered shut.

The next morning Mel was awaken by a different nurse. "How did you sleep?" The nurse brought with her tea and a biscuit.

Mel squinted against the bright overhead light. "What's the time?"

"Five o'clock."

"Gee, why so early?"

"I need to remove your drip. Then you can go back to sleep."

By nine thirty Mel's parents arrived, and Doctor Smith stopped by and explained her medications. Soon she'd be on her way home.

"Good luck, girlie. If you need me for anything, just call. The nurses are going to smuggle you out of the hospital. You don't need to face the barrage of reporters I yelled at yesterday. They don't take no for an answer. Your parents will be here shortly."

"Thank you, Doctor." She lay her head back, thinking about going home. She had scary reservations. She slid out of bed and dressed in the new clothes. She was ready when her parents walked in. Between them and two nurses they managed to get out of the hospital without the press noticing.

"Aah, well done, Dad." Melonie giggled. "I never thought I'd ever be hounded by the press, in fact I never thought I'd live to see home again."

WEAVING their way out of the city, Ivan took a different route home as a precautionary measure. Melonie was a heroine in some people's eyes, but a wanted murderer in the eyes of the terrorists who'd survived the fire. According to Phil, they'd soon be after her again.

"Dad, which way are you going home?"

Ivan sighed deeply. "Mel, we must sell up. It's not safe for any of us to stay on the farm longer than necessary."

"Noo," she cried out. "You can't. Where will we go?"

"It's the toughest decision Mum and I've ever made. We are targets, and if Solomon lived, he'll be back. But even if he didn't survive, the gooks who did will make sure we don't live. None of us could take another attack."

A sadness, bloated with remorse, filled the car. Silent minutes ticked by until eventually Ivan spoke. "Mum's been talking to Gran. Once the farm is sold, we'll move to South Africa. She's too old to run the stud, and the farm. You'd love living there, wouldn't you?" He looked at her in the rear-view mirror.

Mel sat quietly sorting out her feelings then answered. "Yes, I think so. Living with all gran's horses will be fun." Suddenly the thought of being surrounded by so many horses and being far away from the war, made her mood lighter.

"Dad, the war still goes on until we sell, though."

"Because we're so vulnerable, we have militia guarding the house and the sawmill, day, and night. Twelve local farmers got together after the attack, and we jointly employed a vigilante force to patrol the district. You can go out riding as normal but stick with Patric. He said he'd be happy to die protecting you. Isn't that sweet?"

"Aw. Did he really? Amazing. He's so kind to me."

"You asked about going back to school. The headmaster suggested you go back when you're ready. What d'you think?"

"To be honest, I think I'll feel safer there." She laid her head back and sighed. "I'm not going to feel secure anywhere in Rhodesia, anymore."

That was the sad reality of their predicament. "Nor do we. All we can hope for is a quick sale. Our aim is to be with Gran by Christmas."

"Wow. That would be a miracle."

***

Mel never returned to school to the promised hero's welcome. Mel had never felt like one, rather the victim of an unwanted war. But good fortune shone on Ivan's family. The farm had new owners. They were to take occupancy during the last week of October 1978.

A week before their intended departure, Ivan, Mel, and Margaret sat the dining room table enjoying one of their last meals on the farm. "I'm happy and sad at the same time, about leaving." Mel said. "Tonight, I'm going to write letters to all my friends giving them Gran's address in South Africa. I'm also going to pen a letter to Mr Sharp to thank him for being such a great principal."

Ivan looked up. Before he scooped the next mouthful, he said, "What a lovely idea, Mel." Ivan loved Mel's acceptance of the situation and wished he could feel the same. Leaving would be difficult but he needed to keep his family safe. Blue Winds was no longer safe.

The first few weeks of October passed with so many mixed emotions for all of them. Exhaustion, fear of another attack, worry about the future wore on all their nerves.

With only a week before their departure, Margaret wanted to deworm all the sheep so Mel and Patric were bringing in the last of them to the sheep pens situated not far from the stables.

Ivan walked from the mill and joined Margaret. He knew her shoulder may be hurting. "How are you doing? Is the shoulder coping?" Ivan asked.

Margaret inserted a needle into a squealing ewe, held tightly by Enos, one of the shepherds. "I'm managing, but my shoulder can't take much more. You'll have to take over.

"Of course. You've done a titanic job. I'm not surprised your shoulder is sore."

Removing the needle from the irritated ewe, Margaret straightened her back and stretched her arms above her head. "I just want to get out of here now. I never thought I'd say that about the farm."

"I know what you mean. And I never thought I'd agree to leave." Saying the words out loud hurt his heart.

BOOM. A loud explosion shook the ground. They ran into the shed while the sheep scurried about the pen in panic and the ewe in the sheep crush squirmed.

"Jesus Christ, what the hell was that?" Ivan and Margaret stood with their backs pressed against the wall of the shed.

"Landmine?" Margaret whispered.

"Too small an explosion for a landmine. I'll go and see what's happened." Ivan headed down the road in the direction of the plume of dust that rose above the treetops. The same direction Melonie and Patric were likely to be, bringing in the last of the flock.

Enos settled the flock, while Margaret took off after Ivan.

"Jesus wept," Ivan exhaled the words and stood in paralysed horror trying to absorb what he was seeing. Just then, an army Bedford came into view and ground to a stop. The driver, dressed in army uniform, flew out the cab and raced to Melonie, getting to her before Ivan.

"Warrant Officer Brown," he shook Ivan's hand quickly. "On routine patrol. I've just come up from the river road."

Sheep had scattered everywhere, looking about nervously, unsure of which direction to run next. Margaret dodged through them to get to her daughter. Mel was spitting gravel out of her mouth and trying to get her breath back. She'd been winded and couldn't speak, lying ten metres from her beloved horse.

Ivan noticed Patric struggling to stand. He left Margaret to help Mel and ran across the road to assist Patric. He'd got up and was shaking his head. Bewildered, he looked around.

"What happened Patric. Are you okay?"

"I don't know, Mr Ivan. A loud bang and Spindle reared. I fell off, sheep scattered, and I saw Firelight fall. Is Melonie, okay?"

"She's on the road over there," Ivan pointed. Margaret had knelt beside her and was brushing gravel off her arms.

"Firelight must've stepped on an anti-personnel mine. His right leg has been blown off above the knee. I'm going to ask the Warrant Officer to quickly end his life. He's in agony, poor horse."

Patric sobbed.

Ivan nodded to the Warrant Officer. He couldn't bear to see the pain the poor horse was in. Firelight's eyes had rolled back, and he was groaning loudly. Pools of blood smeared the gravel road where he lay.

WO Brown pulled his 9mm from its holster. BANG. He mercifully ended Firelight's suffering. Firelight's body lay still, a woosh of air escaped from his nostrils, as if in relief the pain was over.

"No. No. No," Mel sobbed and screamed, thumping the ground with her fist. "Not Firelight. This....war...," she spat out more sand, "is killing everything. Not Firelight, Mum. Not Firelight too." Margaret rubbed Mel's back. "I know darling. I know. It's all so horrible. But thank God, you're all right."

"My ears are ringing so loudly." Mel tried to stand.

Margaret helped steady Mel.

Holding her head in her hands, Mel hobbled to Firelight, wrapped her arms around his neck, and wept. Shuddering, heart wrenching cries.

WO Brown turned away.

"Thank you," Ivan said to WO Brown.

"Is there anything else I can help with? I'll report this incident on the radio in my truck. The sooner the better."

"No, thanks anyway. Our staff will round up the sheep and we'll get our daughter back to the house."

"Jesus, I'm sorry about that poor horse. Bloody heart breaking for your daughter. I detest shooting animals, but best to put them out of their pain as quickly as possible when there's nothing one can do to keep them alive."

"Yes, I agree and thank you for doing it so quickly and accurately."

WO Brown walked back to the military truck shaking his head. He climbed into the Bedford, talked into the radio mouthpiece, then drove off.

Margaret cooed more words of comfort to Mel. Eventually Mel looked up, her faced twisted with pain. Choked with raw, bitter emotion, she said. "Goodbye my precious boy, you saved my life." Her mum pulled her into her arms, and they cried.

"Another innocent, unnecessary victim of this fucking awful war." Ivan mumbled to Patric. His voice filled with anger and heartbreak. "Are you okay, Patric?"

"Yes." Patric glanced at Mel and spoke softly to her. "I'm so sorry for your loss."

"Let's try and gather the sheep." Ivan said. "Can you manage, Patric?"

"Yes." His eyes still a glazed look. Probably from a mild concussion. Together they gathered the sheep, herding them back to the pens.

That night, lying in bed, Ivan finally accepted the inevitable – Blue Winds was to be his past. He must look to the future in South Africa.

Standing at the graveside, Mel wept. "It's so sad and horrible. I can't get the vision of the blood pumping out of all that remained of his leg."

"Such a terrible end for him, and for us." Margaret hugged Mel.

Ivan wiped tears from his eyes. With all Mel had been through he worried how losing Firelight in such a horrible way would affect her. Mel had endured far too much for such a young girl.

During the days that followed Mel hardly spoke and Ivan worried more. After breakfast she'd sit with Spindle in the stable, groom her and feed her. Then, head bowed, she'd walk back to the house and help them pack.

Ivan was in the sitting room packing up the bookcases. Mel joined him. Margaret had Simon helping her in the kitchen.

"Dad, what about Spindle? Can she come with us? If she stays, she'll be killed. Patric told me he's been warned by someone in the compound who talks to the gooks." Mel put her head on one side, her lips quivered.

Ivan didn't have the heart the keep the plan a secret any longer. "We've organised for Spindle to be trucked to Gran." But Ivan didn't tell Mel they'd applied for Patric, his wife and son, to emigrate to South Africa, just in case it couldn't be done.

"Thank you, Dad." She stepped forward and hugged him. When she pulled away from his arms, she smiled for the first time since Firelight's ghastly demise.

Twenty-four hours later, Ivan and his family left Blue Winds for ever, not looking back as they drove away.

Chapter Thirteen

November 1978

IVAN, Margaret, and Mel met the convoy outside Umtali on the Birchenough Bridge Road. It was 7:00 a.m.

Military personnel waited while cars lined up on the side of the road to join the convoy to Beitbridge.

Standing on the side of the road waiting for the departure at 7:30 a.m. they struck up conversation with other families leaving their beloved country. Many tears were shed. Some sad stories shared.

After hours of driving, the cars in the convoy pulled into the parking bays at Beitbridge border post.

Inside the Johns car a heavy silence hung. This was the end of an era. The war had brought the tranquil, happy life they'd once enjoyed to a bitter end that wrenched at their souls. They'd been forced to leave the country of their birth. Each one of them were dealing with their own heart-breaking thoughts. Despite the war and all the atrocities, they agreed, the hardest part was now.

"Oh God this is awful." Margaret broke the silence. From the back seat, Mel wrapped her arms around her shoulders. Ivan patted Margaret's thigh affectionately. He swallowed hard. This was so final.

The two Labradors seated next to Mel, looked on with curious expressions.

"Goodbye, goodbye," Margaret whispered, holding a tissue in her hand. The tune of the Last Post hammered in Ivans head as she said that. He took a long deep breath and said, "Let's get on with it."

Margaret reached for her handbag and briefcase nestled at her feet and opened the car door. Time to go in and face it.

As they stepped into the dark-red brick Immigration building, they noticed their new friends in the queue ahead of them. Many of the people in the queue recognised Mel. Her face had been in the newspapers across the country on several occasions. She had managed to keep her composure until a little girl ducked out of the queue ahead and came to stand beside her. With wide, shiny blue eyes, and a head of blonde curls, she looked up at Mel. "I cwyed about the story of your horse." In an instant Mel choked on a sob and the little girl wrapped her arms around Melonie's legs. "I yuv'd my pony too, now he's sold to someone else." Tears ran down her cheeks and she went back to join her parents.

Mel held a tissue to her nose. She noticed the tenderness of the moment had affected everyone in the queue that heard the little girls' words.

"Did you leave a window open for the dogs?" Ivan asked, trying to distract Mel from obviously painful thoughts of Firelight.

"Yes, Dad, a few inches. Poor things must be boiling." She wiped her face to dry the sweat off her brow and the tears from her cheeks.

After the immigration formalities were complete, they slowly crossed the vast Limpopo River bridge.

"See how many crocs you can count." Ivan said idly, scanning the sandy banks for crocodile basking in the sun. Islands of rocks and scrub blotted the green-grey water as it snaked its way through the landscape. The river was low, and crocodiles were plentiful.

"I counted twenty-three. How many did you count, Mum?"

"I lost count at nineteen."

"And I'm slowing up traffic, look at all the cars behind us." Ivan speeded up.

The late morning temperatures reached 41 degrees centigrade.

Drenched in sweat and sentiment they cleared customs on the South African side and set off for their new life in a new country. The thought of living in peace, their only comfort.

En route to Chanting Clover Stud, their new home, they stayed over in a pet friendly motel and left early the following morning. Seven hours later Ivan drove down the tree-lined driveway to the house. It had been four years since they last visited. The farm, nestled in the heart of the Natal Midlands where Margaret had grown up after leaving Kenya.

Iris, Margaret's mother had two, always-happy-to-meet-you, golden Labradors, who had heard the car pull up and rushed out, tails wagging and peered through the car windows.

Mel laughed. Benji and Bessie barked, eager to get out the car, meet new friends and stretch their legs. Then two yapping Jack Russell terriers came charging down the stairs.

"Let's not fuss, just let the dogs out," Ivan said.

Mel opened the passenger door. Benji and Bessie jumped clear and stood, hackles up, sniffed out the competition. The curious little terriers swarmed around the bigger dogs' legs but after an occasional snap and growl, they all tore off with their noses pinned to the ground.

"Welcome, welcome, welcome." Hector Willis, the stud manager said as he came down the sweeping stairway to greet them.

Ivan was stretching his tired back when Hector gave Margaret and Mel a welcoming hug, then shook Ivan's hand.

"How was your trip?"

"Not bad at all. Just an awfully long way, but it's good to be here."

"Iris is excited to see you all, she's just on a call. Leave your luggage, the staff will pop down and get it for you."

Mel was waiting for the dogs to return and spied the stables in the distance.

Hector noticed where her stare was directed, and he smiled. "Let's go in. Iris is in the living room. I'll take you round the stables in due course." He said to Mel.

Iris's lovely home was modelled on the Cape Dutch style and had many charming features entirely of its own. When she and Fergus bought the farm, it was Iris who planned the changes. The sweeping stairs that lead up to the front door was one of the features. On either side of the wide wooden front door, stood aged wooden brandy barrels that were now filled with flowering geraniums. Scarlet red blossom covered the plants in a dazzling display of contrast against the backdrop of snow-white walls.

Iris had just ended her call when they walked in, and she hugged her daughter. "Hi Ma, it's so good to see you. Thank you so much for everything. I don't know what we would've done without you."

"Oh, not a bit, darling. It's as much your home as it is mine. I'm delighted to have you all here. How are you after the wretched time you've all had?"

"As good as can be expected, I guess." Margaret said. The tiredness and stress could be heard in her voice.

"Yes, of course," Iris said, concern creased her handsome, broad brow and she hugged Ivan, saying, "You look exhausted. Such an awfully long way to drive."

"It is, but having this to come to is a Godsend. Thank you, Iris." Then she hugged her granddaughter and held her in her arms. "You poor darling girl, you've been through more tragedy than most people experience in a lifetime. How are you coping, sweetheart?"

"I'm alright, thanks, Gran. I'm looking forward to meeting all the horses." Melonie smiled graciously.

"Come on then, let's not stand on parade, sit." Iris motioned. Moments later the dogs came tearing into the sitting room. Smudge and Spot, the two terriers still jostling for an argument.

"Oh, dear, sorry Gran. Are the dogs allowed in the house?" Gran's house was very posh.

"Of course, my girl. They're a special part of the family. They'll settle down shortly. Not to worry." The dogs flew out the room again, leaving their playful energy lingering.

"When can I see the horses?"

Iris laughed. "A girl after my own heart. I knew you'd be itching to have Hector take you around." She turned her attention to Hector. "Is it alright with you?"

"Yes. I'd be delighted."

"Wonderful. Off you go then, there's not much time, it'll be dark soon."

Margaret breathed a contented sigh. "The resilience of youth is enviable." Margaret stretched her arms, "I'd forgotten how comfortable these wrap-around, stay-in-forever, sofas are."

Iris laughed. "You've always loved them, haven't you? Now tell me, how is Mel coping?"

"There's a lot going on in her pretty little head. We're seeing, but she's not telling."

Ivan chipped in then. "But under the circumstances, better than we expected. We hope her love of horses will help her through the trauma."

Iris held her teacup and stared at the floor for a moment. "Yes," she said thoughtfully, "and I hope being here and taking over the management of the farm will ease your heartbreak. You two have suffered terribly too. You must've found it awfully difficult saying goodbye to Blue Winds."

"It certainly was, but the war and all it brought with it, made departing easier. And having this to come to, warms us both with huge gratitude, doesn't it sweetheart?" Ivan said.

Iris smiled. "I cannot tell you how grateful I am that you two are here. The place is yours now, anyway. When I twang my harp, it all goes to you, my dear daughter. Do you remember the dramatics when we left Kenya, or were you too young?"

"I don't remember that much of it, Ma. It's déjà vu, moving back into my old bedroom." Margaret stood up and moved over to Ivan, "And where you proposed to me twenty years ago."

Iris was watching them fondly. "And still as in love now as you were then. I think it's time for a drink, don't you?"

"A whiskey and soda will do the trick. A lot more exciting than tea." Ivan grinned. "Will certainly help me sleep tonight. I think when I close my eyes, I'll still see the road coming at me."

"I'm going to unpack first, Ma. I'll leave you two to reminisce."

AT THE BROODMARE BARN, Mel stood in speechless wonder. In front of her were sixteen spotless, five-meter by five-meter foaling boxes. Eight on either side of a wide passage.

The smell of dried grass and fresh wheat straw bedding caught in her nostrils. She'd always loved the smell. Fresh, herby, and clean. Standing in a stable the bedding reached her knee. It had been drawn down, ready to welcome the mares and foals in for the night.

"Wow, this is a lovely deep bed."

"We like to make it as comfortable as possible for mums and their babies." Hector said while they walked the length of the barn to the opening at the other end. They stood watching the mares and foals being brought in. Soft hues of approaching dusk silhouetted the horses against a pinkie-orange sky and reminded Mel of a postcard she'd once seen.

"Step back a little Mel, make way for them as they come in. These little 'uns can be a bit skittish."

Prancing beside his mother, a beautiful dapple-grey mare, danced an impressive liver chestnut colt.

"What's this foals name? He's gorgeous. I love his four white socks."

"Tropical Sun. He's a stunner isn't he, and the little bugger knows it." Hector laughed affectionately.

"What a beautiful name. Maybe one day I'll ride him."

"I'm quite sure you will. At four weeks old he has the cadence of a champion. Poetry in motion, my girl." Hector's pride sounded in his voice.

"What's cadence?"

"It's a term used to describe rhythmical, naturally good action. When he moves, he looks like he's floating along?"

"I can't wait to see that. I've not been taught all these fancy horsey words to describe things yet."

"It won't take you long, my girl. You have an abundance of natural talent too."

A small smile played around the edges of her mouth. Mel liked the sound of that.

"Sunny, as I call him, is what I would consider a potential Durban July winner in three, maybe four years' time. He'll be a Group One horse."

Mel nodded. Whatever that meant, she'd learn.

Each mare was lead in by a groom, with their foal being guided by the groom. The last two mares hadn't foaled. They lagged, burdened by the weight of carrying a future racehorse.

"In the southern hemisphere the official birthday of all registered Thoroughbreds is the 1st of August, and in the northern hemisphere the 1st of January applies. We like to have all our foals all on the ground by the end of October. These last two mares are a bit late but should give birth within the next few days. Come, let me show you the birthing stable, our new addition since you were last here."

Hector walked back to the entrance of the barn. On their left were two rooms. A single foaling box, six by six metres, and next to it, on a raised platform, an observation room. Three steps led into what Mel thought, looked like a science laboratory.

"Wow, this is fancy."

"It is, isn't it? Cost your granny a pretty penny. Quickly, before it's dark, let me show you what happens here."

Looking down on the single stable through one-way glass Hector explained. "Standing up here allows us to observe the mare without her being disturbed. 'Protects the mare's dignity,' your marvellous grandmother said. This mare is due very soon. Maybe tonight, maybe tomorrow night."

"How do you tell how close they are?" Melonie had never seen a foal being born before.

"Tomorrow, I'll show you what happens in here, but let's go and see. Josia, is the man in with her."

Hector opened the stable door and introduced Josia. Josia took Melonie's hand, "Mr Hector has told me all about you. It's nice to meet you."

Melonie smiled. "It's nice to meet you too."

"Josia is the best broodmare supervisor in the world." Hector said.

Hector put his hand on the mare's neck and smoothed his hand down to her shoulder. "Apart from the obvious," pointing out the mare's enormous stomach, "the udder is a good indicator. On the end of each teat, there's 'wax'. You see it?"

Standing on the left of the mare's hindquarters, Melonie put her right hand on the mares back and bent down for a peep at the engorged udder.

"The pale-yellow stuff?"

"Yes." Hector lifted the mare's bandaged tail, gently holding it to one side. She moved away. Hector cooed and she stood.

"Once a mare is waxed up, rule of thumb is within forty-eight hours she'll go into labour. It's never a guarantee though. The date of her covering is recorded, but that's not guaranteed either, so we look at a few other signs."

Placing two hands, palm down on either side of the dorsal spine, Hector gently palpated her rump. "See how loose and soft, and noticeably dipped it is." Melonie nodded. "And her swollen, sloppy vagina. I wouldn't mind betting she foals tomorrow night."

"Awe, can I see?"

"Of course. I have my alarm set for 2 a.m. Set yours for 1.45 a.m. and I'll come and get you."

"Oh yippee."

"It's not guaranteed, Mel. You may wake up, only to be disappointed and will have to get up again the next night.

"That's okay." She nodded vigorously. Josia smiled.

"C'mon, let's get back. Thanks Josia."

On the way back to the house Melonie and Hector chatted about the mares and foals.

"Hector. How will you know if she has it tonight?"

"There'll be a foal there in the morning." He teased.

"No," she laughed. "I mean does Josia call you?"

"Only if there are problems. He'll call me on the radio. You want to see, so we'll go anyway."

"I was told horses are the best animals to make a fool of you." She chuckled, feeling more relaxed than she had in many months.

"You wicked young lass, but whoever told you that was quite right." Hector answered cheerfully. "It's the maiden mares who surprise us, even though we have their expected birthdate charted."

"Is a maiden mare one who's never foaled before?"

"You got it, gal." Hector smiled. "Our Josia misses nothing. He's brilliant. You will get along famously. He'll teach you a lot about foaling and dealing with grumpy broodmares."

They got back to the house in good time for dinner. Enthusiastic and excited, Mel went to bed early. At 2 a.m. she was in the hall waiting for Hector.

Hector opened the front door quietly and beckoned. Once they were outside, he said, "She's in labour."

The skies were even darker than normal. Heavy rain clouds threatened to burst. Mel kept close to Hector and his torch light. The residues of war had her eyes darting back and forth nervously. She would *never* have gone outside at night at Blue Winds.

Hector noticed the ghosts of what she'd been through were vexing and he put his arm around her shoulders. In a cheerful voice, he said, "It looks promising for our first rains. The pastures need it badly."

Once they got to the broodmare barn, her fears were quickly replaced. They checked in with Josia. The mare was lying down resting her nose in the bedding.

"When a foal is born, we list everything on a birthing chart. The afterbirth is weighed and checked, and the mare's colostrum tested. The time labour began, the duration of labour, any observed difficulties, how long the labour lasted and so on." He ran his index finger down the page.

"Wow. Gran is very meticulous."

"She is indeed and contributes to her success. If the mare does not belong to us, the owner gets copy. Everything is filed and recorded."

Mel pushed her head up against the glass and noticed the mare swishing her tail. While they waited Hector shared a story.

"When I started work here, your gran told me that every horse she bred became a unique family member. Your late grandfather, Fergus, affectionately teased her. He'd always say, 'it would've been cheaper buying you diamonds.' She always answered, 'but they are diamonds, my precious jewels.' From that statement many of the foals were named after precious gems. Isn't that a lovely story?"

"Yes, it is. I think something is happening, Hector." The mare stood up quickly and her waters broke. An opaque bag hung from under her bandaged tail. Melonie watched, fascinated.

The mare lay down again and heaved with the first contraction, then she got up and spun around. A stronger contraction gripped her. She heaved and two little feet appeared. Melonie covered her mouth. Enchanted by what she was witnessing, she felt quite emotional.

The mare's coat glistened with sweat and moaned from the pain, then she pushed the head out. Panting from the effort she waited. Mel watched. Mesmerised. With the next painful contraction and an almighty push, the shoulders passed through the birth canal, and the rest of the body slithered out.

The mare stood up and spun around, nickering to her new-born and began cleaning its head, pulling the rest of the membrane away from the foals' nose, initiating the vital bonding.

Tears rolled down Mel's cheeks. "I've never seen anything more beautiful."

Hector smiled, remembering how he'd felt the first time he witnessed the birth of a foal.

"How does the mother recognise her foal in the wild?"

"The miracle of nature ensures, in the very early process of cleaning, she'll recognise her foal by its smell, then the tone of its nickering."

Mel wiped away her tears, and chuckled. "My body has gone all mushy with emotion,"

The foal lay in the deep straw bedding for a few minutes while the mare licked and nuzzled and nickered, then it stretched its limbs out and attempted to stand.

"Oh, poor little thing, it's struggling to get up."

"It's perfectly normal, and essential we don't assist. It's during the struggles to stand they gain their strength." Hector said.

The foal tried standing again. Wobbly, but determined. After a few more attempts it got up.

"Yes!" Melonie clapped.

The foals' ears and nostrils twitched. It nickered to its mother, then took a few careful steps forward, then slumped to the floor. The mare nickered.

"She's saying, 'come on, get up again.'" Mel laughed. Josia was watching Mel. He was enjoying the banter and her excited antics.

No sooner had her words left her mouth, the foal stood up and wobbled toward its mother, in search of milk. Its little nose ran along its mothers' side. Josia watched, then he left the room, and helped the foal latch. He stood, steadying the wobbly hindquarters, and watched the foal suckle the vital colostrum. Then Josia checked the afterbirth and removed it from the stable. He'd weigh it before disposing of it.

"Gosh, I'm so lucky to have seen this. Thank you, Hector."

"You'll see plenty more, but the first is always special, isn't it? And a very nice foal too." They walked down the steps and stood at the stable door.

"Filly," Josia said to Hector.

"She's a diamond in the making, like Gran said. Can I call her White Jewel?" Melonie asked.

"You'll have to ask. Names must be submitted to the Stud Book for approval. If your grandmother states the name to be her first choice, and no others have used it before, it should be fine."

"Oh! So, you can't just give the foal any name?"

"Not with Thoroughbreds, my dear."

"May I go into the stable?"

Hector nodded.

Mel went to the mare and rubbed her neck, then she squatted next to the sleeping foal and gently played with its soft curly mane. She looked up at Hector with a smile that stretched across her face. Getting up so early had been worth it.

"I am in awe. It really is a miracle."

"It certainly is. I'm delighted you enjoyed watching. I never tire seeing a birth, but I seldom do nowadays."

"My dream has always been to work with horses. At school, when the career aptitude tests were done, they told me there's no future for a woman working with horses."

"Ignore what they said, my girl. This stud is yours. What else do you need."

"Mine?"

"Yes. Yours. That's what your grandmother wants for you."

Melonie's thoughts were whizzing around in her head as she and Hector left the broodmare barn and walked together to the main stable block. Hector checked each horse and by the time they got back to the house the clock ticked past seven.

The smell of frying bacon brought a rush of saliva to Mel's mouth.

"Ooh, that smells good. Are you having breakfast with us?" She asked Hector.

"Great idea, thank you."

Iris was standing in the hall. "Good morning. I'm eager to hear what you thought of seeing a foal being born."

"Morning Gran," Mel kissed her. "I've never experienced anything more beautiful. The foal is a filly. Can we call her White Jewel?"

"Perhaps. After breakfast come with me to my office. I'll show you what must be done."

The rest of the day Mel spent with her grandmother learning about breeding racehorses. Margaret and Ivan drove around the farm, orientating themselves with parts of the farm they seldom ever visited when they came on holiday.

MELONIE RACED to the broodmare barn the next morning and introduced herself to grooms she hadn't met the day before. "Where is Josia?"

"He's off duty." Maria said and shook Mel's hand. "I'm Maria, second in charge."

"Nice to meet you, Maria."

Mel peeked at the newborn, then walked down the line of stables until she came to Tropical Sun's stable. She slid the bolt back and snuck inside. She spoke to the lovely grey mare first, then sat in the straw next to the sleeping colt and gently lifted his head onto her lap.

This is where Hector found her after checking on the foal born the previous night. "What a site to behold." He said, leaning over the stable door.

"He's so beautiful."

"Irresistible, aren't they?" He left her there, while he checked the other brood mares.

Melonie moved her legs slowly and laid the sleeping foals head down, then caught up with Hector. She had a stallion tour with gran after breakfast.

. . .

THE WALK to the stallion barn was slow. Gran, at eighty-three, had dad walking next to her. She offered Mel some words of wisdom. "Always remember, horses are like drugs, the more you have, the more you want. It takes discipline not to collect them."

"I won't forget, Gran." She turned to her father. "When is Spindle arriving?"

"She'll be here tomorrow, we hope."

"Whoopee. Poor thing will be exhausted. Rest and pampering for a week before I take her out and explore the farm. It'll feel weird not having Patric with me."

Ivan and Iris swopped a surreptitious glance.

"Gran, is it true you were voted one of the country's leading racehorse breeders?"

Iris stopped and turned to Mel, "Yes, my dear, it's true, and I'm rather proud of that reputation. Now it's up to you to uphold. I'm sure you will win the coveted title of Breeder of the Year."

"Gee, Gran. I'll do my best. Will Hector and I run the stud and the racehorse training from now?"

"Yes, my girlie." Iris smiled fondly at her beautiful granddaughter.

They stood at the gabled entrance to the stallion barn. "I've always been rather proud of my design, matching this gable with the front of the house. I'm told it's the grandest stallion barn in Natal." She smiled.

The stallion in the first stable stretched his neck toward Mel. "What's his name, Gran?"

"Test of Time. He's a teddy bear, Mel." She put her hand out for him to nuzzle her palm.

"He's so beautiful, Gran."

"He certainly is. My favourite boy." She pulled some chopped apple from her pocket, and he nickered.

Melonie watched the magnificent dark bay horse nibble the apples. His coat shone under the lights, which defined powerful muscle.

"He's an absolute sweetie. Seldom nips and loves attention. He doesn't behave like a Thoroughbred stallion. He'll give you confidence being around stallions, Mel."

Melonie laughed as he tickled the palm of her hand with his muzzle while Ivan looked on with pride. He was watching the old Mel come to life.

"Aah, here's Kagiso. Kagiso, meet my granddaughter, Melonie."

Melonie shook his hand, then he shook Ivans. "It's nice to meet you. Welcome to Chanting Clover."

"Kagiso is our head stallion man. He'll teach you how to handle stallions. They can all be difficult during mating season. They go a bit bonkers." Iris turned to Ivan, "s

hall we walk back, my legs are getting tired."

Mel stayed. Kagiso led her to the next stallion stall.

"This is Eldorado. Your grandmother's first stallion. He adores your grandmother, but he can be unpredictable and may try and give you a bite."

Eldorado wasn't interested in meeting anyone new today. They moved on.

"And this is Affinity. Easy to handle, and a very comfortable ride."

"Oh wow, do you ride them?"

"Occasionally. Mr Hector used to take them out on hacks every day. But now's he's too old. That'll be your job."

"I'd love to ride them. Thanks, Kagiso. I'll see you again." Mel ran back to the house feeling that old sensation of joy renewed. Here there was purpose and hope. She found everyone on the veranda.

"How was that?" Margaret asked.

"Oh Mum, you must see the stallions. They're so beautiful, and Kagiso is such a nice man. He said you used to ride them, Hector."

"Yes, I did, so did your grandmother." That impressed Mel.

"It does the stallions good to go out on a hack. Settles them down."

"Could I ride them?"

"I'm sure you can. Once your legs are fit and strong you can also help with the early morning gallops, if you like." Hector said.

Melonie sat next to Hector. "Really? I'd love it. My legs are strong, Hector. When can I go for a hack?"

Everyone smiled. Warmed by her happiness.

"Once you've been kissed by a Thoroughbred, you won't want to ride anything else. When your dear little Spindle arrives, let's put her to the stallion." Ivan suggested.

"Then who will I ride?" Mel asked, a worried expression appeared on her face.

"My dear old schoolmaster, Dreamz. On him you can focus on getting your legs in the correct position for training racehorses. He's as safe as houses," Gran reassured her using an old-fashioned phrase Mel hadn't heard in a long time.

Hector added. "When you first ride with your legs under your chin they shake like an undernourished beggar."

Everyone laughed at Hector's analogy.

"When can I start?" Mel fidgeted eagerly.

"Any time. It's up to you."

Melonie clapped her hands and reached for a biscuit.

Chapter Fourteen

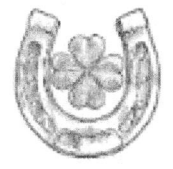

EARLY MORNING MEANT a 5:30 a.m. start for Mel. Today marked her first lesson riding a racehorse and though excitement filled her, so did nerves. Hector waited in the hall and then took her to the stables.

At seven-thirty Mel staggered into the dining room, laughing. Her parents sat at the table smiling. "My legs are like jelly, Mum. Look they're still shaking. Hector's description fits the picture, doesn't it? I never thought riding standing up would be so tiring."

She flopped onto a chair, but her weakened, trembling legs had prompted memories of how her legs felt in Mozambique. She pushed the thought away. "Dad, have you heard what time Spindle will be here? I can't wait to see her."

"In an hour or so." Ivan said.

After breakfast Mel wandered down to the off-loading zone near the feed store. A large circular tarmac area specifically allocated to horse trailers and trucks. Mel paced back and forth, waiting for the horse transporter to arrive, then she heard the grinding down of an engine in the distance and minutes later the truck came into view. She fidgeted excitedly while it drove in and parked, by which time her parents, who'd wandered down from the house, joined her.

"Finally, she's here." Mel stood close to the vehicle and smiled at the thought of being reunited with her horse. The side door of the transporter slid open and Patric stepped out.

"Patric." Mel shrieked his name and ran to him. "What are you doing here?"

"I am here to stay, Mel."

"Really? You're staying here?" She turned to her dad.

Ivan nodded, smiling.

"Oh, Dad. What a super surprise." She hugged Patric and then asked. "Where's your wife and son?"

"They're coming on the train in two weeks." He unhitched the back ramp, guided Spindle out and gave the rein to Mel.

"Oh, my darling, precious pony," Mel kissed Spindle's nose. "You look exhausted."

"It's been a very long journey. For both horses. And this Thoroughbred is a beauty." Patric handed the rein to Ivan.

"No wonder gran wanted this mare, she's gorgeous. Poor thing also looks exhausted but once she's settled, I'd like to see her move." Mel stepped back a bit to have a good look at the dark bay mare, who was at least five inches taller than Spindle.

"I'll lead Spindle to her stable. I know where it is. Next to Dreamz. I'll see you at the stables," Mel said to Patric, leading Spindle in the direction of the main stable block. Most of the other horses were out, but she led Spindle to her stable.

"Now Dreamz, you be nice to Spindle, please." Mel chuckled as the two horses met over the stable door.

After attending to Spindle, Mel found her dad on his motorbike, waiting at the gate to the main stable block. She jumped on the back of the motorbike. He drove them to the housing complex to check on Patric.

***

It took Mel another two weeks to tone her leg muscles for the new riding position and now she loved work riding. The second week in December, Hector put Mel on Sunset Boulevard. A striking, bolshy redbay colt. Mel sensed it was a test.

Ivan had parked the Landcruiser close to the track. Her grandmother sat watching from the passenger seat. This was Mel's first ride in front of Iris.

Circling around the warmup ring with eight other frisky young racehorses, Mel warmed up the colt and after a few good bucks, she settled him. Once she'd settled the horse, she greeted the other riders whom she didn't know by name yet. The other horses were cavorting around too, but they all soon settled into their work.

She glanced at them all, admiring the quality of the horses her grandmother had bred and soon they were leaving the warm-up area. Mel felt the nerves come on. She followed the others down to the start of the turf track. There, one work rider said she could lead the way.

Sunset Boulevard jumped forward, eager to begin the gallop a bit before Mel was ready, but she calmly took up the slack on her reins and off they went. With every stride she remembered what Hector had taught her and the colt responded.

Patric waited for Mel at the end of the track, clapping.

"Very good. Very good." Patric grabbed the reins and held the horse who puffed, his nostrils vibrating from exertion.

"That was so fun, Patric," she said breathlessly.

Patric led the tired horse across to where her family stood. She slid off the horse and into her Mum's arms.

"What a ride. We're so proud of you, my girl." Margaret was grinning broadly.

Hector smiled. "My God, you're brilliant." He sounded a little choked. "I know it's an old, well used cliché, but you've taken to this like a duck to water. It's incredible, having had no previous experience of racing Thoroughbreds."

Pulling out of her mother's arms, Mel uttered, "That.... was... thrilling. Oh God.... I.... love this." Mel moved to the vehicle where her gran sat, tears rolling down her cheeks and hugged her grandmother. Mel whispered breathlessly, "I'm...... so grateful...... to you, Gran. This is what I was born to do." Iris squeezed her, too emotional to answer.

"Brilliantly ridden," Ivan felt the pull of paternal pride.

"Tomorrow, I'll pop you up on Wind Power." Hector turned to Iris. "What do you think, Iris?"

"Watching Mel ride, my heart swelled. Yes, Mel's ready to ride Wind Power, my Durban July hopeful."

"Ooh, Gran, that's an honour. Thank you." Since Mel's first introduction to Wind Power, Mel had made a point of visiting his stable every morning with her pocket full of juicy treats. Now he knickered at her whenever she approached. Mel knew they'd do well together.

Patric walked Sunset to cool him off. Being fit, his recovery was quick. Patric approached the Landcruiser and Iris stood, holding onto Hector. She stroked the horse's nose. "Such a wonderful horse, another of my favourites."

THAT EVENING, the family sat together on the veranda watching the sun gradually drop behind the horizon. Mel cherished these moments. She loved sunsets and now she could watch without the view being blocked by grenade walls, far away from wars and terror and horror.

Curious about Hector, Mel asked. "Gran how did Hector come to be here with you?"

Iris sipped thoughtfully on her brandy, then spoke. "When Hector joined me, he'd just divorced his wife. It was all very nasty." She took another sip. "He was reserved and heartbroken. I only got to know him well by the end of his first year." Iris set her glass down. "The saddest part of the divorce was his wife. She refused to bring their two girls here. To a land filled with savages, is what she'd said." Iris raised her shoulders and her eyebrows. "I owe Hector so much. I couldn't have built this farm and stud without him. He'll teach you well, Mel." She patted Mel's knee and smiled.

Iris then turned to Ivan. "A few years ago, I promised Hector he could live in his cottage until he dies or wants to move. There is no written agreement, but I want to be sure you'll honour that when I am dead."

"Without question," Ivan raised his drink. "To Hector. And to Mel's fabulous ride this morning. Mel looked at her father and felt so proud of herself and her achievement in such a short time. Now she couldn't wait to get on Wind Power.

WINDS OF CHANGE

***

Christmas passed with quiet celebrations. Emotions cracked open and raw. There were constant reminders of the ongoing Rhodesian war on the radio and television. Whenever Mel heard the start of it, she left the room. She couldn't listen. She'd either run to her room or down to the stables.

Hector guided Mel with unwavering commitment at the track in the morning. After breakfast she and Patric would hack out and learn the boundaries, often getting a little lost, but it didn't matter here, there were no terrorists watching. After lunch she'd learn the art of preparing young racehorses, starting stall loading, lunging, early backing, and pre-sales preparations. After tea at four she'd spend a few hours with her grandmother, brushing up on the rules of the Jockey Club, pedigrees, breeding, the names, and places of racetracks across the country, and which were the most important race meetings. At six a tray of drinks was brought to the veranda where the family would meet. There was no time for Mel to dwell on the past.

By early February Hector suggested she was ready to take over the training of Wind Power.

"That is so exciting, but I can't do it without you, Hector." Mel said.

"You ride him every day and I'll give the instructions and watch every training race. After each ride we'll analyse how it went."

"Are you sure, Hector? This is gran's baby. Her dream to win the Durban July."

"I know that my girl. Gran suggested it."

"She did?" Hector nodded his reply.

"Wow, I can't believe it. This is so exciting. So do we start tomorrow?"

"Yip. I think Patric has a good idea where all the sheep paddocks are now, so when you hack out take a different horse each day. They all enjoy a nice easy hack."

. . .

Mel woke earlier than usual, excited about riding Wind Power. She met Hector at the track at 6:00 a.m. She'd ridden down with the string of seven other horses. Wind Power felt like he had the power of the wind under him and bucked and cavorted the whole way from the stables to the warm-up area. She sat him while she giggled and chatted to the other riders completely unphased by the horse's antics.

Hector just shook his head. To begin with he'd wondered if Wind Power wasn't too much horse for her, but Mel proved him wrong. She rode a superb 2000 metre first training gallop and at the end she trotted over to where Hector waited. Her faced flushed from the exertion, but he could see her smiles.

"Gee, I thought... Sunset was fast, but.... this horse. I've never ridden.... anything like him in my life. He makes my body tingle. It's covered with goosebumps. What are those feel-good things called again, Hector?"

"Endorphins." He said and laughed.

"Yeah, those things. Schue, he's so fast." She slid off Wind Power's back and handed the reins to Shadrick, then doubled over, trying to get her breath back. Finally, she stood up and took a deep breath. "Thank you, Shadrick."

"I'm very impressed by the way you rode him. At first, I thought he might pull away from you." Hector said and patted Mel on the back. "Wait till gran sees you on him." He smiled and raised his bushy eyebrows. "His next race is at Clairwood in three weeks."

After a week of training rides, Mel took Wind Power on a ten-kilometre walk/trot ride teaching him about her leg aids. She'd been following all the riding tips gran had been feeding her and they were working well. Wind Power was responding beautifully even though she was a novice, he wasn't wasting energy with silly sideways jogging, though he gave her a few good bucks, but Mel laughed, they were happiness bucks.

At breakfast one morning Mel asked, "Gran, can you come to the track tomorrow? I want to show you how well Wind Power is doing after a week of hacking and teaching him leg aids and listening to my hands."

Iris turned to Ivan. "I'd love to see. Would you take me down?"

"Of course, we'd all like to see, wouldn't you?" Ivan asked Margaret.

"Absolutely." Margaret still marvelled at the transformation of her daughter.

The family gathered at the track at seven a.m. Wind Power had been warmed up and Mel trotted down to the start. His ears flicked back and forth, listening to her voice. This time she wasn't feeling nervous with everyone watching. Even some of the work riders stayed. She felt invigorated. She'd fallen in love with this bold, beautiful horse.

Iris watched with tears streaming down her face. "It's a great shame she can't ride him in the Durban July. This is a winning pair. My goodness Mel's talented. Horses speak to her."

"They do, don't they," Hector agreed as Mel rode over to them.

"How was that, Gran?" Mel asked, keen to know she'd made her grandmother pleased.

"Exemplary." Iris said with a smile. "So good you made me cry watching you two."

Her grandmother's words meant the world to her and boosted her confidence. Training Wind Power she knew was an honour. That evening before dinner, Iris explained to Mel the history of the Durban July. She felt it important she knew the history. It was Iris's favourite race.

"The race has always been run on the first Saturday in July since 1897." Iris paged through a book she had on the history of the famous race. "It began as a one-mile race and changed to 2200metres (10.94 furlongs) in 1970." Iris handed the book to Mel. "If Wind Power wins this year, it'll elevate the status of the stud, the sire, the dam, the trainer, and the jockey."

Mel read bits of the book and got swept up in July fever. It arrived like a pandemic and seized the stud occupants, and the folks in the city of Durban. Everywhere they went the July frenzy hummed for weeks before the race. The line up of horses were hot topic across the nation. The name, Wind Power, was on the tips of tongues and whispered in the racing fraternity was the name Melonie Johns. Anton White, a well-known jockey, and son of Chanting Clover's admin secretary made the odds favourable for a win.

The exciting day arrived. Chanting Clover's horses were trucked to the course early that morning and the family gathered in the Owners and Trainers lounge at 12:45 p.m.

Instead of hobbling along with difficulty, Margaret organised a wheelchair for her mother. Iris Paige, something of a legend in the hallowed halls of racing fame in South Africa, hoped to bag the winner today. Many of her colleagues and friends hoped so too. Sitting in her chair, looking out across the startling emerald coloured turf, she appeared to be lost in thought.

"Mum looks so frail sitting in the wheelchair, doesn't she?" Margaret whispered to Ivan, who glanced Iris's way.

"Yes, she does. Let's hope Wind Power wins. It would cement together her life of breeding and training racehorses."

"He's not the favourite, but we have until four o'clock. It may change."

For many racegoers, the attraction to the Durban July was not only about the horses, but the fashions. A day when models strut the latest couturier designs in dazzling, often outrageous outfits. A place for designers to trigger a new fashion trend. Comparable to Ascot in England, where dressing up is the right thing to do. Except it wasn't on Mel's agenda, nor had she ever seen such outrageous outfits.

"You'd never have seen these outfits at the Borrowdale racecourse in Salisbury," she nudged her mother, staring at a lady hardly dressed in a red sequined outfit, with a dyed ostrich feather ensemble on her head.

"The milliner must have had fun designing her hat. There's more to the hat than the outfit." Margaret commented. A slither of fabric covered her breasts and plunged down the front and the back to the model's waist. A generous cleavage drew considerable attention.

"Scandalous," Iris murmured. "It's no longer about the horses." She shook her head in dismay. "For the last few years, young models have arrived in distasteful outfits like that red one."

"I wouldn't be seen dead in most of the outfits, Gran."

"I certainly hope not, my girl."

Iris was wearing a soft pastel floral suit, matched with an elegant, pale pink brimmed hat, white court shoes, white gloves with a string of pearls around her neck.

"Gran, you look so classy today." Melonie complimented.

"The hat covers my wrinkly, old face." She smiled and held the brim of the hat.

"Well Gran, I think you look terrific."

"Here, here." Margaret agreed. Margaret wore a classic navy-blue skirt suit, while Mel wore a pair of jeans, running shoes and a simple green shirt.

By the time the horses in the feature race came into the paddock at four o'clock, the stud had two winners in separate races and iris was delighted.

A different sort of excitement was mounting now, and the betting had shot Wind Power to second favourite.

"I know he'll win." Mel stated confidently.

"How do you know," Iris asked curiously.

"Cos, he told me, Gran." Mel laughed. "And he likes it firm under foot."

A gentle breeze had blown in off the Indian Ocean and the temperature hovered around 24 degrees centigrade. It was a flawless mid-winter's day in Durban.

Margaret, Ivan, and Iris chatted while Hector and Mel were in the collecting ring watching the horses go round. Margaret put a hand on her mother's arm. "Mum, are you sure you don't want to place a bet, just for fun."

Iris looked at her daughter. "No, my dear, you know I think it's bad luck. This is Melonie's day, and nothing must spoil that."

An infectious energy filled the racecourse grandstands. While Mel stood with Hector she watched as people ran like ants to and from the collecting ring to the bookies and betting booths.

"Good luck Hector, he looks promising." A man slapped Hector on the back.

"Yeah, thanks Basil. He *is* looking good, isn't he?"

"Who's Basil?" Mel leaned in close to Hector when the man was out of earshot.

"The owner of today's favourite, Barbarian. I think he might be worried." Hector whispered. A boyish grin rose on his face.

"Let's hope our darling boy wipes away the Barbarian." Melonie chuckled. "What a horrid name to give a horse. I hope Anton and Wind

Power give it to Gran." She looked at Hector. "I wish I was riding him." She sighed.

"I wish you were too, but Anton's a brilliant jockey. I'm sure they'll make us proud. Come on, let's get back to the others." They hurried back upstairs while the horses galloped down to the start.

Iris had her binoculars up, watching the horses gallop slowly down to the start. "Wind Power went in without a fuss. He's such a lovely boy." Seconds later the gates crashed open, and the commentator began, mentioning Wind Power had jumped clear.

Mel's heart swelled with pride when Anton and Wind Power passed the four hundred metre marker lying in fourth place. She glanced at her grandmother then picked up her binoculars.

Mel couldn't contain her excitement. She jumped up and down. "Go boy, go, go, go." Wind Power was galloping his heart out. "Goooo," Mel yelled again. Wind Power tucked in close to Barbarian and she held her breath, lost in the moment, choked with emotion he crossed the line just ahead of Barbarian. The commentator's voice rose barely audible over the thunderous roar from the crowds in the grandstands.

Wind Power won the Durban July. Melonie hugged her grandmother. "Oh Gran, we did it." Hector gave Mel a hug then they raced down to meet Anton and Wind Power coming in off the track.

Anton, the triumphant champion was standing in the saddle, punching the air, his face showed the joy and pride he felt. Shadrick led the pair toward Hector and Mel. Wind Power, snorting and blowing, caught sight of Mel, and whinnied. The recognition left a stream of tears running down Mel's cheeks as she gripped the left rein and led him into the winner's enclosure. The press loved Mel's open show of emotion. Those standing close noticed the obvious bond between her and the champion athlete and voiced their thoughts and praises.

Caught up in the glory of the moment, neither her, nor Hector noticed the commotion going on not far from the collecting ring. Ivan shouted above the din and waved his arms trying to catch Melonie's attention. She heard the call and looked about her, then noticed her dad beckoning to her.

"Go, I'll deal with the rest." Hector said. Mel darted under the railing. There seemed an urgency to her dad's beckoning hand. As she straightened up, she caught site of a medical officer standing near her dad. Frowning, she wondered what was going on.

"You have gone into the history books, Melonie Johns. How does that feel?" Someone asked. She didn't answer as she pushed through the crowds.

"What's happened?" She asked as her dad caught her arm and led her toward the private entrance to the Owners and Trainers lounge. Without the interference of the swarming crowds, he said, "Gran has slipped away. She had a heart attack minutes after you left."

Melonie stifled a cry. Too shocked to speak she stood gazing at her dad.

"Mum is travelling in the ambulance with Gran. We'll meet her at the hospital." Mel tucked her arm through her dad's. Happiness tears from moments ago were replaced with sad ones.

"At......at least," she sobbed. "Gran saw her amazing horse give everything and win for her." Sadness and euphoria had to find common ground somehow.

"He certainly did. Incredible horse. Granny would not have wanted for a quicker, happier way to go."

Just then a reporter spotted them coming out of the private entrance again and shouted.

"It's been said the miracle rider from Rhodesia turned the horse into a champion athlete. Is it true?" In that moment, the reporter had no idea what the commotion near the ambulance was all about.

"Leave us please, there's been a tragedy in the family." Ivan said, jostling through the crowd with Mel holding onto him as they headed to the car park.

Sounding its siren intermittently for the benefit of the swarming crowds, the ambulance pulled away.

It wasn't long before the news leaked. The commentator requested a minute's silence out of respect for one of South Africa's racing darlings just as Mel and Ivan walked out the main gates.

"Gran will be remembered for being a true champion of the sport, a lady, and one with an admirable eye for a good horse. I hope I can continue her legacy." Mel said thoughtfully.

"Her last moments would've been fulfilling. An ascent to the heavens filled with joy. No better way to leave the planet." Ivan pulled the car keys from his pocket.

Hector followed, struggling to hide his emotions. He'd lost the love of his life. It was a bittersweet win for him. He got to the car, pulled open the passenger door and he spoke. "It's exactly how she would've wanted to go. No fuss, no illness, and a wide brimmed hat to cover her face, departing this life with dignity and her dream fulfilled."

Pictures of Mel and Wind Power covered the front pages of Sunday newspapers across the nation. On the front page of the Natal Mercury, was a picture of Melonie kissing Wind Powers nose. The caption read, *Mel's Midas Touch*.

There were numerous mentions of Iris Paige and her gift to her granddaughter.

Chapter Fifteen

1980

MARKED the end to white dominated rule in Rhodesia. An interim government had been put in place. Ivan watched on TV. A grimace on his face.

"Poor old Smithie, I bet he never thought he'd live to see the day." Ivan referred to the much loved and admired, outgoing prime minister, Ian Smith.

"At least the war is over, darling." Margaret offered her thoughts.

Mel stood. "Now everyone can live peacefully in Zimbabwe, and we can go on living safely here. The last thing that the horrid Solomon said to me, 'When the war is over, Blue Winds will be mine.' I was so incensed, I spat at him. Angered, he slapped me, knocking me off my feet." Tears glistened but never fell. It was the first time she'd referred to Solomon since her remarkable rescue. The main reason for her wanting to leave the room was to escape Ivan's inevitable political tirade, instead he uttered.

"Sorry my angel. I'll switch the tellie off."

Melonie curled up in her armchair again. "Thank you, Dad."

But Ivan still simmered. The anger and sadness within couldn't be switched off like the television. "If Solomon survived the fire and the Hunter raid, he won't get our farm. Besides he wouldn't have a clue how to run it, if he did. Solomon was caught by empty promises. A semi-educated rebel *mujiba,* turned gook." Ivan's face twisted with bitterness. His voice tinged with loathing. "Twenty years of hard work, lost." It was hard to forget.

"That's enough. Let's live for our future with gratitude. If we hadn't left, we'd be dead. Let's treasure the memories of all the good times and move on." Margaret's voice sounded stern.

"You're right Mum. I'm going to the stables. Sorry Dad, but I can't listen. By the way, did Gary Whitaker accept the job offer?"

"He certainly did. He starts next month."

"Oh great. Hector and I badly need help. I think Hector will hang up his boots and feed his wisdom to us from the side-line when Gary starts." Mel turned and left.

"I'm sorry my love. The scars are still raw. I'll bite my tongue next time."

"Good idea. Mel's blossoming. Let's leave Zimbabwe out of our conversations when she's around. It sets her back. Besides, we can't go on hankering over the past either." Margaret's beautiful face showed the sympathy she felt for her beloved husband. "We have a great future here. We couldn't have wished for better, especially for Mel. While you and I are still asleep, she's down at the track galloping a young Thoroughbred over the turf."

***

The sky was just embracing the light of early dawn. Shafts of coloured light fanned the horizon. Mel's favourite time of the day. Two years had passed since she'd sat in his stable with his head on her lap. Now he was being introduced to his early training as a racehorse.

Tropical Sun had grown into a magnificent young colt. Mel spent hours guiding him, teaching him. This morning was her second ride on him at the track.

Mel waited at the start. Tropical Sun pranced eagerly. Calmly stroking his neck, she soothed the excitement. He stood, snorting. She released the rein slightly and trotted down the track to the two hundred metre marker before asking for a slow canter, gently reminding him of his manners. He acknowledged her skill. Mel inwardly rejoiced. He felt better than Wind Power. A poignant reminder of how her life had changed. From terror and war to a super-charged life of everything that was good and safe.

Galloping slowly up the track toward the trees she noticed the moon fading behind ribbons of pink cirrus clouds. The sun shone through the droplets of moisture that fell from Sunny's snorting, dilated nostrils lighting them in clusters, like a sparkly powder puff each time he exhaled.

A hundred metres after the last marker Mel pulled him gently to a walk. A cold wind had whipped at her face pulling streams of salty water from her eyes. Her heart was pumping, oxygen had fed her mind, bringing crystal clarity to her thoughts.

She leant down, dropped her arms around Tropical Sun's neck, and hugged him. "Riding you is the closest I can get to experiencing heaven." Mel whispered and he snorted, as if having her riding him couldn't get better. Mel walked back to the stables beneath the cool canopy of London Plane trees that lined either side of the road.

Happy Thomas was waiting at the gate for her. She slid off and stretched her back, then flipped the reins over the horse's head. Thomas caught them.

"Nice catch, Thomas. Hey! This boy's our next champion."

"Yes Ma'am." Thomas agreed and led the colt to his stable. There he unsaddled him quickly, popped the saddle over the door and ran down the line of stables to collect White Jewel. A small mare by comparison, but Mel had high hopes for her. Granny's crowning glory, she thought. The foal she'd watched being born. It seemed surreal, riding her now when she'd only just turned two.

Thomas legged her up onto White Jewel. Floating down from nowhere, a white feather landed on the pommel. "Granny," she whispered, and goosebumps covered her body. It felt like she was there with Mel. Could the feather be the sign, she wondered. The whimsical sensations were still with her when she finished a slow canter with White

Jewel and walked her back to the stables. Thomas stood at the gate, smiling happily as usual.

"Did she go slowly, Missus Mel?" He asked with a cheeky grin.

Mel was shaking her head. "You won't believe it, Thomas, she did. The best ride since she was backed." Mel imagined it was gran's influence.

Mel ran back to the house, famished. She dumped her gloves and hat on the walnut table in the hall.

"Oh, what horses," she sang. The tantalising smell of toast and bacon wafted up her nose. A rush of saliva tingled in her cheeks.

"Oops," she said, standing at the door to the dining room. Gary Whitaker at opposite her father. Both men stood up.

"Morning. I'm not interrupting anything, am I?" She asked.

"Good Lord, no. Which horses were you singing about when you chucked your stuff on the hall table?" Ivan was curious to know.

"White Jewel and Tropical Sun. Oh my God, what amazing horses. To think I watched White Jewel being born and I named her." Mel dished up her breakfast and sat opposite Gary. "Have you ridden White Jewel?"

"I haven't actually, but I hear she's a classy sprinter."

"Yes, she is. I managed to get a lovely slow canter from her this morning," Mel took a mouthful of scrambled egg. "I'm ravenous."

It wasn't long before she realised the two men were watching her. She put her knife and fork down. "I think Tropical Sun is another Wind Power, but White Jewel has tremendous potential too. Totally different rides. Totally different characters." She loaded her fork with a more lady-like portion. "Granny knew how to breed them, didn't she?"

"She certainly did." Ivan looked at Gary. "It's like this most mornings. I suppose you know work riding makes a person hungry."

"That I do, and I'm looking forward to riding them."

Melonie looked up. "You don't have to watch me." She laughed. "I'm not normally this rude but I got up earlier than normal and took Wind Power for a spin first. I've ridden three horses this morning."

Gary whistled. It wasn't normal for him to be having breakfast in the main house, but Ivan had bumped into him at the broodmare barn and invited him along. "That's some riding. No wonder you're starving.

It's been a long time since I've ridden three horses, one after the other. You must be fit."

Melonie shook her head from side to side. She hadn't taken much notice of Gary over the few months he'd been at the stud. He'd been with Hector learning the system at Chanting Clover. Sitting across from her he watched while she spread peanut butter on her toast.

"So, what are your plans for Tropical Sun?" Gary asked.

"Early days yet. His first race is at Clairwood in six weeks. Ride him tomorrow morning, see what you think. I've been taking him very slowly. I've only stretched him out a couple of times."

"I'd like that."

"I'll take Lady in Red. She's super-hot. Typical chestnut mare." She pushed her chair back. "I've arranged to meet Hector at 10 o'clock at the office." She grabbed her diary and glanced at her watch.

"I think you know I've been mainly with the yearlings and lunging work with Hector. I'm looking forward to the ready-to-runs, but I'm enjoying learning the routine with Hector, He's a walking encyclopaedia."

"That he is." Mel said. They walked together to the main stable block. She had a few moments to spare before the meeting. Wind Power stretched his neck toward her. She gave him his mandatory kiss on the nose and slid a Polo mint into his mouth. Beyond, the elegant White Jewel looked over her stable door. Tropical Sun was in the next stable. They all nickered expectantly.

"This is quite some horse," Gary commented on Wind Power. The horse nuzzled at her pockets for more.

Melonie giggled. "You've already had one." She glanced at Gary. "He's an absolute gent and the most fabulous ride. Have you ridden him yet?" Mel rubbed his muzzle gently between her hands and couldn't resist giving him another kiss.

"No, I haven't. I think Hector has my program nicely planned, but a ride tomorrow would be great."

Mel hadn't had much to do with Gary since his arrival. She was enjoying his company now. Perhaps she'd been too hasty in feeling threatened by him, especially as she scarcely knew him. "I think we'd better get to Hector's office, or we'll be late."

"Yes, of course. It's easy to forget the time when playing with horses like these. You and Wind Power are written into the history books. That's admirable." Gary looked forward to working with Mel.

"Your mother tells me you have very specific ways with horses and won't tolerate anyone who has other ideas."

"Oh Lordy. Did she say that?" Melonie screwed her eyes up against the sun's warm rays and started laughing.

"She said it was *you* who put the work into Wind Power and the reason he won. The praise is well deserved. I'd love to train one of these horses to win the Durban July."

Melonie allowed herself to feel a little modest satisfaction, though she felt the compliment wasn't for her to revel in.

"Follow what Hector teaches, and you will. The only thing I will not tolerate is cruelty and pushing young horses too fast. If you can keep that in mind, we'll get along fine."

"I wholeheartedly agree." Gary liked that sentiment.

A slight smile wrinkled the corners of her mouth. "Hector has taught me so much in the last two years. I don't know what we'd do without him. He told me you remind of him when he was young."

"He did? I'm glad. We met in Johannesburg at Gosforth Park. I remember him tapping me on the shoulder saying, 'You gotta good eye, son.' Over the past four years I've spent hours on the phone picking his brain. He always tried to persuade me to join Chanting Clover and I'm very happy to be here now."

"I can't tell you how many nights he and I have sat on the veranda at his cottage, studying pedigrees, analysing recent performances, weaknesses, and strengths of each horse in training. What races they should be in and over what distances. Tweaking training sessions, and so on. Poor Hector, he's been so patient with me, no wonder he's ready to retire." Mel giggled.

"He's not ready to retire, trust me. Slow down a bit, perhaps. To Hector, this is not a job, it's his life and it's great to have him teach me. If you are anything like the reputation your late grandmother left on the racing world, I guess he's very ready for my help." Gary teased, thinking how beautiful her emerald eyes were.

Mel knocked on the side of the open office door and walked in.

Hector looked up. "Ah, come in, come in." Hector said cheerfully. "I'm glad you are with Mel, Gary. Sit." He motioned.

Since Gary had been taking up so much of Hectors time, Mel hadn't seen much of him recently, but she noticed how exhausted he looked.

"Mel, if it is okay with you, I'm going to hand Gary over to you and disappear into the bush for a week off."

"Go when you want, Hector. You're looking tired."

"Now it's your turn, Mel. Gary never stops asking questions." Hector laughed.

Chapter Sixteen

1982

TIME STOPS FOR NO-ONE, Mel was reminded. She sat quietly in her office preparing the list for the National 2-Year-Old sales. Something she hated doing. Gran's words often hammered in her head about attachment. Sitting here she felt the loneliness of her career this morning since her carefree teenage years had been wrenched away from her. She'd lost her innocence in the cruellest of ways and though her life with horses fulfilled her, a terrible emptiness thrived, and she grew lonelier by the day.

It seemed impossible that four years had passed. Time for socialising had been limited, even though her parents kept reminding her to go out.

They'd radically reduced the numbers of sheep. This made way for extra grazing for her growing herd of horses. Gary took in more outside horses to train, plus she'd increased the number of visiting broodmares for coverings. There wasn't much time for socialising, and she had a friend in Gary.

The sales were scheduled for 19th of August. Running her finger down the list of two-year-olds Gary had given her, she noticed Popthequestion's name on the list.

She jumped up and went to see if Gary was in his office. He was.

"Hey! Popthequestion is not going to the sales. She's a magic little horse. Have you ridden her yet?" Mel leant against his office door.

He looked up and shook his head.

"How about riding her tomorrow morning?" Mel suggested with a grin.

"Great idea. Seven-thirty?"

GARY MET Mel at the track. The ground was covered in a fine frost, and it was icy. He noticed she'd already done the warm-up with Tropical Sun. He was ready. Gary trotted the filly toward her.

"Morning. I'm looking forward to this. You take the lead." Mel urged Tropical Sun into a trot and took the lead. Gary galloped behind her, enjoying the first three hundred metre gallop watching Mel's sexy figure in tight jodhpurs. He lost focus and suddenly the filly took hold, catching him by surprise and he bolted past Tropical Sun. Eventually Gary brought the hot-headed filly back under control and slowed her to a trot then turned around and walked back to the warm-up ring where Mel stood. He slid off her back and doubled over, trying to get his breath back. "Fu...ck. She's... a great filly. Caught me by surprise. Shit, she's strong." He stood, stretched, and noticed a smile on Mel's lips. She was wearing a different expression today, but he didn't dare raise his hopes that she might notice him differently too.

Gary tossed the reins over the filly's neck and bounced back into the saddle. Gary was a big man, but he rode as if he weighed not much more than a jockey. He carried his weight perfectly balanced.

"So, what do you think of her?" Mel waited for an answer.

"She's worth keeping. I agree." He was still trying to regulate his breathing and the filly still had the energy to trot in circles before walking back to the stables.

Later that morning Mel walked into Gary's office and pulled out the chair opposite him.

"So now Popthequestion is staying, who have you put on her for her first official race?"

"No-one yet. I was hoping you'd decide."

"What about Anton. I think she's too much for an apprentice."

"Good idea. Now you are here, there's something else I need to discuss. An associate of mine in Johannesburg called me. He made a ludicrous offer for Kandahar. Are you open to selling him?"

Melonie screwed up her face. "Yeah, maybe. What's the ludicrous offer?"

Gary noticed a cheeky glint in her captivating green eyes. He knew nothing of the horrors of Melonie's past, all he knew was she was stunning, and she'd always intrigued him. Warm and playful like her Labrador's one minute, then as spunky as the Jack Russell's, but in a blink of an eye, she could be as aloof as a Siamese cat.

He shook his head. "He's offered one hundred and eighty thousand Rand for Kandahar."

"What? Sell him!"

It wasn't the answer he'd expected. He smiled. Gary knew when he smiled the dimples on his cheeks were accentuated. Other ladies had told him he was sexy and very good looking. He wondered at her expression now. Did she find him that way? He hoped so.

Mel stood taller and took on a professional aura once again. "How well do you know Andrew Williams?"

"Not that well. Why do you ask?" Gary had just been given a glimpse of the business-side to his gorgeous boss.

"Will he definitely pay that? Because with that money I can add four more stables onto the brood mare barn and eight onto the ready-to-run barn. Please don't let the sale slip. I've got to meet Dad in the weanling paddocks." Gary watched her jump in her truck and drive off.

Mel ran over to where her father stood. "Dad, you won't believe the offer Gary's just had for Kandahar. One hundred and eighty thousand Rand. Can you believe it?"

Ivan whistled. "That's incredible. Are you going to sell him?"

"Definitely. Where's Mum?"

"In her office. You'll be interested to know she wants to sell most of the sheep now. We're not cut out for showing them like your grandmother did. Plus, with your talk of expansion you're going to need even more grazing. Cutting back on the sheep will give you an extra sixty hectares and I can sort out the weanling paddock. Sow some nice red clover in the pastures too." He put his arms around Mel. "You realise you'll have to employ me as your farm manager?" Ivan joked.

"Dad, you can work for me anytime. This is so exciting. We'll save a fortune on winter hay." Mel gazed over the pastures and into the distance, thinking Chanting Clover equalled Blue Winds.

"Before you dash off, a Zimbabwean fella arrived at my office this morning looking for work as a groom. Do you need more staff?"

"A Zimbo? Down here looking for work?" Puzzled, she glanced at Patric.

"Yeah. Seemed nice enough. Rattled off the names of the yards he'd worked at in Zim. Said he'd been dismissed from his last job because the owners sold and moved to Australia."

"Where is he now?" Mel's brow creased.

"I told him to hang around at the farm office until I'd finished lunch."

"Um, okay. Send him across to my office, Dad. Gary and I are meeting at two. Gary can *sus* him out." Melonie felt strangely uncomfortable, and she felt Patric's eyes on her.

"Are you alright?" Ivan noted the change in her.

"Yes Dad, I'm fine. A bit touchy about a Zimbo suddenly appearing from nowhere wanting work. The only Zimbo I want here is Patric."

Ivan raised his eyebrows. Patric smiled.

Ivan didn't comment but her reaction indicated she'd not fully dealt with the horrors of her past. Her ordeal was not a topic they'd raised much since moving to Chanting Clover. As a parent he wondered whether that was a good thing or a bad thing?

"Probably best left to Gary, then." He suggested. This was not the moment to have a heart-to-heart chat about the past, but the arrival of this man had clearly unnerved her. She left deep in thought. In the past, Mel's intuition had proved worth listening to.

When Mel arrived at Gary's office her mood was prickly. Gary nonchalantly suggested White Jewel would also be worth a fortune.

"Firstly, White Jewel is going nowhere." She snapped uncharacteristically. "And secondly, I hear you employed that Zimbabwean?"

Gary frowned. He didn't know what to say.

"Put Owen on White Jewel tomorrow morning. I want to see how they get on." She spun around and left. Gary employing a Zimbabwean had made her ill at ease. She didn't like that feeling.

MEL HAD HARDLY SLEPT. She'd woken around four o'clock, dripping with sweat. The impenetrable darkness in her room unnerved her as much as her nightmare. She'd switched on the bedside light and grabbed her diary. If Kandahar sold for the price the William's man had offered, all her expansion plans could go ahead. She'd sat up in bed and worked out how many years it would take before they'd turn a profit. If her calculations were correct and it went to plan, she'd start to see profit from the expansion in twenty months. That pleased her and eased the discomfort of her nightmare.

She'd got dressed at five. The farm would come alive in an hour. She loved watching the early morning mist shroud the fields and tracks like a bride's veil. She also treasured the quiet time alone to think. As the sun rose, clearing the tracks, the skies turned a milky washed pink. The colours of yellow and orange clashed as the spring dawn arrived. Then she heard the gentle call of the Laughing Dove and felt instantly soothed by its call. The sounds were soon obliterated by the screech of the Hadeda Ibis. Their calls woke everyone, including the roosters, and rose above intermittent dog barking as the Labradors chased them off the dew-covered lawns.

Sitting on the edge of the track she could hear the distant laughter and chatter of children fighting off the cold morning chill as they left for school. The sound reminded her of Blue Winds. Her gut knotted again. But these children had no fears like those at Blue Winds. These children played and cavorted, sang, whistled, shouted and giggled as they breathed out fumes of steam from their mouths. They were such happy sounds.

"Morning Ma'am," Owen greeted her. Mel jumped. She hadn't expected anyone to join her so early.

"Morning Owen. Morning Enos. I've been listening to the school children running down the road. Their sounds make me happy. She stood up and stretched and noticed Gary and Hector walking toward them.

"Owen you're going to love White Jewel." She patted the mare on her rump, covered by a red, white, and yellow quarter sheet.

Hector and Gary joined her.

"I see you have Enos on Tropical Sun." Gary commented after greeting her.

"Yes. I thought that as Owen has never ridden her, she might behave better with her stable mate next to her. She's pretty hot, as you know." Grateful Mel seemed more cheerful this morning. Gary had spoken to Hector about Mel's reaction to the employment of a Zimbabwean groom. Hector had briefly explained Mel's past which had shattered Gary.

"This lovely mare has always been special." Hector had noticed how well Owen rode her in the warm-up. Soon they were on their way down to the start. Lifting her binoculars, Mel watched Owen carefully. She'd made the right decision. The clicked.

"What do you think?" She turned to Gary as Owen pulled her up at the end of the 1600 metre turf track.

"Brilliant." He started clapping as Owen rode toward them. White Jewel blew misty snorts into the air.

"Well done, Owen. Beautifully ridden. You handled her like a master. I guess you know who you're riding in Pietermaritzburg soon." Mel cheered as he brought the mare to a halt close to her.

"Really." Owen shrieked. "Thank you, Mel. Thank you."

Gary turned to Mel. "How about a cup of coffee in my cosy warm office?" Mel agreed. She hadn't noticed Hector smile at Gary. The three of them climbed in Gary's Landcruiser and chatted happily about Owen's ride.

Gary dropped Hector near his cottage then drove to the admin offices. Gary sat and offered Mel a comfortable chair and switched on the kettle. Before Gary had a chance to talk, Mel spoke. "I want to apologise for snapping at you. I don't think you know I'd once said we're not to employ Zimbabweans."

"Hector explained that to me yesterday. I'm sorry. I had no idea. How do you like your coffee?"

"White, no sugar, thanks. Gary, I want to discuss the coverings. Can we ensure, without compromising their health of our stallions that we get through the season quickly. The ready-to-runs born later than the 15th of October are handicapped by the very nature of being nearly three months younger than those born in August."

"You're right. It is amazing what a difference three months makes to a young Thoroughbred." Gary handed her the coffee. "I understand the need for the Thoroughbred Stud Book in Newmarket, England, to control it all, and the system enables standardisation of races by age group, but it can have negative impacts, can't it? It's quite artificial in many ways."

"Yes, it is, but I guess having an official birthday helps planning. In our case it may mean looking to purchase another stallion. By the way I've budgeted for infra-red lights to be installed in each of the stallion's stables. I'm going to leave that to ensure they are installed properly. I promised to spend more time with my mum. You know she's just recovered from a vile bout of flu. I'm surprised I didn't get it. With everything going on I haven't spent enough time with her. We chatted about going to a movie, either this afternoon or tomorrow."

"Great idea. What are you going to watch?"

"A chick flick. An Officer and a Gentleman, I think."

When Mel arrived at the house for lunch, Ivan said was taking her mum out for some fresh air on the farm. He also wanted to show her the new horse paddocks.

"Movies tomorrow then, Mum?"

"Yes. I'm looking forward to that but being on the farm will also do me good." Margaret heard Ivan call. "Are you ready, sweetheart?"

"On my way." She answered and blew Mel a kiss. Mel watched her leave. Happy she was going out with dad. She'd noticed how she was and how much weight she'd lost. She watched them jump in the truck, then they were gone.

It pleased Mel that dad was proud of his design for the new paddock layout. Yearlings could be brainless at times, she laughed to herself, and he'd designed the paddocks for them which such thought. She grabbed a racing journal and plonked down on the sofa on the veranda.

. . .

WINDS OF CHANGE

Driving along, Margaret watched the passing scenery, happy to be out the house. "Mel's awfully excited about what you're doing. And thank you for dragging me out. I needed this. I'll go with Mel to the movies tomorrow."

"Great idea. Mel works too hard, and she never gets out. Even I've not seen much of her while you've been sick. Can you believe that we've been here almost five years? Time has flown by. In November, it'll be five years. I've also noticed just recently that Mel seems to be struggling with the past a bit. I think Gary employing a Zimbabwean groom set it off."

"Oh dear, poor Mel. She and I never speak about it anymore and she's never really divulged what happened to her in any detail. I might ask her when we're out tomorrow."

"I worry about her. She's grown up too fast. She's made very few friends and certainly doesn't accept any offers to go out with young men, yet she's constantly asked. Even Gary has asked her."

"I know. She told me she's too frightened to be alone with a man. So, you must know just from that what she went through when she was abducted."

Ivan's face contorted. Was it sadness or was it anger? Margaret could make out what the expression meant. "Sad, isn't it? She and Gary would make a perfect pair."

Margaret studied Ivan's face. "Yes, they would. I think we should encourage it."

"She may stay single for the rest of her life." Ivan said sadly. "After I've shown you the new horse paddocks, let's take a walk through our remaining ewes."

"What a good idea. I need a good walk. I've had horrid dizzy spells with this blasted flu. A couple of times I thought I was going to fall over."

Even after all this time, Margaret had also found the transition to her knew life, hard. She'd made some new friends here, but none she communicated with on the same level as those she had years of history with.

They drove on passing a narrow stream that ran through one of the paddocks. "Even though we've had rain, the paddocks still look thirsty.

Let's hope we have a good wet season this year." The fields appeared to be suffering the same suffocated sense of anticipation that Margaret felt now. She needed friendship and the pastures needed nourishing rain. Beyond where they drove stretched undulating pastures, soon to turn the colour of Melonie's eyes, she thought.

"Mel is delighted at having the extra grazing." Ivan pulled up near of group of ewes that were huddled together.

"Wow, they're looking superb and it's only a month since I last saw them. Their bellies swelling nicely. Hopefully they'll all have twins again." She gazed out the open window, taking in snatches of fresh air.

"How many have we kept? I can't remember."

"Thirty." Ivan switched off the engine. "Shall we take a walk?"

They wandered among the pregnant ewes, but it wasn't long before Margaret felt breathless and tight chested. They walked back to the truck.

"How many hectares of grazing has Melonie left us with?" A small enquiring smile rippled across her lips, distorting them weirdly.

"Enough," Ivan said. "Twenty hectares of radishes will take us through to the end of October, by then the spring flush will fill the fields with lush grass." He said, resting his folded arms across the top of the steering wheel, gazing at the ewes. "Melonie has put me to work developing better pastures for the broodmares and the weanlings." He turned to Margaret.

"Good God, are you alright?" Margaret was deathly pale and struggling to breathe. She couldn't answer. Her lips were moving but there was no sound. Ivan quickly stopped the vehicle, but Margaret lunged forward, banging her head on the dashboard, and slumped back again, holding her right arm across her chest.

"Margaret, Margaret, hold on," he urged as he jumped out the truck. She was having a heart attack. He laid her across the seat and quickly administered CPR, but he was too late. She'd gone, as quickly as her mother had.

He tried CPR again, but Margaret was not responding. He checked for a pulse, there was none. Shock and disbelief consumed him, but not believing it was possible, he kept checking for signs of life. He laid his head on her chest hoping to hear a faint heartbeat. That too had gone.

Finally, as reality set in, realising his precious, beloved wife was dead a profound grief gripped him. He cried like a child. Blinded by tears and sorrow he eventually lifted his body off hers, tucked her limp legs into the space beneath the dashboard and slid himself back into the driver's seat, then lifted her head onto his lap so it wouldn't loll about. He closed her eyes and rested his forehead against the steering wheel, sobbing in the privacy of the cab. Helpless from despair.

Surely, he could have done more. He grappled with the suddenness and finality of Margaret's passing. How long he'd been crying, he wasn't sure. His heart felt like it had been ripped open revealing a complex mix of emotions. Tears gradually subsided and he stared blankly ahead, dumbfounded, unseeing, wondering how he was going to navigate telling Melonie and the immediate aftermath of her death? He looked down at her lifeless face and stroked her hair and once again gave way to torrential weeping, dousing the steering wheel and his jeans in tears that fell. Spent from misery, he wiped his face and took in some deep breaths. Eventually he drove slowly to Hector's cottage and shared the tragic news.

Hector stood at the car, shattered. He'd agreed to go with Ivan to take Margaret's body the hospital mortuary.

Three hours later they arrived back at the house.

"Mel." Ivan called out, his voice weak and wavering.

"In the sitting room, Dad." Came her cheerful response. When she saw his face, she knew in an instant something terrible must have happened.

"Where's Mum?"

"She had a heart attack, Mel. I couldn't save her." He cried, wrapping Mel in his arms while grief-stricken sobs erupted from them both.

For days after Margaret's untimely passing, Mel still sobbed off and on. She and Ivan never left the house for the first two days. Hector and Gary checked in and took over running the farm and stud in their absence while Angelina continued to run the house and cook their food.

They had a small funeral for Margaret in the village. In her Will she'd requested a cremation and her ashes to be laid beside her parents in the gardens at Chanting Clover. A few days after the funeral, the minister joined Ivan and Mel, a few close friends, and senior staff at the graveside. The minister read a touching verse in her memory and the small pottery vessel containing Margaret's ashes were placed in the ground. A tearful Patric covered it with soil. A sob caught in Mel's throat and Gary took the liberty of comforting her and put his arm across her shoulders, while she held her father's hand.

'I have only slipped away into the next room, I am I, and you are you.... whatever we were to each other, that we still are......' The minister read.

Melonie held a tissue to her mouth. Those who'd gathered were also crying. *'I am but waiting for you, for an interval, somewhere very near, just around the corner. All is well.'*

Heartbroken, Mel felt a part of her no longer existed. She turned to her dad. "Daddy, I'd like to go home to the farm and place a cross in Mum's honour somewhere on the river. There I can lay my past to rest too, or I'll never truly be at peace. Let's go together."

Her face was red, and her eyes were puffy. She felt like a little girl, insecure and terrified of a future without her mother in it. It was in moments like these, she always called her father, *Daddy*.

"I couldn't bear to go back, sweetheart, and you can't go alone. It's not safe." He took a clean handkerchief from his trouser pocket and wiped his face.

"I'll fly to Harare, Dad. Julie and Allan will come with me to the farm."

Their conversation ended as Patric tidied the edges of the small grave. Margaret, Iris, and Fergus lay side by side. Over the next three days Ivan busied himself planting a rose garden in their memory.

Roses had been Margaret's favourite flower.

Chapter Seventeen

May 1983

It took six months before Mel summoned the courage to book a flight to Zimbabwe and in that time, she and Gary had become much closer.

"Are you sure you should be doing this trip alone?" Gary questioned her decision. His mind was filled with what Hector had shared with him. He'd fallen in love with Mel and desperately wanted to protect her. Everyone knew his feelings for her, and he was sure she knew too. They were closer now than ever before. He secretly hoped this year would mark the beginning of a forever romance.

"Things are not great up there, I'm told."

"I'll be fine, Gary." Mel looked at him and saw a different expression on his face and realised how much he cared about her safety.

"It'll be hard, I know but this is a good opportunity to put the ghosts of the past to bed, then I can move on with my life. I'm fine during the day, but since mum died, I often wake at night, always around one o'clock in the morning. That horrid time of night, the hour when fear overwhelms any thought of hope and I lie rigid in my bed, sweating off the exertion of a nightmare. I can't go on like this. I need a proper life. For the last five years all I've done is hide behind my horses. I'm not facing reality. I really must do this."

Gary bowed his head. It was the first time she'd spoken this way with him. He couldn't bear to look at the sadness etched in her face and prayed this trip would help her, not hinder her. He knew there was more to her past than Hector had revealed. Though he didn't want to pry he thought it might help if she talked about it before going back to where it happened, so he asked.

"What happened to you, Mel?" Gary made sure his tone was kind and gentle and matched what he felt for her.

"It's a long and sordid story. I can't talk about it."

"We've got time. Besides, it may help ease the horrors if you talk about it before you go."

"You're so thoughtful. After losing mum, I'm finding everything challenging. I feel like a shattered ornament and there's no glue in the world that can cement me back together. Besides, I've no idea how to start, or even where to start."

Moments of silence followed, then Gary took her hand for the first time and prompted her to continue. Slowly words pieced together and soon they tumbled from her mouth like a waterfall rushing over the cliff after years of drought. An hour and a half later, having sipped on three cups of tea Gary had made her, she said she felt some relief, but deliberately skirted over the real horrors, and it was those that gave her the nightmares and prevented her entering a relationship.

"I'm so sad by what happened to you, but I admire your bravery in telling me." He still held her hand. She'd courageously shed some of the layers and exposed her vulnerable, gentle side to him and he had to stop himself from taking her in his arms. He instinctively knew she wasn't ready. Then suddenly she blurted.

"When I was abducted, my life changed. My teenage years were destroyed by cruelty, greed, brutality, and the war. I grew up very quickly, survival taught me how."

She fell silent again. Gary gave her the space she needed. The soft glow of a winter's evening made them realise how long they'd been chatting. They left Gary's office and wandered down to Gary's cottage. He lit the newspaper bundled between the logs in the fireplace and soon the growing flames had Mel mesmerised, as if they soothed her battered soul.

"You're an incredibly brave woman. It must've been extremely difficult telling me. I'm in awe of your inner strength." In that moment, all the feelings he had for her came together, confirming he wanted this woman as his wife.

"How did you escape the camp? You skirted over those details?" The change in her demeanour made him regret asking. She was on the verge of tears. He saw her body spasm and her jaw clench. Gary held her hand and eventually she relaxed, took a deep breath, and shifted around in the armchair.

"My actions killed more than just the commander. People caught by the fire would've died in the most horrendous way. I'm glad I never saw that, but it preys on my mind." She squeezed her eyes tightly closed. A lonely tear escaped. She felt the pressure increase on her hand lovingly. Then she let go of his hand, covered her face, and sobbed. This time Gary did wrap her in his arms and held her while she wept. Eventually, she pulled back, reached into her pocket, pulled out a tissue and blew her nose.

"I ran and ran and ran with no idea where I was going, or even what direction I was running in, and at the time I had no idea a rescue mission was on its way, until I ran into them. I don't think I'll ever find the words to accurately describe what I felt that night. A desperate race again time, and behind me, nature's fury as the fire spread. Fear was immense. I was convinced I would die in the Mozambique bush."

He reached over and kissed her forehead tenderly for the first time. Mel smiled. "Thank you for being so comforting. Only two men who have kissed me in the last five years. My dad, and Hector." She pushed her head affectionately against Gary's chest. "The commander raped me. I'm no longer a real woman. He took that from me."

Gary was silent for a moment, anger swirled inside his gut like molten lava. "I cannot begin to imagine what how horrific that must've been. I don't blame you for killing the bastard." Gary took a deep breath and played with her hair. Now he understood why she hadn't wanted a relationship with anyone. Why she spoke into his chest, unable to look at him while she regurgitated the memory.

The sun had sunk behind the hills and the last, soft, dusty pink rays of the setting sun came through the window, reflecting on her cheeks when she lifted her head.

"I must go. Thank you for listening."

"I'll walk you home."

IVAN WAS WAITING, worried about her pending trip. "Mel is that you?" He called from the sitting room when he heard the front door open.

"Yes, Dad. Were you waiting up for me?" She turned to close the front door and heard his footsteps behind her.

"Sweetheart, you've been crying." She turned and fell into her father's protective arms." I told Gary what happened to me. All of it."

Ivan pulled her closer to him. "I'm glad you've shared it with Gary. He loves you, you know. And, like me, he's worried about you doing the trip alone. He's a nice man, you two should be a couple." She cried again and couldn't stop crying and they walked back to the sitting room and he asked for her planned itinerary.

"Dad, Gary has offered to take me to the airport, and I accepted. I hope you don't mind."

"Not at all. I could not go back to Blue Winds. You're braver than me. I'm not even sure I want to go back to Zimbabwe. There are too many memories of mum there. I think about her all day, every day. Sometimes I can hardly concentrate."

"Oh Dad," she hugged him tight. "I miss her terribly too. It's the other torments I need to put to bed. I feel the only way I can do it, is to go back to the source."

"Well done, sweetheart. You're very courageous."

"I must go and pack, then get some sleep. I'm exhausted from all the emotion I've spilled tonight."

Chapter Eighteen

Gary opened the front door and shook Ivan's hand. "Morning Ivan, I hope you don't mind me taking Mel to the airport."

"Absolutely not. I think it's wonderful. Thank you for being such a comfort to Mel last night."

"It's my pleasure." Listening to her was extremely difficult. Not only for her to share, but just as difficult to hear. She's a brave young lady."

"She certainly is." Ivan took a few steps from the walnut table holding one of Mel's hats that she'd dropped there. He hung it on the hat stand and just then she joined the two men in the hall carrying her suitcase and handbag.

"Hi Gary. Morning Dad. Dad, I'll let you know when I get to Harare." She kissed and hugged him, eager to set off.

Mel's flight from Durban took four hours. Harare airport hadn't changed much, she thought, dragged her case outside and breathed in the dry air. I'm home, she let out a sigh. Glancing around she waved for a taxi. A *Rixi* taxi, she chuckled, feeling nostalgic. She'd forgotten about the little Renault Four taxis and laughed when a bright blue one pulled up.

The driver jumped out. "Hello, Ma'am. Where to?"

"Monomatapa Hotel, please."

He loaded her bag and off they went in the rattly little car, with the clumsy column shift that had probably done the trip from the airport to the city centre thousands of times but kept going. A rather nauseating smell of tobacco lingered within.

On the journey she realised how much she missed *home*, especially as little had changed except more rubbish littered the sidewalks, and gardens were not as manicured as they used to be, plus informal traders lined the streets in parts of the outer suburbs.

The taxi driver pulled up beneath the covered entrance to the hotel, jumped out, opened her door and offloaded Mel's suitcase. She thanked him and paid the fare. A hotel porter stood by.

At the reception desk, she checked in. "First floor, room nineteen." The cheerful young lady receptionist, smart in a navy-blue suit, handed her the key and wished her a pleasant stay. The porter carried her case up the flight of stairs. Mel handed him a five-dollar bill. His face lit up when he took it from her. It was a generous tip.

Mel closed the door and flopped down on the edge of the bed and dialled reception. She requested an outside line and called her dad, then she called Julie.

"Hello," Julie answered.

"Hi Jules, it's Mel. I'm here at last."

"Hi, how are you doing? How was the trip? Oh, it's so nice to hear your voice."

"All great. I've just got in. The Rixi taxi from the airport brought back happy memories. I can't wait to see you tomorrow." She stretched herself across the king size bed.

"*Mushi*." Mel burst out laughing. She'd not heard the fun slang word for *great*, for so long. "It's so good to hear that word again. Amazing how quickly we forget. It almost sounds foreign to me."

"Well, it's been a while. What time shall I collect you tomorrow?"

"Any time after nine. I'm going to sleep in. I can't remember when I last stayed in bed till eight. It's only four hours to Inyanga, hey?"

"Yeah. There's no rush, we can chat in the car and catch up. I've booked three nights at Troutbeck Inn." Julie told Mel.

WINDS OF CHANGE

"I'm so excited. Incredible to think I never stayed there."

"Hey," Julie's tone changed. "I'm so sorry about your Mum. What a dreadful shock for you and your dad. How's he coping? How are *you* coping?"

"Thanks Jules. Her passing has been a massive blow for both of us. I brought a little wooden cross Dad made. I want to put in the garden at Blue Winds. It's...it's still a bit raw ...." Mel worked to stop her tears. "Dad's okay but he's aged. At least he's busy, which keeps his mind focussed. It's at night we find it hard. You just never know, do you?" She sniffed, "Anyway, I can't wait to see you tomorrow."

"One more sleep, as we used to say at school," Jules said.

They said goodbye and hung up.

MEL STAYED STRETCHED across the bed looking at the ceiling thinking about going *home* to Blue Winds. She missed so many aspects of her old life in Rhodesia, even though it was Zimbabwe now. The slang, the jokes no-one understood in South Africa, popular foods and drinks, friends, Msasa trees and their chaos of leaf colour in the spring. Glancing at the time, she decided to shower, change, and pop down for supper.

One of the hotel's busy restaurants overlooked the pool deck and she found herself a table. A waiter pulled out her chair. Covering her lap with the napkin, her thoughts drifted back to her conversation with Gary last night. She'd felt better after off-loading her terrorist nightmare to sympathetic ears. She liked Gary, a lot. He'd been so kind, but intimacy terrified her. She also worried, that if they did enter a relationship, should she do so with someone she employed?

A waitress appeared beside her. "Ready to order?"

Mel blinked the reverie of thoughts away and answered. "I'd love a Gin and tonic, with a splash of bitters and a slice of lemon. Not too much ice. Thanks. I'll give you my food order when you come back."

The waitress smiled. "Try the Chef's special. Ladies' fillet, topped with shrimps and a lemon-pepper sauce. It's the best."

"Okay, sounds good. Medium rare, with salad and fries. Thank you."

Sipping her gin, Mel's thoughts went back to Gary. The kiss he'd left her with at the airport felt so good, so comforting. After dinner she strolled onto the pool deck. The water glistened in the soft surrounding lights. She sat on the edge, dropped her legs into the cool water, splashed with her feet to create shimmering little waves that sparkled, creating the soothing ambiance she needed.

***

At a table on the far side of the restaurant, away from the pool, Solomon watched Mel intently. Now a decorated Colonel in Robert Mugabe's army, he wielded the powers of a mini dictator, and Samuel, his spy at Chanting Clover had informed him of Mel's itinerary.

His gaze followed her as she made her way to the pool deck. He watched and waited; confident she hadn't seen him. Eventually she left the pool area. He noted the time and ordered dessert. When he finished a large plate of cheese and biscuits, and a pot of coffee, he got up and walked around the pool to settle his stomach then wandered to reception.

"Give me the spare key to room nineteen," Solomon demanded.

The receptionist shot him a *how-dare-you* look. "I'm afraid I'm not permitted to give out spare keys, Sir. That room's occupied by a visitor from out of the country."

Pushing his jacket to one side, he revealed a side-arm, secured in a holster. "Hand over the key."

The receptionist's eyes widened, and her mouth snapped shut.

"Do you know who I am?" He filled his tone with confidence and importance.

"No Sir," she said.

"I'm a very important man of high rank. Give me the key," Solomon said through gritted teeth and unhooked the cover of the firearm and made to pull it out of the holster in a threatening way.

The Receptionist finally handed him the key. "Don't try and call security, or even tell anyone."

Solomon stood at the door of room nineteen on the first floor. By now, Mel should be asleep. His skin prickled with anticipation, and he slid the key into the lock. "Now the white whore will finally pay for what she did." The words thrilled him. He'd often imagined her begging for his mercy.

He entered the dark room with caution. As silent as a shadow, he made his way to the bed.

He stood over her. Faint light from outside filtered through the slit in the curtains. He pounced, covering her mouth with his large hands, pressing down with all his weight. He knew she was a fighter.

She struggled under his grip.

Keeping one hand pressed over her mouth, he switched on the bedside light with the other.

Her eyes widened as she recognised him.

"No sense fighting, bitch. You took away my farm. You let my family starve, you destroyed my comrades. You killed my commander." He seethed. Spittle flew with the words.

She tried to respond, flicking her head from side to side, trying to dislodge his hands.

He showed her his pistol. "You got away and left many dead. Now *you* are going to die." He grabbed a fistful of her hair and wrenched her head back. Her mouth yawed from her head being wrenched back.

He let go of her mouth and stared into her frightened eyes. "Make a sound and I'll twist your head off your shoulders like I do my chickens." He hauled her out of bed and slowly released his hand from her mouth. "Not one sound, or you're dead."

She stared at his pistol.

"Your death, in this room, is going to be a slow one. Shooting you would alert security. I'm not that stupid. I have other things planned." He moved them away from the bed.

"You burned our camp. You killed Antonio. Jacob died next to me when the Hunter's bombed the remains of the camp." He stamped his foot.

She glared at Solomon. "You shot up our house, wounded my mother and abducted me knowing what the commander would do to me, you evil son-of-bitch."

"The commander's, name was Antonio."

"I didn't know that, and I don't care."

Solomon couldn't stand her voice. He struck her face and she fell to the floor, dazed. She hung onto the side of the bed and pushed herself into the sitting position.

Solomon laughed. "Stand up."

"You bastard." She rubbed her cheek and her nose bled. He took a step closer and kicked her. The toe cap of his boned military boot slammed into her ribs.

She didn't cry out. "Why.... now?" Her head hung down and blood poured from her nose, staining the carpeting. "And how did you know I was here?"

"I saw you in the restaurant. My good luck." He wasn't going to mention he had a spy working on her farm.

"What lies." She held her face with one hand and her ribs with the other, but she continued to speak in pained broken sentences. "The war. It's over. You and your comrades got what you want."

Such a stupid girl. "The war maybe over, but you killed my comrades, and I'll never forget that." His voice surged with anger.

"Ask Mr. Mugabe for our farm, if you didn't get one." She continued watching the drops of blood from her nose drip onto the floor.

"I'm a Colonel. I don't want Blue Winds. I was given a better farm."

"So then leave me alone." This ridiculous girl. Doesn't she understand the importance of revenge.

She tried to stand. He launched his boot into her knee, her leg snapped backwards. Mel screamed in agony and collapsed on the floor, grasping her injured leg.

"Shut up." He'd likely dislocated her knee. Good. Pain. She deserved so much more.

But she surprised him. She cupped her kneecap and quickly snapped the joint back into position.

"How did you get away from Antonio? I want to know the whole story," he asked, leaning down, breathing all over her, the same way the commander had.

"I need.... the .... bathroom." Blood from her nose was all over her hands. Pushing hair from her face she smeared blood across her forehead and into the hairline.

Solomon wasn't in a hurry. He planned to make her suffer for hours. "Go."

Mel used the bed and heaved herself to her feet, keeping her injured knee as straight as possible. Once upright, she glared at Solomon and wondered how many hours he'd take to end her life. She wanted to cry, but she would not.

The bedroom looked like a battle ground. Blood on the floor, the sheets, even the wall. Her blood, from her nose. She hadn't won the first fight, but somehow, she would win the war.

The swelling around her right eye tightened and throbbed. She wobbled toward the bathroom. Solomon followed her and laughed, a brittle, insulting laugh. He followed so close she felt his breath on the back of her neck.

At the wash-hand basin she turned on the cold water, bent over and splashed water on her face. The cold water stung to begin with but soothed the swelling around her eye. Taking a face cloth, she wet it, wiped her face, cleansing away the blood. With her face cooled and her mind clearer, she wrapped her mouth over the cold water tap and drank. She straightened and looked in the mirror. He was right behind her, too close for her to lash out.

"Why are you running the hot water now?" he asked.

"To sooth the swelling over my eye." Mel let the hot water run until it warmed, soaked the face cloth, and held it over her eye. Time ticked on. Then miraculously he stepped away from her, likely getting irritated by the length of time she took cleaning her face.

Her planned kick had to be accurate and fast.

Biding her time, she switched off the hot water and stretched her arms above her head.

He no longer watched her.

She spun like a ballerina and launched a kick with her good leg. Her foot connected with his groin, and he went down. She followed with a hard punch to his nose, crashing down on top of him. He was about to retch from the pain between his legs. Mel quickly rolled off him, wrenched the pistol from the holster, and held it to his creepy, oily head.

She enjoyed watching him hold his likely aching testicles. Seemed he'd grown too heavy from the spoils of wealth and a deskbound lifestyle and now couldn't get himself up off the floor.

The gun pressed to his temple, she said, "Don't move or I'll kill you." Keeping her eyes fixed on him and the pistol aimed, she stepped out to the phone. She knew she wouldn't kill him because she could end up spending her life in a Zimbabwean jail.

She called reception and spoke loud and sure. "Security to room nineteen. Now. Hurry."

She opened the weapon, removed the bullets, wiped it to remove her fingerprints, and threw it on the floor next to him.

Still holding himself, he rolled from side to side, groaning.

Melonie resisted the urge to laugh.

The door burst open. Three security guards rushed in.

"Are you alright Ma'am?" said the tallest one.

"Yes, just get this piece of shit out of my room."

It took all three security guards to haul Solomon to his feet and hand cuff him.

"How did he get in?" the tall one asked.

"I have no idea, I was asleep."

Then a voice came from the open doorway. It was the receptionist.

"I gave him the key - he threatened to kill me if I didn't give it to him, or if I told anyone."

"You cannot arrest me," Solomon said, scorn deeply etched on his face. "I'm a Colonel."

The security fellows looked anxious at the mention of rank.

"So fucking what," Mel said. "Colonel or no Colonel, he accessed my room illegally, assaulted me and planned to murder me. Get him out of here before I call the police." She threatened, knowing the police would be no help.

Solomon coughed, moaned, and doubled over.

"Get him out of here. Now!" Mel's voice held raw fury.

The guards pushed Solomon to the door and dragged him into the hall.

. . .

Mel slammed the door and locked it. Minutes later there was a knock.

"Who is it?" Mel asked.

"The receptionist. I.... I want to apologise, Miss Johns." Mel opened the door.

"It's not your fault. Has the bastard gone?"

"Yes. Security removed the handcuffs and took him to his car."

"In a top of the range, government issue, black Mercedes, I suppose." She said sarcastically.

The receptionist didn't answer.

"When you get back to reception, get me an outside line, please."

Mel closed the door and leant her back against it. "I came to Zim to put the ghosts of the past behind me, and the fucking ghost arrived in my bedroom." She spoke aloud then hobbled to the bed.

She dialled reception. "Hi, please send up four Paracetamol and give me that outside line."

Mel dialled Jules's number. It rang and rang. She was about to put the phone down when Julie answered.

"Hello." She said with hesitation.

"Jules, I'm sorry to wake you. I've just been attacked. I've taken quite a beating." Mel choked on her words. "Sorry, hold on, there's a knock on my door." The reception lady had the painkillers.

Mel put the phone to her ear again.

"Did you just say you've been attacked?"

"Yes, by the bastard who abducted me from the farm during the war."

"Oh my God, are you okay?"

"Only just. I'm shattered Julie, and worse still, the son-of-a-bitch is a Colonel in Bob's Brigade and wields a lot of power. He bashed my face in, kicked me about, dislocated my knee and booted me in the ribs."

"What? How did he get into your room?"

"He threatened the receptionist with a 9mm pistol, so she handed him the spare key. I don't blame her."

"Do you want us to fetch you?"

"No Jules. I need to get out of Zim. I'm a target here. I must fly home as soon as I can change my flight, or I'll be killed. Have breakfast here with me tomorrow. I must see you both."

"How did you escape him?" Jules asked.

"I kicked him so hard in the balls he crashed to the floor, and he's so fucking fat, he couldn't get up."

"Good. But why are you a target, for God's sake? The war was over years ago."

"Because I killed his commander, and his best friend died beside him in the Hunter bombings after I escaped. He wants revenge. He said so before security took him out of my room in handcuffs."

"I'm so sorry, Mel. Try and get some sleep. We'll see you at eight for breakfast. Shall we come to your room?"

"Yes. It's number nineteen." Mel blew her friend a kiss down the phone, then she called her dad. He was horrified and assured her he'd call the airlines first thing in the morning.

JULIE AND ALLAN arrived promptly at eight and knocked on her door. Mel burst into tears as she opened the door and hugged Jules.

"Good God, Mel, what a horrid back eye. I'm sorry you had to come back to this," Allan said as they stepped into the room.

"Holy shit, where did all the blood come from?" Julie asked. "It looks like a war took place in here."

"It did. The blood came from my nose."

"Oh, my dear friend. You must be shattered. I can't believe the stupid man is set on revenge. All sorts of horrors happened in the war. He's not Mister innocent, he abducted you. The revenge should be yours."

Melonie nodded. "Hey, sit. Let's order breakfast. I'm having an omelette." She passed over the menu. "You don't mind if we get room service?"

"No, go for it." Allan answered.

The phone rang. It was Mel's dad. He'd managed to change the flight. She had to be at the airport in Harare at 10:45 a.m. She'd arrive in Durban at 3.50 p.m.

. . .

ALLAN AND JULES drove Mel to the airport and stayed with her until she checked in, then she sat alone and waited until called to board.

She settled herself into a window seat and looked out across the runway. It was good-bye Zimbabwe forever. An easy goodbye compared to the last one when they left Zimbabwe the first time.

Now she felt excited to get back to her beautiful stud and horses. There she had a secure future.

When the plane touched down in Durban, the early evening light was murky from a salty wind that had blown off the ocean. She could taste it on her lips, and they stung. Everything hurt, including her heart. She pushed the luggage trolley through immigration and saw her dad pacing about. She ran to him.

"Hello, my precious. You look wretched."

"I am, Dad. Let's get going." She pulled her case off the trolley and slung her bag over her shoulder, and they walked to the car.

During the two-hour road home, Mel shared her grizzly experience with Solomon, then she went on to explain her suspicions.

"Thank God you got out without any more drama. It's a pity you never put a bullet through his head, but I know why you didn't. Was the incident reported to the police?"

"No way, Dad! The police would've been on Solomon's side, and I would've been arrested. Even though my body hurts, I feel a weird inner peace, and a newfound commitment to this country. The yearning to go *home* is gone. This is home. This is where my heart belongs."

"That country was once the breadbasket of Africa. It produced the best beef in the world, the finest tobacco leaf in the world, grain for the whole of the Southern Africa. Soon it'll be like the ruins it's named after, mark my words."

"Dad, I know, and I'm sure you're right. The people seem sad, scared, and suppressed. My heart goes out to them."

"Of course, but they voted the shower of shit in. I can't feel sorry for them."

"Oh, Dad."

"Patric can thank his lucky stars he's not living in Zim anymore."

"That brings me to my suspicions. The Zimbo guy Gary employed, is he still working in the brood mare barn?"

"I've no idea my girl, you'll have to ask Gary. Why?"

"It's just a gut feel. It was no coincidence that Solomon just happened to see me in the restaurant at Monomatapa."

"No, probably not. That's a disconcerting thought."

THE NEXT DAY Mel crawled out of bed late. Every muscle in her body ached. She booked a doctor's appointment to have her knee x-rayed when Gary knocked on the sitting room door.

"Jesus, Mel. I should have come with you." He leant down and kissed her on the cheek.

"Just as well you didn't, we'd be both be in jail."

"You need to see the doctor."

"I've just called. I'm meeting him at the hospital. He's going into surgery now, until two. He's booked me for Xray's at two fifteen. Would you mind taking me?"

"Of course, I'll take you." Gary sat beside her.

"That Zim fella you employed, is he still here?"

"Yes, I think so. Why?"

"Can you find out for sure. Who'll know where he is right now?"

"Probably Thomas or Shadrick. Let me call the stables." Gary picked up the phone and dialled the internal number for the main stable block tack room.

Thomas answered. "Hi Thomas, is Samuel on duty today?"

"Josia reported he never pitched for work today, Mr Gary."

"Okay, don't worry. Thanks Thomas."

Gary put the phone down. "He never pitched for work today."

Mel's whole body visibly shook. "If he's not here tomorrow, he's Solomon's spy."

Chapter Nineteen

X-RAYS REVEALED NO BROKEN RIBS. Her knee required rest for at least a month and enclosed in a knee guard. No riding. Three weeks later, bored and itching to ride, Mel slipped on the knee brace and disappeared on Tropical Sun before anyone could stop her.

Walking through the fields, the wind blew her hair and buffeted against her face. Despite the soothing wind and the sounds of the clip-clopping hooves she wondered how safe even Chanting Clover is. A quiet ride normally soothed her, but not today. The thought that Solomon had ears and eyes watching her in the only place she felt safe, unhinged her.

She wondered if she put Tropical Sun into top gear and test the speed of her equine Maserati, whether it would clear her gloomy thoughts, then she remembered her knee. Another painful reminder of what had recently turned her peaceful, idyllic life upside down. There seemed only one answer to the problem. Internal, undercover security, day, and night. And what would that cost?

The sun shone down on her bare shoulders and Tropical Sun's hoofbeats became her heartbeats. His ears flicked back and forth, picking up different sounds. She felt she should be feeling alive, living the dream, but fear and uncertainty tainted her dreams and destroyed happy sensations today.

Two hours later Mel arrived back at the stables. Her knee was twinging. She lowered herself slowly and felt more relaxed and hobbled with Tropical Sun to his stable and untacked.

"Can't keep you off his back, even when you're injured." Gary stood at the stable door, shaking his head. "You're not supposed to be riding."

"I know and my knee is sore, but I had to get out onto the farm." She rested her head against his shoulder and closed her eyes, the saddle propped on her leg.

"What's the matter?"

Mel opened her eyes and dumped the saddle over the stable door. "I don't think he'll ever stop going after me. We need to make sure we never employ another Zimbabwean. Only Patric and his family are permitted to live here."

"He, being Solomon, I presume?" Gary asked.

"Yes." She unbuckled the throat lash and slipped the bridle off the horse's head and placed it over the saddle.

"Guilt feels like a merited emotion." Gary said as he took the saddle and bridle off the stable door.

"Oh don't." Mel stared at Gary, suddenly realising how much she'd missed him. "I wore the knee guard, but I still couldn't trot. I was so tempted to have a gallop to clear my mind," Mel laughed, "But I knew that would be crazy." She rubbed Tropical Sun's back lifting the hair to cool it off. "Walking didn't help clear disparaging thoughts, though."

"Thoughts about what?"

"That bastard, Solomon, of course. I must budget for internal security to make sure I'm safe and have a future to look forward to here. He will take every opportunity he can to end my life."

"Have you chatted to your dad about that?" He helped her out the stable and noticed she was limping badly. "You need to get off that leg. Let me help you back to your office and I'll call your dad."

Gary offered his arm and got Mel back to her office and she plonked down in her chair, grateful to be off her feet. Gary poured her a glass of water and called Ivan.

"What's up, my girl?" Ivan asked, walking into her office. She explained her thoughts while out riding. "Why were your riding?"

"I just had to, Dad. Out there I began to wonder how safe we are here. I think we should employ a security company. Can we afford a security team on duty day and night?"

Ivan looked at Gary, then back to Mel. "I don't think we have an option."

Mel spent the rest of the week in her office and found a security company in Durban she felt offered the kind of service she was looking for. She dialled Gary's number.

"Hi, have you found the right security company?" Gary asked.

"Yes, but I'm not calling you about that. How about we pop out for dinner this evening."

"What a great idea. Why didn't I think of it?" He joked, though he had, often. "What time?"

"I'll pop down to your cottage at five. Early supper for me, I reckon."

Gary collected Mel instead. The end of the day had become chilly. The type of chill that forces gatherings around a roaring fire and the Green Lantern restaurant lit their fires when the temperature dropped.

Gary and Mel seated themselves beside the main fireplace. The twinkling flames set a romantic ambience and it was cosy and warm inside. They were the first to arrive.

"We're so lucky to have this wonderful restaurant so close to the farm." Gary placed the napkin on his lap.

Mel did the same and after smoothing the napkin across her lap, she looked up. "I haven't been here since Mum passed away." A short silence followed.

"What would you like to drink?"

"I'll have my favourite wine. Nederburg Sauvignon. I'm not one of those connoisseurs who order food first, then decide whether it should be red or white." She smiled.

Gary ordered the bottle and a beer for himself. "Are you riding again next week?" Gary asked. Mel smiled shyly and shifted in her chair, about to answer when the waiter returned and poured the wine.

"Cheers. Here's to many more evenings together. What a splendid idea." Gary's tumbler met her wine glass and chimed delicately.

"I'd like to take White Jewel for a gallop if my knee holds up. Apart from arranging a security company, I also made a list of what needs upgrading in each section. I haven't inspected staff housing. Perhaps after breakfast tomorrow we should all gather in the boardroom. You, me, Dad, and Hector."

Gary nodded with a smile that only lifted one side of his mouth. "Let's leave shop talk for tomorrow." Mel quickly looked away, a little embarrassed, then caught sight of the blackboard advertising, *Specials*.

Gary noticed where she focussed. "Kingklip sounds good."

Gary agreed and then she noticed he gazed lovingly at her. "You're looking gorgeous in that dusty- pink pullover. The colour really suits you."

"Thank you, Gary. I guess this evening, in this romantic setting, we should chat about us?"

It was the opening Gary had hoped for since she'd suggested the evening out. He leant a little closer to her. "I'm intrigued, how did you get away from the brute hell-bent on ending your life?"

It was her turn to lean over, and the chemistry hit her like an electric shock. "I've no idea." She breathed out. An unusually sensual action which even surprised her. "It's a long story, some of which you already know." She sat back, took a sip of wine, and felt her face flush.

Gary watched while she shifted about in her chair. "I got my chance standing at the wash-hand basin in the bathroom. I hadn't intended it that way. I wanted to wash the blood off my hands and face. I also wanted a piddle, but he stood so close behind me and I wasn't going to use the toilet with him watching. I deliberately took my time cleaning my face trying to work out how to save my life. He got bored watching me and moved a few steps away. The extra space was enough room for me to launch into action. It's amazing how one's survival instinct gives the edge. Aiming at his crouch with my good leg, adrenaline did the rest. We smashed to the floor together and I yanked the 9mm pistol from the holster and pressed it into his temple. That felt good." Mel took a sip of wine. "The fat slob couldn't get off the floor. I ran to the phone, keeping the pistol trained on him and called for security. It took three guards to haul him to his feet."

"Good God, you must've been petrified."

"I think I felt more relieved than terrified." She fiddled with her fork and straightened the table mat, then lifted her head and focussed on his beautiful blue eyes.

"The whole episode released me from my yearning to be in Zimbabwe. I guess it's not the way psychologists would recommend getting rid of stored trauma, hey?" Mel's light-hearted humour always simmered at the surface.

Gary loved that about her. "You're amazing. I don't know anyone who could possibly find a situation so frightening, funny." Gary leant over again and couldn't resist kissing her. When he sat back, he lifted his glass, "Here's to a brighter, safer future."

"Thank you, Gary. I hope so." They went on with their meal, enjoying each other's company and the ambience. A gentle hum of classical music played quietly in the background allowing patrons to chat without having to yell at each other to be heard. Gary took her hand, and she kept it resting in his without resistance.

"This has been a magical evening. We should do it more often." Gary said, looking into her glittering emerald eyes.

"It has, hasn't it?" Their hands lingered. "Thanks for listening, and always being there for me."

"I couldn't think of anyone nicer to be with." Gary replied honestly. "Shall we be on our way?"

"Yeah, early start," Mel ruffled her napkin and reached for her handbag. They drove back to the stud comfortably chatting about horses. Gary pulled into the parking in front of the main house, switched off the engine and kissed her. His mouth opened slightly to savour the warmth of her and taste the sweetness of the last of the wine on her lips.

Chapter Twenty

IVAN HEARD Gary's car stop on the driveway and stay for a short while. He hoped it meant the start of their romance. One he'd hoped their flirty friendship would develop into. He'd watched Mel's emotions bounce around like a yoyo. He'd noticed Gary occasionally brought a young lady to the farm, though none had lasted long, and he felt sure Gary had his eye on Mel. Even before he learned of her past, he'd always been the ultimate gentleman.

Once a week Hector made his way to the track and this morning, Ivan met him there. Mel had told him she was having her first gallop without the knee brace. At the end of the track, she pulled Tropical Sun to a walk and noticed them watching her. She trotted over to where they stood.

"Morning Hector. Morning Dad. "It's nice to see you two here bright and early."

"Have to keep an eye you." Hector winked. "Good gallop Sunny gave you."

"He's my soul mate, Hector."

"Gary would be a better one." Hector said in a playful tone, though he meant it.

Melonie didn't respond, instead she trotted off. "See you both at ten."

Ivan raised his eyebrows. He turned to Hector. "You touched a chord."

"It's high time she and Gary started a proper relationship, isn't it?" Hector responded gruffly.

"I couldn't agree more. I think poor Gary's desperate to ask her for her hand in marriage. He's being so patient. How I wish her mother was around to talk to her. Do you know the poor girl was raped in Mozambique."

"Good Lord. No! I didn't. No wonder she's scared, poor darling. Oh, I'm so sorry." She seemed happy this morning, didn't she?"

"Yes, she did. When they got back from the restaurant last night, Gary switched the car engine off. It was a good ten minutes before I heard Mel open the front door. You know Mel wants us all in her office at ten to discuss upgrades of various sections of the stud. I'll see you there."

***

Riding slowly back to the stables a sudden tingling of goosebumps covered her body. *Is that you Mum?* Mel felt a spiritual presence. Mum or gran. It didn't really matter. She untacked, rubbed Sunny down, and lost in thought carried the saddle and bridle to the tack room. Lifting the saddle onto the rack she felt a presence behind her and spun around. "Thomas, you gave me a fright." Her hand went to her heart. "Tell me, Thomas, would it help to have two more junior grooms here in the main block?"

"Oh yes, it would, Missus Mel."

Her brow creased in thought. "If I moved Patric, where do you think he'd be most suited?"

"With the ready-to-run horses."

"Really? Why?" Thomas seemed reluctant to give her an answer. "I'll tell you later." Mel stepped out the tack room and into Gary.

"Ready for the meeting?"

"Yip. If you're heading up to admin now, I'll join you. Hector sent me a bottle of his home-made cherry liqueur this morning. How would you like to have supper with me tonight and sample his liqueur?"

"Yeah, okay."

"We can postpone for another time." He'd noticed her hesitancy.

"No. I'll be there. Sorry. My mind is pre-occupied with where to move Patric. Thomas says the ready-to-runs. What do you think?"

"Let's chat about it in the office."

A few hours later, and a successful meeting behind them, Mel wandered back to the house for lunch with her dad. Instead of going back to the office she sat on the veranda with her diary and made notes. Thomas and Shadrick were joint-in-charge of the main racehorse stable block, and under them were six junior grooms. Twenty-four racehorses in full training.

She'd budgeted for another ten stables to be added to the brood mare barn. These would be reserved for visiting mares in for covering. Up till now they'd only been covering their own mares. Maria had recently joined Josia, and they ran a very happy team of grooms.

There was one spare stable in the stallion block. "Hmmm," she put an Asterix next to that. No upgrades were needed there. Brilliant Kagiso and his team were happy too. She'd pigeonhole the thought of buying another stallion.

Ten more stables were to be added to the ready-to-run barn. This news pleased Gary, plus another tack room on the end, and the installation of infra-red lighting. It was the staff in this section that always seemed to give her the biggest headaches.

The yearlings and weanlings lived out mostly. The paddock shelters had been upgraded and the small block of ten stables were new.

Finally, she pondered the staff housing, the feed sheds, workshops, and pastures, but then discarded them, dad had control of all that and soon the undercover security roving the stud and the farm would fall under him too.

By five that evening Mel felt motivated, hopeful, and content. She'd accomplished a lot sitting quietly on the veranda and looked forward to spending the evening with Gary.

Instead of her usual jeans and shirt, she decided to wear a dress and chose a simple primrose-yellow shift with big cheerful white buttons down the front. A thick white leather belt accentuated her waist. She left the house excited.

The walk from the main house to Gary's cottage took seven minutes. A walk she loved, meandering through the park-like gardens Granny had created and then on through the arboretum Granny had been so proud of. Mel continued past the edge of the brood mare paddocks where banks of Azalea's grew. A tall hedge of Rhododendrons separated Hector and Gary's sandstone cottages. The green corrugated iron roof of each cottage peeped over the top of the hedge.

Mel bounced up the steps and knocked. "Hi, can I come in?"

Gary whipped the door open.

"Wow, you look stunning in a dress. I'm only used to seeing you in jodhpurs or jeans." Mel's mood had taken on the sun kissed yellow of her dress. She reached up and kissed his cheek, then followed him through the sitting room to the veranda.

"What's for supper? Smells so good." Mel sat on the sofa with a view of the yearling paddocks.

"I'm not the most creative cook, I'm afraid. Fresh lamb chops and Hector's wonderful veg with mashed potato. And I got old Martie down the road to make us a lemon meringue pie, which I'm told you love." He arranged the wine glasses.

"Oh yum, sounds scrumptious. How sweet of you." Mel pulled her dress down over her knees.

"I've opened a bottle of your favourite Nederburg." He poured the wine into the two glasses, handed one to Mel and they clinked glasses.

"You're so thoughtful. You're aware of my appetite, aren't you? I burn calories as fast as they enter my body."

"Oh, don't I know it. I'll never forget our first breakfast watching you devour a plate scrambled egg and mushrooms even I wouldn't have fit in my stomach. Are you hungry now?"

"No, not really." She was, but she chose to be polite. Adjusting to being nearer each other in Gary's private space Mel found awkward.

Gary stood beside her and sipped his wine, then he lifted his glass.

"Here's to winning the next race and to all the forecast improvements. You conducted a very good meeting."

"Granny used to say it was bad luck to toast a horse before it runs." Mel raised her glass, then sipped, clearly enjoying the taste of her favourite wine.

Gary's skew smile suggested he didn't believe in old folklore. "Are you superstitious?"

"No. Not at all. I believe everything happens for a reason, even though sometimes I cannot fathom the reason." She said with one eyebrow raised and a curious smile.

Gary sat on the sofa and put his arm across her shoulders. Her first instinct was to tense up, but his arm felt reassuring. "Let me know when you're ravenous. Supper is ready, but it's nice just sitting here sipping wine, listening to sheep calling, and the evening coming alive with insects chatting to each other about their day."

"Oh, I love that – insects chatting to each other about their day. And I love watching the sunset develop." Mel stood up and walked around the veranda enjoying different aspects of the setting sun. "If you don't mind me asking, where are we putting Patric? It's the only subject we never made a final decision on in the meeting this morning." She sat beside him again. "He has my best interest at heart and is a reliable source of information on what's going on among the staff, plus I want to put Spindle to Eldorado when she comes into season."

"Well, as you trust Patric, I'd go with Thomas's suggestion and put Patric in the ready-to-run barn. Why do you want Spindle covered?" Gary spread him arms in a theatrical gesture.

"She's been the most wonderful companion to me all my life. I'd love to have a foal from her. You never know, one day I might have children and Spindle would have the perfect child's pony. And if I never have children, her foal would be a great stock horse." Mel couldn't decipher her feelings in that moment and shifted self-consciously.

"What's the matter? Am I too close to you? Making you feel uncomfortable." Gary leant away from her in case.

"On the contrary. I'm thoroughly enjoying getting to know you better, I'm just nervous. Very nervous." She knew it was time to calm herself or it'd ruin the evening.

With his index finger under her chin, he tilted her head up. "I never thought you'd invite me into your life. I couldn't be happier, and of course I understand your fears." He kissed her nose. "You let me know. You be my guide."

Mel kicked her shoes off and curled her legs underneath her. She patted her cheeks, "you've made me blush." Gary stood up, reached a hand to her, pulled her up and said, "come on, we need to eat. It's better you serve yourself, just leave some for me." He teased.

In the kitchen Mel took a warmed plate and dished up her meal. "This looks and smells gorgeous." Mel waited until Gary had filled his plate, then they went back to the veranda. Once they'd finished supper, Gary took her plate to the kitchen and returned carrying a bottle of Hector's liqueur and two liqueur glasses hooked in his little finger.

"Let's have a liqueur. It may help you relax more than wine." He poured a small glass each.

Mel sipped the liqueur, swallowed, and licked her lips. "Oooh, this is yum." She leaned back into Gary's arm. "Until the Monomatapa experience, I thought I'd dealt with my past traumas, but during my forced rest, I had time to think, and I've realised how devastating the reminder of the past has been." The memory of waking to Solomon's hand pressing down over her mouth made her shudder. "And because I've never really spoken much about the rape to anyone, including my parents, the doctor who said I was in denial, was right." She looked directly at Gary and bit down on her bottom lip to stop herself crying. "I'm only half a woman, the other half was taken away from me Gary."

"Mel, your words tear at my heart. You're all woman. A very brave, courageous, beautiful one, inside and outside. It's obviously sex you're afraid of?" He asked boldly.

Everything about sex was savage, painful and sucks, Gary. I can still taste the fear, visceral and metallic every time I think of what he did to me. I was too weak to fight. He flung me on his desk like a ragdoll, ripped my tracksuit and pyjama pants off and rammed his penis into me with such force I felt like I'd been cut in two."

"Oh my God." Gary cupped her quivering chin in his hands and kissed her lightly on the lips. She never imagined a kiss could feel so tender. She knew she had to be honest. "I know I must get over my fear of intimacy, I just don't know how. Look at me, shaking like a leaf just talking about it, and I don't want to lose you."

Mel rested her head on his chest, savouring the warmth and security of him, then suddenly his radio crackled loudly, and they heard Josia's voice.

Gary jumped up and ran to answer. A few moments later, he rushed back to Mel. "An emergency at the broodmare barn."

Mel grabbed one of Gary's jackets, wondering which mare was having difficulty birthing. She pulled on the jacket and they raced to the brood mare barn a good kilometre from Gary's house. They were quite breathless when they entered the barn.

Josia, the head of the broodmare barn, had moved the mare to the observation stable when he noticed she was having difficulty. The foals two front feet and a little pink nose were peeping out. The amniotic sack hung below the feet and Josia had torn more of the membrane away from the foal's nose. Majestic Crown showed all the stress signs of a difficult birth. Her body glowed with sweat, like she'd been washed. Fear and pain showed in the whites of her eyes. Her nostrils flared, and she breathed fast and hard.

"How long has Majestic Crown been struggling?" Gary asked Josia.

Josia looked at the birthing chart that lay on the desk, clipped to a board. "Forty-seven minutes ago." Josia was known to be precise. "During her last contraction. Just before I called on the radio."

Gary looked at Mel, then the distressed, exhausted mare, then back to Mel. They both understood what they had to do next.

"What do you think, Gary?"

Gary didn't answer. Josia knew too. He handed Gary a pair of long rubber gloves. Gary pulled them on and smothered antiseptic soap up and down his right arm. When the next contraction arrived, Gary eased the foal along helping the head protrude past the ears.

Majestic Crown moaned and raised her head, breathing heavily, then she dropped her head back into the straw.

Watching Gary, Mel realised how lucky she was to have him by her side to help in situations like this where she may not have been strong enough to pull the foal.

With the next contraction Gary eased the foal's shoulders through the birth canal, and between him and Josia, they lowered a huge dark bay foal to the ground.

"My goodness me, that's a big foal, he will probably weight about sixty-five kilos'." Mel said, then frowned.

Majestic Crown stood, but she heaved again as if still in labour. The newborn foal lay in the hay near her, shifting, wanting mama to lick it clean and start bonding. Majestic took no notice of her newborn.

"Oh my God. In the name of everything holy, she's having another foal." Melonie wheezed as she noticed the front feet of the twin appear.

"Good heavens." Gary exhaled, and moved closer to the mare, ready to pull again.

Josia muttered something in his mother tongue.

The next foal was considerably smaller and slid into the world with ease.

"I can't believe they both fit inside poor Crownie." Mel said, feeling some feminine sympathy.

Majestic Crown nickered to her two babies and started licking them clean. The colt stood first and stayed standing. The little filly stretched her legs in an unruly tangle and tried to stand but took four attempts to stay up. She shook herself and wobbled, collapsing into the thick wheat straw.

Majestic Crown spun round to check on her.

Big brother shook his little head in agitation, his milk bar had moved. He nickered and mouthed at his mother. Then the filly finally stood and remained upright.

"What a picture. They're too sweet. What are the chances they both survive?" Mel looked to Gary, worried the filly may not make it through the night.

"Pretty slim, I'm told." Gary cocked his head to one side with a sympathetic expression. "I've never experienced seeing a mare give birth to twins or having to care for twins, we can only hope we get them both through the first week. If we do, I think they will both live."

"Well, nor have I. I'll have to some research on this." Mel watched, her heart swollen with the tenderness shown by Gary as he placed a hand on the hindquarters and the other hand on the point of the shoulder and guided the little filly to the udder. Nosing around, the filly found a teat and suckled her fill of vital colostrum. Milk poured from the mare's teats, so Mel guided the colt to the other side of his mother so both foals could suckle. The soft fluffy hair was like cotton wool and the little swishing tail like an artist's paintbrush.

Mel glanced at Josia who stood watching, looking as proud as she felt.

"Good job, my man," Gary patted Josia on the back. "Keep a close eye on them, especially the little filly. Call me if you need help during the night."

Josia smiled at Gary, happy that Gary noticed how much he loved the mares. "Thank you, Mr Gary."

"Crickey, it's nearly midnight," Gary checked his watch.

It was time to leave mother and twins to get to know each other's smells and sounds, and bond.

Mel and Gary walked back to the main house and entered through the back door into the kitchen.

Without uttering a word, Gary pulled her to him and kissed her passionately for the first time. "Sleep well, my precious. I'll see you in the morning." Mel watched him leave, and for the first time, she felt her heart flutter and her chest tighten.

The next morning before checking on the twins, Mel did the rounds of the yearling stables and to her horror she found Gypsy Girl, a fourteen-month-old jet-black filly dead. She'd rolled too close to the stable wall, 'casting' herself, her legs facing the wall. Efforts to free herself had been in vain. Markings on the wall showed where her hooves had skated in her quest to find a snag that would've given her the anchor so she could roll over. She died trying. Her desperate attempts to get up must've coincided with Majestic Crowns difficulties to produce twins.

Chapter Twenty-One

Ivan made a wooden cross and burned the filly's name, date of birth, dam, and sire details and the date of her death, onto the cross and placed it on Gypsy Girls grave.

"Oh God," Melonie sobbed, "this reminds me of when we had to bury my Firelight. I guess it'll never get easier saying goodbye to horses I love. Losing her could have been avoided if the bloody night watchman had been doing his job."

Gary was standing beside Mel. "I've fired the watchman. This is the third time he's been caught sleeping on duty. One of the other guards had to physically shake him awake."

"Serves him right. I'm going to lie around the house and read. I'm exhausted. You must be too, Gary?"

"I am, but I'm going to check the twins are okay before taking a short nap." He squeezed Mel's arm affectionately.

No-one wanted to wake Mel from her slumber. Ivan checked on her before dinner, she was still asleep. He left her.

When she woke, it was still light outside. She felt amazing, and stretched like a lazy, well fed feline and casually glanced at her watch. Six-forty. She looked again. Six-forty in the morning. Horrified, she bounced out of bed. She'd slept all day, and all night. She quickly dressed, brushed her teeth, and ran to the brood mare barn.

The twins were still alive. "Yesss," she punched the air and rejoiced and named the little filly, Peanut because she was so small. She was also the colour of a roasted peanut. If the darling little twin lived for another four days, she'd find a proper name for her. The colt was lovely and strong, like most of her colts. She wasn't worried about him.

Excited, she raced to Gary's cottage. When she got there, she realised he'd be at the track. She meandered home knowing there'd been a shift inside her. She wanted to be with Gary. She'd have to wait another hour before he returned for breakfast. On her walk home she remembered they had four horses going to Scottsville racecourse today, and the grooming team for the ready-to-run barn were preparing horses for the National 2-year-old sales. She shook her head. The long sleep had disorientated her.

She made herself a cup of coffee and two slices of toast and wandered through to the veranda. Her favourite place to sit and think. The white wicker chairs and sofas with their bulky, blue striped linen cushions were so comfortable. She put her cup on the table, then sat on the sofa and tucked her legs underneath her before nibbling on the toast. She took a small bite and gazed across miles of green fields that stretched toward the middle distance, separated by the Drakensburg Mountain range that rose far away. She felt tempted to stay there all day wondering if this is how it feels to be in love.

The big clock that hung on the wall on the veranda struck eight-thirty. Gary would be at his cottage. She slugged back her coffee and ran down to his cottage.

"Can I come in?" She shouted and seconds later he opened the door. Melonie almost gasped and the blush rose quickly. He stood in the doorway like a Greek God, wearing only a white bath towel wrapped around his waist. Mel's eyes were instantly drawn to his tantalising six-pack which rippled in the morning sunlight.

Mel hesitated for a moment. "May I come with you to Scottsville this morning? Dad is um.... leaving much later. Little Peanut is fine, I've, um......." He stood towering over her, with a smile on his face.

He interrupted. "Come inside. I need to get dressed."

Mel stepped inside and walked straight to the sitting room averting her stare. Seeing Gary half naked had aroused feelings she'd never had before.

Gary came back to the sitting room dressed. "Did you have a good sleep?" He went on buttoning up his shirt. "Josia tells me you have named the twin filly, Peanut."

"It's temporary. I'll change it if she lives." Mel stood awkwardly next to him.

"Coffee?"

"No thanks, I've just had some. What time are you leaving?"

Gary glanced at his watch. "In an hour. Is that good for you?"

"Yup. I'll meet you at the stables."

WHITE JEWEL WAS the favourite for the main race today. It was her fifth race. Cameo, Dream Big and Popthequestion were running their maiden race. The course in Pietermaritzburg looked as immaculate as ever. Standing together in the grandstand, Mel and Gary hoped the two-year-olds would do well in their first outing.

Popthequestion galloped into a stunning first place, ridden by John McIntosh, a junior jockey who'd just started riding for the stud. Mel leapt into Gary's arms and joked, "aren't you glad I kept her." Cameo followed in second place and Dream Big ran fifth.

Still pressed against Gary's chest she looked up at him. "I might sell Dream Big. I don't think she's going to amount to anything, what do you think?"

"I think you are right, and I think you should stay just where you are," Mel's face reddened.

Mel fidgeted with anticipation when White Jewel pranced around the collecting ring, led by Siyanda, dressed in white overalls with Chanting Clover embroidered across his back in emerald green.

Down at the starting stalls Mel saw through her binoculars that she refused to load. "Oh, go in," she moaned. Still looking through her binoculars, she said to Gary, "that mare has a sense of humour. Just watch, in a few minutes, she'll stop and walk in. If she could talk, she'd say, 'What's all the fuss? Let me do it in my time.'"

Seconds later she did exactly as Mel had said. Gary grinned. "You know that mare well."

The trainers' balcony had the best view of the horses as they turned and galloped up the steep bank to the five hundred metre run-in to the finish. Although Jeremy was another newbie to the stud, he rode the difficult mare showing impeccable style and talent. Mel could see White Jewel was enjoying her race and that mattered to her. The mare galloped over the line a whopping four lengths ahead of the horse behind her and the grandstand erupted with cheers.

Mel and Gary raced down to meet them coming off the track.

"What a delightful win." Ivan said, standing behind Mel.

Mel spun around. "Aah. Hi Dad, you made it."

"Congratulations." He kissed her cheek and greeted Siyanda who was walking beside White Jewel, holding the rein, smiling proudly.

"Well done, Jeremy. What a race." Mel took hold of the other rein and patted the mare's sweat drenched neck. They led her to the winner's enclosure while camera's flashed and reporters asked Mel questions about the mare's future.

"You little beauty," Gary patted White Jewel. "Superbly ridden." He congratulated Jeremy.

"With all her idiotic prancing at the gates, she gave me a superb ride. Did you see how the little cow pulled away from me as we got to the top of the hill. She was blowing. I thought she'd lose it but there was no stopping her." Jeremy shouted happily above the loud applause that surrounded them.

Siyanda led White Jewel to the paddock for post-race inspection. While they stood waiting for the vets, an announcement was made over the intercom about the arrival of twins at Chanting Clover Stud.

Mel looked at Gary. "How did that news get out so quickly?" Then they heard the oohing and aahing from ladies close by which triggered Mel's emotions and she couldn't hold back the tears. A cameraman close by captured her tears and the photo made the front page in The Mercury Sunday newspaper. The caption read. 'South Africa's racing pin-up girl in tears over her horse's win."

When Gary saw the newspaper, he said, "And there certainly isn't another owner, trainer, breeder in this country who is as beautiful."

Chapter Twenty-Two

THE READY-TO-RUN BARN buzzed with activity while the two-year-olds were being prepared for the sales at Gosforth Park near Johannesburg. Patric enjoyed the introduction to titivating young, spritely Thoroughbreds. A far cry from grooming sheep for the show ring, he'd told Mel with a grin.

In all the years Mel had refused to attend the sales. It broke her heart, and though it wasn't going to change, Gary insisted she attend with him.

Standing at Dream Big's stable door, she uttered sadly, "I feel nauseous. Gran said I mustn't get emotionally attached, but I can't help it. You guys handle it so much better."

"I think we just hide it better." Gary said honestly. "I hate seeing them go too. I know how hard it is for you have so much to do with them from birth. Just remember your Gran's words."

"I will, but it doesn't make it easier. The most precious little creature grows into a beautiful, glistening two-year-old, then we flog it." She managed a small, cynical sounding laugh. "This business has so many emotional highs and lows, doesn't it?"

"That's for sure." They moved away from the stables and glanced through the catalogue. A trainer Gary knew from his days of training in Johannesburg came up and greeted him. While they chatted Mel's mind wandered to her secret. A place it had been for the last few weeks. She planned to fill the empty stallion stable. If they did well today, she could add another stallion to Chanting Clover asset list. She'd not disclosed her thoughts to Gary, or anyone else. She'd inherited a healthy sum from her mother, but imported, top rated Thoroughbred stallions didn't come cheap.

The minutes ticked by to the start of the auction. Anticipation grew. Buyers and sellers took their seats. Grooms looked as polished as their horses as they waited. A hum fell over the seating as buyers browsed their catalogues, making notes and discussing blood lines.

Mel and Gary took their seats mid-way up the circular grandstand and a few minutes later the auctioneer welcomed everyone. They were seated directly opposite the entrance. Mel noticed Lot No 2 enter the corridor and absent-mindedly wondered where Lot No1 had got to.

The horses carried their numbers on a white disc attached to the browband. The gates to the arena opened and the auctioneer announced the changes as Lot No 2 darted in, startled by the lighting and strange sounds. The filly kicked up her heels, snorted loudly, then stood and looked about. She suddenly jumped forward. The groom lost his footing in the deep pine shavings, though he was quick to rebalance. Bidding gathered momentum and the gavel sounded at seventeen thousand Rand.

Mel snuggled close to Gary. "That's a steel. I hope ours do better."

Ours, he thought sounded rather nice. The next horse, Lot No 1. A red bay colt who oozed presence. Melonie was tempted. She dug her elbow gently into Gary's side. He shook his head.

Lot No 5, Chanting Clover's Pretty Ruby darted in, her number flashing near her eye. Mel's heart swelled. She whispered, "bonuses for all our grooms, the turn-out is magnificent." They listened to the rising bids. Pretty Ruby sold for two hundred and ninety-two thousand Rand. Her sire was Wind Powers' sire.

"Wow, I didn't expect that price for her." Mel said, her eyes wide and her catalogue over her mouth.

"Are you okay? You're not going to burst into tears." He mocked, affectionately poking her side.

The other seven Chanting Clover horses also sold for top prices. While everyone stood to leave, Mel remained seated. Gary patted her leg. "Come on, let's go and celebrate." He stood and stretched. Mel stood too and rubbed her numbed bottom. The concrete seating was cold.

"Next time we bring cushions."

"Will there be a next time for you?" Gary asked, opened the car door, and drove to the hotel. Mel had booked two separate rooms for them. They dumped their overnight bags and met in the lounge near the bar.

When Gary walked over with their drinks, and sat beside her, Mel disclosed she had something to tell Gary.

"Wonderful, do tell."

"Okay, here goes. We did incredibly well in the last Durban July, we even created history with winners in almost every race." She took a sip of her drink. "White Jewel and the babies did us proud at Scottsville, and the prices we got today were way more than I expected. I've now accumulated enough money to fill the empty stallion stable."

"Oh, cheers to that." Gary's face lit up. "We need new blood. Eldorado is at the end of his productive life."

"Yeah, poor boy. Viewing his semen under the microscope there's very little active sperm. I hope Spindle takes. She'll give us a lovely riding horse...."

"Stop! Stop. Did you say she'll give *us*, a lovely riding horse?"

"Yes, I did." She ignored Gary's amazed expression. "Eldorado covered the phantom, (a man-made 'mare' used for semen collection) so we've plenty of frozen straws belonging to him. He's so popular with the dressage fraternity because of his perfect conformation." Gary's mouth opened slightly, staring at her, lost for words.

"Melonie Johns, stop ignoring me. You've just confirmed what you know I've always wanted to hear. I know it's not the right place, nor the right time, but I'll make it up to you. Will you marry me?"

"Oh my God. Yes!" Mel shrieked. The patrons in the bar and lounge turned, smiling from the infectious tone of her voice.

Gary pushed his chair out, went to her and kissed her longingly, then whispered, "I'm the luckiest man in the world." Then he shouted, "she's just said YES!"

Everyone clapped. Those who knew them from the sales earlier came across and congratulated them.

***

Chanting Clover had been hot news recently. Peanut kept her name and romped her way into the country's heart with adorable photos of her in numerous racing magazine and newspapers across the country. *The miracle twin who survived against all odds.*

Then the announcement of Gary and Mel's engagement, though they only shared their happy news with Hector and Ivan for now and when they did, he asked, "where's your ring?"

"Gary's planning a surprise and a second proposal." She laughed with such joy. Ivan felt choked with emotion, and the stallion news was no longer a secret.

When they told Kagiso, he jumped around clapping his hands like a child who's just received a long-awaited gift. Then he chanted something in his native tongue and finally sang, "At last. At last."

A WEEK later Gary and Mel set off to a stud farm in the Karoo to view Bold Warrior. After all the photographs and pedigrees, they'd looked through, Bold Warrior was Gary's first choice. Mel approved and agreed to look at him first.

A top-class Irish bred horse. 3-time Group One race winner in Ireland. He stood 16.3hands in height and was noted not only for his near perfect conformation but his outstanding temperament, and he was so dark bay, he shone black. Gary's favourite colour.

They had a long drive from Chanting Clover to the east of Graaf Reinet in the Karoo. When they arrived, Bold Warrior was prancing around in a small paddock shaded by a cluster of Weeping Willow trees. The stud owner, Mr Kruger, rushed out to meet them and guided them to the paddock.

"Far more captivating in real life than in the photographs." Mel turned to Gary who stood assessing his paces as the stallion pranced around. He'd been vetted and he'd passed. A vital precaution when purchasing a horse going for a hefty sum of money, quite apart from providing peace of mind that the horse is 'clean.' The owner also produced certification that Bold Warrior had been Dourine tested. A venereal disease that can be fatal. Mel watched Gary. She could see he'd fallen for this magnificent stallion. She decided to play a prank on him. Her naughty humour surfacing once more.

"Sorry, Gary. He doesn't do it for me. He's nice, but no!"

Gutted, Gary's frame withered with disappointment. Somehow, she managed to keep a straight face until she drew her cheque book from her handbag and giggled. "You little cow," he poked her side. "You're buying him, aren't you?"

"Of course, I am. I wish you could've seen your face." She chuckled as she moved to a table under the shade of one of the Weeping Willow trees and wrote out the cheque.

"This boy is a fabulous investment. He ticks all the boxes. I'm not passing him up."

"Does that mean you are not going to see Master Vision?"

With a grin, she shook her head. "No, I'm going to see him in a few days. I've booked a flight to George. The owners said they're happy to collect me from the airport. I'll stay with them for the night and fly back the next day."

"Goodness, my darling, you don't do things in small measures."

"Nope." She had enough money to buy both stallions if Master Vision passed all her rigid requirements.

Two days later Mel flew to the Cape to view Master Vision. In photographs Mel preferred him to Bold Warrior. Also, a 3-time, Group One winner, but born and raced in the US. He stood at stud in Plettenburg Bay and as promised they collected Mel at the airport.

Mr. and Mrs. Davidson guided Mel across the stable yard to a paddock on the other side of the stables. Mel took one look at Master Vision. A dark chocolate chestnut with four white stockings. He oozed quality. Mel had to have him. She paid for him while she had breakfast with the owners and on the journey to the airport, they discussed how Mel wanted him transported.

She flew home euphoric. She found it hard to believe what she'd just done. Gary waited in arrivals, eager to hear about the horse.

"Gary," she shouted. She'd seen him before he'd seen her. He spun around at the sound of her voice, walked to her, picked her up in his arms and kissed her.

"So, what's the verdict? Any regrets on buying my favourite?" He asked, still holding her in his arms.

She nuzzled her nose against his and kissed him again. "I bought him!"

"What? Did you really?" He put her down. "What's he like?"

"I'm not telling you, he's a surprise. The only thing I can tell you - he's gorgeous. Way better than the pictures of him."

"C'm on, don't keep me in suspense and how the hell can you afford two imported stallions?"

They stood looking at each other, grinning. "Well Mum left me quite a large sum of money and I've wobbled our cash flow; it's not going to flow for a few months." She revealed with mischief sounding in her voice. "The business can foot the bill for their stables and paddock post and rail fencing."

"You're an endless source of surprises, but let's get home."

"I love surprises, especially this sort. We'll need to get on with building their new stables from tomorrow. We have bricks, sand, and cement, don't we? I've delayed their delivery until their new stables and paddocks are done."

TWO WEEKS later the stallion's new homes were complete. "I'm still in shock," Gary said standing at the first paddock. "These two special purpose-built stallion paddocks and stables went up so quickly. The builders were great, and this position couldn't be more perfect." They walked together to Bold Warriors new stable and stood looking at the view of the pastures and the hills beyond. The post and rail fencing had just been painted white, in stark contrast to the surrounds.

"It's a perfect, tranquil environment for the stallions. The paddocks are well shaded by those lovely grey Poplar trees, and they have enough space to exercise themselves."

"According to Jim, the driver, he'll collect Bold Warrior the day after tomorrow. He's also on a scheduled trip to the Cape two days later. On his return he'll pick up Master Vision. It's hard to comprehend. Gran is probably reeling in shock right now."

Chapter Twenty-Three

The advice Mel sought now, she couldn't get from her beloved father, even though he'd always been her role model and guide. She needed to be alone in the presence of her four-legged soul mate. For the past few weeks, she'd been wanting to sit with him, but other things had got in the way. It was just after five when she slipped into Tropical Sun's stable unnoticed.

She whispered to him and leaned against the stable wall. The soft murmur of her breath mingled with the gentle rustle of straw beneath her feet. He nickered in response, as he always did, which spoke volumes in its quiet reassurance. It was a dance they had performed countless times, a silent dialogue of trust and understanding.

The lighting outside had just come on. The only sounds were horses sneezing, pulling at hay nets, some sighing deeply, others sneezing or nickering to each other. A symphony of sound Mel loved. Peaceful, soulful music that could never be replicated for every tone and note was different, on every single night.

Mel sank into the comforting embrace of the straw bedding. She drew her knees up to her chest, seeking solace in the presence of her horse's breath. Tropical Sun, ever attuned to her emotions, nuzzled her tenderly, a silent invitation into his world of peace and understanding.

In the presence of her beloved horse, she'd try and find the answers to her pressing dilemma - her fear of intimacy.

Closing her eyes, she surrendered to the stillness, letting go the weight of her worries, allowing herself to be enveloped by the serenity of the moment. With each inhale she drew in calmness, exhaling tension and doubt until her mind became as clear as the sky above.

And then, in the sacred space of quiet communion, she felt it – a shift of air, a subtle change in the energy around her. It was as if Tropical Sun was speaking to her with his very presence, guiding her thoughts and emotions with the gentle touch of his spirit.

With a soft sigh, she leaned into his warmth, feeling the brush of his whiskers against her skin like a gentle caress. In that moment, surrounded by the heartbeat of the stable and the comforting presence of her horse, she knew she wasn't alone. In moments like these, everything in her world changed. Transported from the humdrum of the present life to another world, a different dimension. Peaceful and trauma free. In a soft whisper, she asked the burning question of how she'd cope with intimacy.

She felt his soft velvety nose nuzzle her neck. She turned her head and pressed her lips into the hair, sharing with him her most hidden fears. Fears she'd never shared with anyone. After several minutes he put his nose on top of her head and jostled with her hair. In a trancelike state, deep within her psyche, the answers began to filter into her conscience. Eventually she opened her eyes and stretched her arms out in front of her. Tropical Sun still stood beside her, his head dropped toward the ground and his eyes dreamy. As Mel stood, he began yawning. She felt relaxed and confident she'd cope now. His breathing was slow and rhythmical now. She leaned in close and kissed his cheek, then he went back to munching on his hay.

THE SUN HAD DROPPED below the horizon. The skies were lit with heavenly streaks of gold and white against a brilliant cerise backdrop with streaks of cloud drifting across the space. Not dark yet, but she could hear an assortment of birds flying into the trees to roost, frogs croaking in the dam, and crickets in conversation close by as she walked

WINDS OF CHANGE

from the stables to Gary's cottage and opened the front door. Poking her head inside, she called out.

"Oh, what a lovely surprise." He noted her sombre mood. "Is something the matter?"

"No, there isn't. Have you got any of my favourite wine?"

"Of course. I keep crates of it." A gentle affection rose on Gary's face, and he hugged her. Stepping away, he felt the change in her. "My precious, turn that frown upside down, it doesn't suit you like that." She focussed on his eyes, and slowly her brow relaxed. A mellow smile tilted one side of her mouth, but her eyes still reflected the anxiety within. "What's troubling you, sweetheart?"

"You're too receptive to my mood. Get the wine and I'll tell you why I'm here."

Gary quickly left. He returned moments later carrying a tray with her favourite wine in an ice bucket and two glasses. "You look so comfortable there, spread across the sofa."

Mel shifted over to make space for him. He poured the wine, popped a block of ice into each glass and said, "Cheers to this unexpected visit."

Mel lifted her glass to his. She wanted to spit out her fear of sex and crucify all resistance to Gary's affections before her new-found confidence melted. She sat more upright, turned to face him, and took a deep breath. "Now don't laugh. I've been chatting to my precious four-legged soul mate for almost an hour. It's so peaceful at the stables when all the staff have gone, the horses have fed, and they munch on their hay. I left Sunny's stable thinking I should go there at the same time more often. It's so soothing listening to the sounds of happy horses. And Sunny gave me some answers."

"Oh really! Answers to how mad you are for buying two stallions." He mocked playfully.

"No. Answers about you. About us." Now she had his full attention.

"Aah hah. That sounds ominous." Gary dropped his head to one side.

"Let's sit on the veranda and watch the last of the sunset, then you won't see me blush." She put both her hands over her cheeks. "And I'll be cooled by the evening breezes when it gets even more embarrassing, and I'm hit by hot flushes from too much wine and difficult words."

Mel sensed Gary realised her humour and flippancy were a guise to cover the difficulties she was experiencing at expressing her inner self.

"The sounds of the night are harmonising with your breathing, my precious. I'm listening. Let it all out. Tell me what Sunny said." They sat together on the veranda couch.

Tears rolled down her cheeks suddenly. It wasn't the way she intended this conversation to start.

Gary sipped his wine and waited patiently, holding her hand.

Mel wiped her tears, gazed at the evening sky, and curled her legs underneath her. "I always wanted to move into this cottage after my parents and I had been here a few months." She was glad her voice didn't tremble from her cry.

"There's nothing stopping you from doing that now." He smiled, cupped her face in his hands, kissed her and wiped away another tear. "I'm ready to hear the answers from your divine horse."

"I know you think talking to horses is all a bit woo woo stuff." She looked away, feeling the tension return in her neck.

Gary held both her hands in his. Her head turned back to face him. "On the contrary my beautiful fiancé, I connect with them too."

His willingness to believe she had answers from a spiritual source helped her delicate situation. She'd promised herself to give in to intimacy, tonight. It wouldn't be terrifying with Gary, she knew that.

In that moment she looked so vulnerable, he squeezed her hands. "Sunny's answers filtered in as I sat listening. In the past, the answers have never been wrong. The answers come from the soul, gifted by spirit, so they must be right, hey?" She forced exaggerated cheer into her tone, then took a sip of wine.

Mel's hands fidgeted between his, then she held one of his tight, and squeezed. There was no denying she was nervous. She felt the stain of a flush rush up her neck and smear her face. He wouldn't see it in this light, so she continued. "After the quietness with my wonderful boy, I knew I had to come to you. It's where I belong. Dad said we should be living together in the big house, and he'll move in here, but you know my fears, and it's those I've come here to expel."

He surrounded her with his strong arms and kissed the top of her head. "Sweetheart, it's getting cool out here. Let's move inside."

Curled on the sofa in the sitting room, Mel gazed at the sky through the open windows. Someone had tossed a million diamonds across the heavens, and they twinkled at her. She'd not noticed so many before, and suddenly she felt the presence of her mother.

Gary sat beside her, and she stared into his eyes, "I'm so in love with you. I'm sorry for denying the intimacy which should've followed when you asked me to marry you, I'm just so terrified." As the last word left her lips, her fears intensified and she sobbed, falling into Gary's arms.

This time he scooped her up, carried her to his room and carefully laid her on the bed. "Tonight, my love, is on your terms. I've never experienced anything so fragile in my life."

The lamp beside the bed created a warm glow. He'd collected their wine glasses. He carried them through to the bedroom. Mel noticed a twinkle in his glassy blue eyes, the dimples on his cheeks, deeper and sexier with a rosy glow from the wine. "You must be the most handsome, most sensitive man in the country. I cannot think of anyone else I'd want to share my life with, and I don't think I could've overcome my fears with anyone more understanding." Mel sat up and reached for her wine. "I'll have to remember to thank Hector for employing you." She put the glass down and laid her head back on the pillow, forcing herself to relax.

"Are you aware of how exquisitely beautiful you are?" Gary ran his fingers through her auburn locks and noticed her emerald eyes danced like a nervous gazelle.

"Oh, come on. I'm just a horse-loving, farm gal who's feeling helpless, exposed, vulnerable and terrified right now." Which she was, but she held firm to her promise to Gary.

"I'm sure you are, and you're incredibly brave. Such humble grace makes you even more beautiful." He leaned over her. Fear rippled through her insides. *Keep calm. Inhale.*

Gary must've sensed her fear because he stood and left the room. When he came back, he carried two glasses of liqueur. "To help you relax. I remember it worked before."

Glad for the distraction. "Yum, that looks and smells rather good." She held the little glass and sniffed.

"Chocolate, peppermint liqueur to warm you up." He kissed her.

"Actually, I need cooling down." She sipped, savouring the sweet, throat-warming peppermint flavour.

"I don't want you to cool down." He sat beside her.

When she'd left the stables, Mel promised herself to trust the process. She hoped the alcohol would ease the progression, not douse the fire. She wondered if tonight she'd become wholly *woman* again. Could her handsome husband-to-be give back all she'd lost?

Gary sipped his liqueur. "From the day I was interviewed by you and Hector, I was yours in more ways than you could ever imagine."

"Really? But you've brought lady friends here." She felt a jolt from her honest admission.

"Yes, I have but none of them come close to the way I've always felt about you."

Mel knew how much he loved her. He'd waited patiently for well over a year. She hung her head, the thought of making love panicked her even though she'd thought many times of making passionate love with him. The thought of their lovemaking thrilled her, but only in her imagination. Now she faced the difficult reality.

Gary noticed the fear flicker in her eyes again. "My angel, we'll work this out together. Just let me lie close to you and we can talk about what frightens you." He moved onto the bed and lay beside her.

Snuggled close together, he covered her mouth with his, kissing her.

Melonie responded warmly.

"Let's make this union so memorable you'll never remember the past." Gary's tender words caused more tears, she couldn't stop.

"My body is telling me how much I want you. But when I close my eyes, I see *him*, then all I want to do is scream and run and run and run, like the night of my escape. Oh God, hold me tighter. I'm so scared I'll never get over it. Scared I'll always remember. Remember how he raped me." With her jaw clenched she tried to force the memories away.

"My precious I'm going to take away those images for ever." They lay still and silent in each other's arms. "Sweetheart, there's no rush." He kissed her again, then, moved his torso over hers.

Feeling the weight of his body on hers, she stiffened and squeezed her eyes shut, telling herself to be calm. "Relax, sweetheart," he said tenderly. When he spoke, she felt her body release the tension. She knew she was safe, then she felt Gary's desire and froze rigid.

"It's okay sweetie." He stroked her hair and she whimpered. The moment felt so fragile, so poignant, so precious and she didn't want anything to break it apart. He lifted his upper body off her and held her against him until her trembling eased.

Brushing hair away from her face so she could see him clearly, she reached for him. This time she kissed him with a hunger she'd never experienced. Then she stopped. "Gary." She said his name with conviction. "I need you to make love to me, and we need to do it tonight or I may never overcome this horrid fear and that'll ruin our future together, and I can't allow that. I've dreamt of this moment. And.... and you know.... how long.... it's taken me to summon the courage." Her words and lips and body shook.

"No woman should ever have to experience such a violation, but I'm going to make this as special, and as beautiful as I can." He slowly ran his hands inside her shirt and unclipped her bra. Then undid the clasp of her jodhpurs and pulled them off.

Mel shivered with such intensity, the bed shivered too.

"You're doing well, my precious," he looked into her eyes. She saw only tenderness, compassion, and love. He unbuttoned her blouse, slid it off and tossed it and her bra onto the chair.

"Oh Gary, Gary, I'm not sure. Not sure I can do this." She felt exposed, drew up her legs up and covered her breasts with her hands. "Let me get under the covers."

He lifted the bedclothes and she slid under. "You can, my angel. You can do it. I'll make it beautiful." His encouraging and loving tone soothed her, even though she felt she was standing on the edge of a precipice. He shed his own clothing, slid under the covers next to her, gently rans his fingers through her hair and caressed her face. "Don't close your eyes, keeping looking at me. Enjoy the feeling of our bare bodies moulding together and our skin becoming one."

Though she nodded and looked at him with wide eyes at the

thought, she felt grateful to the way Gary was helping her and she loved him even more for his considerate approach.

"Don't close your eyes, sweetheart. Nothing must haunt you now."

She relaxed a little, cuddled closer, savouring the scent of his chest and the hair tickling her cheek.

She played with the hair on his chest. "You're so patient, it must be so difficult for you, my love." She ran her finger over the contour of his chin, then pulled him closer.

He lifted himself on top of her.

Her fingers explored the lines of the muscles on his back. "Your body is so strong and toned," she whispered as her body accepted his weight on her.

"You're doing well, my angel," he whispered.

"Nothing is too difficult for me when I'm with you." Her body softened but she kept her legs tight together.

Very slowly he gently nuzzled her nipples.

He hardened.

Her body stiffened and she moaned with distress. How was she going to cope?

"I.... I..." She fought a fear so crippling it almost took her very breath.

He raised his torso.

"Look at me sweetheart." She opened her eyes. With him guiding her, she could do this. She could conquer the dread of the moment. She heard herself whimper and wondered if the sounds were coming from her violated soul. An indicator that her horrendous nightmare was about to end. He touched her opening.

"Shhhh, my lovely." He pushed himself a little deeper into her.

She gasped. Her body tensed, too terrified to move, even breath.

He held still and smiled. His smile conveyed so much love she knew this was the beginning of the ritual to cleanse away the evil of her horrific experience of the past. As if to confirm her thoughts, he kissed her lips, then her nose, then her forehead. Tender butterfly kisses all over her face which made her smile back at him. She wanted to speak, to tell him to take the sorrowful look off his face while he still held his torso off her. She wanted to tell him how much she loved him and his patience, but he covered her lips with his once more and slowly she felt her body mould closer to his and gently nudge deeper.

Eventually she arched instinctively. She let out a little sigh as he slid in fully. United in love and passion, she quietly rejoiced for there was no pain. Suddenly the fear had melted away. He felt divine. The moment, as she imagined, was real now. She kept her eyes open, fixed on Gary. The man she loved and adored. In slow, gentle rhythms they danced to the waves of passion.

At the crest of the wave, he stopped and smiled. "Are you comfortable, my lovely?"

So taken by everything that she felt, she couldn't answer instead she gyrated her hips gently as he held himself on one arm and pushed tear-stuck strands of hair from her face and he responded with another gentle thrust while she kept her eyes fixed on his. The stormy seas of passion gathered momentum. Mel whimpered through tears of joy as the waves crashed on the edges of heaven.

She felt sure the demons were drowned forever.

Lying spent and exhausted in each other's arms, the light of the moon blazed through the open window. Mel whispered, "I feel whole again. Thank you, my darling." Rebirthed by the gentleness of her saviour.

"Are you sure you're okay, my beautiful?"

"I love you, my precious husband. Yes. Yesss." She hugged him tightly. She never wanted to let him go. "I never thought this would be possible. You were so gentle and considerate."

"Do you know what you've done for me?" he asked softly.

"No," she whispered.

"I'd never be able to find the right words, but I lived your nightmare and your terror, and the moment of your cleansing. The most astonishing experience." They kissed with a passion Mel would never forget.

When she finally let him stop kissing her, he laid his index finger across her lips. "I guess it's what we've done for each other, my gorgeous, beautiful wife to-be." He pulled her to him.

Mel fell asleep, their bodies entwined, her terror finally laid to rest.

· · ·

Gary and Mel never attended the early morning gallops. Instead, they wandered hand in hand to the main house where they found Ivan sitting at the dining room table reading the Farmers Weekly magazine, sipping on a cup of coffee, waiting for breakfast.

Seeing the expression of serenity on his daughter's face, he knew.

"Morning Dad," she greeted, still holding Gary's hand. "We've decided to take you up on your suggestion and move in here. You can have the cottage." She beamed as Gary pulled a chair out for her, and she sat down.

"Morning Ivan," Gary greeted his soon-to-be father-in-law. "We're going to make our engagement official this weekend."

"Finally. What great news."

"Dad, can we have a little gathering here on Saturday night? A few friends and Hector, of course."

"I'd be delighted. You two were made for each other." Suddenly a sad expression rose on his face. "Such a pity Mum isn't here to celebrate with us."

"She is, Dad. She's here in spirit and always will be."

Ivan smiled. Though he liked that thought, he yearned for her physical presence. "She shouldn't have died so young. Taken from us far too soon, dying from a broken heart. Not a heart attack."

Seeing the sadness on dad's face, made Mel want to cry, but she was so happy she couldn't shed a tear, even in sympathy for him, and the loss of her mother.

"So, when do you want to move in here?" He asked, the smile had returned.

"After our little engagement party, if that's okay with you, Dad" Mel said, looking to Gary for confirmation.

"Perfect. Suits me. Fill this bloody great mansion with grandchildren to keep me young." Ivan laughed.

"Not quite yet, Dad. But yeah, this massive house needs filling, doesn't it." She looked at Gary and smiled.

In all the years Gary had been at Chanting Clover, he'd never been through every room in this house, which in a few days would be his home.

Ivan tootled off after breakfast, leaving the two of them to tour the house.

"I'll follow you." Gary said. From the dining room, Mel led the way into the kitchen. He'd been in there, but she was sure he hadn't seen the size of the walk-in pantry and scullery.

"Morning Angelina. Mr Gary and I are going to get married soon and he's moving in here next week. Mr Ivan is moving into the cottage." Angelina's hands flew to her mouth, and she danced about the kitchen expressing her excitement. She'd been the family cook for years and very much part of the family.

"I'll still cook for Mr Ivan," she said, wiping her hands on her apron. Melonie smiled, then showed Gary the walk-in pantry, the scullery, and the laundry. From the kitchen she crossed through the courtyard and walked around the house and up the steps to the veranda. From the veranda she led the way to the sitting room, then to the formal sitting room, through a side door into the grand hall. Gary knew where the dining room was, so she led the way down the passage passing a guest toilet off the grand hall and four guest bedrooms and a guest bathroom. Mel lived in the guestroom with the bathroom ensuite. The master bedroom was at the end of the passage.

"Wow," Gary said as they walked in and stood looking out the bay windows.

"It's a lovely big room isn't it but needs modernising." Iris's four poster bed was still in situ and didn't appeal to Mel. Off the master bedroom was a dressing room and bathroom. From there they popped into the other four bedrooms, one of which also had an ensuite bathroom.

"No wonder your dad doesn't want to rattle around in here on his own. This house is bigger than I thought."

Mel felt a surge of excitement thinking about the master bedroom and its much needed upgrade. Back in the hall she launched herself into Gary's arms and wrapped her legs around his waist.

"I thought the horses were the best thing that ever happened to me and my best therapists, but you are all that rolled into one."

Chapter Twenty-Four

AT BRIGADE HEADQUARTERS IN HARARE, commissioned officers sat through an address from President Mugabe who outlined the details of increasing land reform.

"It's time, Comrades, to remove *all* white farmers from their land. Use our freedom fighters and use force. As we did in our fight for freedom, increase fear. This government offers no land compensation, just get rid of them, by whatever means."

His speech was followed by loud applause. Solomon was delighted. Once the President left, he and fellow officers moved to the officer's mess to celebrate and discuss future operations.

Solomon had been one of the first to have selected a white owned farm. After understanding he couldn't own Blue Winds, he took over a productive tobacco farm in Beatrice. He rubbed his sweaty brow, remembering the day his troops had forcibly expropriated the farm. Except now there was no tobacco being produced and he employed one man to oversee it. Maybe it was the right time to resurrect it, he thought. His mind wandered back and forth in between conversation and planning with fellow officers.

His dearest friend, Johnny Walker Blue Label moved the conversation toward twisted vengeance and the name Melonie Johns was once again on his lips.

"My informant tells me she is to marry her racehorse trainer, Gary Whitaker. I've left her alive too long. It's time to take the necessary action."

One of his major's spoke. "I have friends in Soweto, the sprawling township near Johannesburg who could do the job for you, Sir. They are trained assassins."

"Thank you, Major. I'll keep that in mind, but I want to make her sweat a bit longer. I want her to feel the fear I felt when the Hunters bombed our camp. It'll make her jittery and vulnerable."

"I like that thought." The major said. "And we can look forward to dishing out punishment to many white farmers in the near future."

Solomon thought back to the day he took possession of his Beatrice farm.

"The white farmer who owned my farm had been a leading Rhodesia Front supporter. Ian Smith had been his man." Solomon swallowed a gulp of whiskey. "The staff, much like the people Johns had employed, supported him loyally and provided them with housing, fed them and offered free schooling for their children. Medical care and family planning education for their wives, had also been provided." Solomon sneered. "I hate those who support colonial ideology. They need to be taught a lesson."

"Here, here," the group of officers shouted.

"On that day my feral freedom fighters taught them who is the boss and beat them, which we'll be ordering more of."

Suddenly the room filled with raucous, drunken laughter and the group of inebriated officers wanted to know more, so Solomon continued his story.

"The white woman was standing on the front veranda, screaming. Her two small children clutched her legs, wide-eyed and terrified as one of my men beat her husband. The coward was on the ground, curled into the foetal position trying to protect his head." He cackled. "My man went on striking at him with a heavy stick. Blood poured from his wounds with every strike until he lost consciousness."

Melonie was in his mind suddenly. "On a different occasion, I remember hitting that bitch Melonie and knocking her out. She fought like a crazed animal after I'd grabbed her from the farmhouse. I'd wanted to kill her when she visited Harare, but she caught me off guard and got away." His mouth curled with the anger and resentment the memory brought.

He looked about. He had the officer's attention and he reverted to the day he took possession of his farm. The excessive amount of alcohol made his mind wander all over the place. "The farmer's wife ran down the steps and knelt beside the body of her husband and begged me to ask my man to stop beating him. I looked down at her tear-soaked face and her pathetic sobbing children and revelled in my power. You know that feeling, eh? It's good."

It was a memory worth drinking to; he poured another whiskey.

"I stopped my man from killing the farmer. I told the woman she had four hours to get off my farm. My other veterans danced and chanted while they killed the family dogs. Their dying yelps mingled nicely with the sobs and screams coming from her and the children." His grin conveyed how much he'd enjoyed the sight and sounds of what his power yielded.

"By the following day most of the farm staff had absconded too. One man left a note for me, accusing me of all sorts of things, ending the message with, *'Because of you, all we have to look forward to in Zimbabwe, is starvation.'*

Solomon lifted his whiskey glass. "This is much better than the taste of Chibuku beer we drank when we were soldiers," he laughed, and his belly wobbled. "I love the obscene amount of money we're paid, don't you?" The officers agreed, and why wouldn't they? Disagreeing with their colonel could be dangerous.

Slurring through whiskey fumes, the men continued to share memories of their war days. Many of which Solomon hadn't heard before. Some were more horrific than his and a rage among senior officers erupted. So volatile that some of the junior officers excused themselves. They were frightened by Solomon and his senior officer's wrath.

"Tell us about your most frightening war experience, Colonel." A young major encouraged.

Solomon filled his glass for the eighth time. "Here's to our president. His government is paying for this beautiful whiskey." He raised his glass. "I like this very much," he spat whiskey infused spittle as he spoke.

"Scattered ...... everywhere......" His arm demonstrated the expanse, "were the charred remains of my...... comrades. Scorched beyond recognition. Not a blade of grass...... shrub or tree left untouched by the bombings and the fire." He paused, took a breath, licked the spittle from his lips and rubbed it off his chin. He shook his head. A macabre reminder of the camp where he'd done his training. The camp where he'd taken the Johns girl to, under orders from the camp commander. She'd killed his comrades and the more he thought of her the angrier he got, and *Johhny* was there to fuel the flames of hatred.

"When the smoke had settled, I found the grotesque, distorted remains of many dear comrades. I'm too ...... drunk to find words now, but revenge rose in my blood, like the rancid bubbles of brewed Chibuku. To this day, the smell of burning human flesh is embedded in my nostrils. She must pay." He said with an all-encompassing bitterness.

"Once we'd regrouped some of us went to Blue Winds farm to kill the family and massacre the workers, but they were gone. It took me a long time to find out where they were. Then I read in a newspaper, she was training racehorses, and I activated my contacts in South Africa. Then I learned of her itinerary when she arrived here in Harare sometime back. My mind is too hazy with whiskey to recall how long ago. I went to kill her." He rubbed his enormous protruding stomach. He kept his hand on the shelf at the top of his ribcage, like a pregnant woman. "But she was too quick for me, she got away."

By now, some of the officers had left. Filled with more venom than a thousand vipers, he vowed, in front of the remaining officers, he'd murder her soon.

"She's been left too long, but it's good." A short rope of saliva hung on either side of his mouth. "She'll not be expecting my next move, and it won't be aimed at her, my friends. We were trained well in the art of fear mongering, weren't we?"

The remaining officers nodded vigorously. Most of them were as drunk as Solomon. Powered by greed and revenge, being close to the master of tyranny himself, Robert Mugabe, Solomon would seek ways to disrupt Melonie's life, then end it, with the president's blessing.

Some of the remaining officer's said they remembered the day the camp burned, they were escapees, but hadn't gone back to look. They all agreed, revenge was Solomon's answer.

He stood and wove a few steps, then stopped. "The next time she'll not escape me. I have the means." He thought about the millions of US dollars he had fraudulently squirreled away into a Swiss bank account and smiled triumphantly. His driver rushed to him and guided him slowly to his waiting Mercedes and drove him back to his high security home.

Chapter Twenty-Five

After returning from the track, Gary and Mel did the early morning rounds hand in hand. Sparks of good chemistry bounced around them, even the horses appeared to feel the energy and reached their noses toward them and nickered their greeting.

"I *love* this. No more hiding my feelings for you. We two are one now." Gary kissed her. A lightness to his stride was obvious. "Before we go and join your dad for breakfast, I must give Tropical Sun a big hug and thank you."

Mel giggled and poked him in the ribs. They passed White Jewel's stable and glanced in. Thomas was busy brushing her down after a training gallop. They exchanged a greeting then opened Sunny's stable door and stepped inside together. Mel hugged him first and planted the mandatory kiss on his nose, then Gary put his arms around the horse's neck and whispered, 'Thank you. What a gift you've given me."

They wandered back to the main house. It was Saturday morning. After breakfast Mel and Angelina had a lot to do in preparation for the small gathering to celebrate the engagement.

"Ah, morning Gary. Morning sweetheart. Anything I can do to help today?" Ivan asked.

"Perhaps you can give Gary a hand. The stallions are arriving on

Monday. Angelina and I have everything else sorted. It's only eight of us." She turned to Gary, "shall we have drinks on the veranda then move to the dining room?"

"You decide, my angel, we've already got one surprise in store." He turned to look at Ivan and smiled. Ivan shrugged his shoulders, enjoying the happy, relaxed banter.

The day passed in a blur. When Mel next glanced at her watch, it was six. She'd spoken to Julie earlier and explained the plan, where to park and what to do, now it was time to jump into a shower and change. She ran down the passage to her bedroom and slammed the door happily.

Hector and Gary were the first to arrive at the house. They'd walked from their cottages nattering away about the stallion's pending arrival. Hector stopped on the path and held Gary's arm. "You still haven't put a ring on Mel's finger!"

"Tonight, Hector. The remarkable thing about Mel, she hasn't even asked if I've bought one. I think the arrival of the stallions are on her mind. But I quizzed her the night I proposed after the sales. I think I got what she'd love."

"I'll bet you did, son," Hector said, looking up at Gary. He'd always called Gary, son, "I cannot be happier for the two of you. It's a match made in heaven. Congratulations and all the very best."

EVERYONE WAS GATHERED, except Julie and Allan. Mel surreptitiously glanced at her watch. It was time. She left the veranda, taking the route through the house to the front door. Ivan looked at Gary, he asked with his hands, what was happening? Gary shrugged his shoulders, but he assumed the surprise couple had arrived.

Mel raced down the steps and hugged Julie. "Oh, this is just the most amazing timing." Then she hugged Allan. "Come in, come in. Leave your suitcases, I'll get the maid to pop down and grab them."

They followed Mel through the house and out onto the veranda. "Julie! Allan!" Ivan shouted and rushed to greet them. He'd not seen the couple since leaving Rhodesia. "OH! This is such a wonderful surprise. You're both looking so well."

"Aren't they?" Mel said. Everyone stood to greet the surprise couple. "First, let me introduce you to the man of my dreams. Gary, this is the amazing couple I've always spoken about."

Gary shook Allan's hand and gave Julie a warm, welcoming hug. "It's so nice to meet you, and such a lovely surprise that you can join us."

"I couldn't be happier for you both. We're down here on holiday. When we got to Durban, I called Mel for a chat and obviously wanted to arrange to see her and meet you. And here we are!" Julie said.

When everyone had been introduced Mel popped out to the kitchen. Angelina had everything ready and the little lass helping had already been to the car and popped Julie and Allan's cases in their room.

"Oooh, my goodness, that beef stroganoff smells good, Angelina. You're a marvel. Give us another forty-five minutes, then take everything through to the dining room, please." Angelina wiped her hands on her apron and took Mel's hands. "I'm happy for you, Missus Mel. Mr. Gary, he's a good man."

Mel hugged Angelina. She was so touched, she had to leave the kitchen before she burst into tears.

The veranda was lit by soft lighting. Everyone chatted happily and sipped their drinks. Dave and Sally, friends of Gary's who Mel had never met before were chatting to Allan and Julie. Not only a celebration of the engagement but a celebration of seeing special friends they rarely saw.

Hector stood up and tapped his glass with a pen. The gathering hushed. "Cheers." He raised his beer tankard. "Let's toast to this remarkable couple and wish them a long and happy life together."

"Here, here." Allan also stood. "All of us know the tragedy's Ivan and Mel have bravely faced, and for Mel to have found such a wonderful chap to spend the rest of her life with, makes Julie and I rest easy. We rescued her from the Monomatapa hotel after she'd been attacked, and we pray every day that she never experiences anything but joy in the future." Allan turned to face Mel. "And Mel, in this beautiful home, I'm sure you and Gary will fill it with happy, laughing children. From Julie and I, thank you for having us to celebrate with you."

Then Gary stood. "Thank you, Allan for your kind words. I'm

blessed to have the most beautiful woman in my life, and I have Ivan to thank. But I also want to express my grateful thanks to Hector who employed me here all those years ago. Ivan is moving into my cottage, and heaven knows what he and Hector will get up to living next door to each other." Everyone laughed. Then Gary looked at Mel. "I've dreamed of this moment for years," he chuckled, then looked back at the guests. "I want to tell you all an astonishing story about Mel. There was absolutely no hesitation when I asked her to marry me, which was a relief." A hum of laughter filled the space. "But do you know, not once since then has she asked about a ring. So tonight, in front of you all, I'd like to put a ring on her finger. Mel, come and join me."

Mel grinned, "I'd forgotten all about a ring." Everyone laughed as she stood beside Gary. He opened a little blue box and a magnificent, two-carat diamond cluster engagement ring shone. Mel gasped. The dazzle of diamonds caught in her green eyes, and they lit up. "We could have bought a third stallion with what you spent on that." She roared with laughter and was joined by everyone else. Her comment was so Melonie.

Gary took her hand and slid the ring on her finger. Mel splayed her fingers proudly for all to see, then they kissed passionately to loud applause.

"Phew," feeling giddy with happiness. "Gary said he was lucky, well let me tell you, he's got it all wrong. I'm the lucky one, aren't I, Dad?"

Ivan struggled to hold back the overwhelming emotion he felt. In that moment his thoughts were with Margaret.

After a delicious dinner, endless happy stories shared, and an abundance of laughter and good cheer, they all retired to bed.

The following day the celebrations continued with a tour of the stud and farm, finishing at the furthest point on the farm where they sat beneath a cluster of Natal Ash and White Stinkwood trees Iris had planted years ago, close to the ancient Lemonwood Tree, which grew in the shelter where two rolling hills met. They enjoyed a picnic lunch looking at the most spectacular view of the Drakensburg range of mountains in the distance. It had to be Mel's favourite spot on the farm.

***

The arrival of the stallions coincided with the move. Mel wasn't sure which excited her more and chuckled at the thought. It wasn't long after breakfast that Mel heard the vehicle in the distance and raced to the offloading area.

Anyone who could escape their duties for a moment gathered to watch Bold Warrior's arrival. Gary joined Mel, Ivan and Kagiso. A groom jumped out and unhitched the back ramp, lowered it, then eased the horse from the trailer. He backed out and stood tall and erect, ears pricked, nostrils flared. Mel stared, choked by the magnificence of the animal Gary had chosen. When he moved, his glossy black coat shimmered in the sunlight. Dark dapples rippled beneath his coat like a jaguar.

"Oh... my... God," Melonie exhaled. "He's more stunning than I remember."

"He is, isn't he. What a beauty! Let's hope he produces top progeny."

Kagiso, still shaking his head in awe, took hold of Bold Warriors lead and stood with the magnificent horse, allowing him to take in his new surroundings. A hush had befallen the spectators as if time stood still.

Kagiso took a step forward. "Isn't he beautiful, Kagiso. You look like you're about to burst with pride and pleasure." Gary said.

"I am, Mr. Gary. He is king, his majesty, Bold Warrior." Kagiso grinned. "He's the most beautiful stallion I've ever seen. He compares to the ones I handled in Ireland."

"He was bred in Ireland, Kagiso."

Kagiso laughed. "I know my stallions." Gary heard him chuckle as he led the horse to his brand-new paddock. *His* domain, where no other stallion had been before. It wasn't long before Patric ran down to join them, panting breathlessly. He couldn't miss this moment.

"In Zulu, the name *Kagiso* means peace," Mel said to Patric. Hector stood at the post and rail fence and watched.

Patric added his thoughts, "And it suits him. He's peaceful with the stallion, he's peaceful with the staff, he's peaceful at home. He's a wonderful man." Patric had learned so much from Kagiso. "He taught me that a quiet calm, with the right amount of firmness, earns respect and trust from powerful Thoroughbred stallions. When I watch him work with them, I can see they know he's boss and they happily accept his leadership. To anyone watching he apparently does nothing." Patric said in awe.

Mel stared at the horse for a few speechless moments as Kagiso led him to the gate. "He's certainly going to attract a whole host of ladies. What do you think, Hector?" Mel noticed Hector's legs were shaking. His legs weren't as strong as they used to be. "Are you okay?"

"Yes, I'm fine. Damned pins letting me down. He certainly is a magnificent beast. Great choice. I always get a lump in my throat when I see horses of this quality. Just can't help me self."

Kagiso led the stallion inside his new paddock. He snorted and demonstrated his impatience, pawing at the ground, desperate to stretch his legs. He'd been in the trailer for seven hours.

Kagiso released him. Tail up, he galloped across the paddock, turned, bucked, and farted, then trotted along the rails with his tail raised, displaying perfect cadence, then he stopped abruptly. Something caught his attention. He stood, head up, tail still raised, ears pointed.

"Where d'ya find this beauty, Gary?" Hector asked.

"It took some research. He's exactly what we wanted. Neither Mel nor I could decide which stallion was better, but she bought Master Vision, anyway."

Hector roared with laughter. "Iris will be turning in her grave. Well," he paused, thinking, "Perhaps not, perhaps she is waltzing around up there, rejoicing like we are. I can just picture her face if she'd laid eyes on this magnificent horse."

"I'm sure she would've approved," Mel said "We needed to improve the gene pool. Just wait till you see my boy."

"When's he arriving?"

"We're waiting confirmation. Either tomorrow or the following day."

Walking with Hector to his cottage was a slow walk. "Damn this old age, Gary. Really slows me down."

"You're doing bloody well, Hector. Don't give up on us yet." Hector had been more of a father to him than his own father, whom he rarely ever heard from.

"You're the best horsemen I've ever known. Your brain's like turning the pages of an encyclopaedia on horses. Your weakened legs are testament to successful years in the saddle."

"Thank you for those kind words." Hector dropped into his armchair. "When the next one arrives, I'll get Julia to push me down in that bloody thing." He pointed to a wheelchair in the corner of the room.

"Good idea," Gary said. "I'll let you know well before he arrives."

Hector looked up at Gary. "Can't get much better than Bold Warrior. Iris would be so proud of Mel and so happy for you both."

Chapter Twenty-Six

Master Vision was expected shortly. A flurry of activity happened as people dashed up to the offloading zone. Some to help, others just eager to see the new stallion.

Mel got there just as the driver switched off the engine. Gary had been waiting for a few minutes. "I still have to pinch myself and tell myself this is real." Mel said, out of breath from her run to the parking area.

"It feels that way for me too, and I haven't seen this boy yet." He put an arm around Mel.

"Where's Dad and Hector?"

"On their way. Julia is bringing Hector down in the wheelchair."

"Oh good."

The long ten berth vehicle pulled in and stopped. Jim, the driver swung the door open, jumped out the cab and walked over to where Gary and Mel. Gary shook his hand. Jim tipped his hat to Mel.

"Apologies, my hands are filthy," he said, wiping them on his jeans.

"Not to worry. How did the journey go?" Mel asked.

"Yeah, all good. Perfect horse, this 'un."

Jim lowered the central trailer ramp and spoke in Zulu to his assistant. Mel peered in as the groom untied the rope lead and turned Master Vision to walk down the ramp.

Melonie held Gary's arm as the groom walked the stallion down the ramp. A glistening, dark chocolate tail fell to the floor and dragged along the ramp. As the stallion felt the ground under one foot, he nickered loudly. His coat shone with sweat. He stopped and viewed his new abode, his nostril flared.

Gary groaned, watching Kagiso step forward and take the horse from Jim's groom. Noone spoke.

Master Vision stopped prancing. He sensed Kagiso's leadership as he looked into the animals' eyes while he stroked his nose and he instantly settled. They heard Kagiso whisper something in his native language.

Gary shook his head enviously and glanced at Mel. "Not only is this a huge surprise, but he's also magnificent, sweetheart. And watching Kagiso communicate with a strange horse on such a privileged and practiced level, never fails to inspire me."

"He's remarkable. I don't know what we'd do without Kagiso, but I'm glad you like Master Vision. What I like is they're so different. A worthwhile investment, don't you think?"

"Oh, for sure. Neither is better than the other. I think breeders will be queueing to have their mares covered by them, and important to expand the gene pool in the country."

Kagiso stood. Master Vision sniffed the air, picking up the wafting scent of mares in a distant paddock, then he dropped his head and snorted, ready to explore his new territory.

Keen to see the competition, Bold Warrior whinnied and raced up and down the post and rail fencing that divided the two horses' paddocks. Running between them was a two-metre-wide passage for tractor access between the two paddocks and ensured the stallions couldn't fight each other.

Sniffing the air and nickering with excitement he trotted along the fence. Every now and then Bold Warrior shook his head, and his mane caught the wind. He strutted down the fence like a courting cockerel showing off.

Not to be outdone, Master Vision raised his tail, shook his magnificent head, and snorted louder, jogging next to Kagiso. His hindquarters swung this way and that, showing off the beautiful long tail that flicked from side to side in rhythm with his stride.

Looking at the two stallions, appreciating the immense strength and prowess of both horses, Ivan exclaimed. "I don't know who's better."

"Seeing them together, I can honestly say I don't either. They're both so perfect, don't you think, my love?" Mel asked.

"They're both stunning, my angel." Gary hugged her. "I'm still in awe. There's nothing like a Thoroughbred stallion to get my blood racing."

Hector piped up from his chair, "I think Master Vision is my favourite." He winked at Mel.

"Aaw, thanks Hector." She put a hand on his shoulder. "But there's so much to love about them both."

Once inside the paddock, Kagiso closed the sturdy metal gate. Once he and Master Vision were facing the spectators he stood patiently waiting, making sure the horse stood still before he unclipped the lead.

Master Vision realised he'd been freed and took off. Like a bolt of lightning, he galloped down the side of the paddock next to Bold Warrior. Like two schoolboys trying to outdo each other, they bucked and cavorted, letting off explosions of gas and everyone chuckled. A moment of magical entertainment.

"What do you think, Kagiso?" Mel asked when he joined the group.

"Ma'am. These two stallions are the best. Thank you. I'm very happy." He performed his customary bow.

***

"Oh, what a mess, and the last thing I feel like is sorting it all out." Mel was feeling vile, but she had so many boxes to unpack. She hadn't been feeling well for a few weeks and to keep her mind occupied she spent her days re-organising her home and helping her dad with his. So much had happened in the past few months, she needed time to catch up with herself.

The re-decorating the master bedroom, and the renovation of the old bathroom had been completed. She loved the finished look. She and Gary had bought a hand-crafted Cape Yellow-wood, king-size bed to replace gran's antique four poster bed. Mel had chosen a fresh, botanical look for the theme of their bedroom and looking at it now, it did reflect the peacefulness of nature she'd wanted. Beside her dressing table, the portrait of Firelight hung. Plus, she'd supported local weavers and bought a huge handwoven rug in shades that complimented the soft furnishings. They'd been in their re-vamped bedroom for a week, and she loved it.

"The J&B Metropolitan Stakes are on our doorstep. Where does time go, and I'm still feeling horrid," she moaned to Gary, holding her stomach.

"Pop in and see the doctor, sweetheart." Gary rubbed her back gently.

"I'm not sick, I'm just so tired. Maybe I need a strong multi-vitamin to perk me up. Hopefully I'll feel great when we fly to Cape Town. It would be amazing if we have a few good wins, then our little country wedding and honeymoon will be paid for." Mel walked to the closet. "Seven horses going to Kenilworth for the prestigious race in Cape Town, hey?"

MEL FELT a little better when they landed in Cape Town and took a taxi to the hotel. Mel always booked The View, Boutique hotel close to the racecourse. She loved Cape Town. Once they'd unpacked, they took another taxi to the city centre and picked up their hire car. Cape Town had turned yellow. J&B Met yellow flags lined almost every major street in the city and flapped in the wind at the racecourse. Fortunately, there were none at the stables to spook the horses.

At breakfast they chatted about Wind Power. "I'm gutted he pulled up lame, and it's weird nothing showed on the Xray's." Mel fiddled with her fruit salad. She wasn't hungry.

"I am too, sweetheart. I reckon he could have won the feature race today, and he was the hot favourite. However White Jewel and Tropical Sun will do us proud. While you were in the bath this morning, it was announced on the radio that Tropical Sun is the favourite." Gary reached for her hand. "You'd love it if your special boy romped home with the win, wouldn't you?"

"I'd be over the moon. Two thousand metres is his distance, but White Jewel could win too." Mel spooned a slice of mango into her mouth. "Ooh, such a lovely flavour, how's your Eggs Benedict?"

"Delicious. This dining room is perfectly aligned with the view of Table Mountain. It's a magnificent mountain, isn't it?" Gary looked out the window as he chewed.

"It's one of the reasons I always book this hotel. Stunning views, great rooms, great service, delicious food and close to the course."

It wasn't long after leaving the dining room, Mel's stomach churned with nausea, and she raced to their room. By the time she'd got to the bathroom her mouth had filled with saliva. Holding her head over the toilet, she vomited. Once it was all out, she felt better, except for the burning in her throat and nose. She washed her face, brushed her teeth again and reapplied the make-up around her eyes. While she was putting on lipstick and rearranging her hair, the realisation dawned. She must be pregnant.

Gary knocked on the bathroom door. "Honey, are you alright?" He asked, worried about her.

"Yes," she shouted, then flung the door open. "I think I'm pregnant."

Gary stood looking at her, now all tittivated again. "Are you sure?" A broad grin rearranged his cheeks and altered the shape of the dimples.

"I'm very sure. Isn't this exciting." Mel jumped into his arms.

"You couldn't give me better news, my darling. Are you going to be alright at the track today?"

"I'm sure I will be, sweetheart. We are in the Members lounge and toilets are right there if I need them. Just as well we've planned the wedding for March." Mel glanced in the mirror and flicked some hair from her eyes.

Gary glanced at his watch. "I'm still in shock, it hasn't registered properly yet." He swirled around and put Mel down.

"At least I won't be showing at our wedding." Mel walked to the bedroom window and pushed back the curtain. "The gardens are lovely at this time of the year, aren't they? I think we should get to the track and check on the horses, don't you?"

. . .

Kenilworth racecourse, nestled below the iconic Table Mountain, hummed with excited punters. Gary and Mel wandered hand in hand from the stables toward the collecting ring. The first race still an hour away, but people were furiously filtering into the course grounds seeking a glimpse of the horses.

"This has to be one of the most spectacular settings for a racecourse anywhere in the world." Mel said while looking through the form. "Can we watch the first race from here and then head upstairs?"

They were standing close to the rails. "Of course. Why?"

"I'm a bit concerned about Owen, my love. Buck the System can be a rascal, standing here at the finish line I feel closer to the action."

Owen van der Merwe and John McIntosh, new apprentices riding for the stud, joined them and couldn't stop talking about the course, the going and their mounts. Gary teased them, it was nerves talking.

Before they hurried off to the jockey's rooms to weigh, Gary spoke to Owen. "Keep hold on that naughty boy, don't let him take hold of the bit and haul you down the track like a steam engine." Owen shook his head and laughed.

"No, I won't. He's tried that before. I can handle him, don't worry. Are you staying here to watch?"

"Yes, we are. You two better get to weigh in quickly."

When the two young jockeys left, Mel asked. "Honey, are you really confident Owen will manage Buck the System?"

"Oh yes. He may be a temperamental horse, but Owen rode him beautifully three days ago."

They wandered across to the restaurant and bought a fresh fruit juice and sipped it while the walked back to the rails. They didn't bother to go to the collecting ring, but they watched Owen gallop the horse down to the start. Through her binoculars Mel watched them jump well from the starting stalls, then she shouted, "Jesus Gary, what the hell is that horse doing? Owen's struggling to hold him."

"He's managing, sweetheart. Relax. He's playing with the horse, there, can you see he's calming him." They were passing the three-hundred metre marker, and she could see Owen talking to his mount.

"The start was dramatic, but Owen proved he had the talent to make professional jockey status quickly. Mel relaxed. Then suddenly, as if jet propelled, Buck the System shot forward, almost knocking into the horse on his right. Owen lost his balance.

"Oh my God, what's happening?" Mel heaved. She thought Owen was going to fall, but he quickly recovered took a hard, quick tug at the reins. Gary laughed.

"Some fine expletives pouring from Owen's mouth. Did you lip read the reprimand?" Gary asked Mel.

"I certainly did. Nicely done, Owen." Mel enjoyed that. She was jumping up and down as they passed them, racing into a pleasing second place.

'Trucking paid for', Melonie said to herself. "If he hadn't unbalanced Owen, they could have won the race." She mentioned nonchalantly as they took off to congratulate Owen. They could afford a two-week honeymoon in Italy if their other horses did well. Visiting Rome had always been on Mel's bucket list.

Tossie was mounted on Trialittleharda and John rode Lady in Red in the next race. This time Gary and Mel watched from the comfort of the Owners and Trainer's lounge.

Both fillies ran a pleasing race. Gary's favourite filly, Trialittleharda finished third, and her stable mate, fourth. *My wedding dress paid for,* Mel thought. Not that she wanted a lavish dress, but what she had in mind wouldn't be cheap.

The fourth and fifth races totted up three more places. Owen finished the day riding Popthequestion and won his first ever race.

Whoopee, wedding paid for. Mel quietly rejoiced. Then the crowd noise started ramping up. The anticipation palpable. Mel and Gary had a quick chat to Jeremy Tailor, and Andrew Warren-Smith, the professional jockeys riding for them in the feature race.

Jeremy wanted to please Melonie by romping home on the favourite, Tropical Sun. Andrew, who'd not ridden for the stud before, hoped he could secure the race on White Jewel.

Standing inside the parade ring, Mel's nerves were playing havoc with her already sensitive stomach, triggering the nausea again.

Gary held her arm. "Relax, my darling." He kissed her forehead. "You look so sexy pacing about nervously in that gorgeous cream suit." Mel playfully punched his arm as Tropical Sun pranced past. Shadrick gave them thumbs up. Two more horses passed, then Enos, the head work rider, led White Jewel.

"Did Patric tell you Enos is causing trouble with the work riders? He's been picking on Patric because he's not South African."

"No, he hasn't said a word." They raced back to their seats. Tropical Sun was still the favourite.

"And...... they're off." The commentator announced. Gary and Mel watched through binoculars. The horses had two thousand metres of turf to turn.

Melonie was screaming so hard when White Jewel won the race she could hardly talk.

"I.... can't...... believe it. My...... White Jewel won the J&B Met, closely followed by my beloved Tropical Sun. Now how's that for a race." Gary lifted Mel in the air.

"That's our honeymoon paid for." Mel rejoiced.

Chapter Twenty-Seven

THE WEDDING DATE WAS ANNOUNCED. The news of Mel's pregnancy, only to Ivan and Hector. It seemed that news was more exciting than the wedding date. Ivan was overjoyed. He'd not expected it to happen before the wedding, but he didn't care, he wanted grandchildren to play with. On the same day he announced his days of sheep farming were over.

Carried away by the winds of change, Mel set the wedding date for the last Saturday in April. There was too much to do to have it in March. No longer fighting nausea, Mel got on with organising the wedding.

"You can't do it all alone, my love." Gary couldn't help being concerned. Worried Mel might overdo it.

"We've only invited thirty people. Dad and Angelina are helping. I've found a seamstress in Durban. Marty in Mooi River is organising the marquee, chairs, red carpet, tables, the lot. Plus, a carriage drawn by a beautiful, black Friesian stallion. Won't that be awesome. My only little extravagance. Everything is done."

"You are such a good organiser." He popped a kiss on her cheek. "I'm taking Wind Power out for a hack before he seizes up. He's been resting for two months. Do you want to come?"

"No, I can't. I'm carrying precious cargo, my love. How long will you be?

Gary shrugged his shoulders. "About an hour."

"I'll be finished sending out invitations by then, so I'll meet you at the stables."

Wind Power had picked up weight while in rest, and though he seemed to be enjoying the time off just being a horse, Gary thought stretching his muscles a little would do him good and off he set.

Mel arrived at the stables a little before Gary. Instead of a happy smiling face, Gary looked flushed, sweaty, and irritated. "What's up, honey?"

Gary shook his head and brought Wind Power to a halt. "He's a bit fresh."

Mel didn't expect that response and she didn't dare laugh. Obviously, Wind Power had given him a hard time, but in her mind, *'a bit fresh'*, evoked visions of her father's little lambs frolicking in the field, but Gary looked as ruffled as a cockerel's arse in a hurricane. His hair stuck up as if it'd been jelled. Mel had to look away.

"Bloody horse." He swung his leg over the pommel and slid down. "He nearly planted me straight into a bed of red clover and green grass. Half a tonne of fucking muscle freaked out over guinea fowl flying off, and he flew off to join them, doing several laps of the field, squealing and fly bucking. I hung on for dear life." He flipped the reins over Wind Power's head, but Mel couldn't help herself and doubled over with mirth. Eventually Gary saw the funny side.

"You stupid bloody horse," he patted Wind Power, who stood and snorted. "How the hell I stayed on I have no idea."

Melonie still couldn't speak, and her stomach muscles ached from laughing.

"So much......" she gasped, "for that wonderful ...... um .... quiet hack," she managed to say.

***

The wedding day arrived. Mel looked radiant. She wore a simple, off the shoulder, ivory gown with a long veil that trailed from the back of her head, secured by a slide with delicate white roses woven into it. Long ringlets of auburn hair fell over her shoulders. She looked the picture of femininity. She wore a demure smile as she and her dad entered the garden in a horse drawn carriage. Ivan alighted from the carriage and helped Mel and spread her veil. A red carpet had been laid from where they alighted from the carriage to the front of the marquee.

Mel hooked her arm into her father's, and they walked slowly down the red carpet. Mel's eyes fixed on her man standing at the end.

Mel wanted a short fun ceremony. Thirty guests' side on either side of the red carpet. Gary's brother, Dave was the best man and his wife, Karen and their two daughters were Mel's matron of honour and bridesmaids. The two little girls carried the baskets of confetti. At the end of the ceremony, their vows made, the girls followed Gary and Mel out of the marquee, giggling and throwing confetti at the guests.

"What's it like being Mrs Whittaker?" Gary leaned in close while the wedding guests and bridesmaids covered them with rose petals, confetti, and well-wishes.

"Wonderful. I can't wait for tonight." Gary eyes shone. Mel giggled, "no, I meant we'll be on the plane. The mile-high club is not on my agenda."

The most convenient flight to Rome via Johannesburg happened to be on the same day as the wedding. Boarding time was 10:20 p.m. Once all the formal photographs had been taken, they had two hours for lunch and speeches, an hour to mingle, then change and get to the airport on time.

Mel had booked the honeymoon suite in a beautiful villa in Rome, the city of love and ancient history. A history she'd always been fascinated by during her senior school years.

Though Gary looked forward to touring Rome with his beautiful wife, they'd agreed their next holiday, with their first child, would be to the Okavango swamps. However, Gary agreed - ten days away from horses would do them good, and Gary had never been to Europe.

Chapter Twenty-Eight

Eleven hours later, the plane began its descent to Leonardo da Vinci - Fiumicino Airport in Rome. It was a bright sunny morning. Comfortable temperatures outside, the pilot had said.

Gary held Mel's hand as the plane touched down. Her eyes were wide, and her skin glowed under the fluorescent lighting in business class - another extravagance she thought they deserved. Unbrushed hair fell in a delightful tangle of ringlets that trespassed across her face as she bounced around in her seat looking for her hairbrush that'd fallen out of her bag.

They disembarked before the other passengers and made their way to Immigration. Gary stood behind her and whispered in her ear. "You look more ravishing every minute, Mrs Whitaker." He kissed the nape of her neck, and she shook like a racehorse after a roll in the dirt as goosebumps covered her body.

"Oooh," She whispered. Still chuckling she moved to the desk of a rather bored looking customs official. He did a double take when he saw Mel and stopped what he was doing. A smile, like a quiet, waveless ocean spread across his face resembling the water as it rolled slowly over the beach and stretched up his cheeks.

"You're very beautiful," he said in Italian accented English.

"I agree," Gary said victoriously, stepped forward and handed his passport to the cheered official.

The immigration officer shook his head. He'd been so distracted by Mel. He uttered, "those green, green, eyes. Phew," and he stamped Gary's passport.

Outside, Gary gesticulated for a taxi. Rows upon rows of little yellow Fiats waited eagerly for customers to swell out of the airport automated doors. Gary waved. Engines roared. One little yellow fiat trying to outmanoeuvre another in the rush to get to Gary on the pavement made Mel smile.

Gary opened the passenger door for Mel, and once they were inside, Gary showed the driver their booking for Villa Giorgia. A luxurious Inn built close to the banks of the river Tiber.

The driver nodded and off they went, darting in and out of small lanes, across larger roads and finally came to a stop outside the Villa.

"The long way round." Gary whispered to Mel.

"Siamo qui. (We're here) Twenty-two Euro's."

"Thank you. Grazie," Gary paid. "No tip for dishonest drivers." Gary felt sure the driver wouldn't understand English, but he spun the wheels and sped off. "He must've understood me." Gary shrugged his shoulders.

The front of the Villa was draped in purple bougainvillea. Dried petals and old flowers were scattered by gentle breezes, covering the road. A porter quickly stepped forward and picked up their two heavy suitcases. Gary carried their hand luggage.

"Aah, Mr and Mrs Whitaker, benvenuto in Italia." The happy receptionist welcomed them, then a rather striking, manicured man dressed in black trousers, a white shirt and red cravat graciously beckoned them to follow and guided them up a sweeping, highly polished wooden staircase to the first floor and opened the door to the suite.

"Stunning, thank you," Mel stood looking across the room to the spacious balcony and the view of Rome beyond. The receptionist smiled, bowed, and closed the door behind him.

The honeymoon suite met their expectation, but not their taste. It was very grand, nonetheless. At the foot of the bed, arranged on top of two fluffy white bath towels, were two heart shaped chocolates nestled in a sweep of red rose petals. A navy-blue and gold paisley design bedspread matched the rest of the furnishings. A silver tray with a bottle of genuine French Champagne and two crystal flutes stood on the round table between two royal blue velvet covered wing-backed chairs.

"Wow. Thanks, White Jewel." Gary said and scooped Mel into his arms.

"I wasn't expecting it to be quite so posh. I'm not complaining, even though it's a bit kitschy for our farmer tastes."

The décor didn't concern Gary. He kissed his new wife hungrily and when they did eventually stop kissing her, Mel's legs felt weak.

"Italians seem to like gold, and all that glitters. Let's unpack and look around." She eased herself away from her husband and peeked into the bathroom. "Have a look at this for lavish. What did I say about gold?"

A gilded mirror ran the length of the one wall and Mel caught a glance at her reflection. "Oh my God, Gary, I look exhausted." It'd been a long journey, but for the moment she was caught up in love and opulence and suppressed a yawn.

Gary stood behind her and whistled. The bathroom furniture was also navy blue, and the fittings all gold. An oval bath dominated the room. To the left of it, a glass shower cubicle, edged with gold rim and gold taps.

"Why don't we pop the cork off the champagne and jump in here?" She turned and winked at Gary.

After a long and luxurious bath sipping on champagne, they hopped into bed and blissfully enjoyed each other's intimacies as a married couple.

"I feel so content at last, thanks to you, my gorgeous husband. After a rough beginning to the start of something so heavenly." Mel stretched, then cuddled up to Gary and soon they were both asleep.

Refreshed after a few hours' sleep, Gary ordered dinner to be brought to their room. The smell of genuine Italian Carbonara wafted through the room and Mel's mouth watered. Once they'd eaten, Gary removed the silver tray and spread a map of Rome on the table. They both peered at, then looked at each other, bewildered.

"How can we possibly fit in all these attractions?" Gary shook his head and peeled the red foil off one of the heart chocolates and popped it in Mel's mouth, then peeled the other for himself.

"There must be fifty little red dots that indicate tourist hot spots smudged across the map." Gary's jaw dropped.

"It's the city where love and hope springs eternal, they say." Mel said happily, not perturbed by the number of sites to visit. "It's the mysterious Vatican that I'd like to begin our romantic itinerary. When I studied art at school, I always wanted to see Leonardo da Vinci's works. And here we are, in the heart of a city filled with amazing artistic culture and famous architecture."

"So, the Vatican it is." Gary took her in his arms again. This time they collapsed into bed and slept off jetlag and woke to a bright, sunny day.

They took a taxi to the Vatican.

Wandering through the huge arched gates they joined the tour group Mel had booked. Standing on the side of the Piazza Bernini square, staring at the Basilica of St Peter, a horse and cart trotted past filled with tourists, but soon the monotonous, emotionless droning from their guide became too much. They took a few steps away from the group and edged to the back. The guide continued, 'Constantine the Great commanded the construction of the first Basilica. He had it erected on the site where St Peter was buried after suffering a martyr's death. It begun.........'

Melonie screwed up her face and whispered, "Does this interest you?"

"No, not at all. His accent is so strong I can't get what he's saying."

They decided to look around on their own, keeping the group in their sights so they didn't get lost. They passed through the great doors and heard the guide's boring voice and noticed some of the group yawning. Most of them appeared uninterested that Pope Nicholas V decided to rebuild the Basilica, but everyone looked up at the great dome of the Cupola of St Peter. The opening in the centre of the dome lit the golds and bronzes of the finely painted murals within.

"A peep hole for the Heavenly Father to check what's going on." Mel said with a smile, her neck stretched upward as she spoke. "Don't you think the sparkling brilliance of the interior clashes horribly with the uncompromising Catholic faith?" She whispered to Gary. The lady standing close by pointed a stern look at Mel.

"I was hoping all this wonder would strike different sensations in me, but I have to admit I feel closer to celestial vibrations with Tropical Sun in his stable." Mel confessed honestly. "But I'm in awe of the paintings." It was not the wonder of her surroundings that soothed the darkness and fears within, but the man who stood beside her, and in that moment her instinct was not to speak within the holy sanctuary even though she didn't feel holy. Holy or not she couldn't wait to enter the Sistine Chapel. The most beautiful and famous of halls and the one she'd always wanted to see. Tilting her head she looked up in wonder and admiration. Michelangelo's immense talent was truly something to behold.

"Oh my God," she whispered. "He's a genius. The paintings of the 'Last Judgement' and the 'Volta' are way more spectacular in real life. Overawed, I feel like crying."

"Don't cry," Gary kissed her tenderly, "but I do agree. I'm glad I've seen it. I never thought I'd feel this way about chubby naked ladies and podgy children painted all over a ceiling." Melonie wanted to chuckle but halted it and gave Gary a nudge in the ribs.

"Flawless works, aren't they? The Vatican is a lot to absorb. One needs more than a day in here to really appreciate it." Mel said once they'd got outside.

"I'm famished, aren't you?" Mentioning his hunger pangs, made Mel's tummy grumble. They wandered out the main gates and walked down Via Santamaura to find a place to have a snack lunch. They bought a traditional porchetta sandwich each.

As the sun set over the ancient city, Gary and Mel found a perfectly cosy trattoria to spend the evening in. Their feet were tired. The menu tempted all sorts of dishes they'd not heard of. They clinked their glasses of Chianti and listened to the resident violinist while savouring the pasta filled with spinach and a delicious cheese sauce. A decadent serving of tiramisu completed the meal and they returned to the villa by taxi.

In the morning, they visited a famous Italian cobbler to craft a made-to-measure pair of riding boots each. Gary gasped at the price.

Mel took not notice. After being measured, they went on their way to the next famous stop. The Colosseum.

By the end of the week, they'd seen the Vatican, the Colosseum, the Roman Forum, they'd been up Palatine Hill, entered the Pantheon, wandered through the gardens of Villa Borghese and were about to climb the Spanish steps. Gary was licking at his second ice cream. A whiskey flavoured chocolate ice cream with chopped nuts in a sugar cone. "This must be the best ice cream I've ever eaten. They're so morish, do you think I'd be considered greedy if I had a third?" He joked as they began the ascent to the top of the Spanish Steps.

"Piggy," she poked him in the ribs. "Two is more than enough, you'll be on a sugar high just now."

"I know, but they're so good and a welcome reprieve from all the history lessons."

They climbed all one hundred-and-thirty-five steps to the top. Gary announced. "I've worked off my ice-cream overload," but the sugar buzz left him too sleepy to focus on the view of Trinità de Monti from where they sat, and his eyes flickered closed for a minute or two.

"Wakey, wakey," Mel spoke softly into Gary's ear.

"Hmmm," Gary opened one eye, then the other. "I've enjoyed Rome, but I'm Rome'd out. Too many people. I need the smell of horses and the peacefulness of home."

"I agree, and baba is slowing me down now." Mel ran her hand over the small bulge that was starting to show. With the map on her knees. "The Piazzele Napoleone, the natural meeting place for lovers in Rome is where I think we should have lunch." She read out.

"It's too late for lunch, besides, I'd never fit it in." Mel agreed. They gave lunch a miss and opted for a romantic dinner at Via Margutta. A charming little street romantically lit by lanterns. It was another hot spot for lovers and the following day, visiting the famous Baroque, and Trevi fountains, completed their tour of the city. Just before they left the Villa the leather craftsman called. Their boots were ready.

Standing at the Trevi fountain, Mel watched the crystal-clear rippling of the water and said dreamily, "Apparently, if you throw in a coin, legend has it that we shall return to Rome one day."

"Please don't throw a coin in," Gary begged playfully, holding her arm as she scratched in her purse.

"Has it been that boring for you, my love?" She gave up scratching for loose South African coins lying in the bottom of her bag.

"No, not at all, but I don't need to come back! Besides, the Dolce & Gabbana camel jacket, the shoes, the handbag, the souvenirs, the glassware, and clothing, plus the handcrafted riding boots we're about to collect has set us back what we paid for three classy brood mares." A one-sided smile from Gary said it all.

They hailed a cab and took the taxi to the cobbler. Displayed on his off-the-shelf shoes drew Mel's attention. She purchased two more pairs of boots. Gary winked at the cobbler and shrugged his shoulders.

The next day they were leaving Italy. The taxi waited outside the villa and whisked them off to the airport. Once they were seated in the departure lounge, Mel got the first flicker of a kick and grabbed Gary's hand, but he couldn't feel it. For Mel, the exciting movement rounded off a memorable honeymoon.

Home called. Twelve hours later the salty smell of Durban air blasted into their faces as they raced across the arrivals hall to Ivan who stood waiting.

The tantalising aroma of horse sweat, and leather was a *welcome home smell*. The sound of whinnying warmed their hearts. Now there was a nursery to furnish.

Chapter Twenty-Nine

"It's *so* good to be home." Mel hugged her dad and collapsed into the sofa in the living room. Benji, fast asleep near the fireplace, didn't stir. Seemed his doggy dance of pleasure seeing Mel had exhausted him. Laura, their newest Labrador slept close. Her slinky black coat gleamed.

Gary stroked Laura, who spread herself along the settee indicating a tummy rub. "It is, isn't it. There's no place like home. I'm looking forward to seeing the horses in the morning."

"As much as I loved being in Rome and spending a fortune," Mel shot a guilty smirk Gary's way, "I'm ready to climb into my jodhpurs, slip on my new Italian leather riding boots, and go for a hack."

Gary shook his head. "You sure? You're carrying precious cargo now."

The next day off they went. An hour's quiet amble had been what they both needed. They'd both missed being on the back of a horse even though it had only been two weeks and Mel knew after the visit to her doctor next week, he'd advise against riding.

A week later, during her first non-riding week, Mel spent time with her dad sorting through financial and legal matters now she was Mrs Whitaker. Today, they'd met with Anthony Parks, their lawyer. Ivan insisted on a clause stating in the unlikely event that Mel's marriage to

Gary ended in divorce, Gary would have no claim over the stud or the ownership of the farm, but he would be compensated fairly. Mel reluctantly agreed.

When the meeting ended, Patric rapped on Mel's office door and reported distressing news about Enos.

***

Gary's favourite mare, Trialittleharda was running in the third race of the day at Greyville. The filly looked magnificent galloping down to the start. Gary raised his binoculars, convinced of a win.

All the horses loaded, the flag went down and Trialittleharda jumped away to a disastrous unbalanced landing. Horse and rider crashed to the ground. Gary heaved, as if someone had hit him in the solar plexus. "Jesus. Nooo!"

Mel stood beside him, horrified. She knew the filly had broken her leg. Mel laid a hand on Gary's shoulder. They knew the mare's fate even before the course vet and the team raced across the turf to where the mare limped around.

Owen sat on the grass. "Poor Owen looks disorientated." Mel said, her gaze locked on their rider, silently willing him to get up.

Gary turned away. He couldn't watch.

"Oh, thank God. The medics are with Owen and he's standing." Mel turned to the closest exit and together they rushed downstairs and hurried to the medical block. A white building with a painted blue cross on one wall. They waited for Owen to be brought there from the track. People were buzzing around, asking after Owen and offering their sympathies for the loss of the horse. Gary felt sick. He'd lost his favourite mare, and nothing made sense.

An ambulance stopped near the building. Gary and Mel stepped closer to ambulance while Owen was helped, his face the colour of ash.

"Are you okay?" Mel asked, worried about her jockey.

"Yes, I'm fine, just winded. A bit bruised, but my heart is what's broken." Owen's head dropped forward. He couldn't look at Gary.

Mel hugged Owen, and tears fell.

"Thank God you're not badly injured. I'll let the Jockey Academy know the details of the accident." Mel held Owen's forearm and gave a little squeeze of reassurance.

They'd moved inside the building. The course medical officer checked Owen's vitals. While the young man took Owens blood pressure, Owen cried, "I can't ride anymore, Mel." He stammered out the words.

"Yes, you can. You have the ride at Scottsville in two weeks," Mel said.

"You can do it, Owen." Gary shook Owen's shoulder, reassuring the young man that he had the courage and the talent to get back and ride. "I'm heartbroken too, but you can't let this accident stop you. You're a brilliant young jockey."

"You're one of our best," Mel added while the medical officer removed the blood pressure band around Owen's arm.

But Owen shook his head. "No, I can't. I can't. I can't risk it happening again." Owen sobbed, holding his head in his hands.

The medical officer chipped in then. He rubbed Owens arm after removing the blood pressure machine. "You'll be fine. Look at me." He said, shining a light in Owen's eyes to check he'd not been concussed. "Take a short break for a week, then you can decide. I sense you'll be back in action winning races in no time."

Mel thought that was a nice thing to say to Owen, and to hear it from the medical officer seemed to have more effect. None of them would ever forget that third race.

Later that afternoon, John McIntosh rode Cool King, into a nail-biting photo finish which helped the Chanting Clover crew overcome their immediate sadness. For John, it was likely the most exciting ride of his career but did little to help Gary's obvious sorrow at losing his favourite mare.

Gary went to the collecting ring and met Andrew there. "Jesus, I'm sorry, mate. That was shit luck," he patted Gary on the back.

"Thanks mate. That's horse racing. We win some, we lose some." Gary muttered sadly.

"'fraid so. Where's Mel?"

"She's gone back to the Owners lounge with Owen. The accident has hit us all hard. Poor kid, he's a damn fine young jockey."

"He certainly is. Anyway Gary, good luck for the next race."

The horses filed out of the collecting ring and galloped down to the start. Gary joined Mel and Owen upstairs in the lounge.

"How are you doing, young man?" Gary asked Owen. "As soon as this race is done, we'll take you back to the Academy."

"Okay. Thanks Gary."

Almost a week had passed since Gary and Mel had dropped Owen back at the Jockey Academy when he called Gary.

"Good morning, Gary, it's Owen. My mates here have cheered me up so much, I thought I'd let you know I'm ready to ride again. I will ride for you at Scottsville.

"That's fantastic news, Owen. Thank you for letting me know. I'll pass the good news on to Mel. Do you want us to collect you on Wednesday next week? Have a ride on Cool King on the tracks here before you race him on Saturday?"

"I'd like that very much. The Academy bus is going to Johannesburg on Tuesday. I can get them to drop me in Mooi River, then you can collect me from there."

"Sounds great, Owen. When you get to Mooi River, call me."

Cheered by this news, Gary wandered through to Mel's office.

A bit startled, her head snapped up, then seeing his face, she instantly smiled. "You look happier all of a sudden, my love."

"I am. Owen's just called. He's coming up on Tuesday with the Academy bus to Mooi River. One of us will have to fetch him, but he'll ride Cool King on Saturday. The burden of worrying about the young man weighed me down, but now I don't need to worry. I'm delighted. He sounds enthusiastic again."

"That's great news. I've just got the postmortem results back. Though we both knew Trialittleharda snapped a cannon bone, the results show a very porous bone formation. Now that's a concern, especially as our feed mix is one of the best in the country, designed specifically for racehorses."

Gary frowned. "Then we need to do some more investigation. I'll start asking questions at the track and see what I can find out. Will you check the feed schedule with Thomas?"

"Yes, certainly. I'll pop down to the stables later this afternoon."

"Phil, your dad, and I will check the tracks this afternoon. They may be too hard." Gary suggested, though he felt sure they weren't, but it was still important to check.

After exhaustive investigation, Gary discovered that Enos had put his favourite mare back into hard work too soon. Enos had broken the minimum ten-day rest rule.

Furious, Gary ordered Enos to come to his office. He hadn't forgotten Patric's report on the difficulties work riders had with Enos. And, when he and Mel got back from honeymoon, Phil had also mentioned Enos's bad attitude.

Enos stood in front of Gary, insolently refusing to answer Gary's questions. Gary kept his temper, but demoted Enos immediately and explained the results of the postmortem. "Putting that mare back into work only four days after her last race caused microscopic fractures to her cannon bones and weakened them, that's why she broke her leg. I'm extremely disappointed in you Enos, you should've known better. From tomorrow you'll be a work rider like the rest because I can no longer trust you."

Enos glared at Gary with killer eyes, about turned and left without a word. Though Gary was furious with Enos, he felt he and Phil were also responsible for his favourite mare's death for they should have also checked.

When Gary told Melonie about the demotion, she shared her thoughts with him. "Do you think Enos could be linked to Solomon somehow?"

Chapter Thirty

Hobbling around the house, nearing the end of her ninth month of pregnancy, Mel finished decorating the nursery, and packed a hospital bag.

A few days before her due date a strange stirring at the base of her stomach, woke her. She shook Gary awake. "Honey, I think it's starting." She switched on her bedside light.

"Okay darling. What time is it?" Gary sat up and switched his bedside light on. It was full moon and shafts of light shone through their bedroom window.

Mel had been watching the clock for fifteen minutes, sensing something, but not sure what. Almost 4 a.m. "I'm going to make some tea. Do you want a cup?"

"You woke me saying it was starting, now you want to make a cup of tea." Gary's tone, though sleepy was also exacerbated.

She stood, wrapped her gown around her, and felt a swoosh of warm liquid run down her legs. Her waters had broken. Gary flew out of bed and stood next to her.

"See, I knew something was stirring." She laughed, staring down at the puddle on the floor. Gary joined her laughter. Then he raced to the bathroom and grabbed a towel.

"I'd been awake a while before I woke you. What do I know about going into labour? I didn't know if the sensations were a false alarm or the real deal. I guess we should get to the hospital."

Gary helped pull a large jersey over her head.

"Your bag is packed, isn't it?"

"Yes, just throw in my toiletries."

Gary dashed back to the bathroom while Mel sat on the edge of the bed pulling on her leggings.

"How come you're so calm?" Gary asked, popping the toiletry bag into her suitcase.

"I'm not really. I'm doing my breathing exercises. I hope we get there on time or you'll have to deliver him in the car," she teased, trying to ease the tension in her panic-stricken husband.

"Right let's get out of here." Gary picked up Mel's bag. "It's a forty-five-minute drive." Panic filled his voice.

She shuffled down the passage and through the hall, taking her steps with care. "I feel like I'm carrying a baby elephant."

At 10:49, on the 1st of September their little bundle, Garth Ivan Whitaker made his way into the world. Tears of joy streamed down his proud daddy's face as he held the infant in his arms.

Mel lay exhausted from her intense labour. It had happened so quickly. Now in the main maternity ward, Gary laid Garth next to her and sat beside the bed. After a cup of coffee, he left Mel and his son in peace. He called Ivan from the hospital then drove back to the farm.

Gary pulled up outside his old cottage and parked beside Ivan's Landcruiser. Quickly up the steps, through the sitting room, he found Ivan on the veranda. "Mel's had a boy, as I told you on the phone. Garth Ivan Whitaker."

Ivan jumped up and shook Gary's hand. "That's wonderful news. Congratulations. Have a cup of coffee. Tell me all about it. Do want some toast and avocado?"

"Sure, sounds great, thanks Ivan. Garth weighed 3.6 kilograms and he looks like his mother. I plan to pop back in an hour or so, spend the night in town and bring them home tomorrow afternoon. Seeing her waters break terrified me." Gary almost laughed, remembering Mel's shocked face as she stood with her legs apart looking at him.

Ivan came back carrying a tray with the coffee and toast. "Us blokes don't know how to handle it, do we? We can mostly deal with everything, but when it comes to your wife in labour, we men fall apart. When Margaret went into labour, we were staying in Umtali with friends because it was a two-hour drive from the farm to hospital. Margaret had also had two miscarriages before Mel, so we were extra cautious."

"That must have been very traumatic." Gary said, taking a bite of his toast and avocado.

"It was awful, but along came Mel. And you say you'll be home with her tomorrow late afternoon. Wow. When Mel was born, mothers weren't allowed home until the fourth day."

The next day, Mel brought her beautiful baby boy home, and the house filled with flowers. Neighbours came bearing gifts for the new baby. Their kindness touched them both enormously. For the first six weeks Garth spent his days in a cradle with Mel on the veranda, and his nights in the same cradle next to Mel's side of the bed. Every morning and every afternoon Ivan had tea with his daughter and held his grandson.

Gary got up early and met Phil at the track on the second morning after Mel and Garth's return.

"Morning Phil. Don't expect me at the track early for a few weeks. This baby thing is exhausting." Suddenly, alarmed by a commotion, they spun around and noticed two riders fighting, rolling about on the ground near the warm-up area.

"Let's get over there and pull them apart." Gary said to Phil and they ran to the fighting men and yelled at them. Phil grabbed the back of Eno's shirt and dragged him off Siyanda. While Phil tried to pacify the angry Enos, Gary knelt beside Siyanda, whose face had been slashed with a knife and was bleeding badly. Gary looked up at Phil, still wrestling with Enos behaving like a mad man.

"Be careful, Phil, the pocketknife is still open in Enos's right hand." Gary warned his assistant trainer, then turned his attention back to Siyanda.

"Let me take you to hospital, Siyanda. Stand up." Gary helped him to his feet.

Phil let Enos go and pushed him away, but he spun and ran at Gary and Siyanda holding the knife ready to sink it into either one of them.

"Don't you fucking dare," Gary managed to halt the crazed Enos. Phil pulled him away again and was joined by two other work riders. Between the three of them they dragged Enos away while Gary helped Siyanda to his Landcruiser.

"I'll see you back here in a few hours. Give Mel a call and let her know what's happened and where I am. Thanks Phil." Gary turned to Siyanda. "Are you okay?"

"Yes, Mr Gary, but I'm bleeding badly," Siyanda lifted his arm and Gary saw the blood spread down his shirt. "He stabbed me under my ribs and in my chest." Siyanda feebly pointed to his heart. "It's very painful, but just go Sir, I don't want to bleed to death."

Gary raced to the local hospital in Mooi River. By the time he got to the emergency entrance, Siyanda was barely conscious. Blood was all over the passenger seat and foot well. The emergency team were quick to whip Siyanda away and wheeled him to the theatre on the run while Gary hurried back to the farm and met Phil at the track. The final string of young racehorses were cooling off. Standing on the edge of the ring, Gary asked, "who saw the fight start?"

"I did." Funani spoke in Zulu, spitting Zulu words from his mouth.

"Where's Enos now?"

Phil answered. "I sent him home, and I've let Mel know the story."

"Great, thanks Phil. I'm going back to the house. I'll deal with Enos later. I'd like to see my little bundle of joy, instead of dealing with this nonsense."

"Sure. How's Siyanda?"

"Not good. No good at all. I'll call the hospital after lunch, but he will be in high care for days, I think. I'll see you at the ready-to-run barn once I've called the hospital."

Phil raised his thumb in acknowledgement.

Gary drove the Landcruiser to the main stable block and asked one of the junior grooms to wash all the blood off the seat and the foot well, then walked back to the house.

Mel sat on the sofa feeding Garth when Gary walked in. "Phil let me know what happened. What a drama. Sweetheart, Patric may know more about what triggered Enos's rage. I don't trust Funani, and I don't think Phil does either. Apparently, there's a handful of work riders that give the gentle Siyanda a hard time." Mel looked down as she held her breast to Garth's mouth.

Gary leant down and kissed Mel and popped a kiss on Garth's head. "I've noticed that. Phil also mentioned it, but I assumed his behaviour is because I demoted the aggressive little shit."

"How's Siyanda?" Gary stood at the back of the sofa gazing down at the suckling child.

"Not good. Before Phil and I broke up the fight, Enos had already stabbed Siyanda in the chest, under his ribcage and sliced open his cheek. I didn't realise until I got Siyanda to the car, he had been stabbed three times. I'll call the hospital after lunch."

When Gary called, the nurse told Gary Siyanda would be in hospital for at least a week.

THE FOLLOWING day when Gary got to the track at seven, Enos wasn't riding. After searching the main stable yard, Gary and Funani went to check Enos's house at the staff quarters.

Gary knocked on the door. No reply. He rapped again, louder this time. Still no reply. He turned the doorknob. The door was unlocked. He pushed it open and stepped inside. Funani followed. Enos was lying on his bed, face down.

"Enos." Gary called his name. No response.

Funani moved closer. Gary shifted over to give Funani space beside the bed. Funani knelt and placed his face close to Enos's. He whispered softly in Zulu. Gary understood some Zulu, but he wasn't sure he'd heard correctly. Funani's voice was barely audible, but Gary felt sure he'd heard the name Solomon.

Funani shook Enos, then jumped back. "Enos is dead, Sir."

Gary rolled Enos over. He'd been stabbed in the heart. Gary decided not to question Funani about his whisperings. He'd mention it to the police and question their security. The way Funani had seemingly pretended to be shocked Enos was dead, then the way he ran out of the house was suspicious, as if it was an act.

When Gary got back to the main stables, Phil was there. "Enos has been murdered. I'll deal with the police, but I'm darn sure someone knows who killed him." Gary's expression was dire. He stood at the tack room door and called the police. Once he'd reported the murder, he called for Patric.

Patric was in the stable with Wind Power, grooming him. He answered Gary and joined him in the tack room. "Do you know anything about what has been happening in the staff housing with Enos and Funani and the group of disruptive work riders?"

"Yes, Gary, I do, but it is best I meet you somewhere else. I could be the next one killed if I'm seen talking to you like this." Patric was the one person on the farm that Gary trusted implicitly. He also knew that Patric would go to any lengths to protect Mel.

Gary spoke louder than he would normally have done. "Thanks, Patric." Patric walked back to Wind Power's stable and went on with his task. Gary would find a more appropriate place to chat to him. Over the following days it filtered back to Gary that none of the work riders were saddened by Enos's death, but quarrels broke out because of suspicion.

A few weeks after Enos's death, Patric asked to speak to Gary in private. Gary collected him in the Landcruiser, and they drove off, as if they were heading to one of the broodmare paddocks. In the privacy of the vehicle, far from prying eyes, Patric spoke.

"The work riders think Phila Dube is the suspect. Even though he is well respected for his riding ability. He's like me, he's not Zulu, so maybe they're just wanting to target him and he's not guilty. He's a Union leader and I hear Enos despised him. Though some of riders tell me Funani is a problem, though he and Siyanda have a good rapport."

"So, there's nothing concrete, just talk?" Gary pulled off the road, turned the vehicle and drove slowly back toward the house.

"Just talk. But I'll find out more if I can. Phila's brother-in-law now works in the gardens and Phila's wife, Thando in the kitchen and helping Mel with Garth? I do not trust them."

"Why?" Gary asked.

"I will tell you when I know."

Chapter Thirty-One

GARTH, at five months old, had captured the hearts of everyone who met him. A bonny, cheerful child who'd just learned the sound of his own giggles and found them as funny as everyone else. By ten months old and crawling, his favourite pastime was being led around on Spindle by Thomas or Patric, occupying their time for at least twenty to thirty minutes and when they took him off, he yelled for more.

Mel met them at the stables after hearing Garth bellowing. Then she saw Patric had just lifted him off Spindle and she knew why he was yelling. Nothing to panic about. Then she saw Gary come out of the tack room.

"Sweetheart, I've just seen Anton. He wants to ride Tropical Sun in the July this year. Don't you think my precious boy is too old?"

Gary rubbed his chin. "White Jewel is running her last July, why don't you let Sunny run his. They can retire together, and White Jewel can be covered by Master Vision. Imagine that foal."

Mel wasn't sure. "Maybe, but first I want to see Anton riding him. We haven't had Anton ride for us for a few years, and he's getting on too."

Mel set her alarm for five thirty the next morning. Ivan arrived to look after Garth while she and Gary watched Anton ride Tropical Sun.

At the end of the second circuit, he'd run two thousand metres. After the gallop Anton trotted to where Gary and Mel stood. "What do you think?" He asked.

"There's no doubt he's ready and you two make a fabulous team, so yeah, I'll let him have some fun with you in two weeks' time."

"Oh, super. Thanks, Mel." A happy Anton took Tropical Sun back to the stables.

Dressed and ready to leave for Greyville, Mel packed the bags, toys, bottles and food, and the push chair. It would be Garth's first Durban July. Thando went with them. She would look after Garth for the afternoon.

Sky Dancer, a filly that had climbed into Mel's heart from birth because she'd been born with a limb deformity and, under Vic's guidance, had worked tirelessly to straighten her legs gradually, hence she'd bonded with the beautiful filly. She'd grown into a magnificent racehorse about to run her first. Mel left Gary at the stables and joined Hector and her dad in the Owner's lounge. Thando and Garth stayed at the stables with Gary.

"Isn't Sky Dancer looking amazing, Hector." Mel spoke with her binoculars pressed against her forehead watching Sky Dancer jump from the starting stalls.

"She certainly is. You must be very proud of her."

"I am. Come on girl, go." Mel shouted. Then she saw Sky Dancer gather speed. "Go, go, go. Oh, you little beauty." Mel clapped as she watched the once crippled filly win her first race.

"That little filly is going to surprise us all." Mel smiled proudly and hugged Hector. Just then an announcement came over the intercom. High Court had been scratched. Mel frowned and glanced at Hector and Dad. "I wonder what's going on. I'm going to pop down to the stables and find out."

Mel left the lounge and hurried down the stairs. On her way to the stables, she met Sky Dancer coming off the track and led her into the winner's enclosure, then she handed her over to Siyanda and made her way to the stables.

Mel noticed Gary leaning against the outside of one of the stables. His head dropped between his shoulders.

"What's wrong, honey?"

"High Court's coughing and wheezing like a cockerel on helium, and his temperature is sky high. Fuck, I hope it's not horse flu. I'm waiting for Vic. I've scratched him already."

"I heard. My God, I hope it's not horse flu, that will cause pandemonium, but did you hear Sky won her first race?"

"I did and I wish I could feel as happy as you are, but this is terrible."

Mel peeked into the stable. "Where's High Court?"

"I moved him to one of the empty stables at the end of the block. At least he's isolated there if it is flu."

Mel felt ill. "Jeepers, Gary. Have you called Phil?"

"No, not yet. I'll do it now." Gary called Phil and Mel went in search of Thando and Garth. She found them wandering up and down between the rows of stables. Garth wanted to say hello to all the horses, Thando told her.

"Thando, one of the horses is sick. Can I leave you with Garth for another half an hour?"

"Yes, Ma'am, no problem." Thando smiled and pushed Garth to the next stable. Mel saw him put his hand up to the nose stretched over the stable door. Her heart swelled. It was the sweetest gesture.

When she joined Gary again, he told her Phil had instructed Thomas to take all the horses' temperatures. He was on his way to collect High Court.

"If it is horse flu it must have come in with those visiting brood mares who've been with us for a week." Mel closed her eyes and took in a deep breath. "And if it is what you suspect, it'll cripple the racing industry for months."

Gary had turned around and put his back against the stable wall. They were both very worried.

"Vic should be here soon." Gary said and spotted John Mcintosh walking beside Sky Dancer patting her neck and chatting to her.

"What a smashing race," he shouted to Gary. "What's up with High Court, why's he been scratched?"

"Well done, John. Brilliant ride. I sadly never watched. Not sure what's wrong with High Court, we're waiting for Vic."

John walked past, leading Sky Dancer to her stable.

For Mel and Gary each moment that passed seemed longer than the one before.

"Thank God for a good start. It hasn't really sunk in yet, and Runaway Bride ran fourth." Mel spoke to Gary watching Sky Dancer walk away from her. Just then Vic arrived and pulled his vehicle to a stop near Gary and switched off the engine. "Hi, where's the horse?"

Gary led him to the stable they'd put High Court in. Vic stepped inside and took his temperature.

"Jesus," he said, looking at the reading. "Forty-one and a hell of a fever. In my mind, there's no doubt it's horse flu, Gary. "I'm going to take blood though. Twenty-four hours or more before we get the results." Vic raised his eyebrows. He understood the ramifications of the diagnosis.

"Get him home as soon as you can. Isolate him. This bloody airborne disease travels quick, as you know." Vic inserted a needle into the horse's jugular vein and drew blood. "Oh God. If this *is* flu..."

Gary answered for him. "It's going to screw up our breeding season, not to mention everything else it'll screw up countrywide."

Mel dropped her head into her hands. Her shoulders slumped. This was the worst news possible. "When will you know for sure, Vic?"

"Earliest Monday. But you need to act as if it's confirmed. It'll need to be reported as soon as possible." Vic cocked his head to one side, he knew how difficult this would be for them.

Mel's stomach churned. Influenza was devastating, not just for their horse, but for the entire equine industry.

Gary didn't seem as stressed as Mel. But sometimes he kept his emotions tied down tight. He tapped his index finger on his mouth. "Will do. Thanks Vic. I'll see you at the farm tomorrow."

"Sure. I'll be home tonight after seven, if you need me." Vic said as he walked to his vehicle.

"Right, thanks." He turned to Mel. "This is a fucking disaster. Let's hope Phil gets here soon. I've asked him to put Floss in the isolation stable with High Court."

Mel stroked the horse. "That's a good idea. The poor boy's so stressed. The sweat's dripping off him. The company might help soothe him."

Floss was the only remaining sheep and she loved horses. She was often used as a companion if one of the horses were restless, anxious, or sick. She had an amazing calming effect, though not all horses reciprocated. Floss had been kicked on occasion, but it hadn't dented her affection for the equine species. Mel understood Floss's attitude.

After Phil loaded the sick horse, Mel walked over to Thando sitting in the shade of a tree, where she rocked Garth's pushchair back and forth. Garth was sound asleep. "When Garth wakes, come to the Owners' and Trainers lounge, please. That's where we'll be."

Thando bobbed her head.

Gary and Mel joined Hector and Ivan for the start of the fourth race in the comfortable seating inside the Owner's lounge. Gary's shoulders now hung heavy.

Mel touched his arm. "I know you're disappointed High Court isn't racing."

Gary turned to her, his eyes more worried than sad. "That's true, but I'm worried about the serious implications once the news gets out concerning influenza on the farm. And I'll have to tell the race stipendiaries after this race."

Mel held his hand and squeezed. "We'll tell them together."

Thirteen horses galloped to the start, loaded, and broke well, but as the field turned into the home stretch, Canterbury King collapsed midstride, throwing his rider, John Macintosh into the galloping, pounding hooves of the other horses.

Mel dropped her binoculars and gasped. Her heart stuttered and her chest tightened, imagining the worst, and the pain John must be experiencing. A groan rippled through the stadium, then shocked silence.

Gary and Mel glanced at each other. Too shocked and concerned to speak, and without saying a word, they ran downstairs. Mel wanted to cover her ears to block out the sound spectators were making. Waves of mumbling rippled through the stadiums. As she and Gary descended the stairs, she could see people cover their faces with hands and racing forms. Dread lingered. She knew those sounds. She knew the curtains were being erected around their beloved horse. She'd seen the emergency staff rush to the fallen horse and jockey before they left the Owner's lounge.

Out on the main concourse between the stadiums and the collecting ring, Mel could feel the eerie hush that had befallen Greyville racecourse. The stunned hush made Mel shiver, then she heard the ambulance siren.

They ran on to the stables. Mel needed to see to Thando and Garth first, then get back to the medical centre as soon as she could.

Siyanda saw them coming toward him at speed. "What happened, Mr Gary?"

Thando arrived holding a sleeping Garth in his push chair.

"We'll find out. I'm going down to the track." An agitated Gary paced.

"I'm going with you," Mel said.

"Of course." He turned to Siyanda. "Please collect, The Enchanter as he comes off the track, you'll need to take him for vet checking."

Mel touched Garth's sweet warm cheek. "Thando, please take Garth to my dad and stay there with them. I'll meet you there."

When they got to the edge of the track, they knew there was no point going to where High Court lay. They turned back and made their way to the medical facilities.

Gary stopped and turned to Mel. "You know we've lost High Court, honey," tears dribbled down his cheeks. "I suspect a heart attack."

Mel slipped her arm through Gary's. "Do you think High Court also had the flu? If so, the sudden exertion probably collapsed his lungs which caused the heart attack."

The ambulance pulled up, a young medic jumped out, ran inside. Mel could hear him speaking to a medical officer but couldn't hear his words. He hurried into the ambulance and the vehicle drove off, sirens blaring.

Mel turned to Gary. Her eyes wide. A mixture of dread, fear and concern showed. Her legs felt weak, and she struggled to breath. "Does that mean John has died too?"

"Jesus, I hope not. Let's check with the medical officer inside." Gary's brow lined and his lips pursed from tension.

Mel and Gary stepped into the open waiting room. There was no-one there except the tall medical officer who was standing with his back to them.

"Excuse us. That was our jockey in the ambulance. Can you tell us what's happening?" Mel said, her voice sounding calmer than she felt.

The man turned to the sound of Mel's voice. "The jockey needs urgent medical attention. They're on their way to Addington Hospital."

The words elicited more shock, angst, sorrow, and fear, but Mel held onto hope. John, at least, was alive. "I'm scared" Mel pressed her cheek to Gary's chest. "John took a terrible pounding. It's the worst fall anyone can have off a horse when it drops dead at full gallop." Gary squeezed her and held her close.

Back at the Owners and Trainer's lounge, Mel met the grim faces of a shattered Hector and concerned Ivan. Garth sat on his grandfather's lap. Even he looked bewildered, likely sensing the unhappy situation. Thando busied herself folding and refolding a blanket, over and over.

Moments later an announcement came over the loudspeakers. The two feature race favourites were scratched. This news caused panic among owners and trainers.

Punters threw their arms in the air, furious. Bookies were fretful. Anton and Jeremy looked fretful too. Their livelihood depended on getting the top rides.

No one knew the reason for the scratchings yet, but concern was raised about influenza. After the feature race, another dire announcement. The last race of the day was cancelled.

Chapter Thirty-Two

MEL AND GARY drove to Addington hospital. They waited for any news. But all they learned was that John was in surgery, with no idea how long or when they could talk to a doctor.

Mel decided to call John's parents.

Jill answered after the first ring. "Oh Mel, what on earth happened? I've just heard on the news. A truly ghastly way to hear about my son's accident." Jill's tone was stressed and angry.

"I'm so sorry you had to hear that way. We've just finished filling in all the forms at the hospital and there's been so much to arrange. I never ever thought it would be publicly announced so quickly. Again, I'm so sorry." Mel felt awful for Jill. "What we know is the horse John was riding had a heart attack."

"Oh goodness, Mel. I'm so sorry for sounding angry and accusing. It's just so shocking. Tell me what you know about John."

"He's in surgery and maybe there for a few hours."

"Oh, my God, hours." Jill words shrilled with fear and worry.

"Jill, let me call you back when I've spoken to the doctor. Have a good cry, I find it helps."

"Okay. Thanks. Bye." Jill was already in tears.

John was admitted at 3:25 p.m. and he was wheeled out of theatre at

6:56 p.m. Mel and Gary followed the gurney to the wards and waited for the surgeon who arrived minutes later.

Gary shook hands with the doctor.

"He'll never walk again, Mr. Whitaker." The surgeon said, his tone filled with exhaustion.

Mel covered her mouth with her hands. "Oh my God, he's only nineteen." Her chest tightened. "What are his injuries? I am speaking to his mother next."

"He's suffered spinal fractures in the thoracic and lumbar spine, both tibias, left pelvis, cheek bone on the left side of his face is shattered. His face will need several reconstruction surgeries, and his left arm is fractured. All from racing bloody horses." Now anger mixed with his exhausted tone.

"Is there no hope of him walking again?" Mel asked. She felt sick in her gut. A wave of nausea caught in her solar plexus. How was she going to tell Jill the news of Johns extensive injuries and paralysis.

"No, not likely." No empathy showed on the doctor's face.

"This is incredibly horrible. He was so talented." Gary said.

"He may have been talented before the fall, but he'll never ride again, let alone walk, as I've already explained. Now, if you will excuse me."

Mel felt her face flush with anger at this doctor's abruptness. She called after him. "How long will John be in hospital?"

The doctor didn't have the courtesy to even look back. "Four or five months, maybe longer. Depends."

"Depends on what, Doctor?" Mel said, but he'd already left the room.

Gary wrapped an arm around Mel's waist. "Leave it alone, sweetheart. There is no point in getting angry, he's likely tired or maybe, he's an arrogant prick, and always will be. Let's just go home."

Seated in the car, Mel called Jill and explained exactly what was told to them, but with much more compassion.

Through tears Jill said, "But surely, we'll need to give John some hope. Hope he may walk. Hope he may ride. I'll call the hospital now before the surgeon sees him again."

"That's a good idea. We saw him wheeled into the ward. John won't be talking to anyone on the phone, his face is completely bandaged. I'm so sorry you can't get here to see him. The sound of your voice will help."

"I'm going to try and get on a flight in a few days."

"Wonderful. Gary and I will come through tomorrow afternoon and see him. I'll call you again after that, then you can let me know when you will be here."

At that moment Mel's world felt impossibly messy. She looked at Gary. His face was grey with tension and worry. Tears streamed down Mel's face. "Who would ever have thought today, our favourite race day of the year, would end like this?"

***

The equine flu epidemic, a doomsday panic, had settled down. The financial effects had been sorely felt across the equine industry. Hundreds of horses had been affected, some even died, which triggered speculation about the efficacy of the vaccines.

Despite having John's parents stay for a few days after the accident, and again three weeks later, Mel still felt responsible for what had happened to John. Guilt weighed heavily on Gary too. They visited John as often as they could. Sadly, John's parents couldn't see him more than twice after the last visit for they weren't able to take more time off work. The visits were left to Mel and Gary, Hector, and Ivan. Towards the end of John's fourth month in hospital, Mel took Garth with her. Happy, giggly Garth liked John, and he cheered John too.

The day before John was released from hospital at the end of November, Mel learned she was pregnant with her second child.

"Hi John, how are you doing today? Looking forward to getting out of here tomorrow?"

"Sure," he said. "And going home."

"As I won't see you tomorrow, I thought I'd tell you my good news. I'm expecting our second child." Mel said happily. She knew John felt her happiness by the expression in his one open eye. It seemed like it was smiling.

John's parents were collecting him the following day.

. . .

Two days after New Year, Jill called Mel, distraught. "Hi Mel, I need your help, please," the tone in her voice frantic with worry. "John has plummeted into a dangerous depression and wants to take his life." Mel couldn't answer straight away, but she could imagine how John felt. She remembered the abrupt doctors' words. *He'll need more than hope to walk again.*

"Would you consider having John to stay for a week or two so he can get some horse therapy?"

"Let me chat to Gary, then I'll call you back."

"Thank you, Mel. I'm at my wits end." She sobbed.

Gary wasn't happy, but he agreed. He knew firsthand how therapeutic horses were, he also felt they owed the time to John, but he was worried about Mel and her pregnancy.

Mel let Jill know and a week later John arrived with his parents.

John was itching to see the horses, smell them, touch them, cuddle them, and feel their breath on his face. Toddler Garth jumped up and down and fussed. He wanted to push the wheelchair. Garth's enthusiasm brought a glimmer of a smile to Johns crooked face.

When they arrived at the main stable block, John uttered, "Mel, I'm going to walk again. I'm so happy to be here. Thank you for letting me come."

"Of course you're going to walk again, John, and ride too. It's wonderful to have you and see the joy the horses bring you." Mel cheerfully encouraged. Inside she was thinking it was the least they could do for John.

The initial facial reconstruction prevented John from smiling for the skin was stretched around his nose and lips and across his cheeks in a bizarre crisscrossing of skin. Mel wasn't sure what hurt her more - looking at John's disfigured face trying to smile, or his withered, paralysed legs.

He looked to Mel for hope. "Miracles do happen, don't they, Mel?" There was a pleading for confirmation in his eyes.

"Yes, of course they do, and they're waiting for *you*, John. At the end of this long road of rehab, there's a champion jockey waiting to burst out of that chair."

John attempted to laugh. His mouth was partially open, and the sound resonated through his chest. Only a flicker of movement could be seen on his lips, but it was clear he treasured Mel's words.

Thomas came forward and shook John's hand and opened Tropical Sun's stable. "Chanting Clover's chief therapist is waiting for you John."

Garth raced in and hugged the horse's legs. "It happens often," Mel laughed, unperturbed. Tropical Sun's nose rested near the child's neck and Garth giggled, liquid gurgles only a toddler can make, which made Mel's heart melt, but she took his hand. "Garth, sweetheart, move so John can talk to him too."

Tropical Sun looked at John, only stepping toward him once Mel had picked Garth up, then he poked his nose into John's lap and held it there while John stroked the horse's forehead and ruffled his mane through his fingers.

Jill and Russel had to look away. The moment evoked such deep emotion, they both cried.

"Why cwy, Mummy?" Garth asked, jumping up and down on Mel's hip trying to get down. Mel couldn't speak, instead she passed Garth to Thomas, who took him down to Wind Power's stable.

Mel watched John talking and playing with Tropical Sun. The horse reciprocated exactly as she knew he would. "There's nothing to motivate John with more power, than a conversation with this remarkable horse," Mel said, turning to Jill and Russel, who now stood in awe of what they'd witnessed.

"I've never felt such powerful emotion in my life. In fact, I never knew this was possible." Russel, uttered, still feeling the sensation of the moment. Jill had moved away. She sat on the lawn and sobbed into a tissue.

Eventually John wheeled himself out of Tropical Sun's stable and they all strolled slowly back to the house. Once again Garth insisted on pushing the wheelchair, but it wasn't long before his little legs tired and Gary lifted him onto his shoulders.

Seven weeks later, John was still at Chanting Clover enjoying the therapy. It was Wednesday, mid-week physiotherapy day.

Anne, the physiotherapist arrived as usual and walked down the passage to John's room, but this morning she found him weeping, taking deep shuddering breaths that concerned Anne. Before she began work, she thought she'd better call Mel, and rang the internal line.

Mel left Garth playing with Thando and rushed to John's room. "What's the matter, John? Moments ago, you seemed happy."

"I'm scared. Everything's getting to me. I'm crying for the loss of my legs. I'm crying for the horse that died beneath me. I'm crying because I may never walk again, I may never even ride a horse again. I'm crying because I have no future. There's not even a glimmer of hope. I wish I'd died with High Court, at least I'd be happy. I can't even smile."

Mel glanced at Anne. His words made them both want to cry too. While John wept the skin over the left cheek pulled his face into a strange shape, distorting his once good looks. Mel looked away.

"I miss not riding...." John's chest shuddered as he took another chest juddering breath.

Mel took John's hand and rubbed the top of it with her thumb. Eight months had passed since the fall. "You know you're going home soon, then you'll be back here a few weeks after Easter for the final facial surgery."

John cried louder. "That's a year from now, Mel. Next February."

"No, it isn't, silly. You've lost track of time. Your final surgery is in July. That makes it a year since the accident, as the surgeon said. And what a lot you and Anne have achieved in the time you've been here. Your mum has arranged swimming lessons for you in a pool, and in the sea. That's something to look forward to." Mel squeezed his hand tighter. "Keep telling yourself you'll soon be walking, then riding, then winning races, and while you think about it, imagine it. Imagine the feeling. It's a slow, tough process, but I know your determination will get you up again. Nothing good comes easily, John. Keep fighting on."

Mel handed John a tissue and he dabbed it over his face, encouraged by Mel's determined words. "I'm going to leave you and Anne to get on with your session."

When Mel walked back into John's room he was lying on his back staring at the ceiling. "Gary's going to wheel you down to the stables later. Your mum called. You spoke to her, didn't you?"

"Yes, I did. Thank you, Mel."

"We hope you've enjoyed your extended stay here."

"Yes, I have. I really have. So, in a few months I'll be back. Thank you for all you've done for me. I'm going to miss the horses. I love them all so much. I'm looking forward to swimming, but not the surgery."

"I don't think anyone looks forward to surgery, but when you've had it and your face has healed, you'll be seeing your old handsome face again. Now that's something to look forward to."

"Yes, I suppose so." But the expression wasn't convincing as he looked at his withered legs and placed a hand on each one, wobbled the lifeless limbs that twitched, and he sobbed again.

Mel gave him a moment to let his grief out, then she placed a comforting hand on his shoulder. "You'll be back soon. Seven weeks I think it is. The swimming is going to help, especially in the sea. Make sure you keep at it. The harder you try, the quicker you'll develop back strength to support your weakened limbs, then it'll just be a matter of time, and we *will* get you walking again."

"If you believe that, Mel, I should too, I guess."

"I believe that with all my heart. Remember our thoughts can either conquer us or motivate us. Some battles are harder than others, but positive thoughts are positive energy and that's where you must direct it." Mel put her hands over his.

"I'll try my best, Mel, and good luck with the birth. Don't forget to call me and tell me what you've had and what you call the baby."

"I promise I won't." She gave John a kiss on the top of his head and shook his shoulders affectionately. "You'll be one of the first to know."

The following day Jill and Russel arrived to collect John. It was an emotional goodbye for John, but as Mel had encouraged, he had lots to look forward to.

BRADLEY ARRIVED by an emergency caesarean and entered the world on the 8th of May 1989 after a scan revealed the umbilical cord had wrapped around the baby's throat. Mel spent four days in hospital with Bradley, who, thanks to the prompt delivery, was a cuddly, healthy baby boy.

Once Mel got home, she called John to let him know and they spoke for ages. He told Mel all about the improved strength in his legs and the amazing benefits of swimming in the sea. He was just dreading the last operation. Finally, he ended the call. "I can't wait to be back at Chanting Clover and meet Bradley."

Chapter Thirty-Three

July 1989

"Hold the mirror," the surgeon said to John. The nurse slowly peeled away the bandages and carefully lifted the gauze.

John squeezed his eyes shut. A lone tear made a path over his cheek. He hesitated on opening his eyes. He felt scared.

"Come on John, open your eyes, you look amazing." The nurse encouraged.

"I'm dreading it. I don't want to be disappointed."

"You won't be," she assured him. John opened his eyes, one at a time. Looking back at him was a face he recognised. His lower lip and chin trembled. The old John looked back at him. Speechless, he stared at himself.

"What do you think?" The surgeon asked, whose smile had spread across his face.

"Thank you, Sir. I never thought I'd see *me* again." John said bravely. "Maybe this marks the new beginning for me." He gritted his teeth to stop his chin quivering. "I wish Mel was here to see this and celebrate with me."

"I'll see you tomorrow." Doctor Clarke, the maxillofacial surgeon said.

"Thank you." John picked up the mirror again. The skin was shiny and sensitive, but it was *him* there. He stifled a cry because tears burn.

Later that afternoon, John's parents called.

"Hi Mum, my face is almost me." The excitement in his voice unmistakable.

"That's wonderful news, my boy. We also have some news. Anne is fetching you tomorrow. She's arranged for you to continue swimming. A friend of hers is a swimming instructor and will take you to Durban twice a week."

"Oh wow, thank you, Mum." She handed the phone to John's dad. They spoke for a short time, then John spoke to his mum again. "We can't wait to see the new John. We'll fly up as soon as we can. Enjoy being back with the horses and send our love to Gary and Mel, and please don't worry Mel too much, she has little Bradley to look after now too."

"No, I won't, Mum. We'll chat again soon." John hung up.

The nurse then explained to John how to use the creams and facewash the surgeon had prescribed. "Do not, under any circumstances, pick at the scabs. Allow the healing process to go unhindered and keep out of direct sunlight. These are your painkillers and use them only if you need them." The nurse slid a small plastic sleeve into the top drawer of the bedside cabinet. "And don't forget to see the surgeon in two weeks. Good luck, John."

Just as the nurse left, Anne arrived. She stood in the doorway with her hand over her mouth.

"Oh, my word, John. Just look at you. You're back." She came over and hugged him, careful not to touch his face.

"It's looking good, isn't it? And the best part, I never have to go through any more facial surgery again. I'm never coming back to hospital." John rejoiced. The nurse popped back to help with John's belongings and settle him into his wheelchair, then Anne drove him to Chanting Clover.

But two weeks later, something in John's psyche snapped. Like two wires had disconnected in his brain. No-one could work out what had triggered it. He could wheel himself to the stables whenever he wanted to be with the horses. He had his own room and bathroom, access to the lounge and television and endless books, and he could sit on the veranda and enjoy he views and the sounds, and the house staff were extremely good to him, so were the grooms. There were so many unanswered questions. And when Mel questioned him, he couldn't answer either.

John had changed. And ugly, rude John had taken over. He argued with everyone. He was rude and disrespectful to all the staff and to Gary and Ivan. He foul-mouthed Angelina and downright vile to Anne, and his swimming instructor.

Gary had had enough. "Mel, we need to send John home. I'll not take his rudeness a moment longer, nor will anyone else. He can have his nasty tantrums there. We've done all we can for him."

Mel understood. She couldn't deal with John anymore either. He wasn't rude to Mel but snappy and argumentative. "I don't know what happened in his head. It had been going so well."

"I'll tell you exactly what it is. He's jealous." Mel knew Gary was right. She had two children now and they came first.

Mel called Jill later that day.

"Hi, it sounds like something's wrong?"

"Unfortunately, yes." Mel explained and a few days later Jill collected an angry John.

***

It was the end of April when John turned the corner and urged his parents to send him back to Chanting Clover.

It took a lot of convincing for Gary and Mel to open their doors and their hearts to John again. Before they agreed, Mel had a lengthy heart-to-heart with Jill.

"He's been swimming every day in the ocean, his legs are much stronger, and his old, determined attitude is back." Jill told Mel.

Mel and Gary eventually agreed to give John one last chance and a new John arrived. His face lightly tanned, the dark pink scaring on his face, hardly visible, his upper body was strong and toned, and his legs were visibly larger and obviously stronger, but there was no change to the paralysis.

On his first day back, John spent the morning wheeling himself to each stable in the main block where he knew he'd find Cameo and Tropical Sun.

Mel decided to hide in the tack room and watch his interaction with the staff. He appeared happy and polite though she couldn't hear what he said. Thomas had opened the gate for him, and they chatted. At each stable door he pulled on the brake, pulled himself up and peered in with his face close to the nose of each horse. They all responded with slightly different greetings but watching him not only warmed Mel's heart but assured her the old John was indeed back.

Gary happened to arrive at the stable block before John had finished greeting all the horses. He walked toward John without realising Mel was watching from the tack room. She heard him ask, "Hello John, good to be with all the horses again?"

"It's brilliant. Thank you, Gary for letting me come back."

"Make the most of it this time, young man. I can see how much stronger your legs are. You must've worked very hard on them while you were at home."

"Yes, I did, but I think it was swimming in the sea that helped the most."

Watching and listening to the two men chat, Mel slithered out the tack room and strode toward them as if she'd just arrived.

"So young man, have you had enough of horses for this morning?"

"Hey, Mel, I'll never have enough of horses. You know that." He plonked down in his chair having kissed the last horse on the nose. An inner happiness shone in John's face and creased it beautifully.

"May I go inside Tropical Sun's stable once more before we go back?" Gary and Mel nodded.

"Are you going to show the wonder horse how much stronger your legs are?" Mel asked with a smile on her face, knowing he'd already done that. John nodded, opened the door, and wheeled in. Holding the arms of the wheelchair he stood, let go of the wheelchair and wrapped his arms around Tropical Sun's neck. He closed his eyes and held the horse for a few moments, then fell back into the chair.

"Wow John, what an incredible change. I must admit I was a bit worried you'd topple over. Your legs can almost support you for ten seconds." Mel turned to Gary, "Isn't that fantastic?"

"It sure is. Practice that every day or a few times a day and soon you'll be walking." John turned his head and looked at Gary, "for sure."

Tropical Sun explored John's legs, running his nose up and down his shins, then he moved his nose to John's face, lightly tickling John's chin with his whiskers. John's eyes closed with the ecstasy of the touch. Gary took a few steps away. The sounds coming from John made him want to weep, though he was gladdened by seeing it happen. He could hear John chuckling and saying to Mel, "It's so ticklish."

Mel loved every moment of the special interaction. Tropical Sun jostled John's legs with his nose.

"My legs are tingling, Mel. I've never felt that before." Gary heard and darted back to the stable.

"Really? That's exciting."

"It is, isn't it? But I must admit, I'm getting tired now and besides, doesn't Tropical Sun go out to his paddock soon?"

"Yes, he does. You can come down here anytime you want to." Gary pushed John up the ramp they'd installed for John then pushed him out onto the veranda.

The internal phone rang.

"I'll get it." Gary dashed to answer it. When Gary returned, he was crying.

"What on earth's the matter, my love?" Mel asked, having just sat down.

"Hector's dead. That was his gardener on the phone." Mel and John burst into tears.

"I'd better get down to his cottage," Gary said, knowing Mel would need to stay with the two boys. He ran down the steps and disappeared round the side of the house. He returned forty-five minutes later. "When I got to the cottage, the gardener led me to where Hector lay, all tangled up in the raspberry vines in his vegetable garden. He heard us approach and grumbled, 'get me out of this fucking mess.' I thought the gardener was going to faint." Gary laughed. "The gardener stood there uttering, 'Hau, hau, hau.' I think you need to come with me to his cottage. His arms are bleeding from all the scratches, and he said he thinks he must have blacked out, that's why he fell headfirst into the raspberry vines."

"Oh, thank God, he's alive. Let me call Angelina. Thando's on early lunch."

Mel popped into their bathroom and grabbed the first aid box. She and Gary strode down the path to Hector's cottage.

"You gave us a terrible fright. Thank God you're alive. You need to see a doctor." Mel said.

Hector grunted. "No, I don't, just superficial scratches. They always bleed like bastards." He looked up at Mel.

"Hector, I meant having a black out. That's not good at all." She got to work cleaning Hectors arms and smeared the scratches with an antiseptic cream. "Rest this afternoon and I'll make an appointment for you." She and Gary headed back for lunch and rescued the children from a hungry Angelina.

"Thank you, Angelina. Were they good?"

"Oh, yes, Ma'am. Very good. Is Mr. Hector alright?"

"Yes, he is. Now off you go for lunch, you must be hungry." Angelina smiled and left.

"Hector certainly gave us a fright, didn't he? The poor man doesn't have a single relative in Africa." Mel lay in bed thinking about Hector. "It's so sad most of his friends are no longer around. I think he's outlived them all. He's such a dear, with so much love and knowledge to share and his two daughters never call, and they don't even write. I don't know what he would've done without gran. Probably gone back to England. Should I call Sarah and let her know he'd love to see them?"

"I don't know, to be honest. Would he even want to see them. He never talks about either of them, ever. Don't go worrying about them too. Hector, John, Garth, and little Brad are quite enough." Gary gently warned.

The following morning Mel did call Sarah and got a nonchalant response from her, with no indication they might come and see their father. Mel was furious, but Gary was right. At least she'd tried. She realised how little she knew about Hector's life before Chanting Clover.

"To think he's been here since 1966." She spoke aloud to no one as she brushed her hair. He'd told her once he'd seen the advert gran had placed in the Horse and Hound magazine. He'd been terribly young when he married, and the two girls were born eleven months apart. Mel decided to pop down to the cottage and check on Hector.

"Hector," she whispered, standing next to the couch, her index finger over her mouth warning Garth not to speak. Hector opened his eyes, smiled, and put his hand out to hold hers.

"Hello Mel, this is a nice surprise. And hello, little monster." He tweaked Garth's cheek, who giggled and said, "you're not dead, Uncle Hector."

"No, Uncle Hector was just sleeping."

"How are you this morning?" Mel thought he looked paler than normal.

"Fine, just a bit sleepy still. Those painkillers you forced down my throat did the trick." He teased.

"I've made an appointment for you to see the doctor. I'll take you in tomorrow at two."

"Right you are. I'll be ready. You're so good to me, Mel. Thank you. What a bind for you."

"No bind at all. I wouldn't have it any other way. How are all those dreadful scratches." She checked his arms.

"Oh, they're fine, they're dry already, except the ones you covered with plaster."

"I called your daughter Sarah, to let her know you'd had a fall. She sends her love. (She hadn't, but Mel couldn't help saying that little untruth.)

"That was kind of you," Hector said. A faraway stare took possession of his eyes, as if frozen in thought, then he blinked.

"Most unlike Sarah to send love. Didn't think she was capable. But that's nice anyway. How's John doing? Do you think he'll ever walk again?"

"I can't bear to think he won't. He's spending time in Tropical Sun's stable every morning. It's so special to watch. He's also being extremely polite to everyone which is a huge relief."

"And so he should be. You've done a lot for the young man. How long is he here this time?"

"Until he walks again." Mel said with conviction.

Hector smiled. That was exactly why he adored Mel as he did.

"Come, Mummy," Garth tugged at Mel's arm.

"Okay, sweetheart, where do you want to go?"

"Horsey's."

Hector smiled fondly at the child. "He looks like his daddy. Big blue eyes and blonde curls. He's going to break many a heart. When I was a boy of fourteen, I had a terrible fall off a racehorse. Doctors told my mother I'd never walk again. I struggled for eighteen months. Nothing was going to keep me off a horse. At sixteen I was riding again. The secret is in the mind. John's young and he's got support."

"I'd love you to tell John your story and how you did it. He's very determined now, and his legs are considerably stronger. He'd be delighted, as I would, to hear about your time in Newmarket. How about you have supper with us tomorrow night when we get back from the doctor?"

"I'd love that. Thank you, Mel. You'd better go and get little mister onto his horse."

Chapter Thirty-Four

"Which horse is helping John the best?" Gary asked, standing at the open door to Tropical Sun's stable.

"Tropical Sun, of course. What a crazy question to ask me!"

"Guess I should've known better." Gary's smile tilted one side of his face and deepened the dimples.

"I pray every day for a miracle, especially after what Hector told us last night?"

"Yeah, and we can only hope it happens to John." Suddenly loud raucous laughing and cheering erupted in Cameo's stable. They hurried down to her stable.

John had taken his first unaided step.

"And another," Gary enthused, but John dropped back into the wheelchair. "I'll do three steps tomorrow." The joy and excitement in his voice echoed through the stables. Thomas also ran to see what the commotion was all about.

"Hey, Thomas. One step today, three tomorrow." John's face rosy red from the concentrated effort, but the happiness oozed from him.

Cameo looked on curiously, her ears pricked. She seemed to sense the enormity of the occasion.

"I'm nearly there, hey Mel?" He looked at her. "Hey, don't cry."

"Sorry, John, your happiness and my happiness combined just forced out a few emotional tears, but they're tears of inexplicable joy."

That night John called his parents. "Hey, Ma! I walked a step today." Mel heard him say and left him chatting to his mother excitedly.

The next morning, Mel, Gary, Ivan, Thomas and Patric gathered at Cameo's stable eager to witness the three steps John promised to take today.

"Wait for me," Anne called. Even a few grooms stopped and stood on tiptoes behind Gary and Ivan.

John had placed the wheelchair just inside the opening to Cameo's stable. Mel and Anne were inside standing ready. Gary held the back of the wheelchair.

Cameo's ears were pricked. She knickered to him, urging him to stand. John pushed himself up and stood for a moment, concentrating hard. He took the first step. Gary edged the wheelchair forward. Silence, just John's breathing could be heard. John's shoulders tensed as he took the second step. Mel shook her head. The grooms were about to cheer. She quickly put her index finger to her lips to shush them and John took the third step. Gary was there with the wheelchair. He didn't collapse into it straight away though. He focussed on Cameo who was watching him get closer. She nickered, as if she knew what a momentous occasion everyone had witnessed in her stable.

"Just one more," Mel whispered.

Still looking at Cameo, focussed on her feet, his legs wobbled, but he took that fourth step to loud applause and collapsed into the chair.

"Gee. How was that? We need to go and tell Hector." A tear ran down his rose-tinted cheek like a jewel and landed in his lap.

Two weeks later, John's muscular strength had radically improved. He could walk ten steps comfortably before he needed to rest. Every morning he'd park his wheelchair at the top of concrete walkway in front of the stables. Either Thomas, Shadrick or one of the other grooms would take the wheelchair and walk behind him. Confident that when he needed to sit, he could just fall back into the chair.

"Mel, please will you walk to the stables with me this morning, I want to show you I can do fifteen steps today."

John's grit and determination had been so infectious he had everyone rooting for him. Even Garth bopped up and down on his podgy legs, cheering.

Perspiration dribbled from John's forehead, forcing those extra five steps, but he did it. When he collapsed into the chair he was breathing heavily.

"That's incredible, John." Mel clapped and Garth followed with claps and hoots of laughter. "Soon it'll be twenty." Thomas shouted, "Twenty-five, John."

"There's one thing I'll never forget about this journey. Your changing facial expressions as you've progressed." Melonie had her hand on John's shoulder. "It's been the most endearing experience for us all and I'm sure each of us have learnt from it."

Thomas, Shadrick and two other grooms were nodding. They held their yard brooms and were shaking their heads, even their shoulders bobbed. They'd seen the battle John had fought with his body and his mind and taking fifteen steps today had proved he'd won the war. It was a massive celebration of his fortitude.

Seated, he wheeled himself to Cameo's stable. She arched her neck over the door and John planted a kiss on her nose. Mel heard him whisper, "I'm going to ride you, my girl, and soon."

***

The legendry Hector Willis died in his sleep shortly before seeing John ride Cameo for the first time. John was sad, but he knew Hector had watched from above.

Gary had been nominated Trainer of the Year, and newspapers across the land made John famous with headlines like, 'Local boy wins the J&B Met.' 'Paralysed Jockey beats all odds.' 'Miracles do happen,' were just some of the headlines on the front pages of many newspapers and magazines. His was an inspiring human achievement. Mel cut out all the articles she could find. The first headline she'd cut out and stored, read.

'Jockey paralysed in fall. Horse dies.'

John was riding for Chanting Clover once more. He lived in Hector's cottage and helped teach junior jockey's the way things should be done to become a champion. And who better to teach that, than John.

John, Gary and Mel had joined forces with the Jockey Academy and developed the program for jockeys who struggled with their riding, or those who lacked self-confidence, or had difficult emotional issues the horses they rode picked up on. They took in four jockeys at a time, and they lived in the cottage with John until he felt they were ready to go back to the Academy. It had turned out to be a very successful venture.

THOUGH HECTOR MISSED John's triumph and sorely missed by many, except by his two daughters. The day he died, Marion, head of administration at Chanting Clover, handed Mel a brown envelope. It had been locked in the stud safe for years.

"What's this?" Mel asked.

"It Hector's Will." Mel hadn't thought much about it after Hector passed. She never opened it, assuming Hector didn't own much and what he did have, would go to the two daughters. So, when the company solicitor, Anthony Parks, called her and Gary to his offices and read out the Will, no-one could have been more shocked than Mel.

Hector was a wealthy man. He'd bequeathed his entire estate to Melonie.

All Mel could think about when Anthony read through the will was, Sarah and Gillian, Hector's two daughters. Neither sister had bothered to attend their father's funeral and now a legal battle lay ahead. The two daughters had contested the Will, and they got the news at the stud's busiest time with coverings and visiting mares. Anthony suggested it would be best for Gary and Mel to fly to England and meet with the girl's solicitor.

Hector's Lloyds account had been frozen. This action infuriated the girls. They wanted to get their hands on the one hundred and seventy-two thousand pounds in the account. They also wanted to evict the elderly couple that occupied Hector's flat in Newmarket. They'd lived there for years.

"Jesus, Anthony. Two ugly sisters. If we do fly over, at least we can make use of our membership at Newmarket racecourse. Hector had it all planned for Mel, didn't he? Remarkable old man. We loved him dearly, and we both miss him terribly. I can't believe he pre-paid the racecourse membership for us both for five years. Means we'll have to take a holiday to the UK once a year and make the most of it." Gary was delighted by what Hector had done for Mel. She deserved it.

"How long is this fight going to take, and who pays the legal fees?" Mel asked Anthony.

"The law on contesting Wills is similar in both countries. What I'll try and do is negotiate with their solicitor from here, settle it out of court, if possible, otherwise it's a trip to the UK in the next few weeks."

Gary chipped in. "Give the first a good go, Ant. We've got too much going on to leave."

***

The grand function for the Trainer of the Year awards held in Johannesburg, scheduled to begin in a few hours and Gary dreaded it.

"You should've won this award, not me." Gary said to Mel as they changed and prepared for this formal, rather nerve-wracking event.

"Nonsense, my darling. I don't do much of the training anymore. I'm just mummy." She said as she slipped into a dark green, off the shoulder, body hugging evening gown.

Gary winked at her. "And a very sexy mummy too."

John was also being presented a special award that evening. A new award, in recognition of his gallant contribution to racing, and to inspiring junior jockeys to be the best they can be. The crowd gave John a standing ovation reducing him to tears om the stage and the applauding grew louder. Eventually he gathered his wits through tears and laughter and gave an outstanding, heart-tugging speech. He ended it by acknowledging the Whitaker's.

"Gary Whitaker deserves more than just the Trainer of the Year trophy. I could never have achieved what I have without him, and his wonderful wife, Mel. They are an incredible inspiration, not only to me, but the entire industry." Everyone remained standing and clapped.

TWELVE MONTHS LATER, as if to seal the accolades and blessings of the evening awards, John went on to win multiple Grade One and Two races riding Chanting Clover home bred horses. In July 1990, John won the Durban July on Sunshine Clover, a colt from Master Vision.

Chapter Thirty-Five

"I'M NOT LOOKING FORWARD to this trip, even though we needed a break from the farm, the horses, and the kids. There's nothing as ugly as a bun fight over a will," Melonie sighed, holding their tickets while standing in the queue at the airport, ready to board a British Airways flight.

"Bloody vultures those girls are. They didn't give their father a thought when he was alive, but I'm confident Anthony will sort it out. Thank goodness he's coming with us." Gary inched forward. "It's a pity he couldn't get on the same flight, but we'll meet in Sheffield."

Mel handed over her boarding pass and Gary followed.

THEY MET up with Anthony in Sheffield, having booked the same hotel, and spent the evening dining together and sifting through the details of the case.

The hearing took place at Sheffield's High Court at 10 a.m. Gary and Mel took their seats and listened to Anthony present the case. He'd done his research well. The judge agreed with Anthony's presentation, and the sister's lawyer fought for them, they lost their appeal.

Mel leaned in close to Gary and whispered, "looking at them, they really could pass as the two ugly sisters. They both have the same mean set to their mouths."

"And you, the beautiful and gracious Cinderella gets to wear the slippers," Gary whispered.

"As much as I dislike them both I'm going to ask Anthony to do the decent thing and give each sister twenty-thousand pounds. Hector was their father, after all."

Gary hugged her. "You truly are amazing, my precious, darling wife."

They left the courts forty-five minutes later and found a quaint tearoom on the High Street and Mel called home. "Hi Dad, have you been run ragged by the kids?"

"Not too bad. Garth keeps asking after you both, poor little bugger's missing you. Angelina and Thando have been so good with them. Don't worry, they're fine. How did the court case go?"

"Anthony Parks is such a smoothie," Mel laughed, and glanced at him sitting across the table from her. "But aside from having an admirable command of the English language, he did a master's in research. The two ugly sisters lost their case. They weren't well represented, to be fair, so I decided to give each of them twenty thousand, and never even got a thank you or a glance of acknowledgement. Two most unpleasant sisters."

"Oh, well done Anthony, and how jolly kind of you. Let's be honest, my girl, you deserved the inheritance and shouldn't have really shared a dime."

"I know, but I felt so bad when the judge gave his verdict. You know me." Gary was nodding his head up and down with a smile. He knew exactly what dad had just said without even hearing both sides of the conversation.

"We are seated in a lovely, cosy tearoom, and we're about to have a pot of English brew, scones with clotted cream and strawberry jam." She could hear Garth niggling.

"Yum. Here's Garth." Ivan handed over the phone.

"Hello Mummy, when are you coming home? We're riding, even my bruver's riding. The horses make him giggle." Garth spoke without taking a breath. Mel heart swelled at the sound of his excited voice.

"We're coming home soon, sweetheart. I'm glad you're both riding. Is Thomas taking you out?"

"Yes, and grandpa. He leads Brad and even, um, even... Patric comes too sometimes. Where's Daddy?"

"He's right here." She handed the phone to Gary.

"Hello, my boy. Are you being good?"

"Yes, Daddy, we are, and we're going riding now, bye." Gary burst out laughing, holding the phone that hummed after Garth ended the call abruptly. "We'll give them a ring this evening and find out how their ride went."

That evening Gary, Mel and Anthony celebrated in the hotel pub.

"What an outcome, Anthony. You're quite the suave operator." Gary teased. They lifted their drinks and toasted to the end of the battle of Wills.

"To tell you the truth, the two ugly sisters' total disinterest in their father when he was alive lost it for them, not my suave operating." Anthony smiled, still holding his beer up. "It was so obvious they didn't give a rat's arse about Hector. If it'd been me, I would not have given them a penny."

"Well, cheers anyway. Listening to you, I'm glad you were on our side. The weasel of a solicitor they had was as wishy-washy as a grey day on this island." Gary lifted the tankard of British ale and clinked with Anthony's again.

"The fairy tale ended well. The slipper fits my beautiful Cinderella." Gary said proudly. "Apart from wanting to be in the hallowed place of Thoroughbred racing, it'll be interesting to see the flat and meet the tenants who have cared for the place for so long. Hector certainly was an enigma."

"Here's to that too." Anthony glanced at the menu lying on the table.

Mel took a swig of cider. "Ooh, that's good. Here's to safe travels back for you, Anthony, and thank you so much."

. . .

WINDS OF CHANGE

Anthony flew back to South Africa the next day, and Mel and Gary caught the train to Newmarket. The seven-hour train journey from Sheffield to Newmarket seemed to pass quickly.

Mel and Gary settled into their seats opposite each other at the window.

"As boring as a train trip may be to most British people, I'm as excited as a girl. It's such a good way to see the countryside, and the lovely little villages." Mel folded her coat and placed it on the seat next to her and put her handbag on top of it.

The train pulled out of the station on the second hand - 9: 47 a.m. "Don't you just love how everything operates to the minute here. Imagine if it was like this back home." Mel said while Gary spread the Daily News then folded it in half, glancing from the newspaper to the passing countryside as they went.

Fascinated by watching what past as the train sped on its way, Mel kept her eyes focussed on the countryside. With her head pressed again the window, she could see her favourite olde English houses coming up. "My favourite, the Tudor houses. I love the black and white façade. So quintessentially British and we're about to pass them, Gary." Mel tapped the newspaper to catch his attention.

Gary dropped the open newspaper onto his lap. "They're lovely, aren't they."

They arrived in Newmarket at quarter to five. "Spot on." Mel stood, picked up her handbag and jacket and together they disembarked with Gary carrying their small suitcases.

Standing on the platform they checked the map. They'd booked a room at the White Hart Inn. A ten-minute walk with their luggage and when they arrived Gary had to duck through the reception door. The low wooden beam hung low. The lighting was soft and the interior, cosy and warm. The inevitable ancient pictures of hunting and racing hung on the walls. Mel checked in, and they were guided upstairs to their room. Gary dumped the two small suitcases on the luggage rack. Famished, they decided to have dinner before unpacking.

The following day they immersed themselves in Newmarket's interesting equine history, starting with a visit to the Jockey Club headquarters.

"That is such a beautiful sculpture," Mel pointed to the life-sized statue of Hyperion.

"Exquisite. Must have taken the artist months to complete." Gary stood in awe.

Their newly acquired flat was two streets back from the High Street, adjacent to one of the many stables that unobtrusively fit in with Newmarket's two-legged horse racing fraternity and though a small village, could hardly be described as a one-horse town. They couldn't leave Newmarket without a day at the races, and a tour of some of the racing yards, by kind invitation, and after all the fun stuff. They met with Mr. and Mrs. Stewart, the tenants in the flat Mel had just inherited.

During their meeting, they learned more of Hector's early life. The mystery of why Hector's daughters were so against him, finally solved.

To begin with Mel could see Mrs. Stewart wasn't sure about what she should tell and looked to her husband for support. Silently questioning with her eyes, she received the silent answer from her husband and began the story.

"He never betrayed his children or his wife. No devious or dark misdemeanours in his history. He was the most wonderful man with a heart of gold, and with the eye of the master when it came to horses, as you both know. His only fault as a young man, he had wanted to work and live in Africa." Wondering if she should go on, Mrs. Stewart looked to her husband once more. He nodded.

Mel was enjoying watching the words pass silently between the elderly couple.

"Hector won the fight for Africa, but my, did they argue. Determined to follow his dream he accepted Iris Paige's offer and divorced Hilliary. They'd only been married two and a half years. When I saw Hilliary six months after Hector left, I asked her why she didn't go with him. She replied by saying that she wasn't taking her two little girls to a land filled with savages. Can you believe the ignorance? We never saw Hilliary much after that, but of course we have always been in contact with dear Hector."

"Poor Hector. He truly was the kindest, most considerate man, wasn't he? Gary and I adored him."

"Yes, of course we did too. He'd married Hillary far too young. Poor man left heartbroken at leaving his daughters. I'd write or call Hilliary to find out how they were, then let Hector know. He never missed a month of paying the family living expenses."

Mrs. Stewart poured another cup of tea. "For years, he mailed us copies of what he paid into her account for he didn't trust her. He was sure she'd bad mouth him. He wanted to keep his reputation clean in case he returned to work here one day. In those days Newmarket wasn't the size it is today."

"He didn't deserve that. He was like a father to me, and I've yet to meet a more knowledgeable person." Gary joined the conversation for the first time.

Mr. Stewart went on just listening.

"He paid their schooling and their college tuition. When the girls left home to study in Sheffield, dear Hector bought Hilliary a flat there, so she could be close to the girls. We believe she lived alone." Mrs. Stewart offered Gary and Mel another cup of tea and sliced open two more freshly baked scones and pushed the clotted cream and strawberry jam closer to them.

"The daughters grew up despising their father thanks to Hilliary's embittered influence. We were told the girls became avid men haters. Though not swayed toward lesbianism, we learned they became as unpopular as their mother. They'd inherited her snarky ways. After Hillary died, the girls moved into her flat."

"Do you know why Hector never remarried?" Mel asked, smearing the top of half a scone with cream and jam.

"He'd fallen in love with your grandmother, Melonie. Oh, how he adored her. He loved and admired Fergus, your grandfather, so he'd never have jeopardised the way things were."

"But what about after grandpa died?"

"Hector never revealed why they never became a couple, but they were clearly devoted to each other."

"Yes, they were. Did you ever go to Chanting Clover?" Gary asked.

"Yes, we did. We loved our stay there in his lovely cottage. He paid our airfares." A tear ran down Mrs. Stewarts wrinkled face. "We'll miss him. He spoilt us all these years."

Mr. Stewart leant forward. A worried expression rose on his wrinkled face. "Gary, now that Hector is gone, what about our continued occupation of this flat? May we go on living here, at the same rent?"

"Of course you can go on living here. We'd be delighted. Mel and I chatted about dropping the rental altogether. If you keep the unit in good condition, pay the council rates and taxes and continue paying the water, heating, and electricity rates as you have been, we don't need the rent. If anything goes wrong with the boiler, heating, or there's structural issues, we will handle those expenses, of course." Gary assured them.

The elderly couple visibly shrank from the relief. Being in their early eighties, moving them would have been a terrible shock neither Gary nor Mel would have imposed on them.

"Go on living here until you need to move." Gary said. "Just keep in touch regularly."

"That is incredibly kind of you both. We are ever so grateful. Things are awfully expensive nowadays and with you giving this lovely flat to us rent free we won't have to be a burden on our son and daughter-in-law."

"We are happy to have you stay here. At least we know its occupied and loved. If we fly over, we have a place to stay too, if you'll have us." Gary said and Mrs. Stewart laughed.

They bid the dear couple farewell and went back to the hotel. Shortly after tea they began their tour of Newmarket.

After seeing some enviable Thoroughbreds and pristine stable yards that had stood the test of time, they popped in to see the Stewarts once more before departing for Heathrow the next day.

Gary and Mel flew home business class. Ivan and the children met them at the airport. Two excited children talked, squealed, and chuckled all the way home, then dived into their suitcases to see what surprises and treats they could find.

Chapter Thirty-Six

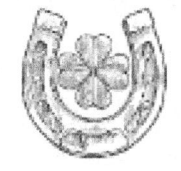

1996

SIX YEARS HAD PASSED since the court case over Hector Willis's estate and their trip to Newmarket. It was all distant echoes in Mel's mind. Time had flown. Mel gazed out the bedroom window. The chill of the morning air dissuading her from abandoning the warmth of her bed. The temptation to linger with her book for another tugged at her.

The house was quiet. Her thoughts wandered to happier times, memories untainted by the shadows of past threats to her life. She rarely dwelt on the past, other than thinking about her mother, or her grandmother, both pillars in her life. Now, surrounded by men and boys, she marvelled at the unexpected resurgence of a carefree, content family life reminiscent of her childhood days at Blue Winds. But here, her children were experiencing even more, a gift from her grandmother's legacy. While she lay in bed, she pondered the profound impact of the inheritance on her business and her family.

Mid-winter in the heart of the Natal Midlands Mel felt its icy grip. This winter was particularly cold. They'd woken to snow covered lawns and the children were already lost in its pristine embrace. Stepping to the window, Mel shivered, yet her heart danced with childlike delight at the sight of the snow. The urge to join her boys in the snow flickered briefly. She went down for breakfast bundled up in layers akin to a walking snowman.

Garth and Bradley raced in for breakfast leaving trails of snow in their wake. Angelina, dismayed at the mess they made, scolded them. They took little notice. After breakfast they dashed back outside and spent the morning building snow men, chucking snowballs at each other, and commandeering makeshift sleds with the help of obliging grooms.

Mel watched the boys frolic from her office window. It was the first winter they'd experienced such a deep fall. Previous winters had only offered a sprinkling of snow, quickly vanishing by noon. Though almost every winter the Drakensburg Mountains wore a mantle of white.

It was a lazy day at Chanting Clover. Most of the horses spent the day in their stables. Gary and Mel savoured a quiet afternoon on the couch, engrossed in their books. The tranquillity short-lived, interrupted by the arrival of two sodden boys at the door of the sitting room, their chattering teeth stopped them speaking.

"You two are blue from the cold. Go and bath before you get pneumonia." Mel shouted.

Gary got up and watched them race each other to the bathroom, elbowing each other all the way down the passage. Garth got to the bathroom first. He heard Brad. Garth had pushed him into the door frame triggering an argument between the brothers.

By mid-day the following day, most of the snow had melted. Garth and Bradley were devastated, but they were going back to boarding school, and it was certainly a story to tell their teacher and buddies. They boarded at Clifton Junior school. The feeder school for boys completing senior schooling at the famous Michaelhouse, the nearby private senior school steeped in history and tradition. Known as one of South Africa's most notable institutions.

At Clifton, the boys were weekly borders and fetched by either one of their parents on Friday afternoon and taken back either Sunday night or Monday morning. During the winter it was normally a Monday morning.

After the melting of the snow and the harsh frosts during July, the lawns and fields were crispy dry. The landscape offered a provocative palate of yellows and browns against cream-coloured rolling hills, scorched by daily frost. Though Mel loved the colours of the landscape in winter, she was looking forward to a vibrant spring. This winter had been way too cold for her.

And at this time of year there was always an underlying worry about runaway fires. Ten-metre-wide firebreaks had been ploughed around the fields and paddocks as early as April. Often, even the ten-metre-wide fire breaks weren't enough protection if a strong wind drove the flames, sweeping the fires across the rolling hills at an alarming speed, causing considerable devastation to thousands of hectares.

Farmers were vigilant. Their trucks were kept loaded with mechanical sprayers ready for action. On the floor of the trucks lay rubber fire beaters and hessian sacks. Everyone kept a keen eye on the surrounding hills. A whisp of smoke spiralling into the air was the give-away. July, August, and September were the primary firefighting months. Despite the heavy snowfall, the pastures and grasslands were tinder dry.

All the farmers in the district were on high alert. The introduction of modern technology made communication easier and faster, and everyone carried cellular phones. Signal strength permitting, it was a great boon.

Gary's radio network within the stud was another quick and easy form of communication, and many farmers in the district had similar sets.

All farm staff in the district were well versed in watching out for the tell-tale spiral of smoke. When alerted, farmers could act immediately, unlike the old days when it took up to thirty minutes before they deployed, nowadays they could be gone in ten.

Two critical factors were location and heading. Whose farm was it on, and in which direction was the fire/wind moving? The farmers' response times, and the effectiveness of their combative next moves made all the difference. Either to stopping its spread early, or back-burning quickly.

This was one of those winter's where numerous fires had already been handled before they got out of control.

A call came through at three o'clock. A fire had started on Little Lakes farm, eight kilometres from Chanting Clover. Mel was busy in the office at home. She'd heard the call for help, and the simultaneous beep on her cellular phone, alerted her to the same message.

Gary had heard it too. His truck was ready. The firefighting crew had gathered in minutes. Ivan's truck was ready too. One person operated the firefighting sprayer and six beaters climbed on board. Gary and Ivan sped off in separate vehicles fifteen minutes after the call. Engrossed in stud paperwork, the boys were at school, Mel went on with her work.

***

Immersed in studying pedigrees, she hadn't heard anyone enter her office. Suddenly, without warning, a thick coil encircled her neck, tightening with a cruel grip, while the searing pain of a blade sliced into her arm and side tore at her senses. Dragged violently from her chair, she found herself ensnared in a desperate struggle for survival.

"NO. Please, no." She screamed as the noose constricted around her throat, cutting her air supply. With flailing arms and legs kicking and fighting, she fought her assailant. Every muscle tensed in defiance as she was forcefully dragged down the passage past the kitchen, towards the interleading door leading to the garage.

Dazed from the initial blow to her head, weakened by the vicious stabs, and suffocating noose, she fought again the inevitable with every fibre of her being. He was too strong, but mercifully, her desperate fighting caused him to falter on the step at the internal door that led into the garage. In that fleeting moment, amid the chaos and agony, she locked eyes with her assailant for the first time.

"Fu.... nani!" She gasped and wheezed in disbelief. "WHY?" She exhaled. Her instant thoughts were Solomon. He'd warned her he'd get her one day. Was this the day, and this the way, she wondered.

Unbalanced, Funani stumbled. Mel squirmed free of his grip and the rope noose loosened. Taking in a deep breath, she reacted quickly in the same way she'd foiled Solomon and Antonio and launched a blow to

Funani's groin, but the kick was too weak to send him to the floor. He doubled over, coughed, spluttered, and groaned.

Fear and panic gripped Mel as she observed another rope dangling menacingly from the rafters, its noose a chilling reminder of her immediate fate. Then she caught sight of a large shifting spanner lying within reach. Acting on sheer instinct, she seized the spanner with trembling hands and delivered a forceful blow to the back of Funani's head. The sickening crack echoed through the air as they crashed to the floor.

With shaking fingers, Mel removed the rope from around her neck and threw it on the floor. Shocked and in pain she expected Funani to rise and kill her. She lay, face down on the concrete floor, the fight had left her. Driven by desperation, she inched her battered body toward the spanner, convinced she may need it again.

Panting from exertion, Mel watched in disbelief as a pool of blood spread from Funani's motionless form, the weight of her actions crashing down upon her. She, a mother, a daughter, a wife, never meant to become a murderer. Shock rendered her speechless, her gaze fixated on the harrowing sight before her.

She had to get off the floor. A surge of determination pulsed through her veins as she forced herself forward. Yet, as moments stretched into eternity, she found herself consumed by uncertainty. Where were Angelina and Thando? Surely, they must've heard the commotion by now.

Exhaustion and pain threated to overwhelm her as she struggled to move. With each effort a torrent of warm blood seeped from her wounds. It was no use. With a heavy heart, she uttered Solomon Tlale's name. His revenge had ensnared them all.

Gasping for breath, she clung to the tool cupboard for support. Her beaten body trembled with each laboured breath. Tears mingled with blood as she grappled with the enormity of the situation, her resolve wavering with each passing moment. She closed her eyes and gathered her wits. With her head bowed she unstuck fronds of hair from her bleeding mouth, and she cried for the first time. When the tears ended, anger consumed her, igniting a flicker of strength in her weary limbs.

Summoning every ounce of willpower, she staggered toward the garage door, her voice trembling as she called out for help, praying for salvation amidst the darkness closing in around her.

"An.... ge.... lina." She waited, then called again. There was no response.

"Thando," She called. No-one was answering. Where were they?

Standing at the door she raised her voice. "Angelina. Thando." There was still no response. She glanced at her watch. It was just after four. The staff knocked off at five.

A cold shiver filled her body. Then a rush of salivary blood filled her mouth. Instead of spitting it out, she swallowed. Her stomach rejected it and pushed it back up. She spewed the contents across the floor and wiped her mouth on her sleeve when an arbitrary thought hit her. The veld fire. Gary was still out fighting it. Had it been lit deliberately as a decoy? A plan laid down by her nemesis.

Funani and Thando were related. Thando had been in their employ since the boys were little. Angelina was a part of the family. She'd worked for Iris for fifteen years before they arrived from Zimbabwe. Surely Angelina wasn't involved in the plan to kill her?

She took her first wobbly step down the passage, edging herself along using the wall to support her, painting a line of blood along the wall. Her legs were like jelly. She could hardly support herself. She progressed one step at a time toward her office. Eventually she made it and slumped into her chair.

"Fuck." She spat, willing Gary to return home, he'd know what to do. She picked up her mobile phone in shaking hands. There was no signal. One of the towers must have been damaged in the fire, she thought.

She called on the radio.

"Gary, Gary, come... in... please." The radio crackled. She panicked and called again, holding her thumb firmly depressed on the call button.

"Gary, go," he clicked off.

"Come home, Funani tried to kill me." Melonie let out a stifled sob.

"Jesus Christ, what? Are you okay? Where is Funani now?"

"Dead," she stammered.

"Fuck. Who killed him?"

"I did." A loaded silence followed.

"I'm on my way. Are you hurt?"

"I'll live." She whimpered.

"Mel, answer me, are you hurt?"

"Not critically, but get back as soon as you can," she said bravely.

Sean Foster, a farm manager from one of the neighbouring farms, heard Mel's call for help. He was closer to Chanting Clover farmhouse than Gary. He called Gary.

"Hi Gary, Sean here. I'm not far from your house, shall I pop in and see what I can do for Mel?"

"Yes please. Thanks bud. It'll take me twenty minutes to get back. Any idea where Ivan is?"

"No sorry, not a clue. Call again on the radio."

MEL LAID her head on the desk. Everything hurt. She couldn't believe she was still alive. She felt like she'd been crushed in a vice.

She pushed her chair back from the desk and noticed blood was trickling down the chair leg. She reached for the box of tissues, pulled out a wad and lifted her jerseys. The stab wounds were deep. Two, close to each other. She placed a wad of tissue over the wounds and pressed hard, looking out the window at the driveway, wishing Gary would get home. A few minutes later she heard a familiar voice call out, but no vehicle in the driveway. The voice called again. It was Sean Foster, the manager from two farms away.

"I'm in my office," Mel answered.

"Oh my God, Mel." Sean stood at the door. The floor smudged with blood. "You're badly hurt, aren't you? Gary's on his way. Is there anything I can get you, or do?"

"Please go to the bathroom and grab a roll of toilet paper and a wet face cloth."

"Yes, sure. It looks like you've just fought a war single-handedly."

"I have. When you get back, look in the garage. I had no intention of killing Funani. I just wanted to stop him killing me."

Sean rushed off and found what Mel had asked for and raced back. "Who the hell attacked you?"

Mel rolled off more tissue and slid the wad down in the inside of her sleeve, then she wiped her face with the wet cloth. "One of our bloody staff. His name's Funani." She turned her chair awkwardly. "The bastard wanted to hang me in the garage."

"I'll take a look." Sean left while Mel cleaned her face and hands. She'd stemmed the flow of blood from the wounds.

Sean returned. "Jesus Mel, he meant business. Luckily that spanner was in the garage or Gary would've found you hanging on then end of that rope. Did he have another rope around your neck?"

Mel nodded. "And I'm convinced the fire was a decoy. It could only have been. He had time to tie that rope to the rafters in the garage without anyone knowing. I heard nothing and the staff aren't here."

"Where are they? And why would Funani want to kill you?" Sean asked.

"I have no idea where Angelina and Thando are. Funani wanting to kill me is because of my past in Zimbabwe. It's a long story."

Sean was shaking his head. "Gary shouldn't be more than ten minutes. I'm not sure where your dad is, but he would have heard the call too, I'm sure. The fire's still raging, but at least the wind changed direction and it swung away from the top of your farm."

"Fires are my worst. They create their own wind, don't they?"

"That's for sure. They scare me too."

"Our staff know I don't get involved with firefighting anymore." Mel shifted painfully in her chair.

"Let me help you up." Sean reached for Melonie's arm. She yelled.

"Sorry Sean, that's too sore. He stabbed me in this arm. We'll have to wait for Gary."

"Ah, there he is." Mel watched Gary jump out of the vehicle and run inside.

"Oh my God, sweetheart." He took one look at his badly beaten, bleeding wife. Taking in the situation he said, "Honey, I must call the cops before I take you to hospital." He turned to Sean. "Thanks for being here for Mel."

He pulled the phone from his pocket. No signal. He raced to the hall and dialled on the landline.

"Mooi River Police Station."

"Hello, yes, it's Gary Whitaker here. I need the police to come to the farm as a matter of extreme urgency. There's been a death."

"Eish! Mr. Whitaker. Where?" The constable asked. Most of the local police force knew Gary and Mel. To learn of a violent death on this farm, however, seemed highly incongruous.

"At my house," Gary stated. Muted vibrations of breath sounded down the line.

"Who?" The constable asked eventually.

Gary shook his head. The constable wouldn't know who, even if he did give Funani's name.

"His name is Funani. He..." Gary stopped himself. "Sorry, can you just get your people out here as soon as possible."

"Yes, we will. Where is the body, Mr. Whitaker?"

"In my garage."

The constable whistled this time. "Eish. Okay. Okay."

"Are you the cause of the death?"

"No, I'm not. I will explain, just get here quickly, please. A man by the name of Sean will be here to show you where the body is. I need to get my wife to hospital."

"Your wife? He asked, sounding shocked. "Is Mrs. Whitaker injured?"

"Yes, very badly."

"We're on our way, Mr. Whitaker. I'm sorry about your wife. I'll send a team out as quickly as possible."

"Thank you." Gary hung up. "I'm packing you a small overnight bag, honey. Hang in there." Gary shouted out and sped to their bedroom, grabbed Mel's gown and nightie, toiletries, a set of clean clothes and her book, and bundled it into a small suitcase. When he got back to the office, he could see Mel's eyes weren't focussing. He panicked.

"Sean, please grab a blanket from one of the spare beds, then help me get Mel to the car. She's going into shock. I need to hurry. Weirdly enough, I parked it outside the garage after dropping the boys at school this morning." He shook his head at the strange thought, rubbing Mel's shoulders gently.

Sean came racing back with a blanket and Gary wrapped Mel in it.

She moaned in agony as he lifted her out of the chair and rushed with her limp body to the car.

"Deal with the police when they get here, please." Gary shouted as he ran.

"Sure thing."

"Hold on honey. I'll get you to hospital as quickly as I can." Mel acknowledged with a slight nod and a groan of distress as he placed her in the passenger seat.

"Can.... I.... have some...... water."

Gary opened the storage box between the two seats and handed her the bottle kept in the car. She took a few sips, screwed the top back on and her head slumped forward.

"Jesus wept," Gary heaved. "Honey, don't fall asleep."

Mel never answered. Wasting no time Gary sped off and focussed on the road, praying all the way until he reached the emergency entrance to Grays hospital in Pietermaritzburg and sprinted inside to get help.

"My wife is lying unconscious in the car outside." Gary's voice sounded the urgency of the situation and in moments two nurses grabbed a gurney and followed Gary.

"Call the doctor." One of them shouted. Gary lifted Mel onto it, and they pushed the bed on wheels back inside and met the doctor on duty.

"Get her to theatre. There's one open." The urgent command spurred nurses into swift action. Gary gripped Mel's hand as they rushed towards the operating room. Once she'd been wheeled into theatre, Gary reluctantly let go of her hand and made his way to admissions to complete the necessary paperwork.

Before settling down to wait and have a coffee he popped out to move the car to general parking and retrieved Mel's belongings. Deeply worried about her, he returned to the cafeteria and indulged in a slice of chocolate cake to go with his coffee and bought daily newspaper to distract himself.

As time dragged on, Gary's anxiety grew with each passing minute Mel spent in surgery. He restlessly ordered another cup of coffee and paced around as he sipped. Finally, a nurse sought him out with news of Mel's condition.

"Mr Whitaker, your wife is out of theatre and being wheeled to Ward 4. She's very groggy, but she's fine."

Gary closed his eyes. Flooded with relief, he thanked her and immediately made his way to the ward where Mel was being transferred.

Gary found Mel asleep in her bed, her face peaceful in repose. He approached her bedside quietly and woke her with a gentle kiss. Their hands intertwined, speaking volumes in the silence between them.

Mel's voice broke the quietude, "I thought I was going to die." Mel expressed, and just then the doctor walked in and provided Gary with a detailed update on Mel's injuries and prognosis.

"Hi, Mr. Whitaker. Two nasty stab wounds in her side could have taken her life had it not been for all the thick jerseys she was wearing. The stab wound in her upper arm penetrated muscle and again, the jerseys prevented the blade going deeper. Physically they will take several months to full heal. Another twenty-four hours resting and recuperating here will do her good. She lost a lot of blood, and shock always takes its toll on the body."

"Thank you, Doctor." Gary shook his hand. Mel struggled to keep her eyes open. "I've got to get home. Police will be there. I can't leave Sean to handle the whole lot." He kissed her gently and whispered, "I'll see you tomorrow morning after ten."

When he looked back at her from the door he saw a peaceful expression on her face and her breathing was steady as she drifted back to sleep.

Chapter Thirty-Seven

"Looking at that rope makes me feel bilious," Gary stood with Ivan in the garage. The excess rope, coiled like a snake, lay in pools of blood as a macabre reminder of the dire need to protect Melonie. Funani's body had been removed by the police.

Ivan turned away. "All I can say is thank the Lord, we never found her hanging in it. I couldn't have dealt with that. This is bad enough. My poor darling daughter. What she's been though."

Sergeant Habebe stepped forward. He shook Gary's hand, then Ivan's. "Good evening, Gary, how's your wife?"

"Good evening Sarg. Thank you for asking. She's lucky to be alive. The two stab wounds in her side could have killed her. But thank God she'll be okay."

"Sean gave us a detailed statement about what he knew. Please read through it to see if it is correct. If you are happy, please sign at the bottom of the statement."

Gary read the report written by Sean and signed it. There wasn't anything more he needed to add. Sean had taken photos of the scene.

"What's the next step Serg?" Gary asked moving away from the garage.

"Well, you realise this is a serious case." Sergeant Hadebe warned.

"Of course, I do, Serg. And it's further complicated because we are convinced this is linked to my wife's past in Zimbabwe. Someone is out to get her, which I think is obvious."

Sergeant Hadebe raised his eyebrows. He knew nothing of Mel's past. "This attempt on my wife's life with the rope hanging in the garage is proof of intent. She had no intention of killing her attacker, but it's just as well she did."

"YES. And we'll get to the bottom of it, Gary. There's no doubt it's suspicious. It's getting late. I'll call tomorrow. We must keep Mel out of jail." Sergeant Hadebe shook Gary's hand and left. The word *jail*, lingered.

"I'm going to head off too," Sean shook Ivan and Gary's hands. "Anything I can do, don't hesitate to call."

"Thanks, Sean. Much appreciated, mate."

Sitting on the veranda Gary lit the gas burner and Ivan popped the cap off two beers and they sat quietly contemplating what to do next.

"Two things. The first, Mel isn't going to jail, and the second, the security company aren't doing their job." Gary stared into the blue gas flame as he spoke.

"My daughter's going nowhere near jail. Here in South Africa? Not a *bliksem*." Ivan used Afrikaans slang to express how he felt. "The poor girl has fought for her life too often." Ivan gulped another mouthful of beer.

"Nope, no jail for my wife, that's for bloody sure. Not now, not ever. There are so many questions, aren't there? I wonder where the maids were. Anyway, there's nothing more we can do until morning. Thank God the boys are at school."

Gary and Ivan wondered through to the kitchen. Ivan threw half a dozen eggs into a pot and whisked them. Gary put the toast on to have with the scrambled egg. They were both ravenous.

ANGELINA ARRIVED at work at six-forty-five and found Gary in the kitchen holding a mug of steaming coffee. In her normal manner, Angelina smiled and said good morning.

"Good morning, Angelina. Yesterday at four o'clock, Missus Mel was attacked in her office. She is in hospital. Where were you and Thando at that time?"

Angelina's mouth dropped open. She stood in shock, staring at Gary, then her hand shot to her mouth. Tears rolled down her cheeks. She lifted her apron and wiped them away. "Sorry my Baas, madam gave me the afternoon off."

Despite her words, Gary could see by her devastation and the look in her eyes, she had not been involved. "Where's Thando?"

"I don't know, Mister Gary. She should've been here by now. Please," she grabbed Gary's arm, "is the madam alright?"

"She'll be fine. He stabbed her a few times, so she'll need your help even more."

"Did the man get away?" Angelina asked, shaking her head in sorrow.

"No, the missus killed him with a spanner." Her eyes flew open. Angelina adored Mel but she had no idea how to respond. She stood fiddling with the lace edging on her apron. Finally, she asked. "Who was the man who attacked her?"

"Funani." Angelina turned away. "I've had a bowl of cereal, so don't make breakfast. I'm going to the office, then to the Police Station and then to collect the madam."

Gary called for Patric. Horrified to hear what had happened to Mel, he asked if there was anything he could do to help.

"You live right beside Funani and his extended family. Please pop down to housing and see where everyone is. Thando hasn't pitched for work either. I need to make copies of their IDs to take to the police station later."

Patric disappeared quickly and it wasn't long before he rushed back to the office and knocked on the door.

"Their houses are empty. Wide open." Patric gestured breathlessly. "Keys are hanging in the doors."

Gary scratched the back of his head. "Funani dead. Phila, Mandla Mabasa from the garden, Jacob Mathuma from the brood mare barn, and Thando, all gone, and all related?"

"It seems so, Gary."

"Thanks, Patric. I'm running late. Ivan is coming with me." Keep an eye Patric. Our security is not doing their job. As Gary picked up the car keys and his briefcase, the telephone rang.

"Warrant Officer van Wyk here. I'm taking on the case, Gary. Can you come through today with copies of Funani's ID document and contract?"

"Good morning, Warrant Officer. I'm on my way, things have changed. The entire family have absconded. I'm bringing all their ID copies through. I'll see you in half an hour."

Gary left to collect Ivan. Waiting outside his cottage, he climbed into the Landcruiser.

"Morning Ivan. This fucking attempt on Mel's life stinks of revenge. The whole family have fucked off. Not one of them at work and their houses vacated."

Ivan fastened his seat belt and looked at Gary, silenced for a moment. "So much for our useless undercover security. I'll get onto them when we get back." Ivan offered.

***

After leaving copies of the five employees IDs, adding another statement and explaining more details to WO van Wyk, Gary and Ivan left the police station and drove to the hospital.

"I'll be bloody interested to see what the cops dig up. Do you think I should call the headmaster and let the boys know?"

"I'm not sure that's a good idea, Gary. They'll worry their little heads off about their mother for the rest of the week."

"But what if the attack on Mel is put in the newspapers, which I'm sure it will be, and they find out from fellow students. You know how news like this, travels."

"Perhaps you're right. Give the headmaster a tinkle. I'll collect the boys from school if it helps."

"Yeah, it will. God, it's been so peaceful for so long. None of us could have foreseen this shocking event."

"Absolutely not. Do you think they'll let Mel come home today?"

"I hope so, the doc seemed to think she would be fine to come home today."

When they reached the hospital, Gary called the headmaster. He promised not to tell the boys about the traumatic attack on their mother.

They found Mel sitting up in bed. The angry rope burns around her neck stood out against her pale skin. Her eyes spoke of the pain and trauma, but she managed a small smile when the two men walked into her room. Gary kissed her, then her dad. They sat in the chairs provided.

"It's good to see you both, but the doctor won't let me go today. I'm only coming off the drip this evening. So, what's happening at home and with the police?" Her eyebrows met the crease of worry between her eyes. It was as if her face changed shape with angst. Gary's chest tightened looking at her.

"Sergeant Hadebe and WO van Wyk have been elected to oversee the case and they're being very helpful. You obviously forget you gave Angelina off. She's mortified. Thando and the rest of the family have absconded, confirming this is a Colonel fucking Solomon, set up. Excuse my language, honey."

"The good thing about that is it takes the pressure off you for killing Funani." Ivan said. "I'd like to know where security was in all this. I think we look for another company."

"WO van Wyk recommended Prime Security. Their head office is in Durban, but he says they're good. I'll call them when we get home." Gary stood to help adjust Mel's pillows, noticing she'd slipped down into an uncomfortable position.

"Thanks, honey. I'm so glad Angelina wasn't involved. That's such a relief."

"More to the point, sweetheart, thank goodness I left that shifting spanner in the garage, or you wouldn't be with us." Gary tucked her in and kissed the top of her head.

"Honey, do you think I'll go to jail?"

"Not a chance of that happening. Don't you worry about that. From here we are going back to the police station," Gary scowled, "Not in a million years. Dad and I will make sure of that, won't we Ivan?"

"Bloody right. WO van Wyk will guide on the procedures. You concentrate on getting better." Gary kissed her lips, they'd cracked.

Dried out from the trauma and anaesthetic. "We'll see you tomorrow before lunch. Sleep, it's the best cure."

The two men kissed Mel goodbye and drove to the police station and learned from WO van Wyk all the ID copies of the five employees were fakes. They *were* all Zimbabwean.

Chapter Thirty-Eight

AT THE POLICE STATION, flustered by confirmation they were dealing with Solomon's connections. Sergeant Hadebe and WO Van Wyk led them through to Sbu Tshabalala, the station commander's office. Gary and Ivan listened to the articulate commander explain the next steps that would be taken.

"However, I advise you see the Magistrate in Mooi River. Even if no-one comes forward to claim Funani's body, it's worth getting his advice. If the body is identified and the family are crazy enough to lay charges, criminal procedures will have to be adhered to. As it stands now, with all employed relatives of the deceased having disappeared from the farm, the chance of a murder docket being opened is slim. Unfortunately, it's a question of wait and see." The station commander said.

"Surely, they cannot arrest my daughter for murder, it isn't murder. The intruder was intent on murdering her. She reacted in self-defence, like any human being would." Ivan spoke, the anger in his voice evident.

"I agree, Mr. Johns, but we must comply with the new laws. It is complicated, we understand that. I'm sure the Magistrate will advise you on what steps to take going forward."

Gary and Ivan returned home. Frustrated, tired and worried. Gary made an appointment to see the Magistrate the following week.

The following day Gary collected Mel. She walked bent, standing straight pulled at the stitched stab wounds in her side. "I'm not sure how I'm going to feel walking into the garage," Mel said as they slowly walked to the car.

"I cannot imagine how difficult it's going to be for you, my darling. I wish I could make it better." Gary said tenderly, trying to contemplate the horrific trauma his wife was dealing with. "By the way, Prime Security have taken over. Your dad fired the last lot and gave them a piece of his mind."

Mel pressed a small grin. "I'll bet he did. But that's a relief."

Gary parked close to the steps at the front of the house. Holding Mel's arm, he guided her up the steps and through the front door. "Are you okay?" He asked, the tone in his voice sounding so sympathetic and filled with concern, Mel's first sensation was to cry. Instead, she answered bravely.

"Yes, I'm doing fine, thanks to you, my love, even though the memory is harrowing." She moved slowly across the hall floor. "Oh, look how Angelina has polished the parquet. I've never seen it so shiny. What a dear she is." Angelina had tirelessly cleaned the blood off the passage walls, shone the parquet flooring but Gary told her she'd refused to clean the garage. A few of the farm workers, armed with buckets of antiseptic water and mops cleaned the garage. The scent of antiseptic clung to the fine hair that lined her nostrils. A stark reminder of the sterile hospital room she'd reluctantly called home for a few days.

"These eleven stitches in my side are going to be a constant reminder I'm still on Solomon's hit list, and even when they come out, all the stab wound scars will stay as a reminder too. Will the son-of-a-bitch ever leave me alone, Gary?" Mel burst into tears as he helped lower her into the comfy armchair in the sitting room.

"What happened to Funani's body?" Mel asked feeling a surreal blend of horror and respite.

"In the fridges at the police morgue until a family member identifies it. If no one comes forward, there's no case. I didn't ask how long they keep the body."

"Do the boys know?"

"I called the headmaster. He wasn't going to share any gory details. He would let them know you are okay."

"Oh, thank goodness. We've enjoyed such a peaceful life for so many years, I wonder what woke the sleeping devil. One thing's for sure, I couldn't go through another attempt on my life. I felt I'd lost it when we reached the garage. Thank God for small mercies. Gary you never leave tools lying around."

A knock on the door alerted them to Angelina's presence. "Come in Angelina." Gary smiled as she stepped closer and dropped to her knees near Mel. "Welcome home, Ma'am. Can I get you some tea? You've had a terrible shock."

Mel reached for Angelina's hands and gripped them affectionately. "I'd love some tea, thank you. Bring a tray with three cups, my dad will be here too."

Angelina rose, straightened her apron and steepled her hands, then left without another word. Her lips trembled as if she would cry. When she returned carrying the tray, Ivan arrived too and kissed his daughter, relieved she was home.

Getting Mel dressed in the morning required Gary's help. "I've never done what my girlfriends do, and binge watch soapies and series, but today, I think I'm going to do just that." Once she was dressed, she hobbled slowly down the passage to the sitting room. Gary switched on the TV for her, made her comfortable and placed her tablets beside her.

"I'm going to call Anthony. He'll know of a good criminal lawyer in case it comes to that." Gary left her.

Mel rested her head against the back of the chair and sighed. She heard Gary talking but couldn't make out what he was saying. He ended the call and came back.

"If, by some horrid chance, a family member identifies the body, Ant put me onto a top criminal lawyer called Brian De la Rosa."

Mel turned the volume down on the TV. "That's comforting. Who was the second caller?"

"The station commander. Fingerprints of the five are back and police have questioned the staff at Little Lakes farm, where the fire started. If there were collaborators, no-one is talking. Cops are combing a wider area, even as far as the tribal lands near Estcourt because of a tip off. The fugitives maybe be hiding there. All we must do is pray no-one identifies the body because of the connection to your nemesis."

Mel shook her head. "Sitting and waiting is worse torture. So, if no-one opens a case, nothing ever happens? They can't come back years later and charge me with murder?"

"Something like that. It's going to be a difficult month ahead for all of us, sweetheart."

Chapter Thirty-Nine

UNDER THE CLOAK OF DARKNESS, the fleeing relatives and their children slipped away from Chanting Clover. Their departure marked the absence of Funani's return. The frightened group ran and ran, laden with heavy bags they fled in fear until they hailed a taxi on the outskirts of the farm. Vehicles were not normally on the farm roads at night, but the taxi whisked them away to Mooi River. There they boarded a train bound for Soweto, five hundred kilometres north of Chanting Clover. A huge sprawling city comprising mainly of the workforce for Johannesburg and Pretoria, but a vibrant bustling city housing millions of people where the family could hide.

The last call Jacob's final communication with Solomon occurred on the train journey, the tension palpable in their terse exchange.

"How's Alice?" Solomon's voice was devoid of sentiment.

"She has cried a lot, Colonel. She's sitting gazing out the window, lost in her grief, though its dark, she can't see anything. She's inconsolable. Her heart is aching, Sir." Jacobs words echoed the despair of their situation.

This was not the outcome Solomon had anticipated. Enraged by this failure, he cursed himself and his relatives. They'd failed him. He should not have left the Whitakers in peace for so long. His spies had not fed him reliable information. He'd have to deal with them.

"What are your plans, Jacob?"

"To hide in Soweto and lie low for a few days, then move to the homelands near Estcourt. We have friends there." Jacob explained.

"Change your contact number, they can trace this one. Dispose of this phone after we have spoken. I'll send money to buy two new phones to share. Destroy every phone the group has. Is that clear?"

"Yes, Sir."

"Call me when you have a new number." With that Solomon ended the call. Alice turned to look at Jacob. Her anguish overflowed, her face still wet from tears.

"I hate that man. I never want to hear from him again. He set Funani up to carry out *his* vendetta." The others could hear the resentment in her voice. "Now my husband is dead and I'm on the run like a criminal. We had a good life at Chanting Clover." Her words cut deep, piercing Jacob's resolve as Thando observed with a glare.

Meanwhile. Solomon grappled with his own dilemma. Any trace leading back to him could spell disaster. He imagined the displaced group, crammed into a single train compartment, their lives upended by tragedy. One Melonie Whitaker had caused. No contingency plan had been put in place. Funani had believed killing Mel would be easy.

Determined to maintain control, Solomon resolved to support Jacob and Alice financially. He had already offered Funani a brand-new car if he killed Melonie. This and some financial support would help rebuild their shattered lives. Thando expressed her disapproval of being left out of the spoken financial assistance, believing that each one of them had taken the risk, they each deserved remuneration.

The rendezvous in Soweto had always been part of the plan, but without Funani, the group were at a loss, nervous and worried. Who deserved the car? They'd need a car between them.

Keep them sweet, Solomon contemplated.

He'd heard the angry Thando. She'd screamed her feelings of discontent while Jacob tried to speak. But Funani had failed him. The family would have to pay for his failure. They were frightened and he intended to keep it that way.

Chapter Forty

IVAN COLLECTED the boys from school. As he brought the car to a stop the doors swung open, and the two boys sprinted through the house to their mother lying on the sofa on the veranda.

"You can't hug me," Mel warned as Garth and Brad almost crashed into her.

"Ouch. Be careful my darlings, mum is rather fragile."

"Oops. Sorry Mum. Grandpa told us you were attacked. That's scary." Curiosity got the better of them. "Can we see where you were stabbed?" Garth asked, proud she'd fought such a courageous battle, and won.

Ivan smiled, envying the resilience of youth. Just as well they didn't know the whole story, he thought.

"I can't show you. They're all covered up, but on Sunday, when Dad takes the dressings off, then you can see."

"Ah, cool." Garth responded. Brad, the more sensitive of the two, had a frown on his face. All he wanted to do was hug his mother.

"Are you going to have battle scars, Mum?" Garth asked boldly. In a small voice, Brad asked, "where did he get you, Mum?"

"In my side and my arm. I'll be better soon."

Garth whistled. "Wow, Mum. Are they really sore?"

"Yes, darling, they are. That's why you can't hug me." Mel smiled fondly at her eldest. Having the boys home made her feel instantly better. "Go and change. Angelina will wash your uniforms."

Garth swung around, but before he left, he shouted, "Hey Mum, I can't believe Thando was involved. Will the police catch her?"

"I don't know my boy. The whole family have gone. Hopefully we'll hear in a few days."

Once they'd changed and given their uniforms to Angelina, they were back on the veranda. "Bye Mum, grandpa is taking us fishing." And they were gone, taking the happy cheer with them.

***

The call they dreaded came through during the fourth week post attack.

"Good morning, Mr. Whitaker. I don't have good news. One of Funani's relatives has identified the body and opened the murder docket." Commander Tshabalala said.

Gary went cold.

"Shit." He uttered, "thank you for letting me know. What happens next?"

Commander Tshabalala explained, then Gary called Anthony.

"Anthony Parks."

"Morning Ant. Bad news. A family member identified the body and open the murder docket. It's time to make an appointment to see Brian De la Rosa, and rather urgently. Shall I call him directly, or do you want to chat to him first?"

"Get onto him now, Gary. He's been primed, he knows the story. He'll understand the urgency. Keep me in the loop."

"Thanks, Ant. I will."

Gary dropped the boys at school and on his way home he pulled over and switched off the engine. He called Brian De La Rosa.

"Good morning, is it possible to speak to Brian?" Gary asked.

"Certainly. Who may I say is calling?" The receptionist asked politely.

"Gary Whitaker."

"Hold on please, Sir."

"Morning Gary, Ant told me about the attack on your wife. I'm sorry to hear that. Explain the sudden urgency."

Gary told Brian of the call he'd just had from the station commander.

"Come to my offices tomorrow, at," Gary could hear him ruffling through some papers, "at nine-forty-five. In the meantime, I'll speak to the station commander and the magistrate."

"Thank you, Brian. See you tomorrow."

When Gary got back to the farm, the knot in his stomach had tightened. How was he to tell Mel? He found her lying on the couch on the veranda reading.

"Hi honey." She looked up, her smile evaporated when she saw his expression. "What now?"

"You're being charged with manslaughter." Gary sat beside her and took her hand. "I've spoken to Brian, the criminal lawyer Ant put us onto. We can see him tomorrow at nine-forty-five. Are you up to it?"

Her eyes were wide, and her chin trembled. She nodded.

"Apparently a family member identified the body and opened the docket."

"Who was the family member?"

"I don't know. The station commander didn't give me those details, but he did tell me the cops followed a lead to Soweto, which was to Jacob's cell phone. The Sowetan police found it on a municipal dump site in Soweto. Apparently, they now think the family are somewhere in the Hlatikulu tribal lands, not far from Estcourt. As the crow flies, no more than fifty kilometres from here. Thank God we have better security in place."

"Being so close means, they could be circling back and someone else in the family will finish me off?"

Gary squeezed her hand. "Don't think like that. Brian will get you cleared of this trumped-up charge and I'm going to have a serious call with our new security company."

Mel had started shivering uncontrollably. "I'm scared, Gary. Very, very, very scared. Hold me. Stop my body from vibrating. If Brian can't prove there's a link to Solomon, I'll be jailed."

Gary embraced her and held tight, but he could slow the shivering. "We will find the link to Solomon. Brian's confident."

Chapter Forty-One

Mooi River. October 1996

"ALL RISE," a voice boomed. The senior magistrate entered the courtroom and took his seat. Attorney De la Rosa, and the government appointed attorney representing the family of the deceased, Mr. Julias Kabaka, were present. Today were the pre-trial proceedings.

"The case of Mrs. Melonie Whitaker versus the family of the deceased, Funani Khumalo." The announcement resounded in the cavernous courtroom.

Melonie, exacerbated by the unknown, stood beside Brian De la Rosa. She'd never been in a court room before. The accusations chilled. If she got off this case, then more attempts would be made on her life. Solomon wanted her dead. Yet, there was no solid proof he was involved. She *knew*. Right now, her future appeared not only gloomy, but more terrifying than ever before. She glanced around the room nervously and noticed only the attorney representing Funani's family was present. She wondered where the family member was who'd identified the body. She wanted to see that person.

A court official's voice rose. He introduced the two lawyers, then instructed all to be seated.

The same magistrate Gary had met a few days after the attack shuffled some papers in front of him and announced he was in possession of the relevant documents.

The magistrate invited the prosecutor's lawyer, Julias Kabaka, to speak first. He opened the proceedings with a raw description of the attack on Funani, suggesting it was a savage killing of an innocent man.

Melonie silently seethed, Funani was no innocent man. She squeezed Gary's hand tight.

The magistrate glanced at Melonie, then back to the prosecuting lawyer. "Where is the family you are representing?"

"They have not been located yet, your Honour."

"What do you meant they've not been located. Who opened this case?" The Magistrate shouted, clearly annoyed. He looked at Attorney De la Rosa and nodded, indicating he was ready to listen.

Brian stood and looked at the magistrate.

"I think it is plain to see the defendant is not of large stature and seven weeks later we can still see the evidence around her neck and on her face of the battle she fought to save her own life. She was attacked from behind by the deceased. There is no question the deceased gained access to the Whitaker household with the intentions of killing Mrs. Whitaker."

Brian turned and looked at Mel for a moment, then went on to describe the barbaric attack. "And in defending her own life, she killed the perpetrator. Not as a wilful act, she had intended to hurt him badly enough for her to escape, and call for help. Had it turned out that way, a police interrogation would have revealed the deceased's reason for wanting her dead."

"Thank you, Attorney De la Rosa. Unfortunately, we cannot proceed." The irritated magistrate turned his attention back to Mr Kabaka. "You are aware, in the criminal courts we cannot proceed without representation from the family of the deceased." The magistrate looked down at his files. "We need to have Mr Theo Tlale present, being the family member who pressed the charges."

Tlale! The name confirmed Solomon's inclusion in the case. She noted a slight grin rise on Brian's face. The surname was all Mel and her team needed to hear. A revenge killing gone wrong. Mel noticed Gary's jaw clench.

"February the 19th, 10 a.m. The next pre-trial date. And remember, Mr. Kabaka, no family representation, no case. Is that understood?"

"Yes, your honour."

When the magistrate left the room, everyone filed out of the court. Mel turned to Gary and Brian. "I knew it. We all knew it. That bloody colonel. What are my chances of getting off this ghastly charge, now that we know who ordered me dead?"

"Though no system is without its flaws, the South African judiciary is in a state of disarray due to the reshuffling of the laws post 1994. According to the new dispensation, the criminal courts are still in early phases of restructure. I know this doesn't really concern you, but it's a fact of life and it is unfortunate that many officials have been promoted beyond their level of competency as we have seen today." Brian put a hand on Mel's shoulder. "I'm confident this case will not be difficult to solve, but let me warn you, it may take years to solve because of the Solomon implications. However, having said that, Mr Kabaka is a government appointee representing the people for free and his limited experience in matters of the court showed today." Brian smiled at Mel. "I'll walk rings around him, and though the magistrate is sharp, he won't be the presiding judge, but from my experience, he was keen to throw your case out."

A WEEK LATER, Brian called Mel. "Morning Melonie, it's Brian. The investigating officer in Mooi River called me this morning. Unfortunately, Mr Theo Tlale will be present at the next session, but do not fret, okay?"

Mel felt her body weaken. "I hope and pray I don't have to fret, Brian. It's all in your hands. Let me know if there's any more information regarding my Zimbabwean past you need, and I'll email it to you."

"I'm sorry to give you this news, but one way or another, we'll get you off this. The police have also picked up the whereabouts of Alice, Funani's wife. She's still in Soweto, living with Theo Tlale. She's been taken into custody for questioning. Hopefully, we'll have more answers for you before the 19th of Feb."

"Well, that is good news. Thank you for letting me know. I'll try not to stress, but to be honest, my head is spinning. Goodbye, Brian and thank you."

Gary walked into Mel's office with a smile on his face. "What's made you look happy?" She asked.

"Well, you know I've been delving into what some of the staff know about the whole gang of fugitives." He pulled a chair out and sat. "We have some very loyal staff, two of whom have confirmed the fire was started by a teenage boy who'd been given instructions from Funani. And, and they provided the names of the boy and his accomplice. I'll email their name to Brian and WO van Wyk for questioning."

"Wow, that's great news. Have you told Dad?"

"Not yet. Patric also has his ears and eyes everywhere. He's teamed up with Kagiso, Thomas and Siyanda."

They walked down to Ivan's cottage hand in hand, and found him in the lounge, reading.

"Dad, I know you've been fretting, but our staff are being a great help. Tell Dad, sweetheart."

"Well, the fire was a decoy to get us all away from the house and was started by a teenager under Funani's instructions. I've let Brian and WO van Wyk know."

"Some good news leaking through at last. Gosh this is so hard for you, my darling daughter." Ivan stood and hugged her. "At least we have Brian representing you and the magistrate is a super guy."

Mel sunk into a chair.

"You'll manage, my darling. You have so much support. In this case, being black or white is of no consequence, I can assure you. And, according to Brian, investigation is heading in the right direction. The police are being pro-active. It's all good news." Gary assured her.

"I pray Solomon is locked up and they throw the key away, otherwise we'll never live in peace." Mel uttered, stress sounding in her voice.

"There's no doubt we have difficult times ahead, but let's try to be positive. You'll come out on top in the end, Mel. I'm certain of that."

"Thanks Dad. I'll come and blub on your shoulder when I need to." She turned to Gary. "Poor you, sweetheart, as if you haven't got enough on your plate. Hand most of it over to Phil, he'll relieve you of the pressure."

Gary mopped the sweat off his brow. "I don't understand why the man is still hell bent on carrying on this evil vendetta, but we have to get to the bottom of it and fast."

Ivan grimaced. "I wonder if we'll ever find out."

Gary's phone rang in his pocket. "Hello, Gary Whitaker."

"These people must be receiving advice from a criminal source, and I have a feeling it may be coming from someone on your farm. We know that fat fuck in Harare has a lot to do with it, but a few things are not tallying." Brian stated angrily. "The cops said they found a relation. A brother, they say. But you know how it is with our African populace, sometimes they refer to friends as 'brothers'. Likely the source is scared Solomon will get to him before we do. I should have more details on the Alice interrogation in a few days, then we can get the runaways arrested."

***

The hearing of the 19th of February 1997 came and went. Something of a non-event. The opposing parties, at least, had the opportunity to look at each other. Mr Kabaka presented the family member, Theo Tlale. The likeness to Funani was disconcerting for Mel.

The final court case date was set. 19th of August 1997. To be held in Durban. Brian was thrilled to have six months for his team to tie up the loose ends.

Outside the court, Brian turned to Gary. "All sorts of things can happen in the next six months, and we don't know which judge will preside, but I welcome this six-month break. Gives me and my team more time. It also gives the family more time to re-group. They're lying low because their plan backfired, but they may appear with their teeth bared. However, I hasten to add, should they be arrested, the lawyer who's assigned for their defence is useless, as you've already seen. Thank the Lord. When we know who is directing Theo Tlale, we'll be home and dry."

"We know who that is." Mel stated categorically.

"Yes, but we must prove it. Stay safe." Brian's parting words.

Chapter Forty-Two

THE 19TH OF AUGUST, 9.00 a.m., in a side room at the Durban Courts, Melonie, Gary, and Brian sat at a conference table, conferring.

Demure and poised, dressed in a khaki shirt dress with a wide white collar and matching white belt, Mel didn't present the picture of a murderer. It took huge will and resolve to remain focussed while she listened again to Brian's planned defence. They'd run through it a week earlier.

She liked Brian, and trusted he'd get her off. Ant wouldn't have recommended him, she thought. "Remember, Mel. When on the stand, never deviate from the *exact* truth, no matter how they try and twist it with devious questioning. I'm not sure Mr. Kabaka is capable of tripping you up, but say the events as they happened, and you cannot be tripped up."

Gary squeezed her hand. She instantly she felt reassured.

"I have no intention of deviating from the truth." Mel said. The truth was all she knew how to tell. Despite knowing the truth, and knowing she'd never intended to kill Funani, the real truth of the matter, Mel believed, is her a God-given right to protect herself if attacked in her own home. Her home, her personal sanctuary where she should be safe. Her stomach twisted and groaned from anxiety.

She held her breath. No matter how innocent, or truthful, the charge of manslaughter preyed heavily on her mind. Fear had driven out the cold logical facts of justified self-defence. Thankfully, Brian was not insensitive to this reality.

Brian, Mel, and Gary walked into the courtroom.

"All rise," the court bailiff announced.

Though the court was smaller than Melonie had envisioned, the energies of justice remained intimidatingly in place. Mel stood beside Brian and her legs shook.

Gary and Ivan stood right behind her.

Angelina, Patric, and a handful of Chanting Clover senior staff joined them in court today. Happy to be called for questioning.

To keep her mind focussed, she looked at the master carpentry of old that surrounded her in the room. The panelling on the walls and the benches, the stand, and where the judge presided, shone with highly polished burnished wood. A beautifully carved emblem of the city, engraved into the wooden counter below the judge's gavel. A random thought of the effort and time it must've taken to carve the symbol took her mind off the curious hum in the court room.

A small woman entered from the judge's chambers and took her seat. Elevated and seemingly unapproachable. The judge placed files in front of her, opened them, and spread them, then looked across the room.

"Be seated." The voice of the judge broke the ominous silence.

Mel's legs still quivered, but she felt relief she had a lady judge. Slight in stature, peppering of grey in her short curly hair, Mel assumed she may be early fifties. Though her face was serious, Mel liked her demeanour. The clerk of the court announced the date and the time of the trial. The case being heard and introduced the judge.

"Judge Elizabeth Dlamini presiding."

The judge nodded and asked council to introduce themselves.

Theo Tlale stood beside the state lawyer, Mr. Kabaka who introduced himself.

Brian stood and introduced himself.

The judge then addressed Melonie. "Mrs. Whitaker, please approach and take the oath, then go to the stand."

Mel took the oath from the stand. The bailiff asked. "Do you solemnly swear to tell the truth, the whole truth, and nothing but the truth, so help me God?"

"I do." Mel answered.

The bailiff then turned to the Mr. Kabaka. "Mr. Kabaka, could you please describe to the courts your representation of the deceased."

Mr. Kabaka stood from the front row of benches and smoothed his suit. "I was appointed by the Moor River magistrate to represent the family of the deceased, Mr. Funani Khumalo, having been slain by the accused."

The judge nodded, then asked, "And what do you know of the deceased's history?"

Mr. Kabaka appeared uncomfortable. "I know he was a Christian man, slaughtered unnecessarily by the accused."

The judge's eyes focussed on him for a few seconds, then she said, "You may begin."

Mr. Kabaka turned his attention to Mel in the stand. "Do you admit to killing Funani Khumalo?"

"I do, but I had no intention of killing him. I was trying to protect myself."

"If you had no intention of killing Funani Khumalo, why did you savagely bludgeon him to death with a heavy spanner? It appears you had every intention of killing him."

"Objection, Your Honour. That is speculation." Brian shouted.

The judge focussed her stare on Mr. Kabaka. "That is an unjust assumption, Mr. Kabaka. Please refrain from further speculation." She said sternly.

If the case wasn't so serious Mel may have smiled. She could see Mr. Kabaka shift uncomfortably when the judge reprimanded him. This gave Mel a hint of confidence. She answered the next few questions without hesitation, briefly explaining the events of the attack as they happened. Courteously, politely, and honestly, she relived the terrifying attack.

"I have no further questions, Your Honour." He said to the judge and was just about to sit when the judge called both legal representatives to the bench.

While they were in quiet conference, Mel looked around and noticed an elderly black woman sitting at the back of the courtroom, leaning up against the wooden panelling. Her short, cropped hair had silver streaks near her brow and there was something about her face which triggered a memory from Mel's past. Mel frowned, trying to remember where she'd seen the face before. The woman noticed Mel watching her and looked down.

Mel refocussed her attention to the bench. The judge and the two lawyers seemed to be in a heated debate. Mel was still trying to work out where she'd seen the elderly lady when it was announced that court was adjourned.

Mel stepped down and walked back to her seat. Brian stormed back to his seat. He said quietly, "It's come to the judge's notice the State lawyer made some error. Too much to explain, but Kabaka is messing up nicely. It's just a waste of everyone's time, and..."

"The woman at the back," Mel interrupted, anxious to point her out. The woman quickly walked out the courtroom doors.

"I only caught a glimpse," Brian said. "Who is she?"

"I'm not sure," Mel said, "but I recognise her from my past.

When court resumed a week later, on the 25th of August, at 10:30 a.m. the elderly lady sat in the same position, resting against the wooden panelling. Elegantly dressed in a maroon skirt suit, and a cream-coloured blouse with ruffled collar. Mel had still not connected her face to the place or the time in her past. It frustrated her that she couldn't remember.

The judge entered. The same introduction protocols were observed and read out. The charges against Mel were repeated. During the introductions Mel noticed Brian taking a good look at the elderly lady and made some notes.

The proceedings had just begun when the judge announced she was called to chambers. She left the courtroom.

Mel turned to Brian with a questioning expression, then she turned to look at Gary and her dad and shrugged her shoulders. She came back and announced, "court is adjourned until the 10th of September at 10 a.m."

A murmur of annoyance rippled through the courtroom. Brian's face turned red with anger. He requested council with her at the bench, and they spoke. Mel noticed Mr. Kabaka looking on, confused. He glanced at Theo Tlale, who appeared flustered.

Mel could see Brian was getting irritated while he spoke to the judge. He shook his head and walked back to his seat. "Can you fucking believe it. Excuse my language. The judge has been called to something more urgent. This is the way it goes nowadays in the new South Africa. It's totally unacceptable, but there's nothing I can do."

The judge gathered up her files and quickly left the courts through the side door.

Brian explained. "Apologies guys. This unprofessional practice happens more regularly nowadays. There's no respect for the correct course the judicial system is supposed to take. I bet she's been called to some politician in trouble who needs the judge urgently. Fraud is steadily rising, these bloody politicians are on the gravy train, big time." Brian gathered up his files and placed them in his briefcase. "I'm sorry Mel. However, we are lucky to have her. She's good, probably the best judge we have in the province."

"It's not your fault, Brian. I must say she also looked annoyed."

"She was seething. She's very correct."

"Before we leave, I must tell you I asked about the elderly lady in the observers' pew. I'll be supplied her name, or at least the one she signed in with. Once we have her name, perhaps we should hire a PI to investigate who she is. It's costly, but worth it. Do you agree?" Mel, glanced at Gary. He nodded.

"Yes, absolutely. This whole bloody drama reeks of my Zimbabwean past. I want to know who she is and I'm sure she's from there, not from Chanting Clover." Mel turned to Gary. "Do you recognise her?"

"No. I don't. I think you're right. She's from your Zimbabwean past."

"I woke the other night with her face on my mind and it's beginning to haunt me. I've seen her somewhere. I think it must be from Blue Winds days."

Brian held his briefcase. "I'll get onto it. I know a particularly good PI. He gets miraculous results, and quickly."

Gary put his arm around Mel and pulled her close. "You do a spectacular job of staying positive, my love. Keep it going. Chin up, we'll get through this soon."

"Yeah, Gary's right. This nightmare will be over soon." Ivan assured her, and the three of them returned to the farm.

During the week Brian called Gary and shared what the PI had uncovered and suggested keeping the new information from Mel for the time being. "I'll surprise her in court." Gary agreed, but they were justifiably excited about the news of the identity of the mysterious elderly lady.

"She's the trump card Mel needs?" Gary stated but Mel walked into his office. "Hold on Brian. Gary could see Mel wanted to ask him something. Mel had a question about one of the horses feed changes, then left.

Go on, she's gone. "The mysterious lady will certainly form a valuable part of the case, but you and I know this whole bloody case is absurd. It's a cut and dry case of self-defence, and the idiotic Mr. Kabaka knows it too. Mel's psychological assessment is rather amusing. I guess you haven't read it?" Brian made to laugh, but it sounded more of a mocking sound of how he felt about the absurdity of the case.

"Let me read it to you." Brian read relevant bits to Gary. "I'm wondering if the judge has read my scribbled notes on the bottom of the report after what Mel said. I'll read out your wife's words.

'My life has taken many radical twists and turns. My hopes and dreams have been challenged all the way through the different phases of my life. It's a work-in-progress, is it not? Excuse me asking, but how would you have coped with what I've been through?'

"I love it. The psychologist never scribed his answer to Mel's question."

The final court date was issued, and the day had arrived.

Mel felt the nerves return to the pit of her stomach while she dressed and sipped her morning tea. Thirteen months had passed since the attack. She still fought the many emotional scars, but none were visible, so she remained stoic.

Outside the court, a barrage of reporters waited for Mel and the high-profile horse-racing family to arrive.

Gary drove Mel and the boys, and parked close to the courts so they could run inside, dodge questions while they protected the two boys.

Her family got out of the car. She tucked Garth close to her side with one arm, and Brad on her other side. It was times like this she yearned for her mother with an ache that felt like a physical vice. Had she been there with her, she knew her mum would have offered the best advice on how to deal with her emotions, but she felt very grateful to her dad, who had been there supporting her throughout the long waiting period.

Judge Dlamini had promised Brian there'd be no interruptions today and there'd be a verdict. Mel straightened her spine and walked with her boys and Gary to the court house. Today, it would be over.

Inside the courtroom, Brian waited. Mel looked about. The elderly lady wasn't there, but Stu Tshabalala, the station commander from Mooi River was with WO Van Wyk and several other policemen she didn't recognise. Many interested spectators sat in the benches, most of whom Mel didn't know.

Mel and Brian took their seats. Gary, Ivan, her two boys, Patric, Kagiso and Angelina filtered into the seats behind them. In the next row, a team of Chanting Clover staff were there to support their employers. Pete and Val, their immediate neighbours, Sean, the farm manager, and a few of the farmer's who'd been firefighting with Gary and Ivan on the day of the attack also filled seats.

Mel turned and spoke to Gary. "There are so many people in court today."

Butterflies erupted in her stomach.

"Relax, Mel. I'm sure things will go well today," Brian assured her.

Only the day before, Mel admitted to Gary she felt scared. Now the thought of being handcuffed in front of her children and all these people shattered what little confidence she had left. Besides, she'd rather die, than be imprisoned in the new South Africa.

She leant forward, filled a glass of water, and sipped. Under the bench her legs shook uncontrollably, even when she tensed the muscles. She crossed her legs and squeezed her calves together tightly which slowed her leg shake but did not sooth her mind.

The air conditioning blasted, and cold air caught around Melonie's shoulders. She shifted. Under normal circumstances she would've welcomed the cool, in the Durban humidity. To calm herself, she'd rubbed lavender essential oil on her wrists before leaving home. She breathed in the scent and filled her mind with silly, random thoughts and continued sipping water.

"How are you feeling?" Brian leant in close.

"I'm petrified, to be honest."

"Understood." Brian nodded.

"All rise." The clerk of the courts voice boomed.

The black-robed lady judge appeared carrying a bundle of files, she sat. She opened a file, then looked out over the court room. "Be seated."

Again, the necessary court readings and protocols were adhered to in the same order as Mel's previous appearances.

The bailiff read out the charges. "The state versus the accused, Mrs. Melonie Jennifer Whitaker of Chanting Clover Stud, Mooi River district. The charges are manslaughter of Mr. Funani Khumalo, on......"

Without raising her hands to her ears, Mel worked to block out the words of manslaughter. The voice seemed far off. The bailiff's voice drifted off. What was she to have done? Stand there and allow Khumalo to hang her and leave her to die with blood dripping from the stab wounds in her side? A sudden rise of anger quelled her shaking legs.

The defence attorney referred to the case as, 'the murder of an innocent Christian man.' Mel knew, now it was up to Brian to prove it was a 'justifiable' manslaughter of a non-Christian man with the intent on ending her life.

Then she was called to the stand. She walked on weakened legs from the quivering and wondered if everyone watching could see how petrified she felt as she took the two steps up to the stand.

The judge began. "Mrs. Whitaker, we've heard the answers to the questions you were asked in the last hearing which unfortunately was interrupted. I apologise for making you wait even longer than you've already had to endure." The judge smiled at Melonie. "I have no further questions to ask you. I'm satisfied with what you answered last time. You may return to your seat." Then the judge focussed on Brian.

"Attorney Del La Rosa, do you have anything further to add?"

"Yes, your honour, we have new evidence to present today." The judge gave a slight nod of acknowledgement. "You may proceed."

"A group of staff skilfully infiltrated the harmonious fabric of Chanting Clover farm as employees. They were Zimbabweans, with a most unusual agenda, and they carried false identity. And they are inextricably connected to Mrs. Whitaker's past in Zimbabwe."

Melonie pressed her hands on her knees. She worried that all her horrific experiences would be regurgitated in court for all to hear and she closed her eyes briefly.

The judge tilted her head in interest. "You may continue."

Attorney Kabaka stood. "Objection."

"Overruled. You may continue." The judge nodded at Brian who breathed in deep and smiled, showing a measure of gratitude.

"Thank you, your honour." Brian stood.

"We do know, Mrs. Melonie Jennifer Whitaker did kill the deceased, Funani Khumalo. She killed him in the garage of Mr. and Mrs. Whitaker's family home, but only as an act of self-defence, after he'd brutally attacked her from behind while she worked in her office."

Brian looked around the courtroom and puffed up his chest while Mel quietly prayed that he'd not give too much detail of her past.

Brian continued. "We know Funani Khumalo dragged her from her office, down the passage, passed the entrance to the kitchen and on toward the internal garage door which had been opened. He had every intention of killing Mrs. Whitaker by hanging her from the garage rafters." Brian stopped speaking, leaving his words to penetrate those that listened with interest. Mel shuddered as she thought of herself hanging there.

"Your honour, you have the photographic evidence on file showing these events. We know that during the ensuing fight, the deceased tripped at the entrance to the garage, faltering. This afforded Mrs.

Whitaker the time to reach for the shifting spanner she'd noticed lying on the floor." Another dramatic pause as Brian focussed his attention on the judge, then to the audience in the seats.

"Mrs. Whitaker hit the deceased on the back of the head to stop his attack of her, and the blow killed him. This took place on the afternoon of the 3rd of August 1996, and was clearly an act of self-defence."

Brian glanced to the back of the courtroom. Mel followed his gaze. The elderly lady sat in the same place.

The judge shuffled through her files, acknowledged the information was correct and there were no deviations from the previous reports.

Despite feeling nervous, she enjoyed watching Brian present her defence. She noticed everyone keenly listening to him.

Brian went on. "From further recent investigations, we can now provide proof the fire and the labour unrest of the previous year, was all instigated by the deceased and his family."

Feet shuffled and murmurs stirred in the courtroom.

For the first time today, Mel felt more assured that Brian would win this case for her.

There was silence in the courtroom as everyone waited for Brian to continue. "Let me take you back to a well-documented kidnapping which took place in 1978. Many of us will remember the newspaper reports of the plight of a young schoolgirl who was taken by Zimbabwean Freedom Fighters from an Eastern Highlands farm in what was Rhodesia. She was marched into Mozambique, to a training or staging camp. It had been front-page news here in South Africa." Stopping at this point, Mel noted Brian had everyone captivated, including the judge.

He asked her if she recalled the incidence and all eyes reverted to the judge.

Judge Dlamini answered. "Yes, I do recall reading about it in the Sowetan newspaper all those years ago."

Mel closed her eyes trying to shed the memories and Brian went on. "The young schoolgirl miraculously escaped from her captors. Terrified and alone. Somewhere in Mozambique, expecting to die, she fled. With the help of friendly forces, she was restored to the safety of her parents. In the process of her escape, she displayed extraordinary courage. She left the Freedom Fighters with casualties. And it was this, that led to an undying determination for revenge from one of the survivors of the camp."

Mel felt her bottom lip begin to tingle from the memory of that night. She bit down hard.

The judge nodded. "Go on."

Brian curtly gave a slight nod in the judge's direction. "She and her family were forced to leave their cherished farm in Rhodesia and emigrated to KwaZulu Natal to the safety of her grandmother. That young schoolgirl sits here in this courtroom with her father, her husband, her two children, and many of her staff seated behind her in support. Sadly, Mrs. Whitaker's mother has since passed away. But it was her mother's mother, Mrs. Iris Paige, who provided this displaced family with refuge and a livelihood. The mention of the two most precious women in Mel's life made her want to cry. She stifled the desire.

Attorney Del la Rosa went on. "Mrs. Whitaker has since taken over the famous stud and racehorse training facility. She has enjoyed enormous success at the top level of racing in South Africa. She herself is a three-time winner of the Durban July, amongst other prestigious races across our beautiful country. She not only provides employment to many, including Funani, providing him and his family with work and comfortable housing."

"Objection." Julius Kabaka leapt to his feet.

"Overruled." The judge responded.

"Your Honour, my client's notoriety, thus described, commenced as early as the Durban July of 1979. Mrs. Whitaker was still single, a mere year after her abduction, and went by her maiden name, Johns. Her face was blazoned across many South African newspapers. This did not escape the notice of her avenger, Funani who was operational as a freedom fighter, and even they read newspapers."

Mel sat in her chair loathing every minute of this recount, but she could see Brian was enjoying having such a captive audience and she felt sure he had the judge on his side too for every now and then the judge would glance at Julius Kabaka. Mel wished she knew then what she was thinking.

"Furthermore, we now have proof, the deceased, Mr Funani

Khumalo was instructed by one of his family members, to murder Mrs. Melonie Whitaker."

Mel thought she might faint. Knowing where the instruction came from, but in that dizzy moment she noticed the expression on the judge's face alter from a rather bored expression to a look of confirmation that she'd heard enough.

Looking at Brian, she thought he'd noticed the judges change of expression too. "Our proof shows, this family, naturalised South Africans, born Zimbabwean, are directly related to the man who abducted Mrs. Whitaker from the family farm, Blue Winds, in Rhodesia during the terrorist war in 1978."

Brian paused and took a deep breath. "This man, who ordered Mrs. Whitaker's abduction, then subsequently tried to murder her in a hotel room in Harare in 1982 when she visited, ironically, to see if she couldn't put her terrible past behind her."

The memories of that night had never left her. She shifted in her seat and looked down at her hands.

Brian's expression changed now too, like he was delivering the final blow to the family, and he felt the pleasure of it. "The man's name is Solomon Tlale, who is a colonel in Robert Mugabe's army, and uncle to Mr. Theo Tlale, who is present here today." Brian pointed to him seated beside his attorney.

Mel fidgeted at the sound of Solomon's name.

"It should be noted Mrs. Whitaker was a mere teenager at the time of her abduction. It's reprehensible she should be pursued like this over the course of her life."

Julius Kabaka's face had lost any angry flush and now paled. "Your honour, this is not relevant to the case."

"Continue." The judge said to Brian.

"That elderly woman," Brian pointed, "who has just stood at the back of this court and looks like she wants to leave, is in fact, the mother of Phila Dube, one of the employees who absconded after the attack on Mrs. Whitaker. He remains at large."

Mel heaved a sigh. She was finally learning who the woman is, but she still couldn't work out where she'd seen her before. Maybe Brian would enlighten the courts as to where she had come from.

"Phila Dube was a work rider at Chanting Clover. It was he who instructed the young boy from Little Lakes farm to start the fire on that farm as a designated spot. A deliberate distraction to get Mrs. Whitaker's husband and father off the farm.

Mel put her hand over her mouth. She'd always suspected the fire had been started to get Gary and her father away from the farm.

Brian continued. "His wife, Thando Dube, was a domestic worker in the Whitaker household. She also absconded the same day. She too, remains at large and she happens to be the youngest daughter of Solomon Tlale, the man hell-bent on ending Mrs Whitaker's life."

"Objection." Kabaka's pitch rose again as he likely realised, he was unprepared for this information.

"Overruled," the judge said, once again.

Commotion broke out at the back of the court. Two policemen confronted Phila Dube's mother.

"Silence please." The Judge hammered her gavel on the wooden counter.

The crowd ignored the instruction.

"Silence please," she shouted louder.

Phila's mother was removed from the court.

Mel couldn't believe what she was witnessing. Order restored the judge requested Brian to hand over all documentary proof.

Brian stood and gathered the documents, walked across to the benched and handed them to the judge. "Your honour, the facts don't end there. The deceased, Funani Khumalo was Solomon Tlale's son from his second wife. He changed his name to Khumalo with a false South African Identity document. You'll find proof of this in the documents I just gave you."

Mel wished she could hear what Brian had just said to the judge.

Brian returned to his seat but remained standing. "Further intel has provided information Khumalo was acting under instruction from Solomon Tlale to murder Mrs. Whitaker. This was an act of pure vengeance, your honour."

Brian continued. "No killing is condoned, but the evidence proves that to save her own life, Mrs. Whitaker, in the fight against Funani Khumalo, was forced, once again, to defend herself. She had no intention of killing him, she reacted on our human survival instinct. If she had not done so, Mr. Gary Whitaker would have found his wife hanging from the rope the deceased had premeditatedly suspended from the beams in their garage. She would be dead. A pre-meditated murder."

Mel watched Brian as he presented the facts and watched the judge carefully. At this point she was sure the outcome would be favourable, but she didn't want to show relief yet.

"Mrs. Whitaker's act was in self-defence. Her nature and her exemplary human relations record at Chanting Clover Stud, is proof she would never intentionally harm anyone."

The staff seated in the courtroom rose.

"Yes, that's true." Patric shouted.

"Silence, please," the judge said.

The staff remained standing defiantly. "She's, our mother. She's, our mother," they sang.

Kabaka seemingly lost for anything meaningful to say in response withered in stature.

The judge motioned to Brian to come to her bench. They spoke in hushed tones, and he returned to his seat.

Then the judge called Attorney Kabaka and Theo Tlale to the front. She spoke to them, and then they too returned to their desk and chairs.

She called Brian forward again and spoke quietly.

Mel heard Brian thank the judge and he walked back to Mel.

The judge ruffled through the paperwork. She slowly raised her head and looked at Mel. "This case is closed. Mrs. Whitaker, you are free to go." She banged her gavel. "Court is adjourned."

The staff cheered. Mel was momentarily dumbstruck and stared blindly ahead of her. A single tear rolled down her cheek as the crescendo of cheers rose. The relief so great her body shook. She'd waited so long to be free.

Garth and Bradley scrambled and hugged her.

"Come on Mum, let's go home," Garth said and tugged her arm. She stood, her legs so weak they hardly supported her.

She grabbed onto Gary's strong arm and said, "When your past calls, don't answer."

Want More?

BENEATH THE LEMONWOOD TREE
The second book in the Whitaker trilogy.

Melonie survives the attack her nemesis, Solomon Tlale orchestrated, but when the news of the court decision filtered back to him, he was furious and vowed she'd not get away again.

The result of the court case made him more determined to wreak havoc in her life, her family's life and he began to work on changing tactics. He would target what Melonie loves most.

The plans he devises are insidious. His intentions are deadly, and he sends someone to spy on the family. Solomon learns of their every move.

Melonie's sons, her employees and even her horses become the recipients of his evil ways.

The story punctuates the terror the deranged Colonel from Zimbabwe dishes out. His puppets, family and friends become the assassins and the spies, while he sits in his offices at Army HQ in Harare enjoying the life of the mega rich. His friend, Johnny Walker Blue Label, remained close at hand to help concoct the terrifying deeds he unleashes on the Whitaker family.

WANT MORE?

The wheel turns slowly, and though the Whitaker's endure heart wrenching losses, eventually the hunter becomes the hunted.

Another fast-moving page-turner.
Available on Amazon and in bookstores.
Visit the author website to see what is coming soon.
www.dianakrobinson.com
Diana K Publications